RAVES FOR TONY GIBBS AND *SHOT IN THE DARK*

"A smart, sexy series launch chock-full of boating lore and lingo.... Both Neal and Tory are fully realized characters.... There's nothing cozy or cute about their relationship.... Gibbs is one of those rare writers—Tom Clancy and Patrick O'Brian come to mind—able to draw a bond of technical trust with readers so that even arcane details are compelling. Gibbs deftly sketches in scenes from the complicated social life of the Santa Barbara harbor."

—*Publishers Weekly* (starred review)

"The nautical descriptions are deftly and excitingly handled.... Gibbs is as masterful [about sailing] as Dick Francis is about horses.... Gibbs has a lot going on in SHOT IN THE DARK.... He keeps the novel moving and generates a number of suspenseful sequences before the wrap-up. Neal Donahoe is a classic maverick hero.... The best thing about SHOT IN THE DARK is Gibbs's ability to transmute his love and knowledge of boats and sailing directly to the printed page. That is the strength that will make readers remember SHOT IN THE DARK and look forward to the next Harbormaster mystery."

—Mostly Murder

more ...

"Tony Gibbs has the copyright on seagoing suspense, so we were happy to read his latest, SHOT IN THE DARK . . . This is the one to take to the beach."

—*Bookviews* (NJ)

"Holds together . . . reads and works well, one learns some lore of the sea, and Santa Barbara seems welcoming."

—*Boston Sunday Globe*

"Gibbs sets a fresh scene in SHOT IN THE DARK . . . Authentic and colorful."

—*New Smyrna Beach Observer* (FL)

"Gibbs manages to maintain interest in his characters and keep the plot rolling at a steady pace . . . .an engrossing and entertaining mystery."

—*Saint John Telegraph-Journal* (New Brunswick)

"A wonderful fun read . . . very well-written and well-rounded."

—*Ellenville Press* (NY)

* * * * *

TONY GIBBS is the senior editor of *Islands*, an international travel magazine. He is the author of five previous thrillers and a dozen nonfiction books, all but three with a nautical background. A resident of Santa Barbara, he spends most of his free time afloat.

SHOT IN THE DARK

SHOT IN THE DARK

TONY GIBBS

THE MYSTERIOUS PRESS

Published by Warner Books

A Time Warner Company

MYSTERIOUS PRESS EDITION

Cover design and illustration by Daniel Pelavin

Mysterious Press Books are published by
Warner Books, Inc.
1271 Avenue of the Americas
New York, NY 10020

Visit our Web site at
http://pathfinder.com/twep

A Time Warner Company

Printed in the United States of America

Originally published in hardcover by The Mysterious Press.

First Printed in Paperback: July, 1997
10 9 8 7 6 5 4 3 2 1

Thanks to Julia Hazard Peyton, Harbormaster of Santa Barbara; and Commander Chet Hartley, USCG, for technical advice

. . . And to the family, for being themselves

Santa Barbara Channel, 2030 hours

For more than an hour *Blue Thunder* had been lying dead in the water, one big diesel rumbling softly at idle to feed the batteries. Though the wind had died with the sun, the heavy westerly swells still marched down the channel, swinging the DEA chase boat's narrow hull until she was taking the seas broad on the quarter—a corkscrewing pitch-and-roll that draped young Tim Huggins over the gunwale and faded even Cowboy Daniels's surfer tan to an ugly yellow-green.

Christian Ericsen, slumped bonelessly in the padded helm chair, pretended not to notice. After ten years in assorted Coast Guard small craft, it took more than a ground swell to bother him, and privately he was enjoying the skipper's obvious misery. At last Cowboy snarled, "Jesus, Swede, will you for chrissake turn the goddam boat, before the kid ralphs all over the cockpit."

Without answering, Ericsen slipped the idling engine into gear and swung the bow away from the seas. The southeaster was just beginning to creep in, he noticed—swatches of ripple flitting over the swells. The sky overhead was still clear, and the lights of Santa Barbara, twenty-five miles to the north, were bright, but off the starboard bow the angular spine of Anacapa Island had lost its sharpness. The front had got ahead of the weather guessers, then: the haze wasn't supposed to set in till midnight. He heaved himself to his feet, his knees creaking like rusty hinges. Arthritis, they said—but he was barely forty. It wasn't fair.

"Where you goin'?" Cowboy demanded.

"Below. Check the weather."

Cowboy growled something under his breath, but Ericsen ignored it. He slid aside the thick, tinted plastic companionway hatch and felt his way down the steps. The cabin's sour smell—stale diesel, bad plumbing, and very old wet suits—was sharp in his nostrils, and the engine, five feet away behind a poorly insulated bulkhead, throbbed like a migraine.

Without bothering to click on the overhead light, Ericsen slid the hatch closed and dropped into the navigator's chair. It was a twin to the helm seat, its upholstery stained and scarred but still giving off the faint, rich tang of real leather. Like much of the chase boat's more exotic equipment, the chairs had been liberated from a seized druggie—in this case a quarter-million-dollar Bertram that had trashed itself trying to outrun a Coast Guard helo through an eight-foot chop off Catalina.

Ericsen had no tears for the Bertram's skipper, any more than he did for the previous owner of *Blue Thunder*'s radar, a longline fisherman who'd decided to stuff plastic-wrapped cocaine suppositories up the frozen bluefin in his hold; he too had lost his boat—and contributed his top-of-the-line Furuno to the DEA boat's battery of electronics.

No, those guys had no complaint coming, Ericsen reflected. They'd gambled big and paid big, and that was just. But it was different with the little guys—like the sea urchin diver last week whose buddy had stuck three tokes in a can of teabags and forgotten them. Sure, it came under the law—"measurable amount of a controlled substance"—but seize a guy's boat for three smokes? To someone like Ericsen, who'd grown up among commercial fishermen, taking a man's workboat was rape and robbery both at once.

And how had Cowboy known where to look for those joints, anyway? Twelve urchin boats at anchor in San Miguel Island's Cuyler Harbor, and he'd gone right for this one. The answer had popped into Ericsen's head immediately: betrayal was, after all, behind nine drug busts out of ten, and when Ericsen thought back over the six months he'd been part of *Blue Thunder*'s crew, he realized that tipoffs could account for nearly all their successful missions.

But it didn't make sense. *Blue Thunder*'s skipper always found enough for an arrest, but the amounts were penny-ante shit—not the hundred-key loads that tempted a guy to rat on his buddies. Busts like Cowboy's were never going to get on the TV news or even make a front-page story in the local paper. And if there was one thing Ericsen had learned in the Drug Enforcement Administration, it was that the hot-shot agents lived (and sometimes died) for headlines. Cowboy Daniels was the biggest grandstander of them all, from his custom-made crocodile-leather boots to his two-hundred-dollar bush hat with the brim turned up on one side.

So how could he be satisfied with cases built on a few funny butts or a handful of PCPs? It didn't compute, and that made Ericsen unhappy. His blunt, broken-nailed finger stabbed at the radio's keypad, and the voice of the NOAA weathercaster cut through the low rumble of the idling diesel. The forecaster was boring his way through the synoptic picture for Southern California, but Ericsen ignored it. He was waiting for the nuts-and-bolts data, the hourly reports from the automated weather buoys up and down the coast, from which he could build a mental picture of the oncoming weather system.

But by the time that part of the forecast came on, his attention had switched to the radar. The set was a beauty, though the antenna was mounted lower than Ericsen liked, to keep it from snapping loose when Cowboy put the pedal down and *Blue Thunder* started to bounce across the wave-tops at fifty knots.

Ericsen kept the range on sixteen miles, which provided a nice, sharp picture right across the screen. The east end of Santa Cruz and the western tip of Anacapa filled most of the picture, and the rest was pretty much a blank, aside from the big blip—a container ship, probably—moving steadily along the channel's westbound traffic lane. But a new target had appeared in the screen's upper right hand quadrant, something small and slow that was just clearing San Pedro Point, the eastern end of Santa Cruz Island.

It could just be a skipper who'd been anchored around the corner in Smugglers Cove and had second thoughts because of the southeaster. If so, he'd begin changing course in the next few minutes, heading for Potato or Chinese or one of the other west-facing anchorages on the island. But Ericsen doubted it: this guy was coming in toward the coast, heading straight for Santa Barbara at about six knots. Ten to one it was the quarry that had brought them out here.

Ericsen watched the blip for ten more minutes while listening with half an ear to the forecast. The southeasterly wouldn't really fill in till dawn, they were saying, but after that the weather would deteriorate all along the coast. By afternoon the channel would be swept by heavy showers and fifteen- to twenty-knot easterly winds that would raise square-sided seas running across the westerly swells that rolled in from the open Pacific.

But by then *Blue Thunder* would be home and dry—their victim tied up to the Coasties' pier at Channel Islands Harbor, her hapless crew in the slammer, and the chase boat's own complement in some bar, listening to Cowboy explain his own wonderfulness to Tim and anyone else who'd listen. In the dark cabin Ericsen grimaced. Why hadn't he stayed in the Coast Guard at the end of his twenty years? Everybody said what a cold, cruel world it was outside the service, and they'd been right. After six months at jerk-off jobs, he'd been glad to get the billet jockeying one of the DEA's cigarette boats. Glad for about a week—until he'd met Cowboy Daniels.

The hatch slid open and the too familiar peckerwood voice echoed down the companionway: "So what's happening, Swede? How about waking up and finding me my target."

Swallowing his anger, Ericsen said, "You expecting a sailboat, skipper? Not too big, motorsailing offshore from the south?"

It was not much more than an informed guess, but Cowboy's silence told Ericsen he'd hit it on the nose. "How the hell—" Cowboy began, and Ericsen cut him off.

"He's on the screen: maybe two miles off, bearing one two zero."

"Yes!" And then: "Heading?"

"Three twenty-five, about. He's coming to us. We don't hardly have to move."

"I want to pace him a little," said Cowboy. "You get on up here and take the wheel, while Tim and me slip into something comfortable."

"Something comfortable" meant flak vests under orange PFDs with "DEA" in big white letters fore and aft. Cowboy would leap aboard the other boat, waving his long-barreled Magnum, while Tim Huggins would back him with the stainless-steel automatic shotgun. Ericsen's job was to bring the chase boat right alongside and hold her there, while flashing the blinding sodium lights into her cockpit and deafening the other crew with *Blue Thunder*'s PA. It was the kind of performance Ericsen hated, and he told himself he went along only because it was better to terrorize the other crew than have them do something stupid and get hurt.

On deck he was momentarily blinded: the radar screen had killed his night vision, and all he could see were the dozen round, red-tinted instrument dials flanking the padded steering wheel. As Tim lurched down the steps, Cowboy turned on one of the cabin lights, and a shaft of brightness shot from the companionway, so tangible it looked as if you could cut chunks out of it.

"Stupid bugger," Ericsen grumbled, kicking the hatch shut with his foot. The tinted plastic cut the light to a barely perceptible glow, and Ericsen switched off the instrument lights. Bracing himself against the boat's roll, he stood so his head cleared the low windshield. It was like entering another world: the chase boat's smells—diesel exhaust, human tension, old sweat—were instantly gone, replaced by the cleanness of salt water and kelp. And though he could feel the idling engine's vibration coming up through the floorboards and the soles of his seaboots, the sound that filled his ears was the sea at night—the slow, easy break of surf on the rocky shore, punctuated by bird cries.

The stars were dimmer, but overhead the Big Dipper looked close enough to touch. Orienting himself on the North Star, Ericsen stared out to the southeast, past the looming blackness of San Pedro Point and two fingers' width to the left. The other boat was there someplace, no more than a mile away now. As his eyes strained, his ears caught the faintest mechanical muttering, wafted to him on the night breeze.

They must be running without lights, he thought. It was so natural if you were doing something illegal, and such a giveaway. As the other boat's engine grew louder, Ericsen shook his head in wonder. An old gas four-cylinder, probably an Atomic-4, running wide open. Few more hours of that, and the cylinder head would pop right off.

Moments later he saw the ghostly triangle of a sail—no, two sails—off the bow. A ketch, he told himself. Maybe thirty, thirty-five feet, with the main and mizzen sheeted in hard to steady her and the jib roller furled or lowered to keep it from luffing. He pulled the night glasses from their padded holder. The ketch was no more than three hundred yards off now, cutting right across *Blue Thunder*'s bow. He focused the rubber-covered 7 × 50s on her—a distinct glow in her cockpit, probably from the instruments, silhouetted a vertical human blob just behind the mizzen, but he couldn't see anyone else on deck.

A mom-and-pop boat, almost for sure, he thought. There'd been fleets of them a few years back. Ericsen had been stationed in the Coast Guard's Seventh District then, aboard one of the last ninety-five-footers working out of south Florida. On patrols in the Bahamas was when you'd see them—ordinary citizens with extraordinary debts and a boat eating them out of house and home. A couple of bales of grass brought up from the islands seemed like a quick way to get ahead of the finance company.

Now, of course, it was nearly all cocaine or heroin—more buck per bang, and if you got chased and had to dump your load, at least it sank, unlike baled marijuana.

The ketch was past them, and Ericsen nudged *Blue Thunder* into gear. Even on only one of her two engines, and that idling, the chase boat was moving faster than her prey. He swung in behind the ketch, then let his boat slide off to a position on her starboard quarter. It was one of the first things he'd learned: most people were right-handed, and a nervous right-handed helmsman would keep glancing aft, but always over his left shoulder.

But *Blue Thunder* was moving much too fast. Ericsen pulled the shift lever back out of gear, felt his boat slow. At his right elbow he heard the companionway hatch squeak open a foot or so. "I can't see them on the radar," whispered Cowboy. "Where the hell are they?"

"We're too close," Ericsen replied, aware of the dim cabin light—at least Cowboy'd had the brains to switch on the red bulb—but taking care not to look down into the glare. "A couple-three hundred yards off their starboard quarter."

"Two masts, right?" said Cowboy. "Thirty foot overall, white hull, teak cabin, white cabin top?"

"You got it," Ericsen said. "You guys ready to go?"

"Can you see the sail?" Cowboy asked.

"Both of them. Why?"

"Should say B-30 on the sail. Bravo dash three zero. On the main sail."

Ericsen raised the night glasses. "Can't tell. Angle's too sharp."

"Well, swing out to starboard, then," said Cowboy. "I want to be certain."

Was it really necessary? Ericsen wondered. But he wasn't going to get into a hassle with his superior. He put the engine in gear and eased *Blue Thunder* to windward, out of the ketch's wake. A hundred yards, two hundred, and he lifted the glasses again. His lips were parted to speak, when the cockpit radio squawked out: "Unknown vessel! Unknown vessel! What do you want?" It was an old man's quavery voice, Ericsen decided, and clearly near panic.

"Jesus!" snarled Cowboy from the companionway. And then a heartfelt, "Fucking *shit*!"

"I see you tracking us!" said the voice again. "If you don't identify yourself, I'm calling the Coast Guard!"

Ericsen picked up the microphone. "Want me to—" he began, but Cowboy, emerging from the companionway, snapped off the radio.

"Go for him," he snarled. And as Ericsen hesitated, "Now!"

You're the skipper, Ericsen thought, and he pushed the throttle all the way forward. As *Blue Thunder* leaped ahead, he spun the wheel against the single engine's torque. "Their starboard side," he said, keeping his voice flat and emotionless. "Ready to board?"

"Ready." Cowboy was already braced against the gunwale, knees bent. Beside him, Tim Huggins, the shotgun tucked awkwardly under one arm, was working at the snap catch on his PFD. "Will you watch that goddamn gun?" snapped Cowboy. "You're gonna blow somebody's head off."

"Sorry," said Tim. "I can't get this—"

"Stand by!" called Ericsen. With his free hand he toggled the switches for *Blue Thunder*'s spotlights and loud hailer. They were closer than he'd thought: the overpowering lights lit up a cockpit only a few yards away. The hailer launched into its recorded message—"Freeze! Freeze! Freeze! This is a boarding! Don't move or you're dead!"—a deluge of bellowed orders meant to paralyze the hearer.

And it was working, Ericsen saw: clutching the long tiller, an old woman in a yellow foul-weather jacket was open-eyed, slack jawed with surprise. Halfway out the companionway, an even older-looking man was staring blankly into the spotlights' glare.

With accustomed skill, Ericsen dragged the throttle back, then popped the shift momentarily into reverse, spinning the wheel as he did so. *Blue Thunder* decelerated sharply, sliding alongside the sailboat. But the old woman, sensing rather than seeing the other boat, yanked instinctively at the tiller. The ketch's stern swung sharply to starboard, slamming into the DEA boat's hull with a hollow, gouging crash.

Tim and Cowboy had leaped up on their boat's wide gunwale, were crouched to spring. The collision threw the younger agent off balance, and he lurched forward, clutching automatically for the ketch's mizzen shrouds. Cowboy, a natural athlete, absorbed the shock easily, half turning to grab at his staggering crewman.

Beyond him, bathed in the blinding glare of the spotlights, the old man in the yacht's companionway was jarred into movement. A double-barreled shotgun appeared in his hands—a small, detached part of Ericsen's mind noted it was streaked and pitted with rust—the muzzle swinging wildly.

"Watch it!" Ericsen heard himself scream. "He's got—"

A deafening roar that drowned out everything else, and a pink halo, streaked with dark red, appeared around

Cowboy's head as he was lifted clear of the gunwale and hurled back into *Blue Thunder*'s cockpit. Ericsen, his hands frozen on throttle and gearshift, had no time to dodge as Cowboy's full weight crashed down on him. The impact tore the helm seat clean out of the deck, but Ericsen was unaware of falling, of hitting the unyielding teak planking with a solid thump that drove the breath from his body.

All he saw was Cowboy's ruined face, inches from his own; all he felt was hot, spurting blood on his skin; all he heard was an endless high, thin shrieking that had no connection to his own wide-stretched mouth. Something was wrong with his left arm, and it seemed forever before he could drag himself from beneath Cowboy's dead weight.

But it could only have been seconds: the old man was in the same position, still holding the shotgun. The old woman had half turned toward Ericsen, her eyes wide with horror. Tim had simply disappeared.

Got to get help. Ericsen pulled himself to his knees, pain flooding up his arm. The VHF: get off a Mayday. His good hand seized the microphone, keyed it. "Mayday! Mayday! Mayday!" His own voice, hoarse and urgent but no longer a manic scream, steadied him. "This is DEA boat *Blue Thunder*. We're . . ." His voice trailed away. The damn radio wasn't on. Cowboy had switched it off.

He tried to raise his injured arm, and the pain took his breath away. He dropped the mike, groping for the volume switch. From the corner of his eye he saw movement, but he didn't dare take the time to look. He drew a gasping breath, forcing a calm he didn't feel. "Mayday! Mayday!" he called again. "This is *Blue Thunder*. Off San Pedro—"

The force of the blow was like an immense fist in the middle of his back. A red-hot fist that slammed him off his knees onto his face. He never heard the shotgun's second roar.

SANTA BARBARA HARBOR; 11:45 P.M.: NEAL

For Neal Donahoe, the harbor was at its best at night, and the place to see it from was the harbormaster office, upstairs in a nondescript, two-story wooden structure—one of three the city had dropped, seemingly at random, between the old Naval Reserve Building (an all-purpose WPA palazzo with a Spanish tile roof, that could as easily have been a post office, a courthouse, or an opera set) and the Yacht Club, an oversize chalet on pilings, right on the beach.

The office itself was nothing special—a big, low-ceilinged room, cluttered with unmistakably municipal desks and filing cabinets—but its east-facing picture windows commanded a panoramic view down the harbor's main channel, flanked on both sides by a maze of floating piers and slips, the whole wedged between the massive stone breakwater along the harbor's south side and Cabrillo Boulevard's restaurants and motels on the north.

By night, the twelve hundred yachts and commercial fishing craft that filled the slips were a dimly apprehended mass jeweled with walkway bulbs and crowned by a forest of masts, derricks, and antennas. From where Neal stood, the harbor's mouth, beyond the floating piers, was apparently sealed by the two-hundred-yard-long extrusion of Stearns Wharf thrusting out from shore, the brightly lit windows of its shops and restaurants reflecting off the dark, unruffled water.

It was a vista that sucked you in; Neal could not have said how long he'd been standing at the window, when he became aware of slow, heavy footsteps climbing the outside stairway. Reluctantly he lifted himself off the desk he'd been sitting on, rebuckled the wide, stiff, heavy gunbelt that had been sawing him in two, and moved toward the chest-high counter that separated the harbor staff on duty from the customers—mostly slip holders with a question, a gripe, or a problem, but also tourists (usually Germans) determined to explore the harbor's every cranny. Or just looking for a bathroom.

He was barely halfway across the room when his boss's massive head appeared in the window. Christ, he looks terrible, Neal thought. Ten years older than this morning.

But he forced a smile as the door opened. "*Buenas noches*, peerless leader," he said. "Have trouble sleeping?"

"As a matter of actual fact," said Walt d'Andrea, "I was sleeping better than I have in weeks, until Jacobson called in sick." The flu that swept through Santa Barbara every winter seemed especially baneful to young adults: Bill Jacobson, the third Harbor Patrol officer to be infected, was a musclebound twenty-six-year-old. Neal, almost a decade older, had not come down with it once in five years, and even Walt, closing sixty and a bronchitic chain smoker, seemed immune.

The Santa Barbara harbormaster was a big man, nearly as tall as Neal and half again as wide, Smokey the Bear gone to fat. D'Andrea wore no uniform: there was none for the harbormaster, unlike the chief of patrol, who was supposed to set an example for the ten men and women under his command, the youthful officers whom Neal privately thought of as the kids.

D'Andrea pushed open the partition's swinging gate. He was breathing heavily—a lot more heavily than one flight of stairs called for. But Neal wasn't about to say so: they'd torn that script to bits two days ago, when Neal had caught Walt smoking, dead against doctor's orders, behind the maintenance shed.

"Anything going on?" D'Andrea asked.

"Dive boat in 2-B-23's real low in the water. Joanie reported it, end of last watch, and I took a look myself. Another six inches and he's a submarine."

D'Andrea pursed his lips. "B-23," he repeated. "That wouldn't be *Whirlaway*, would it?" It would, of course: Walt carried a blueprint of the harbor in his head. "T. J. Wellcome just got her last week. You call him?"

"Three times," Neal replied. "No answer. His van's in the harbor lot, though."

"You tried Brophy's, of course. And the Breakwater." D'Andrea was really talking to himself, and Neal didn't bother to answer. "He's got a girlfriend, hasn't he? Works in one of the shops on Stearns Wharf?"

How the hell did he do it? Neal wondered, not for the first time. If you figured that each of the permanent boats in the harbor had an average of three people connected to it, and you added all the working people and hangers-on who made the harbor their headquarters, and then did the same for the staffs of the motels and restaurants along Cabrillo and Stearns Wharf—not to mention the shops and apartments for three blocks back, to where the freeway cut the waterfront off from the rest of the city—you had a population of maybe five thousand, and Walt seemed to know all of them. Not just their names and faces, either, but who was sleeping with whom (and more important, who wasn't), who was flush and who was broke, and why, down to the most unimportant details—relatives and birthdays and anniversaries.

Five years before, when Neal had just arrived in town, a temporary employee of the Waterfront Department doing general maintenance, Walt had come up to him one afternoon, out of the blue, and said: "There's a slot opening up on the Harbor Patrol, Neal. Why don't you apply?"

At that moment Neal, slimy with grease and sweat, was head down in a patrol boat's engine compartment. He had just about decided to go back to sea, maybe sail west to Hawaii if he could find a yacht that needed a skipper with a hundred-ton ticket. He hadn't even straightened up. "Harbor Patrol? No, thanks, Mr. d'Andrea."

Neal was perfectly aware that people in California seldom called each other "mister." But it was a way of holding on to his Yankee persona, and at that point he didn't possess much of anything else, barring some patched dive gear and a Japanese sextant with a minute's error knocked into the arc.

Walt had simply ignored his reply and pressed on: "Your middle name's Machado, they told me. Is that for real?" Neal had pulled himself out of the hatch and blinked in the bright sun a couple of times, trying to decide if he ought to take offense. But Walt's broad, flat, friendly face was unrevealing, the deep-set brown eyes blankly inquisitive. At last Neal said, "It's real."

Walt's infectious smile invited you to blabber on. But Neal had just stood there, waiting.

"I wasn't sure," Walt said. "You look, like, kind of Hispanic."

"Oh?" said Neal, on the verge of annoyed. "What's that look like?"

"You know—that actor in *Wrath of Khan*, only younger, before he sold Chryslers on TV."

"You mean Ricardo Montalban?" said Neal incredulously. "You think I look like him?"

"Well, maybe like him if he had an Irish father," said Walt, laughing. "Thing is, some people figure a Hispanic name looks better on a city job application."

Just play it as it lays, Neal had told himself. "It was my mother's name, before she married."

Walt had nodded with satisfaction, as if Neal had just answered a difficult question correctly. "Machado," he said. "There's a bunch of Machados here in town, but you're not one of them."

Neal had fallen neatly into the trap. "Yes, I am. More or less. My grandfather . . ."

Walt was nodding again. "Eddie Squid," he said. And then, seeing the amazement in Neal's face, added, "No, I'm not that old. But how many Hispanic abalone divers' kids—or Anglo ab divers' kids, for that matter—grow up to be hotshot New York lawyers? Edward Machado, esquire, the Chicano F. Lee Bailey: your grandpa was a kind of legend around here."

Not a legend that Neal had wanted to be reminded of. He'd shrugged and leaned back into the engine compartment, but Walt could be relentless when he wanted. "About the Harbor Patrol: why not give the job a shot?" he asked innocently. "You got something against cops, Neal?"

Looking back, Neal could see that was where he'd lost control of the situation. Just as he'd lost it again, two years later, when Walt had maneuvered him into taking the advanced law enforcement courses at City College. "It's not *for* anything," Walt had insisted. "But it's free—the city's paying."

Of course, Walt had already known—probably the goddamn microbes had told him—about old Ray McInery's recurrent colitis, and as harbormaster he was aware none of Ray's officers had the qualifications to step into the chief of patrol's job.

Because going along was easier than being niggled to death, Neal had taken the courses and passed them easily enough. And, when the time came, he'd accepted the promotion, too. An uptight guy, Neal reflected, might bristle at being manipulated so often—but if you thought of Santa Barbara as nothing more than another of life's way stations, getting uppity was hardly worth the trouble.

Now Walt was waiting for a response to his semi-question. Not that Neal could offer much help. T. J. Wellcome, a boat mechanic who worked out of the back of his van, wasn't one of the harbor's brighter lights. He'd taken the urchin boat called *Whirlaway* as payment for a bad debt, and now that he had his pound of flesh, he probably didn't give too much of a damn about it.

Neal shrugged his ignorance, and Walt seemed prepared to accept it, for the moment.

"Anything else?" he asked.

"Nothing local. A funny kind of Mayday off San Pedro, a little before nine."

"San Pedro?" Walt's eyebrows rose. "Down by Long Beach, and you picked up the call this far away?"

"That was the funny thing," Neal admitted. "It was loud and clear on sixteen, though. Coast Guard Channel Islands heard it, too—they called right back, but there was no reply. Probably another false alarm."

"Channel Islands heard it," said Walt slowly.

"That's what I said." Neal could feel himself starting to get annoyed.

"But Long Beach didn't," Walt continued.

And Coast Guard Station Los Angeles/Long Beach was a stone's throw from where the Mayday was supposed to be coming from, while Station Channel Islands was closer to Santa Barbara than to Long Beach. A lot closer. I should have picked up on that, Neal thought. "So it must've been a false call," he said.

"Maybe." Walt eased his huge frame onto one of the desk chairs, which creaked painfully. "What exactly did the Mayday say?"

Here at least Neal was on firm ground. He picked up the office log and held it under the light. "Mayday twice," he said. "Then 'This is blue under . . .' " Seeing the surprise in Walt's eyes, he added, "Sounded like 'blue under' to me. Maybe 'blue thunder.' Blue something, anyway. There was a lot of engine noise."

Walt's lips were pursed again, which made Neal nervous. "What else?"

"That was about it. Just the position: 'Off San Pedro.' Then a hell of a bang and he was cut off."

Walt was nodding. "Cut off in, like, mid-sentence?"

"Might've been," said Neal cautiously.

Walt heaved himself out of the chair with a grunt and waddled over to the chart of the Santa Barbara Channel tacked to the office wall. "Come here," he said.

Neal saw it was lesson time, knew he'd missed something important. "What?"

"Come over here," Walt repeated, and, when Neal was standing at his side, pointed to the eastern tip of Santa Cruz Island. "What's it say?"

"I'm an idiot."

"It doesn't say that yet," replied Walt, with a deep, wet, remarkably bearlike chuckle. "For the moment it just says 'San Pedro Point.' "

"But how come Channel Islands—"

"Who knows?" Walt cut him off. He picked up a phone and began punching a number. "But those Coast Guard kids cycle through so fast, they hardly have time to learn all the names on the chart. If there wasn't a senior petty officer right there when the call came through, the watchstander probably made the same mistake you did."

"Only I should know better."

"You said it—I didn't." His voice changed pitch as he spoke into the phone. "Let me speak to whoever's in charge. This is Walt d'Andrea, the harbormaster up in Santa Barbara. I think you may have a problem." He paused, waiting, and glanced at Neal. "DEA," he mouthed silently.

Neal looked a question, but Walt was talking again. "Do you people have a chase boat named *Blue Thunder*?" He stuck out his tongue at the clearly abrupt answer, then continued: "Well, have it your way, buddy. But I heard you were running a boat with that name, and one of my people picked up a Mayday that sounded like '*Blue Thunder*.' " Walt, suddenly grinning, held the receiver away from his ear. Neal could hear the voice gabbling excitedly.

"That's all we got," said Walt, raising his voice to cut through the other's. "It was aborted in midtransmission. But the guy might've been calling from off San Pedro Point . . ." No, the east end of Santa Cruz Island. Look, why don't you call Coast Guard Channel Islands? They'll have the whole transmission on tape."

From across the room Neal heard the click as the DEA hung up. "You're welcome. Any time," said Walt to the handset. To Neal: "I love those guys."

"Personally," said Neal, "I hope their fucking boat sank like a stone." His stomach, he realized, had tied itself in a knot. To Walt's raised eyebrows he said, "Listen, when I first came here, I was bringing a yacht up the coast to Long Beach, through the canal from the Caribbean. . . ."

"I know. DEA boarded you."

"Boarded us?" Neal could hear his voice trembling with fury as the memory returned. "Waving guns under our noses, slapping my crew around—and when they couldn't find anything, they ripped the wires off the distributor cap so we had to sail in without the engine." And then the penny dropped: "You knew?"

Walt's smile was bland. "You think I hired you without checking? And I also heard the DEA was tipped. That was why they were so pissed when they came up dry."

"Yeah. Well . . ." Watching Walt's eyebrows rise, Neal felt his ears go hot.

"But you're no druggie. Those years in the Caribbean: never a whisper." Walt paused, as if about to add something, then seemed to think better of it. "The thing is, you're a peace officer now, and DEA are your colleagues, just like the Coasties. . . ."

"Not like the Coasties."

"Just like the Coasties," Walt repeated, "and the Customs and the county mounties and the SBPD." He waited, saw Neal wasn't going to object, and added: "Even if they are arrogant pricks."

Neal held up his hands in surrender. "Whatever you say, peerless leader."

"That's what I say," said Walt. The phone at his elbow jangled. "Now get out of here."

"Want me to answer that?"

Walt picked up the handset. "Harbormaster. Wait one, please." He hit the hold button. "It's going to be a busy night. Why don't you go home while you can?"

"But—"

"This is my part of the job," said Walt. "Explaining why we aren't going to send an outdrive boat out twenty-five miles in a rising easterly to look for their lost lamb. You think you can do it better?"

"Hell no."

"So get going." He reached over, finger poised to press the hold button again, and said: "She's waiting for you. In the shadows next to the Chandlery."

There was no point to a rhetorical "Who's waiting?" so Neal merely shrugged an acknowledgment.

It seemed to irritate Walt. "It's a sucker move, Neal. Not only is she married to a well-known reptile, but she's got some reptile blood herself."

Stung, Neal could only say, "They're not living together."

"Just watch yourself, is all I say." He stabbed at the phone. "This is the harbormaster. How can I help you?"

Standing at the bar on the far side of *Finish Line*'s ornate main cabin—all smoked-glass bulkheading and slippery-looking white Naugahyde, decorated to within an inch of its life—Jannice McKay slammed down her empty highball glass on the Corian countertop. "Well, I don't see how Walt could've expected you to know," she said. "Half the places in California begin with San, and the rest begin with Santa. I can't keep them straight myself, and I grew up here. He was just trying to put you down."

As if for emphasis, she tossed her head so her shoulder-length hair shimmered like a crow's-wing waterfall around the oddly sharp planes of her face. It was one of her best effects, and Neal could watch her do it all evening long. Watching the rest of her wasn't too painful, either: her skin, tanned to its winter café-au-lait, was still as smooth as a teenager's. She was wearing black stirrup slacks that were tight across her muscular behind, and a black top so loose it looked as if one of her quick, nervous movements might take her right out of it.

Jannice was wrong about Walt, though. Neal was sure of that—though not at all sure why she was so wound up about it. Maybe it was her idea of how to stand by a man. She and Neal had been lovers—bedmates, anyway—for two weeks, but he had the feeling he'd known her better before they'd come together, in a blaze of lust and tequila, right on the fake fur carpeting of the yacht's main cabin.

At the time, Neal had assumed *Finish Line* was her husband's property. That had been part of the excitement, no question about it, though everybody knew Rudy and Jannice McKay had had an open marriage long before they started living apart. Rudy, whom Neal had met only once or twice, was an investment counselor, specializing in the well-off retired folks who comprised ten or fifteen percent of the city's population. Jannice was just Jannice, and that seemed a career in itself.

Until recently they'd lived on the Riviera, Santa Barbara's fashionable cheek-by-jowl strip of homes overlooking the city, the channel, and in clear weather the nearer offshore islands—Anacapa, Santa Cruz, and Santa Rosa. Now Rudy had moved up into one of the canyons above and behind town—a bigger place, people said, though he seemed to be living alone. And Jannice had just received a live-aboard permit for *Finish Line*, which turned out to have been her property all along.

One thing Neal was sure of: he didn't want to talk to her about Walt anymore. He mumbled something noncommittal into his margarita and shifted his weight, trying and failing to find a comfortable position on the slippery settee.

"That's right," she said, dark eyes glittering. "Let him walk all over you." She sounded genuinely angry, but she used her slightly husky voice like a musical instrument, and sometimes she got so wrapped up in the melody that he had the feeling she wasn't paying much attention to the words. Abruptly her face cleared, and the vertical grooves between her finely plucked eyebrows disappeared. "Okay," she said. "I'll lighten up. Here, I made you another." She held out the shaker, but he shook his head.

"I'm still working on this one." Jannice made the best—and probably the strongest—margaritas he'd ever tasted, using undiluted frozen limeade, tequila she kept in the yacht's freezer, and practically no ice at all. Neal was already feeling a warning tingle in the tips of his fingers and toes, and he'd only had one and a half.

She set the shaker on the counter and came across the cabin, dropping beside him on the settee. She leaned into him, her head on his shoulder. "I know, I know. But you're such a softy. I hate it when you let people take advantage of you."

Her pose was relaxed, almost boneless, but she was trembling against his arm. By now he knew what that meant, felt his own breathing quicken. Before he was quite ready for it, her long fingers had taken him by the chin, turned his face to hers.

It was less like kissing than being devoured, but you couldn't be indifferent to it. After a long minute they broke apart, mouths still half open. Jannice recovered her voice first. "God, you turn me on," she said.

"It's mutual," he replied, his voice uneven to his own ears. And that was entirely true: he felt like a teenager about to score for the first time. He knocked back the rest of his margarita, barely tasting it, and set the glass on the deck. He slid his hand under her blouse, and she arched her back in response.

As his fingertips felt for the catch of her bra, she bent forward, probed his ear quickly with her tongue, and whispered, "Here? On the floor again?"

"The deck," he said, barely managing not to gasp. "On a boat we call it the deck."

"You're the only man I've ever known who could undo a bra without a fuss," she said. "One of your many talents." She pulled back, lifted the blouse over her head, her eyes locked to his. "What's the matter? Nobody can see in."

"I know." But knowing and believing it were two different things: the brocade drapes were drawn tight across *Finish Line*'s cabin windows, but Neal felt the unseen presence of thousands on the pier's concrete walkway just outside. "Let's use the aft cabin."

She rose to her feet in a single sinuous ripple. "You just like to watch," she said, grinning. "Well, so do I. Come on."

The owner's stateroom, under *Finish Line*'s afterdeck, ran the full width of the yacht and was occupied mostly by a king-size bed that stood a full three and a half feet off the deck—the better to accommodate the 250-gallon fuel tank beneath the mattress. Into the low overhead above the bed Rudy had set a plastic mirror six feet square that provided an unnervingly rippled version of what was going on below it. The cabin's small ports, three on each side, were closed and covered, and Jannice, on tiptoe, pulled the deck hatch shut. "I suppose you want music," she said. "There's a tape in the player."

He certainly did want music, the noisier the better. And she had anticipated him: as he pressed the switch on the bulkhead-mounted tape deck, Gaieté Parisienne surged into the cabin. When he turned, Jannice was facing him, propped against the bed, feet spread apart, the zipper of her slacks partway open.

Apartment #3, 200 Elise Way; 0015 Hours: Tory

The soft burr of the telephone beside her bed brought Tory out of an erotic dream starring Gilles Everard, so real she came awake feeling his hands on her. But that, she reminded herself firmly, was in a previous life. Clearing her throat, she picked up the phone and said, "Lieutenant Lennox."

Lieutenant: even half asleep she enjoyed hearing it—so much better sounding than "Lieutenant Junior Grade Lennox"—and it stopped telemarketers and other obscene callers in their tracks.

"Tory? It's Dave Blanchard. Listen, I'm sorry for calling so late—"

For heaven's sake, stop apologizing, she wanted to say. You're an officer in the United States Coast Guard, or supposed to be.

"—but we just got called out, and I wondered if you felt like a ride. . . ."

"When have I not? I'll meet you at the boat."

"Give you a lift down to the harbor?" he offered.

Five minutes alone with him. It was, she supposed, the least she could do. "That'd be nice. I'll be outside in ten minutes."

"That's great. And I won't honk if you're not."

"See that you don't," she said. Last time he'd turned up ten minutes early and leaned on his horn till she'd come out, which had necessitated a formal letter of apology to the condo board. If there was one thing Tory disliked more than other people apologizing, it was doing so herself.

She gathered herself, hurled back the covers, and sprang from bed. Pulling her nightgown carefully over her head so as not to tear the lace (one might be a commissioned Coast Guard officer, but one was also a woman), she stepped to the counter at the end of the bedroom. While brushing her teeth, she decided a shower—even an in-and-out navy shower—would take too much time, and so would any makeup beyond lipstick.

Her working coveralls were hanging next to the sink. With a windbreaker, they'd do well enough. She stepped into panties and eased into a notably unseductive jogging bra. For a moment she considered long johns—it could get damned cold in Santa Barbara Channel in January—then decided the *Point Hampton*'s wheelhouse would be warm enough.

Taking the coveralls off their hanger, she caught her profiled image in the mirror. Too many of the Breakwater's strawberry cones. But she'd told herself that before. A grease pencil was lying on the counter, and she picked it up. On the glass, just to the left of the scrawled "Order more FV inspection forms," was larger, heavier lettering that read "125 lb by Easter!" Beneath it, neatly indented, she wrote "No More Cones," but not the codicil, "At Lunch-time," that formed automatically in her mind.

She zipped up the coveralls and turned sideways, patting the fabric over her belly. The deadly phrase "corn-fed good looks" leaped from memory's ambush, dripping acid, as it had when her roommate, that slinky round-shouldered bitch, had used it their first night at boarding school. Picking up the grease pencil again, Tory added "Or Other Desserts" to her admonition. She pulled on wool socks and heavy black boots, gave her short, blond curls two quick passes with the hairbrush, glanced at her watch, muttered, "Oh, shit," and raced down the stairs to the apartment's small living room.

In the hall closet Tory's civilian coats and jackets hung on the left, her Coast Guard gear on the right. She chose the blue float coat as being warmer than her windbreaker and, from the row of three baseball caps on the shelf above, the one lettered *USCGC POINT HAMPTON* that Dave had given her—forced on her was more like it, and didn't she wish it were true.

Rasp of tires on the asphalt turnaround outside. Speak of the devil. She opened the door with one hand, to show him she really was ready to go, while groping with the other for the black leather gloves with the wool inserts that she was sure she'd remembered to put back on the closet shelf.

Dave's car horn gave a strangled, as if it were semiaccidental, squeak. Hell with it, she decided. She pulled on the float coat and discovered the gloves tucked neatly in its pockets. Grinning at herself, she stepped out into the night.

As she slid into the passenger seat of his Chevy, she could feel him getting up the nerve to try to kiss her. "Rain before morning?" she said.

"What? Oh, the easterly." He thought about it for a second. "Could be," he said, his voice flat. He put the car in gear.

Don't be a bitch, Tory. "It's sweet of you to ask me along, Dave," she said. As the car rolled down the condo development's twisting drive, she leaned over quickly and pecked his cheek.

For a moment she was afraid he would pull over, but he didn't. "My pleasure," he said, beaming.

As he paused at the condo's entrance gate, the streetlight lit his round face. He'd just shaved—two small cuts were still gleaming wet—but he'd missed a spot at the corner of his jaw. And the silver J.G. bar on his jacket's right shoulder strap had lost one of its clutch pins. This was so usual for him that he carried half a dozen extras in the ashtray. Tory fished one out and resecured the insignia. She asked, "What's happening?"

"Thanks," he said absently. At the corner he stopped again and carefully looked both ways, yet only just avoided a weaving pickup rolling lightless down Shoreline Drive. As Tory released her held breath and the Chevy turned onto the main road, her companion—oblivious of their narrow escape—said, "Somebody transmitted a partial Mayday, maybe off Santa Cruz, and the Los Angeles DEA office thinks it might be one of their boats."

From the Coast Guard housing enclave on the right—small, cramped ranches with million-dollar views of the Santa Barbara Channel—two cars squealed onto the road ahead of the Chevy, heading down toward the harbor a mile away. One she recognized as the Bronco belonging to Mike Svoboda, the surly first class who was the *Hampton*'s boatswain. Rise above, Tory, she thought. He's just an enlisted man. "So it's a SAR mission, then?" she said.

"Search, anyway. Rescue, I don't know."

But at least it was on the water, doing what Tory had joined the Coast Guard for—not sitting in the Santa Barbara Marine Safety Detachment's airless office filling out forms or trying to keep hostile commercial fishermen from killing themselves, which was what the service was paying her to do.

Strictly speaking, Tory had no business riding aboard the *Point Hampton* on a mission. In fact, you could make a good argument that having her aboard—outranking the eighty-two-footer's legitimate skipper—was a poor idea. Especially when that skipper was so eager to defer to her, in the hopeless hope that it would somehow get him into her bed. She could ignore Dave Blanchard without difficulty, but she couldn't ignore the fact that she was undermining his already wobbly authority in his own boat—and making a potentially dangerous enemy in Mike Svoboda, who could salute and call her ma'am all day and half the night, without in any way hiding his disdain for women officers generally and Lt. Victoria Alexandra Lennox in particular.

Well, screw him, she decided as Dave swung into the harbor entrance and parked almost in the slot that read "C.O. Point Hampton," behind the two-story cinder-block building that housed her own office and the *Hampton*'s workshop on the ground floor and the cutter's shoreside base above.

She followed Dave between two gray-painted wooden buildings—dark at this hour, except for a faint glow from the second-floor windows of the harbormaster—and out onto the high wood pier where the fishing boats unloaded and the *Hampton* tied up. There was movement aboard the cutter and the suppressed rumble of her twin diesels. Dave quickened his step.

Relax, she wanted to say. They can't leave without you. But that would only have embarrassed him, so she matched her stride to his—no problem, since they were nearly the same height and Tory's legs were, if anything, slightly longer.

As they came abreast of the eighty-two-footer, she saw that Svoboda had singled up the lines and had hands stationed fore and aft. The boatswain's mate himself, a blocky ghost in the semi-darkness, was standing amidships, radiating impatience.

The *Hampton*'s deck, depending on the tide, was anywhere from level with the pier to a good six feet below it, and a steel ladder had been set into the pier's timbers to make boarding the cutter relatively easy. Dave went first, swinging clumsily over the gunwale and throwing a gesture that was half salute, half wave in the general direction of the stern. Behind him, Tory paused on the ladder, saluted Svoboda, and said, "Permission to come aboard, sir."

"Permission granted," he said, returning her salute.

She stepped to the deck, came to attention, and threw her best highball to the flagstaff at the cutter's stern—aware all the while of Svoboda's expressionless stare and the nearly visible amusement of two of the crew nearby. But it was, she felt, important for her, both as an officer and a guest, to set a good example, regardless of how over the top it might seem to the cutter's own crew.

In the cramped pilothouse, the QM2, Paul Abrams, was at the wheel, with Dave standing beside him. "Welcome aboard, Lieutenant," Abrams said. "You want some coffee? It's ready."

"I'd kill for coffee," she said, and heard a chuckle behind her. It was Wilson, the cutter's cook, with two steaming mugs.

"Cream, three sugars—right, Lieutenant?" he said.

"Exactly right," she said, taking the mug he held out to her. "You're a lifesaver." She took a long swallow, savoring the taste: two-thirds double-strength instant, one-third evaporated milk, and enough sugar to make her heart race. It was ferocious, dreadful stuff, and she loved it.

"Ready any time you are, sir." Svoboda's flat, hostile, Brooklyn voice came up from the darkness below.

Dave turned to her, and she knew before he opened his mouth that he was going to ask her to take the *Hampton* out;

knew she could do it, day or night, better than he. And knew, absolutely, it would be a big mistake. "I'll hold your cup, skipper," she said.

But it was Tory's owllike night vision, three hours later, that picked out the tiny, greenish glow in the choppy water off the starboard bow. In the absence of any precise information about where the missing *Blue Thunder* might have got into trouble, the *Hampton* had been working a creeping line search pattern, criss-crossing a straight course between San Pedro Point and the DEA boat's home base at Long Beach.

In Tory's five years as a Coast Guard officer, she had participated in enough SAR missions to know that the search data you started with was always fragmentary and often dead wrong. But seldom as fragmentary as in this case, where the Los Angeles DEA seemed to have no idea where its chase boat had planned to be and a considerable reluctance to admit it even existed.

But the light on the water was real enough, even if no one else in the *Hampton*'s wheelhouse could see it at first. "It's pale green," she insisted. "Like one of those chemical things. At two o'clock."

"Cyalume," said Svoboda. And then, "I've got it."

The *Hampton* had already rigged the outboard-powered inflatable she carried on deck, and at Tory's hint one of the junior petty officers was suited up for rescue swimming. The cutter, with Abrams at the wheel, eased to a rolling halt about a hundred feet from the green glow that appeared and disappeared with each small sea. Svoboda, raising the night glasses, said, "The light's on a PFD. The guy looks unconscious."

Or dead, Tory corrected. The water temperature was only fifty, and a skinny man without a wet suit could be unconscious in three hours. The official name, Personal Flotation Device, was often ironically accurate: the person floated all right—but if he couldn't hold his head up, he drowned.

In case the figure in the water was still alive, the *Hampton* put her rescue swimmer over the side, and the inflatable, too. But it was no good. Three minutes later the young man's slim body lay face up on the deck. He was wearing dark coveralls not unlike the Coast Guard's—but, Tory noticed, tailored to fit tight around the hips and loose across the shoulders. One foot was bare, the other was still shod in a garish cowboy boot. The useless life jacket, with the still phosphorescent plastic cylinder clipped to one shoulder, lay to one side, as did a second vest, of bulletproof Kevlar with *DEA* in block letters across the back.

A circle of Coasties stood staring down as Valdez, the cutter's EMT, examined the body. "You want me to call in a Medivac, Mr. Blanchard?" Svoboda prompted.

Valdez looked up. "I s'pose we better, but he's deader'n shit, sir. Back of his head and half his ribs are smashed. Nothing's going to bring him back, short of the Second Coming."

Tory had placed herself in the circle of observers, more because she thought it proper than out of any curiosity. She had seen a few bodies, including a couple that had been in the water more than a week, and she had learned she could look straight at pretty much anything as long as she kept her eyes slightly unfocused.

But Valdez's remark was so unexpected that, without intending to, she found herself staring straight down at the dead man's outflung right arm. "Look at his hand," she heard herself say.

"What about it?" Svoboda demanded.

She forced herself to drop to one knee and took the chilly, slightly rigid, amazingly dead hand in her own. The wrinkled, blue gray palm was scored diagonally by a deep purplish pink groove running from between thumb and forefinger to the heel.

"Man, that's some friggin' gash," said an uneven voice she didn't recognize.

But it wasn't a cut, she saw—at least not in the usual sense. It was too wide, for one thing, and the edges were abraded.

"You know what that is, don't you?" Svoboda was looking across the body at her.

"I think so. Yes," she said. Almost idly, she turned the dead hand over, heard herself gasp.

"Sonsabitches tortured him," said somebody.

"Yanked out his fingernails," said somebody else.

"Don't be dumber than absolutely necessary, Watkins," said Svoboda coldly. "Those nails are busted, not pulled out. Poor bastard was in the water, trying to claw his way up the side of the boat."

"Or stuck between two boats," said Valdez. "Trying to push them apart."

"The head and the ribs: yeah," said Svoboda.

For the first time, Tory allowed her gaze to take in the young man's face. Not a young man, she corrected herself, a boy, like these kids. He looks peaceful enough, she thought. She was glad his eyes were nearly closed. A deep discoloration marked his forehead. She bent forward to look more closely, pressed it with two fingertips.

"It's a bruise all right," Svoboda said. "Hell of a whack. Probably got it when he went overboard."

"So he hit the water unconscious," said Tory, working it through. "The cold woke him up, and there were these two hulls . . ."

"Squeezing him," said Svoboda. His hard tone softened. "That's a bad way to go."

The surge of pity and sorrow caught her completely unaware, and for a moment she was afraid she'd burst into tears. Strangely, it was Svoboda who rescued her: "Maybe you'd better get on the horn, Lieutenant. There's people ashore gonna want to know about this." As if reading her mind, he added: "The skipper's not feeling so good, I think."

She looked around. A figure was sitting on the deck, its head between its knees. From one shoulder strap a silver bar swung loose.

Finish Line, Santa Barbara Harbor; 4 a.m.: Neal

Ten years earlier, a college dropout in flight from his dead-end New York office job, Neal had washed ashore on the French-Dutch Caribbean island of St. Martin, where for a while he made a living as mate aboard large sailing yachts. Just when nautical subservience was becoming more than he could take, he stumbled into a job as off-the-books mechanic for a bareboat charter firm teetering on the brink of bankruptcy. The pay was meager and occasional, but one of the perks was accommodation aboard a derelict sloop, dismasted in a hurricane and surviving as the company's floating shop, pad for employees without work permits, and source for cannibalized spare parts.

The job endured, surprisingly, for nearly five years. By then Neal had learned, usually by trial and error, how to jury-rig almost any broken part or system on a sailing yacht—without either the correct parts or the proper tools. And because his floating home had a habit of subsiding unexpectedly beneath the harbor's surface, he had picked up another, more subtle talent: the ability to remain subconsciously in tune with his nautical surroundings while focusing his overt attention on the job at hand—whether it was fiddling a sticky float valve or interpreting an obsolete French chart.

Thus he was able to enjoy Jannice's demanding, even painful, passion to the hilt (and play his own part with enthusiasm), while at the same time registering the gradual increase in the southeast wind, the departure of the *Point*

Hampton, and even the too frequent kicking in of *Finish Line*'s battery charger.

When Jannice, who liked to wind up on top, had at last collapsed sweatily beside him, he felt himself sliding down the pleasantly steep slope into unconsciousness. And that was the way he wanted it, he told himself. There was nothing that soured classic, white-hot sex more completely than an earnest postcoital discussion studded with terms like "relationship" and "co-dependency."

But since Neal's arrival in Southern California, that kind of intellectual tofu had become inescapable—another awkward, deeply boring aspect of what he thought of as the safe-sex culture. He himself had come of age sexually in the last unfettered years before AIDS changed everything, and his Caribbean, an enclosed world of charter yachts and nubile vacationers, had remained a carnal time warp. Dutifully, he mastered the new vocabulary and the new rules, but he mourned the vanished, casual lust of his twenties.

Until Jannice. She'd come up to the office—her magnetized key to the marina gate had got bent and wouldn't fit in the lock—one evening when Neal was holding the fort alone. She was wearing a souvenir T-shirt from the defunct charter firm Neal had worked for, and it quickly became obvious that they needed to compare experiences over dinner.

Not since Neal's days on St. Martin had an encounter progressed so fast. A couple of beers and chowder upstairs in the noisy conviviality of Brophy's—where they'd compared life histories and decided that Neal's long-ago divorce carried the same weight as Jannice's semi-official separation—was followed by an hour in a nearly deserted joint on lower State, drinking ersatz dark-and-stormies. But even lacking the proper ingredients, the drinks must have had impact, because suddenly the scene had changed to *Finish Line*'s main cabin, where Jannice was introducing him to her high-octane margaritas. They were on the second batch, dancing to a tape that Neal would normally have scorned as elevator music, when Jannice lifted her head from his shoulder, looked him straight in the eye, and said, "I hope you're clean, because I like it bareback."

From there to the carpeted deck was a blur of motion, the rest of the night unsafe sex at its old-fashioned, dangerous best. And if he and Jannice didn't have a great deal to say to each other between engagements, was that really so bad? If nothing else, it made for a deep and dreamless sleep afterward.

Not so deep he failed to note the first drops of rain on the deck above, and he was dimly aware later of Jannice slipping quietly out of the bed. And out of the cabin—some part of his mind, about three levels down, heard and remembered the distinctive click of the catch on the engine compartment door.

But the scream brought him up to the surface fast, his heart pounding and the sweat starting fresh. A second scream, barely human in its agony, and the throat-catching smell of burning fiber. By then he was pulling on his pants, trying to remember where he'd dropped his belt with the sheathed walkie-talkie. The third scream came from right outside the cabin door. It burst open, and she was standing there, wreathed in flame.

The quilt was a heap on the deck, and he grabbed it up. As she stepped forward, screaming again, he threw it over her, embraced it, pulled her to the deck. She was struggling feebly and moaning. From the quilt came the smells of Jannice's perfume, burnt cloth, and—he would never forget it—cooking meat.

On his knees, he looked up and saw a flickering light down the passage, heard the pulsing roar of a well-established blaze. He lurched up, slammed the door shut, and opened the overhead hatch to the deck. Someone was shouting—was it his own voice?—"Fire! Fire!"

There wasn't time to be gentle. He lifted Jannice's wrapped body—she was jerking convulsively under the quilt—and managed to find in the moment a strength that surprised him. He pushed the bulky cylinder of her out the overhead hatch, but the quilt caught on the latch, and he had to tear it free. Then he pulled himself up through the opening, cracking both kneecaps in the process.

It was raining, a cold and driving drizzle, and the boat was perceptibly rising and falling. The smell of burning was thick in his nostrils as he lifted Jannice, by now barely twitching, breathing with dreadful, hoarse snores.

A handful of half-dressed figures were milling about on the walkway, well back from the finger pier next to *Finish Line*, and none of them was showing any willingness to come closer. Neal risked a glance over his shoulder: no sign of fire in the yacht's wheelhouse, but on the dashboard three or four dials had lit up, and alarm bells were going off below decks.

Down the pier he saw two running figures; his heart lifted when he recognized the Harbor Patrol's khaki under their yellow rain gear. "Get off, Neal! Get off the boat!" one of them yelled. He recognized Taffy Hegemann's clear soprano, so the larger officer behind her had to be her partner, Lance Dalleson, the patrol's newest and least experienced member.

Taffy pelted out onto the finger pier, puffing like a beached whale. She must have run all the way from the marina gate, he realized, a good two hundred yards, with her belt cinched far too tight. "Whole forward end's on fire!" she gasped up to him. "You can see it through the portholes."

Lance, beside her now, was barely breathing hard. "We called the Fire Department. They're on the way."

"Here," said Neal, falling again to his knees and extending the still smoldering bundle. "Take her. Get an ambulance—she's burned, I don't know how bad."

Between them, Lance and Taffy managed to grasp Jannice's body without dropping it between boat and pier. Neal's senses seemed to have been sanded to a preternatural edge, and he noticed the quick glance that passed between the two officers, realized they knew who was in the quilt.

He was on his feet, three long steps to the wheelhouse controls, his mind racing. *Finish Line* was a diesel boat, of course—two big GMs—but the generator that powered her electrical system was gasoline-driven, with its own twenty-gallon tank. It could go anytime, and with this wind blowing, half a dozen yachts could be in flames. The strategically placed fire extinguishers and hoses that dotted the pier wouldn't do much against that kind of blaze.

Jannice seldom took the big yacht out of its slip anymore, but she kept the ignition keys in a drawer next to the wheel. Neal slid it open as he heard Taffy calling from what seemed like miles away, "Neal! Will you get the hell off of there?"

He was stabbing one key at a slot, and of course it was the wrong one. Now the other key was in. Was the deck warm under his bare feet, or was that just his imagination? The starboard engine's starter ground and ground without catching; Neal jammed the first key in its slot, and the port engine started almost immediately, in a pungent cloud of diesel fumes. As he gave it a minute to steady down, he tried to recall where the generator's fuel tank was located. In the engine room, he thought. Not good.

Lance was calling now, from right alongside. "What're you doing?"

"Going to take her out of here! Cast me off!"

Lance, he remembered gratefully, had been a marine before he'd drifted west and joined the patrol: an order was an order, even though it took him an extra thirty seconds to figure out how to get the spring lines free from Jannice's mystery knots.

No time for knots. Neal pulled the gear lever aft, and the boat began to move. Taffy was jumping up and down on the finger pier, trying to get his attention. She was jabbing her pointed finger at something on *Finish Line*'s side, just below the gunwale. Had the flames broken through? No, that couldn't be. . . . And then the two yellow shore-power cables she'd been pointing at snapped simultaneously in a shower of sparks.

But *Finish Line*'s stern was swinging to starboard under the uneven thrust of the single propeller. Neal spun the wheel all the way over before the boxy hull began to straighten out. By then it was a little late: he heard the grating sound of metal against fiberglass, and the unoccupied boat in the next slip shied away. The high squeal of rubber fenders was followed by a loud explosion as one of them popped under pressure.

The harbor's slips had been arranged and rearranged to allow a bare minimum of maneuvering space between each pair of rows. Normally, a twin-screw boat like *Finish Line* would turn completely in its own length simply by running one engine ahead and the other astern. But with only a single propeller, and that well off center, the boat could turn in only one direction, unless there was about a quarter mile of open water ahead.

And backing the big, square stern into the wind was making it worse. There was only one way *Finish Line* was going to get free of the cul-de-sac she was in. Putting the helm hard over, he let the port screw drag the stern sharply to starboard. The big yacht pivoted somewhere around her midpoint, and the bow slammed into the concrete piling at the slip's outer end, ripping several hundred dollars' worth of stainless-steel rail out of the deck.

But *Finish Line* was free, in the narrow slot leading to the main channel. Neal spun the wheel back to straighten her, and she began to slide crabwise and backward toward open water. The southeaster was still pushing her down on the leeward slips, where Lance was standing on one boat's after-deck with a huge boathook in both hands. A puff swung *Finish Line*'s high bow down toward him, and he braced himself, the pole out like a lance. There was no point yelling at him, Neal saw: his jaw was set for the impact.

Lance weighed perhaps 180 pounds, and it was solid bone and muscle. *Finish Line* had no muscles at all, but she displaced twenty-five tons. When her hull struck the outstretched boathook, Lance went over backward so fast his determined expression didn't have time to flicker.

Two more slips to pass, with *Finish Line*'s bow falling farther and farther off the wind. It slammed another piling—wood, not concrete—and left it tilting dangerously; dragged across a sailboat's transom, amputating the dinghy in davits that hung there; and left the debris draped around the last piling.

But she was still pointed in the wrong direction: toward the tangle of floats where the Harbor Patrol's boats tied up and, more dangerously, toward the fuel dock. *Back out or try to turn?* Neal couldn't decide, knew he must. And then, like a guardian angel, the running lights of *Harbor 3*, the patrol's twenty-five-foot inboard, flashed on. Taffy, who'd grown up on her father's fishing boat, must have seen what Neal's problem was going to be and was risking her life to help him out.

The patrol's three fiberglass boats had all been fitted with solid rubber cylindrical fendering that completely encircled the gunwales. Skillfully, Taffy set *Harbor 3*'s padded nose against *Finish Line*'s high bow and began to push it around. But could she do it quickly enough? Even as the heavy yacht began to swing, both boats were blowing down on the gas dock.

Now Neal, glancing down the companionway, could see the flames were invading *Finish Line*'s main cabin, licking hungrily at the furry nylon carpeting. There was only one thing to do, one gamble to take. Neal turned the steering wheel all the way to starboard, jammed the throttle all the way forward. As he'd hoped, the yacht's stern lurched sharply to port and kept on swinging, with the wind now helping instead of hindering.

Turn, you big cow. Come on, you can do it. She was moving ahead now as the bow swung, but she was going to clear the gas dock by a good twenty-five feet, he saw. Taffy was still pushing *Finish Line* around, oblivious of the fuel dock's steel guard-rail reaching out for *Harbor 3*'s stern. Neal pumped the yacht's horn, again and again, until he saw Taffy's face turn to him. Without a word, he pointed to her boat's stern. She looked back, slammed both *Harbor 3*'s engines into full reverse. The little inboard jumped backward as if scalded, just in time to slide between *Finish Line*'s swinging transom and the guard-rail.

The yacht could complete her turn unaided, Neal saw. He stepped to the afterdeck as *Harbor 3* pulled alongside. "Thanks, Taffy," he yelled. "Now get clear!"

"Throw me a line," she called back. "I'll tow you. . . ." Her face changed, and Neal looked over his shoulder. The flames filled *Finish Line*'s cabin and were flickering out the open companionway. Through the windshield he could see the fire had burst two of the three hatches up forward. "Better jump!" Taffy yelled.

Damned if I will. He dashed forward, gave up the idea of trying to close the companion door, and sprang for the ladder that led to the flying bridge. A flame reached for his ankle as he climbed, but then he was safely up on top. *Finish Line* was still turning, past the heading he wanted, and he quickly spun the wheel back until she straightened more or less and began to pick up speed.

With only one engine to push her, *Finish Line* was mushing heavily, throwing a wake that looked like a tidal wave. The pierheads slid by on both sides, each one alive with spectators—live-aboards who'd been dragged from their beds by the commotion. Off to Neal's left, a city fire engine was pacing *Finish Line* along Cabrillo Boulevard, heading for Stearns Wharf.

Now he saw the high silhouette of the live-bait boat and its floating pound, permanently moored just inside the channel's right-angle turn to the sea. The last of *Finish Line*'s deck hatches chose that moment to explode, and a column of reddish flame shot several yards into the air.

He put the helm over and *Finish Line* answered slowly, open water ahead of her. Stearns Wharf was on his left, with the fire truck rumbling noisily over its loose planking. And just in his wake Taffy had *Harbor 3* almost climbing his transom.

The flying bridge deck—which was also the wheelhouse roof—was burning his bare feet. He climbed into the helmsman's seat, his hand still on the wheel. Only a hundred yards more, he told himself. Well, a hundred and fifty.

And one more decision to make. The rain was hissing as it hit the deck. *Finish Line* would burn to the waterline before she sank—unless, of course, she exploded first. But there would be a hulk left either way. A hulk that might contain evidence of how the fire had started. And the shallower the water in which the yacht sank, the easier it was going to be for the salvagers to raise her. But the shallow water was directly to windward of wooden Stearns Wharf and its wooden buildings.

On *Harbor 3* Taffy was stabbing the horn furiously. Yeah, I want to get off, too, he thought. But he deliberately put his mind in neutral, slowly and carefully headed the flaming boat straight out to sea, and switched off the port engine before he jumped from the helm seat, yelling at the fierce heat that seared his callused bare feet, and leaped over the side.

CGC *Point Hampton*, Santa Barbara Channel; 0645 hours: Tory

Dawn arrived without a perceptible sunrise, just a gradual easing of the soupy blackness until the sky had assumed the sullen gray of wet cement. The southeasterly was into its stride, gusting to thirty knots or so, but the rain still came only in bursts that slatted across the *Point Hampton*'s bridge windows every few minutes.

For the past two and a half hours, since the body had been hauled aboard, the cutter had been running an expanding square search pattern, in which each leg was at right angles to the previous one, and a quarter-mile longer, using the spot at which the body had been found as the base point. A little after dawn, the port lookout had spotted another life jacket like the one on the dead man, but empty. Aside from that, the channel had yielded nothing useful at all.

The steep, wind-driven waves were now cresting at about four feet, but far larger swells—twelve feet high or more—were marching down the channel from the west, pushed by the storm center up in the Gulf of Alaska. The resulting cross seas were pitching and rolling the cutter simultaneously, and her six-knot search speed seemed to emphasize the uncompromising shape of every wave.

Tory had stationed herself at the small nav table, on the port side of the eighty-two-footer's U-shaped bridge, an open-backed shelter about fifteen feet above the water. It was dry, but that was about the most you could say for it. Tory, who almost never got seasick, was feeling distinctly puce, but as long as the apelike Svoboda continued to hold out beside her, she would stick it out.

She had volunteered to handle the cutter's navigation after two successive crewmembers succumbed to the combination of small print, poor lighting, and a motion that combined the worst features of a roller coaster, a rocking chair, and a pot-holed roadway. That was bad enough, but the previous navigator had left as a legacy what appeared to be his last three meals, mostly on the deck but a certain amount sprayed across the chart itself.

One of the cutter's radios crackled to life. The *Hampton* was running a regular comms schedule with Long Beach, which was acting as coordinator of the search, but this was a new voice, a high-pitched tenor. Tory recognized it quickly—she had, in fact, lunched with its owner, a Coast Guard helo pilot, not three weeks ago.

"I've got a visitor for you," it said after the formalities had been completed.

"Seven three one, *Point Hampton*. Say again?" said Svoboda, who was handling the call.

"A visitor," the pilot repeated. "Somebody who wants to play boats with you guys."

What was it, Tory wondered, that made so many pilots talk silly on the radio? Svoboda, at all events, was not playing: "Seven three one, *Point Hampton*. Explain, please. Over."

"Okay, *Point Hampton*: It's some heavy from DEA in L.A. He insisted on coming out, and my CO figured a helo transfer at sea would serve him right."

Svoboda's expression of disgust made his face look like a Notre Dame gargoyle's, but his voice remained even and passionless. "Seven three one, *Point Hampton*. I'll have to check with the skipper. It's pretty bumpy for dropping personnel on the deck."

"I can see that from here," the pilot's voice came back. "Feel it, too—and it's going to get worse before it gets better. But I don't think you've got a choice."

"Wait one." To Tory's amazement, the petty officer turned to her. "What do you think, Lieutenant?"

Several thought patterns were moving through her head, and it required a moment's concentration to isolate the correct one. "If *Hampton* were to tuck in behind Potato Harbor," she said slowly, "we ought to be able to find flat water at least."

Svoboda nodded grudgingly. "Right in close to shore? It's plenty deep."

"No." She didn't have to think that one through. "This southeasterly'll be coming off the hills like gangbusters. We'll just have to poke around till we find a flat spot without too much wind," she said, remembering to add, a second late, "If the skipper approves, of course."

"Agreed." Though his expression never changed, she could feel Svoboda relax. You hardass, you were testing me, she thought. And in your position, I'd've done the same. The petty officer picked up the mike. "Seven three one, *Point Hampton*. I think we can find a lee behind the island. Make your drop a little easier. How on that? Over."

"Fine with me, *Point Hampton*. But I don't much care if we soak this turkey. Might cool him down."

Svoboda's eyebrows shot up nearly to his hairline—admittedly no great distance. He glanced at Tory, and she shrugged incomprehension. But she was thinking that the helo pilot must be furious at his passenger to be so careless with his transmissions.

"Seven three one, *Point Hampton*. Wait, out." Svoboda got to his feet, swaying. "I'll run it by Mr. Blanchard."

"Yes," said Tory. A DEA heavy from the Los Angeles office, she was thinking. Somebody with enough juice to muscle himself onto a Coast Guard helo. It's got to be Feltrini. And if you were going to list people you didn't want to match wits with while trying to keep your stomach behind your belt buckle, Mr. August Feltrini would be close to the top of any selection.

She knew a good deal about him, considering she had yet to lay eyes on him. He was, after all, her presumptive target, the reason she'd spent the last month spreading her behind on a Santa Barbara office chair. And he was also, she hoped, going to be her ticket out of there, to where she knew she belonged—the bridge of one of the Coast Guard's new 110-foot cutters.

It went back to her previous assignment, at headquarters in D.C., where she'd been in the public affairs office. On the one hand, she had to admit, the job looked like a perfect fit: where better to place a personable young lady whom the Masters School of Dobbs Ferry had brought to a pitch of social savoir faire and the Coast Guard Academy had taught to look and act like an officer?

But the job turned out boring almost beyond belief and, some days, dangerous to one's career. Particularly when some congressional creep was demanding a favor that was impossible to grant—often because the same creep had just voted to further geld the service's already tiny budget. Patriotic by upbringing, Tory had arrived in D.C. with a carefully neutral attitude toward her nation's legislators; after six months in the capital, she wouldn't have trusted one of them with a rusty nickel.

Perhaps sensing her frustration, Tory's indulgent boss set her up as tour guide for a troupe of representatives investigating military expenditures. The senior among Tory's charges, the ferocious Rep. Linda Goodell, R-Calif., had decided she wanted a ride on a Coast Guard cutter, and when a congressperson of Goodell's seniority (six consecutive terms, ranking minority member of her subcommittee) said "Jump," the military only whimpered, "How high?"

They had flown down to Miami and embarked aboard CGC *Reliable*, a 210-foot dowager older than most of her crew, for a routine exercise in fishing Cuban refugees out of the Caribbean. Two nights out, *Reliable*'s radio picked up what might have been a fading distress call, in semi-hysterical French. As luck would have it, Tory was the only person aboard the cutter able to understand the language when it was being shrieked at supersonic speed by a panicky yachty.

While *Reliable* worked through the formalities of obtaining permission to board a foreign-flag vessel—District to Area to Flagplot to the State Department—Tory reflected she could have cut through it all with a single patched call to the French embassy, whose handsomest and most efficient second secretary was her regular escort in D.C.

The requisite Statement of No Objection came at last, and Tory had led the boarding party, straightened out the problem—a cocaine overdose, exacerbated by calvados—and earned Rep. Goodell's loudly expressed approval.

The skipper of *Reliable* put Tory in for a commendation, and that would normally have been the end of it. But one evening a week later, back in D.C., Tory's home answering machine had taken a message from Rep. Goodell herself. Please call—immediately—a number in suburban Maryland. The call arrived just as Tory was on her way out to dinner with Gilles Everard, but the young diplomat insisted she phone back right away.

"When the Republicans win in November," he said, "Goodell will be chair of the Merchant Marine and Fisheries. She can make you an admiral, *chérie*."

Well, that was just Gallic hyperbole, of course: Tory was as far from flag rank as the GOP was from taking Congress. But Gilles's reasoning appealed to her, as he well knew. He had confided to her that someday he would be *la grande nation*'s ambassador in Washington; in the same spirit, she'd confessed her intention to make admiral before she retired.

So she had returned Rep. Goodell's call and got an invitation—an order, really—to meet the representative the following evening, at a restaurant she'd never heard of. And not in uniform.

Technically, as Tory knew very well, she should have gone straight to her boss in the public affairs office, but she could argue—barely—that this was purely a social occasion. And if (as she confidently expected) it turned out to be something else, she could always throw herself on the mercy of her easygoing leader.

Gilles, when she explained the situation, was dubious—but not about the service's rules. "I don't know if you want to go there, *chérie*."

"It's that bad?"

"Actually, the food is nearly acceptable, I am told. But the clientele . . ." He paused in thought. "It is possible Mme. Goodell has something other than business in mind," he said with obvious reluctance.

"Do you mean what I think you mean?"

"*Mais enfin*," he continued, "it is probably worth the gamble. I will drive you there, and wait outside."

"Oh, come off it, Gilles. I'm half her age and twice her size."

"I was thinking," he said mildly, "that you might have need of a character witness."

La Goodell, in unobtrusive dark slacks and a blazer, had been all business, however. Having sworn Tory to secrecy, she got right to the point. One of her other subcommittees, as it happened, had strongly backed that embarrassing political flop, the Zero Tolerance war on drugs. The public—most of them—were passionately on her side, Goodell believed, but too many enforcement agencies saw the drug war only in terms of how it might swell their departmental budgets. Or as the representative put it, in her open-voweled California accent, "They want to catch just enough druggies to make a splash on the six o'clock news, but they don't really want to stop the flow, as long as the appropriations keep coming."

Tory was inclined to agree, so she nodded and said nothing. That was enough for Goodell to lay her proposition on the table: One of the most suspect agencies, in her opinion, was the DEA, a collection of cowboys who were often in business for themselves. Goodell had tried and failed to get an inside peek at the agency by suborning one of the DEA's people, but if she could obtain the help—off the record, of course—of someone in a supposedly cooperating organization, it might be possible to winkle out the information she wanted.

By this time alarm bells were going off in Tory's head and her stomach had tied itself in a knot around the dreadful gnocchi she had managed to swallow out of politeness. "I couldn't possibly—" she began, but Goodell, riding her own enthusiasm, pressed in for the kill.

The kind of person required, she continued, was smart, brave, and ambitious. Too junior to attract attention—or have a bureaucratic ax to grind. She fixed Tory's eyes with her own. "That's you to a T. And the fact you're a woman and already in law enforcement is even better camouflage."

"Look," said Tory desperately, "even if I wanted to . . ." The representative's eyes narrowed dangerously, and Tory switched to a feeble, "Public Affairs isn't exactly—"

"Of course not. It's the wrong place entirely. But I can fix that—put you where the action is."

Action. Tory's mind flashed back to the moment of boarding the French yacht. In the midst of the sodden, pitching, hysteria-streaked chaos, she had felt fully alive, for the first time in months.

"And you'll be doing something important, Tory—for the American people."

Tory, struggling to keep her emotional footing in the wash of rhetoric, had felt herself being swept away by the sheer force of Goodell's will. "I can't," she said. "It's—"

"Too risky?"

Suicidal, if you really want to know. "It wouldn't be ethical," she said feebly.

If Goodell even heard what the younger woman was saying, she gave no sign of it. "I'll set things up. It'll take a few weeks."

"But—"

"No commitment. All I'm asking is that you keep your eyes and ears open." She paused. "I'm assuming you wouldn't object to a transfer from D.C. to Southern California. . . ."

At that point in her life, Tory would cheerfully have fought a roomful of lieutenant-commanders to get away from Washington, but she managed to say only, "It's not Southern California that's the problem. It's—"

"Then that's settled," Goodell said quickly. "Trust me."

That was something she would never do. But Goodell had delivered and, more remarkably, had stayed off Tory's back—so far. But at odd moments, especially in the hours before dawn, Tory would wake up wondering when the reckoning would come. And here it was.

The Coast Guard helo, a French design with a nose that always reminded Tory of a dragonfly's big-eyed, inquisitive face, was holding position with some difficulty above the *Hampton*'s after deck, its main rotor *thwacking* the air viciously. Its personnel basket, which looked from below like the framing for a medieval iron maiden, swung and twisted overhead as the wind gusts caught it, until at last a deckhand was able to grab its guide line and bring it down. The man who struggled free of it was streaming water. His beaky face was suffused by rage and his iron-gray hair stuck up in spikes that looked so much like feathers, Tory heard herself say without thinking, "The proverbial wet hen, I do believe."

Next to her Svoboda, who was supervising, gave a startled bark that might have been laughter. "You got that right," he said. And to the passenger: "Sir, you want to clear the basket, please?"

On his feet, the man tore off the PFD he'd been wearing and hurled it to the deck. Wearing a blue windbreaker and sodden trousers molded to his body, he was revealed as being of middle height but remarkably skinny. He stepped gingerly away from the basket, which promptly lifted clear of the cutter's deck and superstructure.

Catching sight of Tory's silver bars, the visitor demanded in a snarl that cut through the helo's ear-splitting noise, "You the captain? I'm Feltrini, DEA Los Angeles. Where's the body?"

Basic Bronx, she thought. And used to having his own way. Rather than try to explain, she pointed to the black body bag secured to a couple of railing stanchions. From the *Hampton*'s bridge, Dave Blanchard's voice called down: "The pilot wants to know if he's released."

Feltrini, who had dropped to one knee by the rail, looked up at the swinging personnel basket and farther up at the hovering helo. "Shit, yes," he said. "You're not getting me back in that thing."

A professional tough guy for sure, and yet his face, when he had unwrapped the dead man's head, was momentarily as tragic as a Goya sketch. Then it hardened, and he turned to Tory. "He's mine all right. Name of Huggins. What killed him?"

Tory, in a complete set of the *Hampton*'s foul-weather gear, was feeling cold and soggy. Feltrini, she thought, must be on the verge of pneumonia. Yet he wasn't even shivering. "I think you'll need an autopsy to answer that for certain, Mr. Feltrini," she said. "But I can give you some contributing factors." Unexpectedly she sneezed. "Wouldn't you like to get inside, where it's warm?"

"No," he said. "I go in that tin box, with this toy boat of yours hopping up and down, and I'll be sick in five minutes."

"Suit yourself," Tory said. "But if you're going to stay on deck, you'll have to wear a PFD—a life jacket."

"Have to?" His eyes narrowed dangerously. "Is that supposed to be an order?"

She wasn't sure she had his measure, but she couldn't back down now. "Yes, sir. Our boat—our rules."

Something that might have been a smile flashed across his hard face and disappeared. "Whatever," he said.

"Boats," she called to Svoboda, "a dry PFD for Mr. Feltrini. And a cup of coffee."

Ten minutes later the DEA man, though still soaked, seemed somewhat mollified. "You said something about 'contributing factors,' Lieutenant. What was that supposed to mean?"

"Well," she began, quickly arranging her thoughts, "I'm pretty sure Mr. Huggins was alive when he went in the water. It's about fiftty degrees, and he was in it for at least three and a half hours—"

"How do you figure that?"

"We got called out at midnight, on a possible Mayday. If we assume the call was real, that's probably when he went in. We found him at about zero three-thirty. Okay so far?"

Feltrini nodded.

"That water temp and that immersion time wouldn't kill somebody young and strong. But Petty Officer Valdez, who examined him, says the back of his head's crushed, and so are most of his ribs—"

"I saw that," said Feltrini. "What do you think happened?"

Was he really taking her seriously, or did it just sound that way? Nothing to do, she decided, except press on: "Here's how I see the sequence, Mr. Feltrini. Your agency's boat was in the process of boarding another vessel, probably a sailboat—"

"How d'you know that?" Feltrini snapped.

"If you'd let me finish, sir. This is just a theory—my own theory."

"Okay. Go ahead."

"As I said," Tory continued, "your boat came alongside to board. Mr. Huggins takes a step across, or starts to. Something happens—the boats swerve apart, I don't know—and he loses his balance. He grabs one of the sailboat's shrouds—"

"He grabbed *what*?" said Feltrini.

"A shroud. It's part of the rigging, a wire that runs from the top of the mast to the side of the boat. He grabbed it, and it slashed the palm of his right hand, almost to the bone. Obviously, he couldn't hold on after that, and he fell between the boats. I think that was when he bruised his forehead."

A spasm of pain creased Feltrini's face. Maybe there's a little human left in him after all, Tory thought.

"The cold water woke him up," she continued. "The two boats were still side by side, and he saw they were going to crush him."

"Jesus God," said Feltrini softly.

"With a PFD on, he couldn't dive—even if he thought of it. But he clawed at one or both of the boats. Lost some fingernails. Didn't do any good—they came together and . . ." A sailor herself, she saw it clearly. She had to swallow hard before she could finish: "Came together hard enough to break his ribs, crush his skull."

"I see," Feltrini said slowly. Abruptly, he shook himself. "Yeah. But what about my other two men?" he said. "And my boat—forty-seven-foot Magnum, had two five-hundred-horse diesels. You got any bright ideas where that is?"

"I wish I did, Mr. Feltrini," she replied. "All I can say is that if it didn't sink, it's no place within radar range."

COTTAGE HOSPITAL, SANTA BARBARA;
8:40 A.M.: NEAL

"How they feel now?" the emergency room resident asked.

Sitting on the edge of the examining table, Neal cautiously wiggled his bandaged feet in midair. "Like a real bad sunburn. Could be worse."

"It will be," said the resident, smiling grimly. "Wait'll you put your weight on them."

"I thought you told me to stay off them," said Neal.

"I did, but you won't," the resident replied. "I know your kind."

"Just another macho martyr," Neal agreed. "Listen, what about Mrs. McKay?"

"Sorry, she's not my patient."

Neal could tell from the doctor's nonexpression that he knew—and what he knew was bad. "Look," he said, straining to keep impatience out of his tone, "this lady may be a material witness—the *only* witness—in a major felony. I need to talk to her. As a police officer."

"There's already police officers up there with her," the resident said. From the way he was measuring his words, Neal suspected the young doctor already saw himself a hero of the witness stand, maybe even *Court TV*.

"Can you find the officer in charge?" Neal asked. "I need a few minutes of his time."

"For what, Neal?" The voice came from behind him, at the curtained entrance to the little cubicle.

Neal swung around slowly, lifting his legs over the table. In the process, three more bruises made their presence known. The man watching him was thin, heavily freckled, and pale—for Southern California—with washed-out blue eyes. He looked to be in his forties, mostly because of his thinning hair, which he wore in an old-fashioned crewcut that emphasized the loneliness of the stragglers in front. He was dressed like a tourist, with a short-sleeved shirt worn outside his pants, presumably to hide the holster on his belt and the SBPD lieutenant's badge clipped to a leather fob at his waist.

"Morning, Steve," Neal said. "Are you the one?"

It was a guarded relationship on both sides: nominally, Neal was Steve Merriam's professional equal. But a certain tension existed between the city's regular cops and the Waterfront Department's small, low-profile force. In the presence of outsiders, the two groups tended to treat each other with exaggerated politeness, but Neal knew that Merriam, whom he'd met half a dozen times, was a spokesman for the department's faction that wanted to absorb the Harbor Patrol entirely—which made him Walt d'Andrea's mortal enemy.

"We're not officially in this yet," the police lieutenant said. "But I know the victim, so I came down."

Now that Neal considered him more closely, Merriam looked as if he'd dressed in the dark and been up for hours. He was, Neal recalled, that rare bird, a native Santa Barbaran, and he'd probably known Jannice for years—hell, he might have gone to high school with her: they were close to the same age.

For those who'd been born there before about 1970, Santa Barbara was two places at once: the sleepy small town of their childhood memories and, superimposed on that, the wealthy, tourist-oriented city of 85,000, wedged between the sea and the mountains and blocked on the west by the untidy sprawl of Goleta and on the east by the mansions and estates of Montecito.

But the vast majority of Santa Barbarans had come to the city from someplace else, and they had grafted to the original social root system an elaborate web of organizations and relationships that would have fit a place three times Santa Barbara's size. When it came to knowing how things worked and who worked them, a native started off with advantages, but longtime connections cut both ways, too: the same social network an insider like Merriam could usually exploit might sometimes pressure him in unexpected ways.

"You've seen her, Steve?"

"*Seen* is the word. They've got her pretty heavily sedated." Merriam was one of the open-faced school of Southern Californians, and his reluctance to meet Neal's eyes was worth remembering.

"Well, I want to see her myself," Neal said. "Look, I know she's in bad shape—I saw her on fire."

Merriam shook his head. "Not a prayer. The doctors just threw me out of her room. Maybe later on today, they said." He paused, and Neal wondered if the feeling of guilty relief showed on his face: he did not in fact want to look at Jannice's face as he'd seen it last—reddened, blistering, swollen; her lustrous black hair scorched away. He'd do what had to be done, when it had to be done, but the postponement was more than welcome.

Merriam's lips pursed, and Neal could tell he'd decided to offer a little information, maybe as an investment. "Third-degree burns. Hands, arms, face, chest, abdomen. Like something blew up in her face." He waited a few seconds, perhaps to let it sink in. "So what happened, Neal? You were with her, right?"

With her. Something in Merriam's tone made Neal wonder if he and Jannice had a history, too. He glanced up at the young MD, who was trying to impersonate a piece of furniture. "I could use a cup of coffee, or six," Neal said. "I'm about a gallon behind, for this time of the morning."

"Fair enough," Merriam replied. "They got a coffee shop here."

"What I was hoping was you'd give me a lift back to the harbor. We can talk in my office."

"Sure. You're planning to go like that?" The ghost of a smile flicked across Merriam's face and vanished.

In his impatience, Neal had forgotten he was wearing only an open-at-the-back hospital gown. "Yeah, well, we're informal, but maybe not that informal," he said. Carefully, he eased himself off the table. For a moment, when his feet touched the cold floor, he felt nothing. Then the pain kicked in, fierce enough to make him speak through clenched teeth. "Walt brought me some clothes. I wouldn't want to shame you in public."

As Merriam's black-and-white, one of the SBPD's Ford sedans known to waterfront regulars as killer whales, pulled into the harbor entrance, it found itself nose to nose with a genuine monster—a thirty-ton-capacity Travelift with *Finish Line*'s blackened, dripping hull suspended in its fabric slings.

The Travelift, a huge, wheeled quadrilateral made of steel beams, pivoted sharply, crossed in front of the police cruiser, and chugged through the open gates of the Boat Yard, where the supports for the dead yacht's temporary bier were already in place on the asphalt.

"That's the boat, right?" said Merriam. "Christ, what a mess." He watched, shaking his head, as the Travelift positioned itself with elephantine grace and slowly lowered the wreckage to the ground.

"Let's have a look at her," Neal heard himself say.

For several seconds the only sound inside the car was the slow flap-flap of the windshield wipers. "You sure?" asked Merriam, sounding almost as surprised as Neal felt. But the question had confirmed Neal's resolve. The charred, sodden hulk had to be inspected, and he was determined not to let someone else be the first.

Merriam pulled the cruiser into the yard and parked between *Finish Line* and a big dragger up on blocks for rudder repairs. As yard personnel chocked the burnt-out wreck on her keel, the two men watched in silence from the car. The after end of *Finish Line* barely existed above the waterline, and her deckhouse and flying bridge had disappeared entirely. Her forward half, which had looked undamaged when she was up in the slings, was revealed, once she had been lowered to the ground, as nothing but a gutted shell. Below the waterline she was intact, but the hull, props, and rudders were covered in green growth.

Neal opened the car door and carefully swung his bandaged feet out into the rain.

"What're you—crazy?" Merriam demanded. "You'll get soaked—your feet'll get infected. . . . ."

Neal pulled free of the lieutenant's hand. "No. I want to look."

The asphalt was streaming with wet, and the thick bandages soaked through in seconds. But the water felt cool, and the padding insulated his blistered feet from the old screws, bits of fiberglass, and sharp pebbles that littered the ground. Neal limped around to what was left of *Finish Line*'s transom. What had been the master stateroom was now a chaos of charred rubble. But if he looked carefully, he could still see the stubs of bulkheads and frames.

Amidships, the big diesels were entirely recognizable, even with most of the paint burned off them. The starboard engine was considerably more blackened than its companion and seemed tilted slightly out of plumb. The generator, which had been outboard of it, was gone. So it blew after all, he thought. Funny I didn't notice.

As he stared at the shambles, something heavy and dry—a blanket that smelled like damp closet—fell across his shoulders. He looked around. Merriam, in an old raincoat, was standing behind him. "Thanks," said Neal.

"*De nada*. So, does all this tell you anything?"

"Not a hell of a lot," Neal admitted.

"We've got the specialists coming in. Surprising what they can piece together." Merriam was clearly organizing his next questions, and Neal found he couldn't make himself wait for them.

"We were in the aft cabin," he began, his voice sounding harsh and cold. "Back here at this end of the boat—"

"Alone, just the two of you." It was not a question.

"Right. We were asleep—anyway, I was—and I heard her get up—"

"When was this, Neal?" Merriam interrupted.

"I'm not sure. I heard the *Point Hampton* leave harbor, and I'm pretty sure I remember the rain starting. . . . Anyway, Jannice got out of bed, quietly."

"Like she didn't want to wake you."

"Yes. And she went out the door, closed it behind her."

"Also quietly," said Merriam. "But you heard it."

"If you're a sailor, you do. On a boat, you hear everything."

"Okay, she went out the door and closed it behind her. Then what?"

"Few seconds later, I heard a click. I'm almost certain it was the latch on the engine compartment door." Neal leaned forward over the blackened transom. "See there? That's where the corridor was. That little sill is what's left of the engine room doorway."

"Let me see if I've got this straight, Neal: It's the middle of the night, you hear your . . . lady friend getting out of bed. She goes out of the what's-its-name, the bedroom cabin, but not to the bathroom, which might make sense. No, you hear her going into the engine room." Merriam's tone was even, reasonable, almost gentle. "Didn't that make you curious, Neal? The engine room at—what?—three, four in the morning?"

"Not really," he said. "Not on a boat. . . ."

"What was she wearing?"

"Wearing?"

"For this midnight jaunt among the machinery. Coveralls? Tights? An evening gown?"

Neal felt his ears redden. "Nothing."

"I see. And you weren't curious enough to follow her."

"No." There was no way of making a landlubber understand that a sailor would wake up two or three times in the night, for no reason at all, and have to prowl the boat.

Merriam sighed. "Okay. What happened next?"

"I heard a scream," Neal replied. "In fact, it woke me up."

"But you were awake—awake enough to hear a latch open ten feet away, through a closed door."

"That wasn't awake, Steve. That was . . . Oh, forget it."

"Whatever you say, Neal. And then?"

"Another scream, in the corridor. I got out of bed, started climbing into my pants, when she screamed the third time." Neal glanced at Merriam, but the lieutenant seemed to be fascinated by something in the middle distance. "Then the door popped open, and there she was. On fire."

"You mean her hair."

"No, I mean she was on fire. Burning."

Merriam shook his head. "How could that be, Neal? She didn't have any clothes. People don't just burn."

The memory of it, blocked so firmly from his consciousness, flooded in. He turned from the charred boat and threw up on the ground.

Santa Barbara Harbor; 1500 hours: Tory

Sometime during her first, ceremonial visit to Walt d'Andrea's private hideaway, at the end of a short corridor from the patrol's main office, Tory had decided the room was a remarkably accurate reflection of its proprietor. Its door was a mosaic of colored Post-it memos from Walt's staff—long-defunct phone messages and felt-tip scrawls expressing varying degrees of exasperation at Walt's habit of never getting back to callers. The wall to the left as you came in was standard bureaucracy: floor-to-ceiling steel shelves stuffed and sagging with the reports, regulations, and edicts that government emitted in endless quantity—though Walt's collection was in total disarray. She suspected he'd deliberately avoided filing the contents in any coherent order (a suspicion fortified by a half-dozen bulging cardboard cartons on the floor, from which leaked more windrows of crumpled, yellowing paper).

Facing the door was a second wall—half of it a window overlooking the northwestern corner of the harbor and half an oversize aerial photograph of the entire harbor, almost covered with thumbtacked postcards, snapshots, Christmas cards, wedding and birth announcements, and yellowed newspaper clippings.

The wall facing the harbor's axis was almost filled by a wide window, and against the remaining partition was Walt's desk, which usually looked as if large, paper-eating birds had been nesting on it. Today, however, the desk was at first glance far more businesslike—forms, memos, and letters in moderately neat stacks, each a couple of inches high, each held down by some piece of marine hardware. But then Tory noted that the topmost item on the pile nearest her, under a bronze shackle lacking its screw pin, was a two-year-old note addressed to Walt and signed by a now deceased Santa Barbara county supervisor. It confirmed her suspicion that the arrangement of the desk was purely cosmetic, a desperate last-minute gesture for the benefit of Walt's present guests. If so, she feared, it was a waste of time: three of the four other men wedged into the small office were unlikely to be impressed by bureaucratic scenery. And the fourth, alas, didn't count.

Walt himself had swiveled his desk chair around to face the room, but it was Gus Feltrini, perched on one corner of the desk, who dominated the group without saying a word. He seemed to be vibrating with barely suppressed impatience, but it wasn't communicating to either the deputy—she thought his name was Mendez—representing the Santa Barbara County Sheriff's Department or the rumpled, tired-looking lieutenant from the city police, both of whom were slouched on chairs borrowed from the main office. Their postures expressed equal parts boredom and indifference as they traded city-official small talk with Walt, while the wind-driven rain sheeted across the office's single window.

Between them sat Dave Blanchard, following the conversation with quick, anxious head movements that suggested a bird who'd found itself seated between two cats. His tropical blues—a spare set carried aboard the *Hampton*—were unnaturally neat and clean, while Tory was still wearing the coveralls (damp, wrinkled, and salt stained now) she'd blithely leaped into some fifteen hours before. The cutter had made port only half an hour earlier, but Feltrini had used the time running in from the channel to organize this meeting—a meeting that was now waiting on one missing party.

Just when it seemed that even Walt had run out of county gossip, the office door opened. "Sorry I'm late, folks," said Neal Donahoe. He shuffled into the office—for some reason he was wearing sandals and bulky white athletic socks with his otherwise immaculate khaki shirt and blue pants—and lowered himself stiffly onto the remaining chair.

By God, he is a handsome man. It was exactly the thought that had run through Tory's mind the first time she'd met the harbor's chief of patrol, three weeks before. And, maddeningly, each of the dozen or so times she'd seen him since—even though he was not in any way her type. Still, if you liked your men tall and lean, with a boxer's shoulders and a mechanic's corded forearms and big, competent hands, Donahoe certainly filled the bill. And the deeply tanned face fascinated her—broad across the cheekbones, with almost oriental dark eyes set in a web of sun wrinkles; large nose, straight except for a bump at the bridge; wide, thin-lipped mouth and too perfect teeth; and straight black hair cut short on the sides and in the back.

An interesting face, coupled with a polite, almost ingratiating manner—so what about the man had put her off in their brief, formal encounters? She'd dismissed her feelings as disdain for yet another pleasant California lightweight, but now, watching as Walt introduced him to Feltrini and Mendez, Tory saw the faintly amused detachment that assessed the others, kept them at arm's length. Subconsciously she must have been aware of it during their previous meetings, and suddenly she was not so sure she'd read him right.

"Any word from the hospital, Steve?" Donahoe was addressing the city police lieutenant, who shook his head and started to answer, only to be interrupted by Feltrini.

"I asked you all here because we've got a problem," the DEA man said. "That is, my agency has a problem, and I want your cooperation clearing it up."

The city cop, whose name Tory now remembered was Steve Merriam, had raised his eyebrows in surprise at the DEA man's bluntness, while Mendez, whose appearance suggested a fire hydrant carved from a chunk of teak, just looked more wooden than ever. Dave Blanchard was nodding vigorous acquiescence, and for some reason it annoyed her. She threw a quick glance at Donahoe, but his face was an expressionless mask.

"We hear you lost a boat," Mendez said.

"I lost three good men," Feltrini snapped. "One murdered, the other two presumed dead."

"Why don't you fill in the details, August," said Walt. A fleeting expression of surprise and annoyance shadowed Feltrini's face; Tory wondered if he disliked his full first name or just the automatic California use of it. "I mean, most of us know something, but you're the only one with the complete picture."

If Walt had meant to flatter the DEA man, Tory saw, it wasn't working. She found herself feeling sorry for the harbormaster, who looked old and ill and worried. "That would help, Mr. Feltrini," she said.

He looked at her as if he'd forgotten her presence and managed to pull his lips back in something he probably meant as a smile. It would, she thought, look more convincing seen over a gunsight. "Right, Lieutenant. Okay. Here's the picture."

Feltrini had apparently decided to come more or less clean. The first part of his story she'd already learned from him on the way in: Daniels, the senior of the missing agents, had been using *Blue Thunder* to compile a solid record of drug arrests, nearly all of them in the Santa Barbara Channel area. And he'd been working with an informant, whose tips had enabled him to set up his busts alone.

"No other units?" asked Mendez.

Feltrini shook his head. "Not necessary."

"Not till now," murmured Donahoe.

Feltrini's hard face darkened. He seemed on the point of objecting when Mendez spoke again: "No cooperating agencies, either," he said. It was not a question.

"No headlines for anybody, except Mr. Daniels," said Donahoe.

"Neal, that's not necessary," Walt put in quickly. "We're talking about a missing peace officer."

"So who's the informer?" said Merriam.

"Daniels keeps—kept his sources to himself," Feltrini said. "But we know it's somebody here in Santa Barbara."

"Somebody who might have changed sides?" Merriam offered. "Instead of the DEA staking out the bad guys, the bad guys ambush the DEA: is that how you see it?"

"It's a possible," Feltrini admitted.

"How do you know the source is here in town?" asked Donahoe, his voice studiously neutral.

"Daniels told me so."

"And presumably at the harbor."

"Or plugged into it," Feltrini agreed.

"Why don't you go over the cases, August?" said Walt. "Maybe we could brainstorm some kind of pattern."

"Uh, right," Feltrini replied. He took some papers from the desk, began handing them out as he continued. "First, I apologize for these copies. I had a summary of Daniels's recent cases faxed up here, and Mr. d'Andrea—Walt—kindly ran it through his copier, but it's a little fuzzy."

It certainly was. Tory, who already felt as if her eyeballs were coated with sand, knew that trying to concentrate on the blurred dot matrix print would only lead to a shattering headache. But it appeared that Feltrini intended to read the entire list, item by item.

"Okay, number one was off Carpinteria"—he pronounced it like cafeteria, the mistake most newly arrived easterners made—"on twelve Feb. The, uh, schooner *Wild Thing*, coming from Puerto Vallarta, going to San Francisco. Three point two keys of cocaine. Number two: three March, fishing vessel *Alice T*, home port Monterey, boarded off Anacapa Island. Six marijuana cigarettes and an unlabeled container of capsules, turned out to be medication. Number three: eighteen March, power yacht *Mabel's Mink. . . .*"

He read without inflection, in his harsh baritone. Despite Tory's best efforts to concentrate on what he was saying, she felt her eyes closing.

"Well, it's pretty obvious, isn't it?" The voice was Neal Donahoe's, without any filter of deference, and it snapped Tory out of an almost complete stupor.

"Is that so?" Feltrini's tone was acid. "Maybe you'd enlighten us, Officer Donahoe."

Just the slightest emphasis on "officer"—why? And Donahoe seemed to redden, though he was so tan it was hard to be certain. He looked like a man who was ready for a fight and Feltrini like a man ready to oblige him.

For the others, Mendez was blinking, as if he'd been asleep, too. Merriam, his head cocked to one side, was watching Donahoe. Dave looked attentive but puzzled, and

Walt miserable, like the host at a party where all the guests were misbehaving.

Donahoe took a visible breath, as if to steady himself. "Well, there's two kinds of busts on this list—local boats on out-and-back trips and long-haul cruising boats, mostly on passage from Mexico." He glanced quickly around the crowded room; as his eyes caught Tory's, he blinked and looked away.

Merriam, who was considering the paper in his lap, said, "I don't get your categories, Neal. This *Alice T*, for instance: came from up north. And number ten, *Longliner*, out of Redwood City, the same."

"Sorry, Steve," Donahoe said. "I should've explained: I count those two as local. I remember both of them were working out of Santa Barbara when they were boarded. A lot of commercial fishermen move up and down the coast, take a temporary slip here, maybe for a month or two—isn't that right, Lieutenant Lennox?"

"What?" *Wake up, stupid.* Tory groped for his last observation, finally snagged it. "Oh, yes. We've got three kinds of commercials using the harbor: transient deep-water boats, like the two you just mentioned; small ones—mostly sea urchin divers—that live on trailers when they're not in the water; and the slip holders—that last bust, *Three Sisters*, that's a slipholder."

"*Was* a slipholder," said Neal, cold anger apparent in his tone. "Thanks to the DEA's mighty hunters, *Three Sisters* is now impounded, for a lousy bag of grass that'd fit in your shirt pocket."

Feltrini was off the desk snarling, but Walt, with surprising speed, grabbed him by the shoulder and was pulling him back. For a long moment, the only sound in the office was the DEA man's breathing, and then Merriam observed, as if nothing had happened, "The local guys got tagged with what they brought along to snort themselves, but the ones coming north were bringing stuff in—is that how you see it, Neal?"

Donahoe was nodding agreement when Mendez put in, "Unless some of these local guys were linking up with carriers, meeting them offshore."

"Carriers bringing in six spliffs?" Donahoe said. "Or half a bottle of amphetamines? Get real."

Mendez bristled. "Hey, maybe they got snagged before the transfer. . . ." His voice trailed off.

"The passage-making boats," Donahoe said, addressing the room at large, "aren't local—no, number eight, *Teresita*, is—and the quantities seized aren't quite as chickenshit as the—"

"Wait a goddamn minute!" Feltrini snapped. "These were all good beefs. Convictions or nolos on every one. Maybe you'd better decide which side you're on, *Officer* Donahoe."

"They're chickenshit and you know it," Donahoe said. Two pale spots had appeared on his cheeks, and his eyes glittered dangerously. "You add up the drugs you seized—"

"I didn't hear you answer my question, Donahoe: Whose side you on?" Feltrini demanded.

"You add up the drugs and shit you seized," Donahoe repeated evenly. "Pot, coke, uppers, the works. Hell, throw in the capsules that turned out to be Dramamine." His voice was still level and calm, but he was on his feet, towering over the seated Feltrini. "Your best street price for all of it probably comes to less than *Blue Thunder*'s fuel bill, never mind court costs and the rest of it. Your operation isn't even chickenshit, Feltrini. It's mouse crap."

But Donahoe's speech had given Feltrini a chance to get a grip on himself, Tory saw. He smiled up at the taller man. "You left out the boats we seized. I mean"—he extended his feral grin to include the rest of the room—"it's not like we're in the used-boat business, but every little bit helps." The smile disappeared, and his mouth snapped back to its former animal trap conformation. "And maybe—just maybe—there's a principle involved here. Something called law enforcement."

"Gentlemen, gentlemen," said Walt. "And lady, of course. Come on guys, please."

He looked pleadingly around the room for an ally, and Tory heard herself say, "Can we table the philosophy and just talk about the murder?"

She felt the tension in the office back off several notches, and Walt thanked her with his eyes. "The murder, yes. I think we can all get behind that."

Slowly Donahoe turned on his heel. As he did so, his face twisted momentarily with what might have been pain. He saw Tory watching him and gave her a sallow imitation of his usual grin, then lowered himself onto his chair, moving like a man twice his age.

Briskly, Feltrini took the floor again. "Lieutenant Lennox here came up with a good explanation of what probably happened out there," he said. "You want to run it past them, Lieutenant?"

Tory Lennox, girl lightning rod, she thought, seeing the relieved expressions around her. She rose, resisting the urge to straighten her coveralls. "Thank you, Mr. Feltrini," she said, pulling her thoughts together. "Now, this is just a theory. . . ."

One thing the academy taught you was how to think on your feet while an audience tried to shred your argument. And being a female officer in a mostly male service put you frequently in the spotlight. Tory knew she had a good, well-organized mind, and she'd already rehearsed her theory for Feltrini. She laid it out now, as concisely as she could. But while she spoke to all of them, there was only one face she was watching, surreptitiously.

". . . so that's the way I see *what* happened," she concluded. "And I think Lieutenant"—the name came to her with barely a half second's search—"Merriam may have put his finger on *why* it happened." Her gaze panned around the office. "Comments?"

"Congratulations, I think," said Walt. "Anyone else?"

They were all waiting for Donahoe, she saw. And he saw it, too. "Makes sense to me. Have you got a theory for what happened to *Blue Thunder* and the other two guys?"

"I'm afraid I do," she said.

"Yeah," said Mendez. "If they didn't come looking for this kid Huggins, it's because they couldn't."

"And, as Lieutenant Blanchard can tell you," she said, "our radar couldn't find anything that might've been *Blue Thunder*."

"That's right," said Dave, a second late.

Tory and Feltrini waited for him to go on, but he didn't, and the DEA man finally said, "Plus we heard on the way back here the Coast Guard's finished a helicopter sweep over all the islands—from Anacapa clear to what's-its-name—"

"San Miguel," said Walt.

"Right, San Miguel. No *Blue Thunder* in any of the harbors. Hell, practically no boats at all out there."

As if in punctuation, an especially strong gust rattled the window frame. "And that's why," Donahoe said.

"Understood," said Feltrini. "So we have to assume *Blue Thunder* was sunk, and Agents Daniels and Ericsen are dead. But Lieutenant Lennox tells me there ought to be some trace of the boat on the surface, and maybe the bodies, too."

A tight smile hovered on Donahoe's otherwise closed face. "Seems reasonable," he said. "Hell of a job finding it, in this weather."

"Well, that's what we do," she replied.

"The Coast Guard's got one of their boats out there now," said Feltrini. "Plus two helicopters. And Lieutenant, uh, Blanchard's going to go back out as soon as his cutter refuels."

"That's right," said Dave.

"So I'm not asking the rest of you—that is, the Harbor Patrol or the sheriff—to join the search now. If necessary, we'll call on you later."

"A whole lot later," said Mendez, not quite under his breath.

"What you can do now," Feltrini continued as if he hadn't heard the other man, "is put a full-court press on this harbor and the area around it. We want to find Daniels's tipster—or tipsters, could be there's more than one. That's where I'm looking for help from the SBPD. And maybe somebody saw *Blue Thunder* or the boat that sank her. Some boat owner here in the harbor. That's where we need help from your people, uh, Walt. And from Lieutenant Lennox, with the commercial fishermen."

Nobody spoke for nearly a minute. Then, "We'll do what we can," said Merriam. "But that full-court press . . ." He shrugged.

A knock on the door and Officer Joan Westphal's round face appeared. "Lieutenant Merriam? Phone call for you."

"Take it in my office," said Donahoe. "Two doors down."

"I'll talk to the sheriff about sending out our boat," said Mendez when Merriam had edged his way out. "You've got to realize it's not a Coast Guard cutter, though—the weather's going to have to be a lot better than this before we can justify sending a crew all the way to the islands."

You could cut Feltrini's displeasure with a knife, Tory thought, but he only turned to Walt and said: "Your people are the ones we're counting on."

"Yes, well," Walt said, avoiding Donahoe's icy stare. "Of course we'll be glad to help. . . ."

"We do have a case of our own," the patrol chief said.

"Oh, right. Of course." Walt was looking flustered, Tory thought. But what was Donahoe talking about?

"A case?" said Feltrini. "What is it—a loud party on a boat? Somebody parked in the wrong slip?"

"Maybe arson, maybe attempted murder," said Donahoe.

The door had opened behind him, and Merriam, looking paler than ever, was standing there. "Maybe murder," he said. "She died ten minutes ago, Neal. I'm sorry."

3:45 P.M.: NEAL

"My car had to go back to the cop shop," Merriam said, looking out at the rain, which was now slashing diagonally, the drops exploding on the asphalt. "Where's your pickup?"

"In the harbor lot," Neal replied. He zipped up his foul-weather jacket all the way to the throat and thought wistfully of the orange sou'wester and the foul-weather pants in the locker back on his boat. Back home (as he still called it) in New England, Neal had grown up knowing that fair weather was a fluke, not to be expected and certainly not counted on. But his years in the sunny Caribbean and theoretically sunny California seemed to have eroded common sense, and now he was going to pay for it. He could feel the icy water running down the back of his neck already.

Over by the picture window, the two officers and the clerk on duty seemed preoccupied with the view down the harbor. Since there was nothing to look at, their attitudes told Neal they knew all about him and Jannice but couldn't think what to say. In their places he wouldn't have known, either.

"Give me the keys. I'll go get it," Merriam said.

"What do I look like, the Wicked Witch of the West?" Neal said. "If I melted in water, I'd've disappeared long ago."

"What you look like," grumbled Merriam, "is a pig-headed asshole. When they amputate your infected feet, don't come whining to me for sympathy."

Neal didn't attempt an answer. The rain seemed to have slackened for the moment, so he pushed open the door and started down the outside stairs. The bandages under his socks were still wet from their earlier soaking, and the new wetness seemed a lot colder. He stifled a sneeze, but Merriam, right behind him, wasn't fooled. "What'd I tell you," he said.

Heads down, the two men hurried along the harbor's edge, past the Chandlery, the yacht brokerage, and the sushi bar. Out alongside her pier the *Point Hampton* lay ready for departure, her engines idling. Santa Barbara Channel would be brutal by now, even for an eighty-two-footer. Over his shoulder he said, "You're the asshole, Steve. You could've waited while I got the truck."

"What, and let my prime suspect out of my sight?" Merriam replied.

"I hope that's a joke," Neal said.

"So do I."

Hobbling past the old naval reserve building, Neal glanced automatically down at the floating pier in front of it, reserved for the urchin divers' boats that now jammed it. A slight figure in a too large black raincoat was standing next to one of the small fishing craft, talking to its skipper, who was sheltering under the open-ended wheelhouse. Neal took two more steps before memory kicked in. Fumbling at his belt, he unsnapped his key ring and tossed it to Merriam. "Truck's parked in the slot right in front of the Marina Two gate. There's a guy on the float I need to talk to for a minute."

Merriam picked the keys out of the air, but his eyes were on Neal's face. At last he nodded, turned on his heel, and squelched away. Watching him go, Neal realized he felt empty inside—or was that just another version of apprehensive?

The raincoated man on the float had finished his conversation and was trudging up the ramp, head down to keep the rain out of his eyes. Halfway up he caught sight of the Harbor Patrol jacket and froze in midstep.

"Afternoon, T.J.," said Neal. "I've been looking for you."

For a man who worked mostly outdoors, the mechanic had strangely pale skin, emphasized by a permanent five-o'clock shadow. And even paler eyes, set close to his long nose. Neal had never seen a ferret, but he knew that if he ever did, it would have T. J. Wellcome's face.

"Lookin' for me? How come?" The Ozark voice had a perceptible note of wariness.

"That boat of yours—"

"Boat? I ain't got no boat."

T.J. was one of those who denied everything on principle. It made for very tedious conversations. "*Whirlaway*. In 2-B-23. The urchin boat you squeezed out of Mitchie Boyd."

"Oh, *that* boat."

"That boat," Neal agreed. "It's sitting real low in the water. Maybe you better check the bilge."

T.J. bared his teeth in a conspiratorial smile. "Hell, let 'er sink. I got insurance up the wazoo."

It was the attitude that got to you, Neal decided: T.J. had an angle on everything, and he assumed everyone else did, too. "You're forgetting one thing," Neal said.

"What's that?" Wary again.

"Well, if *Whirlaway* sinks, chances are she'll leave an oil slick. And you're responsible for it. Cost of cleanup plus fines to half a million."

"Bull*shit*, man," said the mechanic.

Neal shrugged. "You don't believe me, look it up yourself: Oil Pollution Act of 1990. The Marine Safety Office'll have a copy—they're the enforcers."

"That bitch lieutenant. She'd do it, too."

She might, Neal thought, if T.J. tried some of his attitude on her. "Just trying to save your ass, my friend," he said.

T.J. regarded him suspiciously, but he said, "Well, thanks, man. 'Preciate it."

"*De nada*," Neal replied, thinking that just talking to T.J. made you feel you ought to wash your hands. How could people do business with such a scuzzball?

"Yeah." Halfway past Neal, the mechanic paused. "Hey, I was sorry to hear about your girlfriend," he said.

Jesus H. Christ. Aloud, he managed an unnatural-sounding, "Thanks."

He started to turn away, but the mechanic clearly was not finished. "See they got the boat up. Any idea what made her blow?"

"Not yet. But the experts'll be all over her tomorrow, like ants at a picnic. They'll work it out."

"For sure." T.J. flashed his carnivore's grin. "See you, man—I'll go check out old *Whirlaway* right now."

Neal watched him walk away. *Made her blow*. Interesting way of putting it. But maybe that was just T.J.'s turn of phrase. Behind him, he heard the sharp beep of his pickup's horn.

"She's a real pistol, isn't she?" Merriam said as they waited for a light to change. When Neal didn't respond instantly, he added, "The Coastie, I mean."

The green arrow lit up and Neal swung the pickup around the corner. "A pistol? I suppose so." But he realized Merriam had hit on the exact word.

"You've got to wonder, though," the other man continued, "what someone like her's doing in the military."

"Oh?" said Neal in an encouraging tone. It was a question that had occurred to him several times before, without the shadow of an answer. And even though Lieutenant Lennox was no concern of his, he welcomed the idea she might be deflecting Merriam's attention.

"Definitely a big league young lady," the cop said as Neal slid the truck into the homebound traffic on 101 north. "Of course, money always helps."

"Money?"

Merriam didn't try to hide his surprise. "Sticks out a mile, even to me. I figured you must have noticed, being an easterner yourself."

Merriam was right, Neal realized: Lieutenant Lennox did have the poise and self-assurance that went with money—old money, at that. And he certainly should have spotted it, since the distinctions of affluence had been drummed into him from childhood. Neal's own mother had been born wealthy, but it was first-generation money, a social disqualifier in Fairfield County, Connecticut. Her resentment at being frozen out was what had impelled her into the arms of the bewildered Irish mechanic who became Neal's father—and given her a stick to beat him with ever after.

"I guess the uniform threw me off," Neal said.

"Never mind she looks like a recruiting poster," Merriam said with enthusiasm. "She'd look right in whatever she was wearing."

"Probably," Neal said. His memory served up a picture of the lieutenant two or three evenings ago, coming out of the yacht club. She'd had on what Neal thought of vaguely as a party dress—black and expensive-looking, the skirt high enough to show off her legs. And she'd certainly fitted with the laughing yuppie crowd she was with. The mental image sharpened to include her escort, and Neal suddenly felt as if he'd been slugged just below the rib cage. Because the arm Lieutenant Lennox had been on belonged to Alex Tallant, Santa Barbara's most eligible bachelor of the moment—and Jannice McKay's brother.

"No *probably* about it," Merriam said, and then: "Hey, that's the turnoff."

Neal yanked the wheel sharply. *Jannice*: The past twelve hours collapsed on him. His hands were slippery wet, and suddenly he thought he might pass out. He managed to guide the pickup onto the backwater street, three blocks short of the hospital, and pull in to the curb. "I'm okay," he said, but his head sagged forward till his forehead was touching the steering wheel rim.

"You sure you want to do this?" Merriam's tone was as neutral as a human voice could get. "It might be pretty rough, with Rudy there."

Have you got the nerve, Merriam was really saying, *to face your dead lover's husband?* The SBPD had tracked down Rudy McKay at an investment counselors' convention in Denver, and he'd been able to get a flight straight into Santa Barbara.

"Just give me a minute, Steve." *Christ, was that my voice?*

"Take your time." Neal could feel the other man watching him. "You want to tell me anything?"

A confession, you mean? Aren't you rushing it a little? "Not that I can think of," he said, straightening up. "Let's do it." He put the truck in gear, even remembered to hit the turn signal and look in the rearview mirror before pulling away from the curb. He could feel Merriam watching every movement.

* * *

The hospital's lobby was vaguely modern, with puffy leatherlike settees in clusters, for families waiting to hear the bad news. Neal spotted Rudy McKay immediately—he was on his feet, reading a newspaper, the only man in sight wearing a business suit. Rudy was one of those big, loud, reddish men who instantly put Neal off, but a lot of Santa Barbarans, especially older ones, seemed to find his manner reassuring.

"He's so, I don't know, positive," Jannice had said one evening, after three margaritas. "I mean, he always does seem to know exactly what to do."

It was the first time Rudy's name had come up since the night Neal and Jannice had met. For some reason she seemed to be feeling the need to reexplain the terms of her private life. No, everything was just fine, she insisted. Rudy knew about her and Neal, and he didn't mind. Now, Neal found himself wondering.

He and Merriam were halfway across the lobby before Rudy saw them. He was paler than normal, but his rough, freckled skin still had a semicooked appearance, and his thinning, reddish blond hair seemed to float in wisps around his head. His lightweight gray suit was wrinkled, as usual, and though his tie was pulled all the way up, you could still see that the top button of his shirt was undone. Looking right past Neal, he held out his big, freckled paw. "Steve, how are you? It's tough on you, I know—but I'm glad you're the one who's handling this." The sad, noble smile was just about perfect.

"Rudy, I'm sorry," said Merriam. "What else can I say?"

"I appreciate it." And, as if Neal had that instant risen out of the terrazzo, "How are you, Neal? They tell me you tried to save her. Thanks."

Probably he couldn't shut off the manner even if he wanted to, Neal thought. He mumbled something noncommittal.

"Where are we, Steve?" said Rudy, turning back to the lieutenant. "I've called the funeral home, but they say you have to release her."

"Under the circumstances, Rudy," Merriam began, then tried again. "I mean, we don't really know what happened yet. . . ."

"Of course. An autopsy." Rudy pursed his lips judiciously. "I should've realized. We want to know how this dreadful accident—"

"If it was an accident," said a voice behind Neal—a husky, musical voice so much like Jannice's that he felt his heart jump. He spun around awkwardly, realizing halfway who it had to be: Alex Tallant resembled his sister so closely that they occasionally turned up at formal parties dressed as twins, in identical dinner jackets. They'd shared the same inky black hair, the same angular features, even the same long-waisted slenderness. And definitely the same smoldering sensuality, though Alex was as arrogantly masculine as his sister had been feminine.

Today, like Rudy, he was wearing a suit, though Alex's looked as if it had sprung, fully accessorized, from the pages of *GQ*—some pale tan, obviously expensive fabric that Neal couldn't identify, but with the raw silk shirt open at the throat, showing just a glitter of gold chain that echoed the heavy gold band on his Rolex. Like everything Alex wore, the outfit had a hint of costume about it, but there was nothing fake about his trembling, barely contained rage.

"Well, that's what we're going to find out," Merriam was saying. "Unless," he added, "you know something I don't."

Alex's dark eyes were red rimmed. He regarded the three men before him for several seconds before he responded. "No," he said slowly. "I don't know anything, yet. But I will."

MARINA 2, SANTA BARBARA HARBOR;
1730 HOURS: TORY

"Today? You got to be kidding." The bearded young man stared at Tory incredulously. "Take a look over the breakwater: no boat this size was at the islands today." He turned his attention back to his VHF transmitter, slung in brackets from the wheelhouse overhead of his dive boat. With a tiny screwdriver—even tinier in his huge, square-fingered paws—he removed the last machine screw holding the faceplate to the case and popped it into his mouth.

"How about last night?" Tory asked, knowing what the answer would be.

The man shrugged. "Me, I haven't been to the islands for a week," he said, his attention still focused on his work. "But they've been forecasting this southeasterly for two days. Everybody's waiting it out." With painful care he revolved the radio's faceplate 180 degrees and reseated it on its gasket. He spat a screw into his palm, inserted it into a hole, and began tightening it. "You're the new marine safety dame, aren't you? From the Coast Guard?"

"That's me."

"So what's this latest shit about life rafts?" He turned, suddenly antagonistic, his tanned face darkening. "I mean, for shit's sake, look around you. How much money you people think I've got—"

"Whoa, tiger," she said, holding up both hands, palms out. "You only go for urchins, right?"

The fisherman nodded slowly, as if a verbal response might be held against him.

"Then you're exempt," she said. "Those regs don't apply to you." He was, she saw, still dubious, and she leaned forward, locking his eyes with hers. "Do. Not. Apply," she said very slowly and distinctly.

The fisherman's open anger had subsided, Tory saw. But he was still a long way from friendly—for which she could credit both the personality of her predecessor, one of the Coast Guard's few commissioned bastards, and the natural antipathy between the anarchistic commercial fishermen and the crotchbound rule writers in Washington.

Tory had learned to ignore hostility from the mostly young, mostly macho fishermen she tried to think of as her customers. But it was a major pain in the tail when you had so much ground to make up before you could even start doing your job.

She stepped over the gunwale onto the finger pier, forcing what she hoped was a brisk, businesslike, not too soggy smile. "Any time you've got a question, just swing by the office and ask for me: Tory Lennox. You'll get a straight answer. That I promise."

"Yeah," said the fisherman, and there were half a dozen possible meanings built into the one syllable. "Listen," he added. "Did you try the big boats in Marina One? They might've been out yesterday."

She had, of course, but it was an olive twig of sorts. "Thanks," she said, meaning it.

The whole exercise was a waste of time, though. Fishermen of all people knew what a winter southeasterly was like in the Santa Barbara Channel. Tory hadn't been here long enough to see a really big one herself, but she'd heard that once or twice a year the rollers would break clear across the harbor's entrance, sealing it off completely.

This afternoon, most of the fishermen weren't even aboard their boats—wouldn't emerge from wherever they hid out until the weather moderated. And except for the few live-aboards, the pleasure-boat owners had better places to be, too. But Tory had told Feltrini she would cover two of the harbor's four pier complexes, and she would. She wondered if the Harbor Patrol was fulfilling their part of the assignment; doubted it: Walt d'Andrea was not the man to push his people out of a dry office to chase someone else's will-o'-the-wisp.

She looked down the length of the pier, saw another of the stubby, flattened bows with its chain roller windlass peeking out from behind a cruising sailboat's bowsprit. She sighed and squelched forward. Abreast of the boat she paused as the rain slowly trickled down the neck of her coveralls. Nobody home, she thought. Thank God. Too tired even to turn around, she stood for a moment, staring dully at the little craft.

When Tory had first arrived in Santa Barbara, she'd thought the urchin divers' boats were perhaps the ugliest small power vessels she'd ever seen. Locally designed and built, they seemed to her sailor's eye graceless fiberglass oblongs about twenty-five feet by eight, with a brutally boxy shelter cabin forward and a rusty air compressor aft, the whole thing painted whatever color the owner had got a bargain on. But after she'd watched a few of the boats belting their way back to port against a stiff chop, her opinion slowly began to change. If ever there was a case of form following function, the dive boat was it—a deeply veed underbody to cut through the water without pounding the crew to pieces, topped by a spare, functional working platform, with just enough space in the cabin for a couple of bunks and maybe a small stove.

Dive boats were for tough young men who wanted to make their money fast and didn't mind expending a lot of energy doing it. A few years back their quarry had been abalone, but most of the abs had been pried off the undersea rocks they clung to, and the new prize was sea urchins—black pincushions filled with slime, which Japanese seafood connoisseurs would pay a fortune for. Enough of a fortune—$2 a pound to the diver—that far too many hunters were scouring the bottom. The harvest was already thinning out, but in Tory's experience fishermen had no more self-discipline than alcoholics. They'd scoop up all the urchins they could grab until there weren't any more, and as the pickings got slimmer they'd take longer and longer chances, convinced of their own immortality.

Aboard the boat she was staring at, a jet of water shot out of a hull fitting six inches above the waterline, snapping her from her numb reverie. The water was coming in single spurts rather than a steady stream: a hand pump, then, rather than an electrically driven one. She walked reluctantly down the finger pier until she could see that the companionway door was closed but not locked. And now she heard the wheeze of the pump's diaphragm marking each stroke.

"Anybody aboard?" she called. No answer. She rapped the fiberglass cabin top with her academy ring, and the pumping stopped abruptly.

The door swung open and a narrow, pale, sweaty face appeared in the opening. "Afternoon," she began. "Mind if I ask . . ." As she swung into her prepared speech, she noticed that this skipper—a vulpine citizen with oddly pale eyes—was hanging on her every word, unlike all the others she'd spoken to this afternoon.

"Why d'you want to know?" he asked, the instant she'd finished.

Tory considered a reassuring smile, decided she didn't have the energy. "You're not in trouble or anything. I just need to know if you were out at the islands today or last night."

"What if I was? There some kind of new rule against it?"

The urge to pick him up and shake him till his teeth rattled was almost irresistible. "Of course not," she replied. "There's a boat missing, and we're trying to find somebody who may have seen it."

"Missing? Who's missing?" He didn't look like a fisherman, Tory thought. In fact, he didn't look like someone who got outdoors much at all—though the hand she could see was a workman's hand, with filthy black crescents under the broken nails.

"Nobody from this harbor," she said, hearing the fatigue in her voice. She waited, but he said nothing. "So, were you out by the islands?"

"Me? Hell, no," he said, grinning quickly. "This boat ain't been out of the slip in a couple months—ask anybody."

"Thanks a lot," she said. His sly grin told her he'd heard the exasperation in her tone. He popped back out of sight.

From where she stood on the finger she could see there were no more commercial boats on this pier. No boats with people aboard, as far as she could see.

Tory glanced at her Rolex, one of the few visible indulgences she allowed herself: nearly 1800. Only live-aboards would be around at this hour, on a miserable evening like this. And live-aboards, almost by definition, never took their boats anywhere. One more line of slips and conscience would allow her to call it an afternoon.

The last pier was one she'd seldom walked. Its occupants were nearly all pleasure craft and thus seldom the Marine Safety Office's concern. Tired and wet as Tory was, she found herself moving more quickly past the slips. The fragment of her mind that was still on duty noted a bowsprit stabbing over the walkway at just about eye height, an empty slip whose regular occupant had left his docklines in decorative flemished coils, a ketch with a light showing in its cabin, from which also drifted the faint sound of classical music.

The boat was somehow familiar—a chunky, dark hull nearly forty feet long with a low deckhouse and an oversize cockpit—and was quite large and seaworthy enough to go to sea in nearly any weather. Tory reached through the lifelines and knocked on the cabin top without stopping to consider why the boat's appearance was ringing a distant bell in her memory.

The music stopped and the hatch slid back, dimly revealing a head and shoulders in the companionway. "Good evening, Lieutenant," said Neal Donahoe.

"Oh, I didn't mean—" she began.

"Come aboard. You look like someone in need of a hot drink." She would have declined his invitation, but the smell of cocoa wreathing out the hatchway was more than she could resist.

Two steps down the companionway ladder, blinking in the light, she remembered how soaked she was. "I don't want to drip all over your cabin."

"Don't worry about it," he replied, wry amusement in his voice. One measured look told her why. Even the warm glow from gimbaled kerosene lamps mounted on the bulkheads couldn't soften the cabin's starkness. A low-roofed square about twelve feet on a side, it looked like something that had escaped from a boatbuilder's production line about halfway through: the hull's interior and the deckhouse structure were raw, rough fiberglass, and the bulkheads fore and aft were unpainted marine plywood from which someone's scribbled measurements, in thick black carpenter's pencil, had never been erased. Fat beads of bedding compound protruded from around the rims of the heavy smoked-glass deckhouse ports, while the worn house carpet underfoot had obviously been rough cut to fit without any consideration of its faded floral pattern.

The space was dominated by a U-shaped raw-plywood galley that occupied most of the starboard side, and an oversize teak chart table—a cabinetmaker's masterpiece, almost certainly from another boat—had been fitted alongside the companionway to port. Forward of it a low settee, upholstered with unmatched life preserver cushions, ran along the boat's side and then at right angles across the forward bulkhead, providing a single L-shaped seat for two sides of a battered folding card table.

The only attempt at decoration, tacked to the forward bulkhead, was a grainy, black-and-white blowup of the ketch herself, sailing a close reach on a bright, breezy day, off thrusting cliffs that looked like one of the offshore islands. Leaning close, she could just make out the lettering on the boat's transom. "*Carpe Diem*," she said aloud. " 'Seize the day,' isn't it?"

"Good for you," said Neal, pulling the hatch closed and moving to the galley. "Sit down anywhere. Whatever isn't waterproof is already ruined."

Tory had a feeling that once she sat she might never rise again—and she didn't care. She subsided, squelching, on one of the settees, leaned back against the cool, rough fiberglass of the hull. In here, the storm was noisier than it had been outside—rain thrumming hard on the cabin top and a halyard slapping staccato against the aluminum mast. Good manners called for some kind of complimentary remark about the boat, but none came to mind. "So you're a live-aboard," she said at last. "I didn't know."

"That's me," Neal replied. "One of the freeloaders."

The reference, which took Tory a moment to place, was to a recent remark by one of Santa Barbara's city council, a body torn by affection for the harbor as a tourist attraction and distaste for its unruly inhabitants, of whom the live-aboards were the most fiercely independent. The crack about freeloading live-aboards had drawn a firestorm of protest from every corner of the harbor, and the council had retracted. But their hostility remained a constant presence even an outsider like Tory could sense. Neal's clear contempt for the people who paid his salary said something about him, but Tory wasn't yet sure exactly what.

"Here," he said, setting a heavy earthenware mug on the card table. The smell rising from it was primarily chocolate, but with a strong, unmistakable subtext.

"Rum," said Tory, sniffing. "And I can almost identify it, too. Not Caribbean . . ."

"Gosling's Black Seal," he said, just as she added:

"Bermuda—the dark stuff."

They grinned at each other, momentarily joined by recollection.

"But on an empty stomach?" she added. "I don't know if that's so smart."

"No problem." He reached into a galley bin and produced a bag of tortilla chips and a bowl. "These'll soak it up."

One delicious moment on the lips, she thought. Three weeks to get it off the hips. To hell with it. She raised the mug to Neal, took a healthy slug. It was like inhaling a sugared flame. "*Whoof,*" she gasped.

"Think of it as medicinal."

That wasn't difficult. Two swallows and she could feel her cold, wet toes going numb. She bit off half a tortilla chip, savoring its crisp, lethal greasiness. Her host put his palms on the galley counter behind him and with a single, easy movement hoisted himself onto it, to sit with his bandaged feet dangling. The bandages and the smudges under his eyes—smudges darkened by the oil lamps' muted light—reminded her that she wasn't the only one who'd had a difficult day.

Tory had heard three different versions of the fire aboard *Finish Line*, and according to the most overheated of them she might be sitting with a murderer. Those big hands, wrapped now around a cheap mug, might a few hours ago have killed a woman.

No, she decided. That's ridiculous. But the other accusation—carefully wrapped in venom and laid on her by Feltrini—that, alas, was a lot more believable.

"More chips?" Neal asked.

She looked down and saw with horror that she'd emptied the bowl. "Lord, no. Thanks just the same," she said.

They eyed each other for a long minute. She knew what he was going to say before he spoke. "Any luck with your . . . assignment?"

His neutral tone made her bristle more than an overt sneer might have done, but she was not about to show it. She shrugged. "A long shot. But a necessary long shot."

"True," he said, and multiplied her surprise by adding: "We covered Marinas Three and Four. Only a handful of boats had been out, and none of them saw anything." He was watching her as he spoke, and she had the uneasy sense that her thoughts were showing in her face. It would not be the first time—duplicity had never been Tory's long suit.

When he spoke again, she realized she'd been right. "I expect Feltrini told you to watch out for me," he said evenly.

"Yes." She waited.

He was not about to fall into the trap of self-justification. "You'll have to make up your own mind about that. But I won't try to hide my opinion of the DEA: goddamn *bandidos*, in it for the thrills. And those are the straight ones."

Tory had heard the same opinion, if not quite so bluntly put, in the corridors of Eleventh District Headquarters in Long Beach. And she knew the defense, too: "You don't think a little"—she had to search for the right word—"a little aggressiveness is necessary? To protect themselves?"

"Not theirs, I don't. Far as I'm concerned, that kick-in-the-door attitude just gives all cops a bad name." His tone was even, but the feeling behind it, she saw, was visceral: his hands, gripping the counter, were white-knuckled, and the muscles stood out in his corded forearms. Again his eyes read hers. He grinned, and the cabin's tension slackened abruptly. "I really am an easygoing guy, Lieutenant. Being boarded, though—that really gets to you."

"It must," she said. *But five years later?* Time to change the subject. "You could bag the 'lieutenant,' I think. Try Tory—now that you've bought me a drink."

"Tory, then."

She could see he was assembling a comment on her nickname, but she'd heard them all. "What about your case?" she said quickly, then felt her ears go hot as she realized how her question might sound. "The one you're working on. The fire."

"My case. Yes." Three long beats. "What do you know about boat fires?"

It sounded like an unloaded question, but his dark eyes were too intent. "Just some basic stuff. D'you have a theory?"

"About what started it? A couple, I guess—but I don't want to get too attached to them until the experts go over the wreck tomorrow morning."

"I might join you," she said. And quickly added, "For my own education. If you don't mind."

"Not at all," he said. He eased himself off the counter, like someone slipping reluctantly into cold water. "Ready for another?"

"Certainly not." It sounded too abrupt, so she added, "Home is a little far to crawl, and one more of those . . ." She heaved herself to her feet, shivered as the wet coveralls rearranged themselves on her skin.

"How about dinner?" he said.

CARPE DIEM; 6:45 P.M.: NEAL

His invitation, he saw, had taken her by surprise—as it had Neal himself. Even more surprising, she seemed to be seriously considering it.

"I'd like to," she said almost wistfully. "I'd really like to." A moment later she sneezed. "But that's why I'd better get home."

He wanted her to stay. Wanted it more than he could easily explain. "You'll only get colder on the way," he said. She was wavering, he saw. "There's dry clothes up forward," he continued. "Just sweats, but they're fresh from the laundry."

"Well, I don't know about appearing in public in—"

"Who said anything about public?" He sensed she was on the point of giving in. "We'll eat here—it's no trouble. I was making my own dinner anyway. In fact, it's already started."

"But . . ."

A pro forma "but," for sure. "It'll be ready by the time you've changed. Just a matter of bulking things up a little."

It was the first time he'd seen her laugh. A good laugh, if a little uncertain. "Okay, okay," she said. "Now, where are these fresh-from-the-laundry sweats?"

But as he pulled aside the faded curtain that separated the main cabin from the forward quarters, misgivings swept over him. They must have shown in his face, because she laughed again and said, "What're you hiding up there, Neal?"

Nothing, he thought. That's the trouble. But if he started apologizing about the boat's condition, there'd be no end to it. "Right this way. Let me get a light first."

Behind him, she said in a carefully neutral tone, "Nice big head compartment."

It wouldn't look so big, he reflected, if it contained more than a toilet and a temporary shelf clamped to the bulkhead. By way of response he said, "I use the marina bathroom up on the pier. They've got showers, too."

"So I understand," she said.

"This space across the way is going to be a hanging locker," he continued, realizing as he spoke that his entire wardrobe was already on display—two more sets of khaki shirts and blue trousers, a couple of sport shirts, a slightly mildewed blazer, two wet suits, and the promised sweats, all on plastic hangers suspended from a sagging pole between the fore and aft bulkheads. On the bare deck beneath them sat a pair of knee-high boots and two plastic laundry baskets—labeled "clean" and "dirty"—of socks and underwear.

"And that's your sleeping cabin," she said, looking past him. Not that there was much to survey: most of the space was taken up by the triangular shelf forward—raw plywood, chest high, and large enough to accommodate two or even three human bodies, but occupied now by a single air mattress, a sleeping bag, and a spread-eagle paperback. At the berth's after end, a built-in step that also served as a seat was the only other cabin furniture, unless you counted the worklight suspended from the overhead hatch. Here, where the galley's comfortable warmth didn't penetrate, the atmosphere was cold and damp, pervasively scented with the chemical tang of badly cured resin.

Regret for his impulsiveness was bitter and complete. He'd felt amused, even superior, watching Tory's carefully controlled expression as she came down the companionway and took in *Carpe Diem*'s main cabin. What he hadn't appreciated was the small distance—three steps, it seemed—between spartan and squalid. "I'm sorry. . ." he began.

"If I could borrow a towel, too," she said. "I'm that soaked."

"Oh, right. Of course." He ducked out into the passageway and fumbled in the laundry basket. When he reentered the cabin, holding out the frayed beach towel like an offering, she had already peeled off her windbreaker. Under it, the sodden jumpsuit clung to her like a rough, navy blue skin. The line of her bra was unmistakable, and her nipples thrust out like bullets.

Her blue eyes, wickedly amused, met his, daring him to make a remark. He didn't, and she took the towel, saying, "Give me ten minutes."

He was bending over the stove when she appeared in the doorway. The old sweatshirt was stretched tight across her magnificent, clearly braless chest, giving a new, unconvincing meaning to the shirt's souvenir slogan, "Do it the Tongan way—tomorrow."

She met his rigid non-expression with a grin and said, "There is absolutely nothing more unpleasant than cold, wet underwear." A two-second pause. "How can I help? With dinner."

He spooned a ravioli square from the bubbling pot and considered it. "You could make the salad." He indicated a hatch in the galley counter. "Stuff's in there, in a plastic box."

Tory tipped back the lid and peered inside. "Wow," she said. "Mammoth Cave goes to sea."

"You may have to root around a little," he agreed. *Carpe Diem*'s top-loading icebox was built around a fiberglass casting taken from the wreck of a much larger yacht. It could engulf a hundred-pound block of ice and still leave room for half a dozen cases of beer and food for a week. Setting it up for refrigeration was a project about halfway down the second page of Neal's project list.

She was on tiptoe, her head, arms, and most of her torso inside. "Should be near the top," said Neal, eyeing her rump.

"I've got it, I think." She surfaced a moment later, face pink, clutching the box. "You don't want to give that test to short people. Especially ones with vertigo. Or big tits."

Had she really said that? No question—but the brisk way she was sorting through the salad greens told him she regretted it. "Some of these leaves I don't even recognize."

"I like to cook," he said. "Especially when it's a challenge."

"Well, you certainly rise to the occasion," Tory said ten minutes later. "This is delightful."

"It's not too bad," he agreed. In fact, he was pleased: the ravioli—bought, luckily, that afternoon—had more than its usual flavor, the tomato sauce had turned out exceptionally well, even the garlic bread had survived *Carpe Diem*'s unpredictable oven with flying colors. Only Tory's notion of salad seemed unimaginative, given the possibilities. "On a boat, I think, the rule is 'Keep it simple.' "

"You're right, I'm sure," she said. Suddenly she grinned. For a moment her boyish face matched the oil lamp's glow. "Tell you the truth," she said, "I can barely boil water. Love to eat, but cook . . ." She shrugged.

With a body like yours, you can forget cooking, he thought. But what came out was, "How about some more wine? Before it gets warm." He filled her plastic cup, adding, "It's a theory I have: Nothing works better with Italian food than bad Chianti, as long as it's really chilled off."

"You're wrong, but I'm not in the mood to argue," she said. He saw she was preparing a personal question. "If you don't mind my asking, Neal, why does Feltrini hate your guts?" She was watching him narrowly over the rim of her cup.

"Just a basic difference of opinion about law enforcement. Hang 'em high versus lighten up."

"Baloney," she said sweetly. And waited.

"Well, partly baloney," he agreed. "Feltrini and I go back a ways."

"I had a feeling that might be it. Tell me."

Oddly, he found himself almost eager to explain. "Five years ago," he began, speaking slowly as he arranged his thoughts, "no, five and a half, I was bringing a boat to California from the Caribbean. I was a delivery skipper, then," he explained.

She nodded. "So it wasn't your boat."

"Right. It was a big, old schooner called *Baby*. Bermudan main, gaff foresail, seventy-two feet long, not counting the bowsprit. Belonged to a movie actor named Johnnie Brett."

"I remember him," said Tory. She tilted her head in thought, and Neal felt his long-frozen heart stir. "Didn't he make a bunch of silly action movies? Lone hero shoots up the whole Mafia—or was it the Viet Cong?"

"That's the guy. He was into sailing that year, in between rescuing POWs from Vietnam, racing motorcycles, kung fu, and right-wing politics."

"A man's man," said Tory.

"A major dork," Neal snapped before he saw the mischief in her eyes. "Anyway, he bought *Baby* down in the Virgin Islands. She was an old-timer—had already bankrupted three owners, including the film director who'd had her before Johnnie."

"But he's dead, isn't he? Johnnie Brett, I mean."

"That's part of the story," Neal said.

"Sorry. Please continue."

"*Baby* was hauled out in a yard in Virgin Gorda when Johnnie got hold of me. I was working out of Road Town—in Tortola, just across the way."

"I've been there."

He wasn't surprised. "Anyway, the boat was pretty tired, but Johnnie seemed to think if he could just get her to California, everything would be all right. Didn't make much sense to me, but he was ready to pay whatever it cost to move her there. I put together a crew—a couple of other pros—to help me prep her, sail her across the Caribbean, through the canal, and up to Long Beach, where he'd take her over." Was that a faint, knowing smile? he wondered. "Did Feltrini already tell you this?" he demanded.

"A parallel version, you might say. We can compare details when you're finished."

"Oh." He emptied his now warm wine, wincing at the sour bite. "Well, while we were getting the boat rigged for an ocean passage, old Johnnie put the three of us up at—what's the name of that big resort, something bay?"

"Little Dix."

"That's the one."

"He was no cheapskate."

"He wanted us off the boat," Neal said. "Only we didn't know it at the time." He paused, but she only gestured for him to continue. "Well, we set out all right, made one broad reach to about two hundred miles off the coast of Mexico, then flopped over and headed straight for the canal."

"You didn't want to get too close to shore," she said. It was not a question.

"It's a tough stretch of coast," he agreed. "We cleared the canal like shit through—well, there were no problems except a leaking stuffing box. So we headed north. About halfway up the coast of Baja—"

"You found it," she said, smiling. "Cocaine?"

He was smiling himself, partly at the recollection and partly because her own grin was so contagious. "The leak wasn't dangerous. But it was definitely getting worse. So I crawled down into the shaft tunnel, and there they were, those flat, plastic-wrapped packages we all know from the TV news, lining the shaft."

"And you three guys—professional sailors in the Caribbean—you hadn't suspected *anything*?" Her eyes were dancing with amusement.

"Let's say those packages explained a few things we were wondering about," he said, grinning helplessly. "Like our greased-pig clearance through Panama, the light plane that overflew us twice, and the boat that'd been shadowing us off the port quarter for three days—we could just see its superstructure from the crosstrees." He shook his head ruefully at the memory.

"Anyhow, the three of us had a little conference and decided Johnnie's piece of free enterprise was already blown. As soon as it got dark, we put all those packages of white powder in a big sail bag, tied it to the spare anchor, and sent it down to cheer up the halibut."

Her lips were twitching with barely suppressed laughter, but she managed to ask, "So when did they board you?"

"About five minutes after we finished scrubbing down every inch of the boat—"

"You were lucky it wasn't grass," she put in.

"Damn straight," he agreed. "You need a steam hose to get that residue off—or so they tell me." He and Tory exchanged a look of perfect understanding, and he continued. "It was just short of San Diego. Effing DEA roared out of a fogbank a little before sunset, coming at us like the cavalry, waving guns and shouting. They tore *Baby* apart—knew just where to look, too. Threatened us, roughed us up a little, and when they couldn't find thing one, tore half the wiring off the engine. But they had to let us go."

"It was Feltrini on the DEA boat," she said.

"His very self. He was brand-new out here."

"They were tipped off," she said thoughtfully. "I'm surprised he didn't tow you in and really take the schooner apart."

"So were we," Neal agreed. "Figured it was Johnnie Brett's name on the papers that stopped him. Johnnie was pretty much a back number by then, but he'd made a lot of political friends with that POW grandstanding."

"Maybe," she said. But something was bothering her, he saw. "What happened then?"

"We finally sailed into the anchorage just off the Long Beach breakwater, cleared customs, and called Johnnie. He came aboard, took one look at his boat, and started to cry."

"Because of the damage or the missing dope?" she demanded.

"Oh, it was the coke," said Neal. "He was no sailor. But what could he say? I told him the DEA must've been in on the secret, and if they'd found anything, he'd've been in the slammer along with us. It didn't seem to make him any happier."

"And that was the end of it?" she said.

"Not exactly. The next morning he was out jogging in Malibu, and a hit-and-run driver got him. Or so the papers said. My two sailing buddies got on the first plane back to the Caribbean. I just got out of town—cashed in my return ticket, rented a car, and came up here."

"Here, as in Santa Barbara?" she said. "To live?"

"Not at all. The LAX Avis office had a San Francisco car on their lot, and I wanted to see the coast. I figured it was a message from the universe." She was looking dubious, and he added, "No drop-off fee: it was too good to miss. Everything I owned was in the duffel on my back."

"So you settled here more or less by accident," she said slowly.

"Totally. I was in my motel room, grazing the TV, and I hit one of those access channels—the one with the city job listings?"

"I've seen it."

"The Waterfront Department was advertising for a handyman. I answered the ad, and the rest is history."

"You didn't take the car back to San Francisco, then."

He laughed. "Let me guess: you don't do spur-of-the-moment much."

She looked so startled that he thought for a moment she was going to take offense. Then a private smile spread across her face. "Only once," she said.

He waited until it was clear she didn't intend to explain. "So what did Feltrini tell you?"

"Is it worth another glass of wine?" she asked.

He shook the bottle. "It's almost gone, and besides, it's warm. Tastes like battery acid that way."

"Tastes just a little like battery acid anyhow," she said, taking the bottle from his hand. She filled her glass, frowning with concentration, and he realized she was slightly drunk. "It's basically the same story. Just the emphasis—emphases are changed." She chuckled softly. "Yes. Feltrini knew about the dope a couple of days after you'd left Virgin Gorda. Thieves falling out, he said." She took a determined swallow, grimacing.

"So why'd he wait—" Neal began.

She held up a finger. "He wanted the credit, of course. The whole thing. And then he struck out. Publicly. No wonder he was furious—he's sure you must've landed the coke before he boarded you. And now you're a cop, which makes it worse."

"And getting in his way," said Neal, "which makes it—"

"No," she interrupted. "Not just getting in his way. Obstructing justice."

"To him it's the same thing."

"Maybe." She inspected the empty cup owlishly. "Not only does that stuff taste terrible," she said, "it's remarkably powerful."

"Coffee," he said, getting to his feet. "A little espresso will sober you up."

"A little espresso will just make me a wide-awake drunk. But I'll have some anyway." And then, as he turned to the galley, she added very quietly, "There seems to be a mountain lion on this boat."

He looked around. The immense tabby was sitting at the top of the companionway ladder, staring at Tory. The expression in its single green eye was not reassuring. "Oh, that's just Atrocious," Neal said. "Belongs to my neighbors." He was about to say, "She's really very friendly," when the cat began emitting a low, hoarse, sirenlike noise from somewhere down its throat.

"What—" Tory began.

"You're in her seat," Neal said apologetically.

"Not for long," Tory replied, sliding quickly to one side. With majestic deliberation Atrocious gathered herself, then leaped easily from the ladder to the settee, where she sat ignoring both humans, her tail lashing slowly from side to side. "She seems a little tense," said Tory.

"She does," Neal agreed. It was not like her: in Neal's experience, only large dogs could break through Atrocious's regal composure.

"So do you think Feltrini's on the take?" said Tory suddenly.

In the process of measuring coffee into the espresso maker's filter basket, Neal was completely taken aback. He meticulously brushed spilled coffee into the sink as he considered her question. "No," he said at last. "I really don't." He screwed down the machine's cap. "Why do you ask?"

He could feel her powerful desire to tell him—feel the equally strong caution that fought against it. In the end, caution won. Or seemed to. "I'm not sure," she said. "But you certainly put your finger on something."

"Put my finger on it?" he repeated. The espresso machine gave a sigh and a burble. "You mean when I went at Feltrini in the office today?" His words were a little slurred—was the booze hitting him as hard as it had her?

"Yes," she replied. "D'you remember what you said?"

He grinned disarmingly, and she wondered again if his teeth had been capped—and if so, why. "I seem to recall some fairly hard language. Something about mouse crap. Didn't faze him, though."

"He didn't let you see it, is all," she said. "But you had a point: all those busts by *Blue Thunder* didn't amount to beans."

"So?"

"So why is Santa Barbara County up to its ears in white stuff?"

He regarded her thoughtfully, and it was as if a veil had dropped between them. "Is it?"

"You're supposed to be a cop. You tell me."

"Well, maybe Feltrini was right about us Harbor Patrol folks," he said. "Loud parties and boats in the wrong slip: that's about our speed."

"You don't want to know, do you?" she said, not bothering to hide her scorn. "As long as nothing rocks your own little boat, you don't care about the rest of the world."

For a moment she thought she'd got under his skin, but he shrugged and poured out two cups of steaming, oily, inky black fluid. Setting one in front of her, he propped himself against the galley counter. "What I sometimes think," he said, "is that if more people worried about their own little boat and weren't so eager to stick their nose in everybody else's, we'd all be better off."

There were days she felt the same way, and sometimes more so, but this was not one of them. "So John Donne got it backward, then? Every man is an island?"

"I'm afraid so." He grinned at her. "Unless they're having a loud party in the wrong slip—in this marina. Then they are definitely a piece of my main."

She raised the cup of espresso and sniffed at it.

"A little strong?" he said, reading her expression.

"Smells kind of like . . ." She hesitated. "Caffeinated diesel fuel" was trembling on her lips, when she was saved by footsteps on the finger pier alongside *Carpe Diem* and a loud female voice.

"Neal? You aboard?" The speaker had a strong New York accent and, it seemed, no qualms about sticking her nose in other people's boats. The face that appeared in the companionway was gaunt, deeply tanned, and seamed with a thousand lines. Her eyes passed over Tory in a single appraising sweep and lifted back to Neal: "I just heard about Jannice. I'm so sorry."

No, you're not, Tory thought.

"Thanks, Bea."

And you're sorry—but not heartbroken. In a flash of intuition, Tory understood the relationship between Neal and Jannice and guessed that he and the woman called Bea had agreed to disagree about it.

"So, are you all right, Neal?" said Bea. "What's with your feet?"

Genuine concern there, Tory decided. But she's trying not to overdo—I'll bet he hates being mothered, and he's let her know it.

"Just scorched a little," he said, and, changing the subject with clear intent, added, "This is Tory Lennox. Tory, Bea Seligman, my neighbor from two slips down."

Feeling like an eavesdropper, Tory dropped automatically behind the shield she privately referred to as Best Behavior. "How do you do? I'm a colleague of Neal's."

The old woman's brow wrinkled as she considered Tory. Age and harsh sun had faded her eyes, but Tory suspected she didn't miss much. "Colleague?" She snorted derision. "Since when is the Harbor Patrol hiring girls from the Seven Sisters?"

Taken flat aback, Tory was speechless, but the other woman's eyes had lighted on Atrocious: "So there you are, you bad kitty. You had Mommy scared shitless." And to Tory: "Pardon my French, dear. She only understands bad language. It's from being around sailors."

"Come on inside and stop performing," said Neal. As Bea slid the hatch forward, he added, "Tory really is a colleague. She's a Coast Guard lieutenant."

One boot on the companionway ladder, Bea lost her footing. In a flurry of wet yellow foul-weather gear, she half slid, half fell down the ladder to the cabin deck. With a baritone yawp, Atrocious leaped straight past Tory and through the curtain into the forward part of the boat.

Her brain still registering the vision of scythelike claws, fully extended a couple of inches from her face, Tory missed the exchange as Neal helped Bea to her feet. "Are you all right?" she managed at last.

"I'm fine," said Bea. She lowered herself gingerly onto the opposite end of the settee. "Neal, give a clumsy old woman a drink, would you, please?" She shook the hood from her head, revealing an explosion of thinning white hair.

"Coming up." No further instructions seemed to be required: Neal produced the bottle of Black Seal and poured a stiff double into a cup. "When did you guys get back in?" he asked, passing it over.

Bea held the cup in both hands as she took a swallow. "Yesterday evening," she said. The harsh molasses smell of the rum began to fill the cabin.

"I was on till nearly midnight," said Neal. "Didn't see you come in."

"Maybe it was later than that," Bea replied. She swallowed some more rum. "It was a rotten voyage—Sid's been in bed all day."

"Where were you coming from?" Tory asked.

"San Francisco. We sailed up to visit friends. We got as far back as Port San Luis when the forecasts started talking about this storm. So we thought we'd better hurry on home."

Tory had seen the open roadstead San Luis Obispo called a bay. It was not a place she'd want to ride out a southeasterly, but the options for a small boat weren't attractive. Between San Luis and Santa Barbara were fifty miles of rock-ribbed coast, with a right-angle turn at Point Conception, nicknamed "the Cape Horn of the Pacific" (though not by people who had seen the original).

She eyed Bea with new respect. How old was she, anyway? The hands cradling Neal's plastic cup were twisted by arthritis, but they looked powerful and competent. Close to seventy, Tory guessed, but she could be a decade off. "What kind of boat?" she asked.

"A little old ketch," Bea replied. "Thirty feet—just about right for two golden-agers, you know?"

Just about right in harbor, Tory thought. Out at sea a boat that size would feel like a bathtub toy. "How'd you pass Point Conception?" she asked. "Take a tack out to San Miguel and hang a left?"

Bea's lined face split in a sour smile. "That's okay for you young people, and a younger boat. There was almost no wind when Sid and I started, so we decided to just motorsail close to shore."

"You were taking a risk," Neal put in. "That's a long lee shore, once you round Conception."

Bea waved him off irritably. "When you're our age, every day is a risk. Anyway, it worked out all right. Flat calm till five miles out." She looked around her. "Where's that damn cat? Time I got back to Sid."

"She's up forward," Neal said. "She can stay here, if you like."

"I'll get her," Bea said. She got up stiffly, stepped through the curtains calling, "Here, darling. Come here, sweetie," in a harsh, flat tone that belied the words.

"Point Conception in a thirty-footer," Neal said softly, shaking his head. "And they do things like that all the time."

"Just the two of them?" Tory asked.

"More like one and a half. She's the sailor. Sid was in real estate out here. The crash took a lot out of him. Besides most of their money."

"So she's—" Tory's question was cut off by nearly synchronous human and feline shrieks. Atrocious, her ears flat against her skull and her tail like a bottle brush, shot through the main cabin and through a low curtained opening next to the companionway.

A moment later Bea appeared, eyes blazing. "Tabby bastard. Look what she did to me." She held up her right arm, scored by three parallel scarlet lines. "Where is she?"

"In the aft cabin," said Neal. "You'll never find her."

"Not in that junk pile," Bea agreed. "Not in the dark. Let her stay already." She turned to Tory. "It was nice meeting you."

Ten minutes later Tory emerged from *Carpe Diem*'s companionway with Neal right behind her, still expostulating. "I think you're nuts," he was saying. "That coverall must feel like . . ."

"Like yesterday's wet suit," said Tory through clenched teeth. As the wind struck her, she doubted her reputation was worth the effort of changing from warm, dry sweats back into a clammy, icy, clinging garment the consistency of fiberglass matting. Who would know she'd arrived on Neal's boat in her own clothes and left in his? Half the harbor, was the answer. The jungle drums were probably already throbbing. By dawn, rumor would have installed her as Jannice's replacement—and that, at least, she was not about to be.

"I'll see you tomorrow morning, then," she said.

"Tomorrow morning?" he repeated.

"At the Boat Yard."

"Oh, right," he said.

The wind had gone out of his sails so completely, she found herself feeling sorry for him. "It was a wonderful dinner, Neal. A lifesaver."

"Any time," he replied. In the chiaroscuro of the walkway lights, his face looked as old and lined as Bea's.

The question, Tory decided, was whether to jog back to where her car was parked, outside the MSD office, and get it over with quickly, or walk back slowly and carefully, to minimize the incipient chafe between her thighs. In the event, she decided in favor of speed and warmth; the rasping cloth almost kept her mind from unseemly thoughts of Neal Donahoe.

In the trunk of her Honda Accord—a compromise between the second-hand econobox appropriate for a young officer living on her salary and the Beamer she could have bought out of pocket—was a piece of plastic sheeting, kept for just such occasions as this. As she was spreading it over the driver's seat, her eyes caught a flash of light from behind the Boat Yard's chain-link fence. She checked her watch: nearly 2100. Nobody should be poking around in there.

What business is it of yours? she asked herself. From where she stood, she could see only one darkened window of the harbormaster office, but somebody would be on duty up there.

Yet here she was, boots kicked off, padding silently toward the open gate. I don't do spur-of-the-moment, she reminded herself. So how come I'm doing this?

Her eyes had had plenty of time to adjust to near darkness, but she could make out only vague, looming shapes around her. Ahead, just beyond the bulk of the yard's workshop, was a shape both longer and lower than the rest: the topless hulk of Jannice McKay's *Finish Line*, waiting for its autopsy.

And on it a momentary glow, like a flashlight flicked on and quickly off. Tory felt her breath catch in her throat. Go get the cops, she told herself. They've got guns. This is what they're for.

She was only a few yards from the blackened hull. Now she could hear someone moving, a grating noise that she realized must be feet treading on charred debris. Whoever it was seemed to be roughly amidships, standing where the yacht's engine room had been—where, if what she'd heard was true, the fire had started.

Louder movements. Tory shrank back, her shoulder against the roughness of a wooden hull. A round silhouette appeared above the irregular edge of *Finish Line*'s burnt-out side. Someone's head, she decided, and then his shoulders—he was trying to climb up over the edge of the hull and having a hard time of it. No, he'd made it: he was straddling the edge, swinging his other leg over . . .

Now or never. She stepped away from the other boat, pitched her voice to its most commanding, and snapped, "Hold it right there!"

Without a second's hesitation, the figure on *Finish Line*'s gunwale sprang down on her. In the instant before he landed, Tory realized she was much too close. Yet not—luckily for her—quite as close as her opponent thought. He'd jumped at her feet first, but he landed off balance on his heels and fell back against *Finish Line* with a thump and a grunt. Tory lowered her shoulder and drove it into his middle—a substantial gut—with all the force of her 130 pounds.

The air went out of him in a gasping wheeze, but he was nearly twice her weight, and one flailing arm caught her a glancing blow that sent her staggering. With a wordless roar, he lurched toward her. There was something in his right hand, and he was swinging it.

She ducked back, and the object—a three-cell flashlight, she thought—slammed into her upper arm. Her opponent crouched, collecting himself for another blow. *If he hits my head with that thing, it's all over.* The thought freed her voice, and she heard herself shout, "Help! Police! In here!"

Instead of frightening her assailant, the cry seemed to madden him. Snarling something that sounded like "Kill you!" he hurled himself straight at her. She dropped nearly flat, slipping between his outstretched arms, and pulled herself into a tight ball. One of his feet kicked her in the ribs, and his other shin collided with her hip, as he sailed headfirst over her, landed with a gritty thud and a bellow of outraged surprise. Something flew from his hand, hit the asphalt in a tinkle of breaking glass.

Tory rolled forward and to her feet as he struggled to his knees. Yelling at the top of her lungs, she kicked him as hard as she could, aiming at his side, just above his hips. For a moment she was sure she'd broken all her toes, but her enemy had had enough. He heaved himself upright, one arm clutching his side, and began to stagger off. Without thinking, Tory leaped at his back—but he must have seen her from the corner of his eye. Half turning, he swung at her. The flashlight caught her just below the ribs. The force of it knocked her flat, but it snagged on a pocket of her coveralls and pulled free of his hand.

With the last of her strength, Tory rolled away from him, shielding her head with both arms. She heard uneven footsteps on the gritty asphalt, but it took her several seconds to realize they were receding. When she pulled herself to her knees, he was gone.

A figure was advancing cautiously toward her, behind the beam of a powerful light. "Police," said a woman's voice. "What's going on here?" The voice was determined but slightly unsteady, and Tory, guessing how the speaker must feel, suddenly felt herself torn between tears and laughter.

"I still think you ought to see a doctor," said the young Harbor Patrol officer, whose brass nametag identified her as T. Hegemann. She typed in the last sentence of her report with painful care and looked up. "You look kind of green to me."

"I'm fine," said Tory for the fourth or fifth time. "Really I am." It was a very relative fine—her shoulder ached, her ribs felt like a well-thumped xylophone, and she didn't dare wriggle the toes of her right foot—but she was reasonably sure the damage was superficial, and the thought of a physical examination was more than she could bear.

"Do you want to read this over—make sure I got it right?" Officer Hegemann was earnest, heavily freckled, and about ten pounds overweight. She wore her long, mouse-colored hair in a complicated French braid that had the effect of making her round face look even rounder. She seemed to be somewhat in awe of the older woman, which Tory found amusing, considering who had rescued whom.

Tory accepted the report as gracefully as she could. One glance told her that Officer Hegemann was well on her way to mastering police prose. Something was missing, though—something she'd forgotten to say. But the words were swimming on the page before her, like the fragments of thought in her head. "Looks fine to me," she said, handing it back.

"Thanks." The young cop set down the report, squared it carefully with several sheets beneath, stared at it intently.

Come on sweetheart: spit it out, Tory thought.

"You had dinner with Neal," the young cop said, concentrating fiercely on the paper she was holding.

Ah, so. "That's right," Tory said after a long silence. "I was soaked, and he took pity on me."

"He's like that," said the other quickly. "He doesn't hang out with the rest of us—well, he's a lot older, of course—but every time you think you really need him, he's been standing behind you all along."

Why doesn't that surprise me?

"Some people think he's completely laid back. Like, he doesn't really care about anything. But they're wrong."

"They are?" In spite of the exhaustion that had drained her, Tory found herself unwillingly fascinated.

"Absolutely. Take last night: anybody else would just've let *Finish Line* torch off in her slip. Wait for the firefighters. Not him. He got her out of the harbor, even though he practically fried himself doing it." Her wide brown eyes were moist with sincerity, Tory saw. And then the nametag jump-started her memory.

"The way I heard it," Tory said, "you were right alongside him all the way. He wasn't the only one who cared about the job."

A wave of scarlet rose out of the young woman's open-necked khaki shirt and disappeared in her hairline. "That wasn't the job," she said, looking first away and then, defiantly, straight in Tory's eyes.

No, I can see it wasn't. "Whatever. It took a lot of guts, just the same."

The scarlet, which had faded to pink, flooded back. "Well, I grew up on boats. I knew what to do—like, it's in my bones."

"And tonight? Was that in your bones, too?" asked Tory.

A slow, delighted smile spread across the young woman's face. "I guess that was the job," she said. "I guess I really am a cop."

"No question in my mind," Tory said, pushing herself slowly to her feet. She could sense the young woman was ready to settle down and discuss her self-discovery at length, but she'd just have to find herself another Southern Californian for that exercise.

"You positive you're okay to drive, Lieutenant?"

It was a professional question, Tory realized, and deserved a professional answer. "I'll do fine, Officer."

But by the time she reached the foot of the stairs, she wasn't so sure. She managed to maintain an even—almost stately—pace until she was around the corner, out of Officer Hegemann's sight, then allowed the gathering aches and bruises to shape an ungainly, crablike shuffle for the few remaining yards to her car.

She had opened the door when she remembered what had been bothering her. "Oh, fuck it," she said, and slid behind the wheel, crumpling the protective plastic hopelessly. She started the engine, flicked on the headlights, and backed the car around until it was pointing into the Boat Yard. "Double fuck it," she said, but she inched the Honda through the gate. Her assailant's flashlight lay just where it had fallen. *Then where's the other thing he dropped?* Moving as if she were hip deep in syrup, she put the car in park, opened the door, and got out.

She forced her nearly drained consciousness to visualize each step of the fight, but in reverse: *Here's where I jumped him, like a dope. Here's where he went tail-over-teakettle . . .* At the very edge of the head lamps' arc she saw it, a bit of glass that caught the light.

Bending over nearly finished her. She had to drop to one knee until her head stopped spinning, but she took the object—about the size of three packs of cigarettes, porcupined with jagged, sharp edges—hefted it, and got to her feet. Back in the car, she flicked on the overhead light and considered her prize. "I thought that's what it might be," she said.

For a moment she weighed the idea of driving over to the

harbormaster office and leaning on the car horn, then decided another hour of interview was beyond her. Besides, it could wait till tomorrow.

Carpe Diem; 7:15 A.M.: Neal

"You always liked pancakes before," said Neal to his companion, who rewarded him with a silent glare—especially baleful, coming from that single eye. She was sitting bolt upright on the settee across from him, on two cushions that raised her head and shoulders above the card table's edge. On the plate before her, the pancake, cut into neat squares and awash in grade C Canadian maple syrup, remained untouched.

Some of Neal's friends said he was crazy to share his meals with a cat—someone else's cat at that, and one noted throughout the harbor for its hostility. But when Sid and Bea were in Santa Barbara Neal was a regular dinner guest on their *Iolanthe*, so it was only fair for him to cat-sit Atrocious when they were cruising.

Jannice, he suddenly recalled, had objected the most strongly, though she spent practically no time on *Carpe Diem.* Bea put it down to simple jealousy: Atrocious and Jannice, she claimed, were very similar personalities—direct, passionate, and humorless—so naturally they grated on each other. Even now, with his memories of Jannice already gilding themselves, Neal had to admit Bea might have been right.

Atrocious turned her single eye back to Neal's pork sausages and emitted a deep, ominous murmur.

"You had yours," he replied, his mouth full. It was not a line of reasoning that carried much weight with Atrocious—or, come to think of it, with Jannice. Theirs had been a strange relationship, he reflected. A sexual intensity beyond anything Neal had known, an often brittle mutual amusement, but no deep affection on either side, not even the pretense of it.

Over the years, Neal was aware, Jannice had been involved with a dozen more eligible men, among them some of the city's most notorious sexual athletes. "So what did she see in me?" he asked. Receiving no answer, he got up and poured himself a second mug of coffee. The tarry, penetrating aroma of French roast filled the cabin. Without warning he found himself thinking of Tory Lennox—the look on her face when she'd sniffed the espresso, which he'd made about twice too strong. An amazing body, he thought. And a sharp mind to go with it. But why the military?

He lowered himself back onto the settee, speared the remaining sausage, and had the fork halfway to his mouth when he remembered there'd been two. Deliberately Atrocious extended her tongue—the texture of eighty-grit sandpaper, as Neal knew all too well—and began to lick one of her forepaws. There was no point yelling at her—like every other cat Neal had known, she was totally unhampered by any sense of guilt.

Again like Jannice, he thought. And why didn't that occur to me till now? He collected the plates, rinsed them, and stacked them in the sink with the last two days' dishes. Thanks to garage sale purchases, *Carpe Diem* had utensils enough for a large family—or for one person to accumulate for nearly a week between washings.

He scooped Atrocious off the settee and set her in the hatchway. "Back home you go," he said. As a rule, the big cat would stalk down the walkway to *Iolanthe* without a backward look, but this morning she spun in her tracks and leaped back into *Carpe Diem*'s cabin. When Neal took a step toward her, she vanished into the sleeping quarters forward.

He stood a moment, irresolute, then decided it didn't matter. What did matter was getting to the harbormaster office by eight, when the day officially started. See who's called in sick, he thought, climbing the companionway. He dropped the hatch slides in their slots and engaged the combination lock, then stepped gingerly over the lifelines to the box that served as a step. His feet were still too tender for boat shoes, though he'd managed to slip dark socks over the bandages, so the black sandals didn't look quite so strange.

For a guy who says he hates uniforms, he told himself, you sure take enough trouble with yours. Again he found himself flashing on Tory—how she'd managed, even in wrinkled, soaking coveralls, to look vaguely military and amazingly neat. Money, as Steve Merriam had said—but there was more to it than that.

The rain had decided to take the morning off, though the wind was still in the east and the clouds massed over the coastal range hung dark and heavy. It had taken Neal a couple of years to get used to the self-contained weather systems of the Santa Barbara Channel, where a barometer was nothing more than a hood ornament. By now he could read the more obvious signs—the cloud streamer on Santa Cruz's peaks or the sudden blast of warm air coming down the canyons—but the nuances still escaped him. Probably you had to be born here.

A flash of movement aboard *Iolanthe* caught his eye, and he turned down the finger pier alongside her. Bea must be shipshankying—her jokey term for the polishing, scrubbing, and oiling that seemed to obsess her. But when he came abreast of the cockpit, it was empty. He paused, considering. He'd skipped Sid and Bea with his inquisition yesterday, and that was hardly professional. Besides, Bea ought to know that Atrocious was locked away on *Carpe Diem.* He reached across the lifelines to knock on the cabin top just as the hatch slid forward and Bea's head appeared, a finger to her lips.

"He's asleep," she whispered. "Tossing and turning all night, until an hour ago."

"Right," he whispered back. "I need to ask you some questions, but I can do it on the pier."

Something flashed in her eyes, gone too quickly to identify. She eased herself out *Iolanthe*'s companionway, closing the double doors behind her with exaggerated care. She climbed over the lifelines, feeling with one foot for the step on the pier. Neal, who knew better than to offer a hand, said, "Did you and Atrocious have a fight or something?"

"No, of course not," she said. She looked up at him warily. "Why do you ask?"

"She seems to have moved aboard *Carpe Diem*. She's playing hide-and-seek in the forepeak, but I'll bring her back later."

"It doesn't hurt my feelings," she replied. "A cat always recognizes a sucker—and you're a sucker, Neal."

"As you've said," he replied, and suddenly he remembered the context in which she'd said it.

So, apparently, did she. "What did you want to ask me?"

"Night before last, when you and Sid were sailing back to Santa Barbara . . ." he began.

"Yes?"

No nervousness that he could see. No visible apprehension at all. Relieved, he continued: "Did you see any other boats in the channel? Anyone at all?"

"To tell you the truth, we weren't looking for boats. Ships, we were looking for. We saw only one that I remember. Westbound."

"Before you rounded the point?"

"After. An hour or so. A container ship, I think."

"And you were close to shore?"

"Three miles." She shrugged. "That's as close to Conception as I want to get, especially in the dark."

"Amen," he said. "You stayed about that distance off for how long?"

"Past Harmony. We were inshore of it—and the other oil platform, too: Heritage." She narrowed her eyes, remembering. "We were steering seventy-five magnetic, I think. When the shore trended south, we just let it close us." She gave him a sour smile. "You can check the logbook, if you want."

He felt his ears go hot: exactly that thought had been forming in his head. "Maybe later. Now, when you were anchored in San Luis Bay, did you talk to anybody?"

"You mean, did we say, 'Write down *Iolanthe* in your log, please, so we can prove we were here'? No. And we left before dawn, so nobody saw us go." She laughed. "Sorry, Neal."

His own smile felt wooden. He hadn't expected to dislike this so much. "The people you visited in San Francisco. Can I have their names, please? And a phone number?"

"Of course," she said. "Do you mind if I get it for you a little later, when Sid wakes up?"

"That'll be great," he replied far too effusively. "What's wrong with him? Nothing serious, I hope."

Bea rolled her eyes upward. "Who knows? Ever since two years ago, he gets these spells. This is a bad one."

Two years ago, he remembered, was Bea's code for the day Sid's investments had started their terminal slide. Neal knew, as no landsman could, the kinds of small economies the Seligmans had been reduced to—economies in *Iolanthe*'s maintenance that were nearly invisible only because of Bea's meticulous care.

Even he hadn't got the full impact until the day Bea had asked him—studiously avoiding his eye—if he could maybe just check *Iolanthe*'s anti-corrosion zinc the next time he was scrubbing *Carpe Diem*'s bottom. One look at the little ketch's underbody told him it hadn't been touched for months. On an impulse he'd called the local dive service and was unsurprised to learn Bea had canceled the hull cleaning contract.

He'd put a new sacrificial zinc on *Iolanthe*'s propeller shaft, then made the mistake of telling Sid, who insisted on paying for it. Since then Neal had simply replaced the corroded collars without mentioning what he'd done, but he hadn't quite summoned the nerve to scrub the ketch's hull, too.

"I hope Sid's well enough for dinner tonight," Neal said. "I've been looking forward to it ever since you left."

"I don't know," she replied. "I'll call you at the office later—maybe you could pick up a dessert on the way home." It was another of Bea's codes: When Neal went to dinner aboard *Iolanthe*, it was understood that he brought the food—enough for the entire meal and generous second helpings, which he never asked for. The only problem with the arrangement was that he didn't dare return the invitation—the two times he'd done so, Sid had turned up bearing preposterously expensive bottles of wine, presumably the only kind he knew how to buy.

"I'll count on dinner, then, unless you call," Neal said.

"All right," said Bea, adding, "You could bring somebody, if you want."

It was how Bea automatically capped her invitations, a bit of meaningless static he'd always ignored. Before he thought, he heard himself say, "Maybe I'll ask Tory—the woman you met last night."

Bea looked at him hard. "Yes," she said at last. "You bring her, Neal. She's a good person." She shaped a twisted smile. "You could both look at the logbooks."

"Morning, Walt," he said. "*Point Hampton*'s still out, I see." And to Bill Jacobson, slumped at his desk, "You look as if you'd died last Thursday. I hope to hell you're not infectious."

Officer Jacobson, who'd learned how to read Neal's tone of voice, managed a wan smile. Walt looked up from his newspaper. "The *Hampton* won't be back for a while. Dinged a prop on some driftwood, running those search patterns. She's on her way to the yard, limping along on one engine."

Feltrini probably thinks they did it on purpose, Neal thought as he flipped quickly through the pages of last night's log. And froze: "What the hell's this?" he demanded. "Is Tory—Lieutenant Lennox—all right? Why wasn't I called?"

He looked up, realized he was literally shaking with anger. Jacobson, his eyes like saucers, was clearly shocked speechless. Even Walt was taken aback, but words had never yet failed him.

"She's fine, Neal. I asked Taffy specifically, and she assured me." Walt sketched a tentative smile. "I'm glad you're so concerned about your colleagues."

The smile, as much as Walt's heavy bonhomie, warned Neal he was overreacting. "Somebody could've called, though," he grumbled.

"We could've," Walt agreed. "And you'd have come hustling down here and lost most of a night's sleep—which, I may say, has clearly done you a lot of good."

Trying to start a fight with Walt d'Andrea was like punching a feather pillow, as Neal knew from experience.

And his boss was right. Eight hours in the rack might not have made Neal a new man, but he felt like a reasonable imitation of the old one. Anyway, Taffy Hegemann was the most conscientious officer on the patrol. She would never have let Tory leave if there was any possibility she'd been injured. But Taffy's report, like the woman herself, was utterly without imagination. He had to know more, and right now.

"Hey, where you off to, Neal?" the harbormaster demanded. "You just got here."

His voice said it all. Halfway out the door, Neal barely glanced back. "You know where to find me," he said.

THE BOAT YARD; 1000 HOURS: TORY

Something about the scene around *Finish Line* suggested an operating room, though the surgeons, wearing soot-smeared coveralls, were standing on and inside their thoroughly deceased patient. And the surroundings, in the raw, gray morning light, were more like a nautical version of the blasted heath than a hospital: lines of mostly battered fishing boats blocked up on the asphalt, with ladders propped against the higher hulls and well-used power tools and chunks of machinery scattered here and there.

What was happening aboard the burned-out hulk, Tory decided at last, was a generic professional performance: an aura of total concentration, punctuated with meaningful nods and pointings, a muttered obbligato of technobabble, and floating over it all a slightly pompous mutual deference. The stars of the show—a Santa Barbara fire marshal, a sheriff's deputy, and a tiny, sparrowlike man from the insurance company—seemed at last to be homing in on something, as she remarked to Neal, standing impatiently at her side.

"More likely they're getting ready to break for coffee," he replied. He had been surly, verging on childish, from the moment he'd burst into the Marine Safety Office, nearly flattening Chief Boatswain's Mate Braddock Washington and scattering the pile of fishing vessel examinations he was moving from one desk to the other. The chief (himself a front-runner in anyone's surly sweepstakes) blew up, Neal flared right back, and Tory found herself in the ridiculous position of calming both of them down without taking sides.

Of course, it was sweet of Neal to be so concerned—but why did he automatically assume that in any fight with a man she'd have come out second best? It was the kind of attitude Tory was used to meeting in some of the old shellbacks she worked with, but she'd expected more from Neal. Maybe that kind of chauvinism was locked in the male DNA, though. Even Gilles Everard, the standard to which Tory held all subsequent men, had sometimes been unbearably patronizing.

Well, Neal might have learned a few things if he hadn't been such a kid—might learn them yet, when she felt like telling him.

Steve Merriam, on Tory's other side, looked like a child left out of a birthday party game as he shifted from foot to foot. Finally, unable to bear his exclusion, he stepped to *Finish Line* and leaned on the charred gunwale. Eventually the deputy acknowledged him with a curt nod and, after another minute or two, bent over to hear his sotto voce question. (What, she wondered, was the meaning of the deputy's hard stare at Neal, as he whispered his answer to Steve?)

Walking back to Tory and Neal, the police lieutenant shook his head. "They don't know yet." But she had the strong feeling he'd received some information from the deputy, some piece of news that wasn't necessarily welcome.

"Jesus," said Neal. "They could've rebuilt the damn boat by now."

"Any theories, Steve?" Tory asked.

He wavered under her innocent stare and finally yielded slightly. "They're pretty sure it was deliberate."

"Anything to do with—"

"That's all for now," he said quickly. "Tory, I've got to get back to the store. I'll talk to you later. See you, Neal."

"What was that all about?" said Neal, scowling at the police lieutenant's departing form.

In the middle again, Tory. "Beats me."

He didn't believe her, she saw—no big surprise, since she was lying through her teeth, and badly. For an unpleasant moment she was sure he was going to call her on it, and then he flung away without a word.

But they—Steve—couldn't suspect Neal. Or could they? she asked herself as she walked slowly back toward the safety detachment office. Earlier that morning, when she'd handed over her two trophies to the police lieutenant, his first question had been if she'd recognized her attacker. When she'd said no, he'd asked if the man could have been Neal. He'd seemed to accept her shocked negative, but now she wondered.

In the office, a gloomy cave with too many desks and too few windows, there was a phone message for her, from Alex Tallant. "Just three words," said Chief Washington. " 'Lunch.' 'Today.' 'Urgent.' "

"Urgent?"

"That's what he said." The chief seemed uninterested in her perplexity. He was black, which was still rare among Coast Guard chiefs, and an ex-marine—one of the Coast Guard's numerous transfers from the second-smallest service—much given to abrupt messages. He and Tory had not hit it off, and she was at a loss to understand why. "He's coming by at noon," the chief added.

Alex Tallant? she thought. Urgent, after two plain-vanilla dinner dates? What on earth . . . Oh, God—it must have something to do with Jannice.

At which point Feltrini gusted in like a chill nor'easter and blew Alex right out of her head. "A fifty-foot boat," he was saying before he was even through the door. "A fifty-footer, and you people can't find it. Not only can't you find it," he went on, ignoring Chief Washington's rising fury, "you can't keep your own goddamn boat off the rocks or whatever. Some cooperating agency you guys turned out to be. What's that motto of yours, *Semper paratus*? Should be *Semi paratus*, you ask me."

He paused, savoring his own anger, and Tory said, "Finished?"

"Finished? Hell, no. There's Daniels's informant. You people haven't found him, either." Feltrini was addressing her, but he was watching Chief Washington from the corner of his eye, as well he might be. The chief's normally cocoa-colored face was now a shade Tory thought of as Concord grape. He looked ready to kill.

Feltrini's mouth was opening for another blast when Tory got to her feet. "I think that's enough," she said. She ached from neck to shins, and the pain had the odd effect of focusing her mind. "You say we can't find your boat, Mr. Feltrini—but who lost it in the first place?"

She held up her hand to stop his furious reply and pressed on, pitching her voice a little louder. "And just how did your people lose it? Amateur grandstanding, that's how. No cooperation, no backup, and piss-poor performance. If your DEA didn't exist, the druggies'd fall all over themselves inventing you." She paused deliberately. "Now, shall we try a real discussion?"

Feltrini, to her unspeakable relief, was smiling. No, he was laughing. When his grating wheeze subsided, he said, "You don't by chance have a little Sicilian blood, Lieutenant?"

The explosion had cleared the air. Feltrini might still be frustrated, angry, and largely helpless, but he seemed to realize that his problems weren't going to be solved by bullying. Or not, at all events, by bullying the Marine Safety Detachment. The Harbor Patrol was another story, and when Feltrini hustled off, his outrage rebuilding with every step, Tory found herself pitying Walt d'Andrea.

"No fingerprints," she repeated.

"Only yours," said Steve Merriam. They were drinking coffee at a far corner table in the Breakwater, and none of the other half-dozen customers was paying the slightest attention. "The flashlight is a three-cell Maglite," he continued, dropping his voice slightly. "A little upscale for your average mugger, but this is Santa Barbara, after all. And it makes a dandy club."

"Tell me about it," Tory said.

"The other thing, though . . ."

"Don't play games with me," she said. "It's a clock, right?"

"It was a clock," he corrected. "Now it's scorched, partly melted, blown-across-the-engine-room junk."

"The timer," she said, feeling a surge of triumph. "A bomb blew up *Finish Line*, and that was the timer."

"That's what it looks like," Steve replied. "Now, I have to ask you again, Tory: that guy who jumped you—could it've been Neal?" He rode down her objection with a gesture. "Footprints—well, foot marks—in the boat. They're about the same size as Neal's, allowing for bandages . . ."

"You think Neal jumped five feet to the ground with his feet burned like that?" she demanded.

She could see her point had told, but Steve shook his head stubbornly. "He was tough enough to stand on the roof of Jannice's boat while his feet were frying. He could do whatever he had to. Anyway: you walked back to your car—"

"I jogged."

"Okay, but you were still on foot. Neal has a truck . . ." He saw her shaking her head and let the question die.

"I was on the bike path by the harbor," she said. "He'd've had to drive through the parking lot—right past me. Nobody came past me."

"You're sure?"

"I'm positive. Believe me, a woman alone at night pays attention to what's going on around her."

"Most women at night don't pick fights in unlit boatyards," he said with a tired smile.

"That was temporary insanity," she said, matching his smile. "Brought on by booze. Tell me, Steve: Why're you so hot to tie Neal into this?"

"I'm not. Far from it. But Jannice McKay's death is a major event in this town. Her father was a county supervisor back in the early eighties, and her brother's got a piece of every development for miles around. She had a lot of important friends who want this cleaned up fast."

A lot of former bedmates running for cover, you mean. "I see," she said slowly.

"I doubt it." The waitress swooped down with more coffee, and Steve said, "I could do another pastry, if you've got something with red jam in it." When she had retreated behind the counter, shaking her head, he continued: "There's other things. More issues than just Jannice's death."

"Let me guess," she said. "If the top cop on the Harbor Patrol were to get nailed for killing another man's wife, some people uptown might not be heartbroken."

"I *hate* that!" he exclaimed. For a moment his sallow face went blotchy red, and faces turned to stare at them. "I just hate it," he repeated, his voice dropping to a whisper. "Look, my opinions about the Harbor Patrol are a matter of record, but if anybody thinks I'm going to stack a deck—"

"In case you care, I don't," she said.

"Of course I care. And I believe you. But there's people who wouldn't. And this case just gets messier the more you find out."

"You like your murders simple," she said.

"Damn straight," said Steve feelingly. "Give me your classic sex slaying every time: man gets girl, man loses girl, man pops girl—and maybe, if it's fancy, pops the other man, too."

"You're sure this isn't something like that. Jannice's husband—"

"Jannice and her husband between them have screwed half the city," he replied. "For years. Jealousy is not a factor here—that's the one thing I'm sure of."

"Well, what *are* the factors?" she asked.

"What's your interest? Neal Donahoe?" His eyes seemed to be focused on the contents of his cup, but she knew all his senses were on full alert. He looked up quickly as the waitress reappeared with a saucer.

"Danish with red jam," she said, setting it down. The pastry looked as if it might glow in the dark.

"Thanks," Steve replied. He lifted the Danish gingerly.

"That color doesn't occur in nature," said Tory. "It'll eat through your stomach lining."

"Actually, it only attacks tooth enamel," he said. "Real cops know these things by instinct." He took a massive bite, chewed it thoughtfully, and swallowed most of it. "My question's on the table," he mumbled around the rest.

"Neal Donahoe is a colleague," she said, choosing her words carefully. "Almost a friend. But I'm a Coast Guard officer first of all, and there's a chance he's involved in something that concerns me professionally. I want to know everything about him." She leaned across the table and fixed his eyes with hers. "What you tell me doesn't go further."

"No," he said slowly. "I don't think it would. Okay, here's what I've got, in all its messy confusion: Jannice owned

Finish Line free and clear, and Rudy, her husband, owns the house they used to live in. That was the deal when they agreed to live apart. Each is responsible for their own property."

"But if they got divorced . . ." Tory put in.

"If they got divorced is a whole other thing," said Steve. "No reason to think they were going to. This status quo's been going on for years. Recently, Jannice has been talking about selling *Finish Line*—that's kosher information, by the way: I checked with both yacht brokers."

"The boat's listed for sale?"

"No. But she definitely talked to them about it. She wanted too much, they said. Much too much." He took a sip of coffee, made a face, and set down the cup. "Rudy says she needs money. He said she even talked about torching the boat, but he assumed she was joking."

"And does she need money?" Tory asked.

"Everybody needs money. I'm getting a court order to see just where Jannice was at financially. The real question is that bomb."

"Ah, yes: the bomb," said Tory. "I suppose you're going to say a mere woman couldn't have built a bomb. She had to have a man to do it for her."

"I didn't say that at all," he replied, exasperation clear in his voice. "And it's not what I think."

"I apologize," Tory said. "Provisionally. Continue."

"The explosion was definitely caused by a fire bomb," said Steve. "The details aren't entirely clear yet, because it seems to have been plastic—a plastic casing, that is, not plastic explosive—and a lot of it's melted. A standard five-gallon container of gasoline was the fuel, and the igniter seems to have been something like blasting caps, sealed in a plastic tube suspended in the gasoline, and set off by electricity."

"The clock I found was an electric clock," said Tory.

"Right. An old travel alarm—worked off an internal battery or house current," Steve said. "It's a pretty complex set-up."

"Too sophisticated for Jannice, you're saying."

"No, that's not what I'm saying," he replied, laughing. "You never quit, do you? 'Complex' was what I said. Maybe it should've been 'clumsy.' "

"What's that supposed to mean?"

"I don't know yet. You know how experts are—they never want to commit themselves until they're absolutely sure. But there's something funny about that bomb. Maybe Jannice built it wrong and it blew up in her face—or maybe somebody built it wrong for her."

"Somebody like her husband?" said Tory.

"He was in Denver," Steve said. "Had been for the better part of a week. In front of thousands of witnesses."

"There's no motive for Neal to kill her," Tory said. "He was getting what he wanted—I assume—and he could leave anytime."

Steve regarded her in silence for several seconds, and she could feel the smile lurking just beneath his wan exterior. "I never let myself get locked in by motive," he said at last. "Everybody's motives are different, and sometimes they're plain nuts."

"You're the expert. I have got one question, though: Why did that guy last night, whoever he was, want the clock?"

"Now, that's a *good* question," Steve said warmly. "Of course, it may not be the right question, but it shows you're thinking."

He was teasing, she saw, and maybe he was entitled to. "Explain," she said.

"Explain what?" said a husky, musical voice from above and right beside their table.

Tory's heart skipped a beat, but she saw Steve go ash gray. They looked up together at Alex Tallant's pale, angular face framed by the hood of a foul-weather jacket. A thin smile shaped itself, and he said, "I'm not interrupting anything . . . personal, am I?"

Within minutes of meeting him, Tory had decided that bitchiness was Alex Tallant's dominant characteristic. But because he was clever, often amusing, and a change from the straightforward men and women she worked with, Tory had indulged herself with small doses of his company. Now she had the feeling she was about to become a central character in one of his notorious anecdotes.

"Cop business," said Steve. "What brings you into the Breakwater, Alex? Not your usual style of place."

"Oh, I don't know. It's got a certain earthy je ne sais quoi," he replied. "Actually, I thought I'd made a lunch date with Miss Lennox, but perhaps I was mistaken."

If Steve's ears had been long and furry, Tory thought, they would have lifted straight up. "You two lunch together?"

"So far, we've only dined together," Alex replied. "I thought we might extend the relationship." His dark eyes flicked quickly to Tory's, and she caught an unmistakable hint of warning.

"Then I guess you'll want to be private," said Steve, getting to his feet. He produced a handful of change and began to sort through it, but Tory laid a couple of bills on the table.

"My treat," she said. "I'll take a rain check on that question."

Harbormaster Office; noon: Neal

He knew something was up as soon as the call came in. The admin assistant, Shirley Dodge, fielded it, and Shirley's face (as Walt himself had once remarked) exactly mirrored whatever she was feeling. Extreme apprehension in this case, and though she quickly swung around so Neal couldn't see which extension she was punching in, there was only one other office she could transfer a call to.

About five minutes later, Walt came down the hall and made a production of scanning the room. His expression of surprise—indeed, amazement—at seeing Neal was a minor masterpiece, but Neal was in no mood to enjoy it.

"Oh, there you are, Neal. Feeling better? Feet on the mend? Hope you're keeping those bandages dry. . . ." He ran down at last, and his "Oh—could I speak to you in my office?" seemed almost a depressed afterthought.

Once the door was closed, though, he got right to the point. "Maria just called," he said. "She wants you suspended."

It wasn't an overwhelming surprise: Maria Acevedo, the head of the Waterfront Department and Walt's boss, was widely considered the most sensitive political weather vane in city government. A lushly handsome woman with deceptive, heavy-lidded eyes, she had fought like a tigress to reach her post, and she made no secret that she intended to climb a lot higher.

"She said it's just temporary," Walt continued when he saw Neal had no instant response. "Till you're . . . till the police untangle it. She wouldn't have insisted, she said, except the public would have a fit if she didn't."

"She may have that one right," Neal said.

"It's a foolproof move," Walt admitted with reluctant admiration. "She's even got somebody at SBPD to bless it. Or so she said."

Steve Merriam? Backstabbing wasn't his style—at least it hadn't been in the past. But the temptation might have been too much for him: Maria had made no secret of her two job goals—turning the harbor into a profit center for the city and getting rid of Walt d'Andrea and all who sailed with him.

"When am I suspended?" said Neal. The word tasted just as bad as it sounded.

"As of this morning. But you're not suspended—you've already taken a leave of absence." Walt was grinning. "I outfoxed her on that one."

Neal felt himself bristle. "Say again?"

"You need time to convalesce from your injuries," said Walt, grinning more widely. "Heroically sustained above and beyond the call of duty."

From Walt's point of view, Neal realized, it probably looked like a coup. Not only had he finessed Maria, he would also look good to city insiders, who would assume he was the one who'd forced Neal's leave.

"I suppose it's without pay," Neal said.

"Looks better that way. We'll make it up to you—trust me on that."

"What choice do I have? But I want something in return."

"Return?" said Walt, looking aggrieved. "I do you a favor, and you want more." He sighed. "What is it?"

"Not a whole lot. I just want to know what the hell's going on. What the true word is."

"Well, you've come to the right place," said Walt. "Though you won't like what you hear."

I'm just not equipped for this, Neal thought as he limped past the Boat Yard and the Marine Safety Detachment's office. I can sail a boat through a gale single-handed, but by God, I can't navigate the fucking city government. If I get out of this mess in one piece, it's Hawaii for me.

At least the storm was ending, trailing off into the usual blustery nor'wester. The patches of blue lifted his spirit, and then a chill gust drove right into his open jacket. Anybody who thought Southern California never got cold had another think coming.

His feet directed him into the Breakwater, warm and fuggy and somehow welcoming. He was about to slide onto a stool at the counter when he saw Tory, at a table by the window, deep in conversation with a yellow foul-weather hood. Conflicting emotions froze him where he stood: reluctance to be seen by her, as if his suspension had left a mark of Cain on his forehead; annoyance, even anger, that she should be talking so earnestly to someone else, when he wanted desperately to confide in her; and anger at himself for being a fool.

"Coffee, Neal?" said the woman behind the counter.

Her usual greeting—but was that a different tone in her voice, like someone speaking to a friend with a fatal illness? *I must be getting paranoid.* "A double," he said. "And double strength, too."

She looked on the verge of comment, then clearly decided against it. Someone had left the second section of the *News-Press* on the counter, and he picked it up idly.

"There's a story about the fire in the front half," said the waitress, setting down his coffee. "Should be around here someplace."

"I'll read it later, thanks," he said, forcing a smile.

"You're lucky you didn't fry," she said, and added, leaning across the counter, "We're all with you, Neal." An obvious tourist two stools down, scenting a new attraction, turned to stare.

"Thanks," Neal said again. "I appreciate it." What he really wanted to do was run, but he pivoted carefully on the stool, looking right through the tourist, until Tory was at the corner of his vision. Her companion had all her attention, he saw, but her expression was one he hadn't seen before: alarm with a strong base of distaste. The hamburger on the plate in front of her was untouched. Suddenly she pushed back her chair and rose in a single movement. "All right, Alex," she said, her voice clear across the restaurant. "I'll think about what you said."

Her companion had risen, too, and now Neal could identify him. Alex Tallant looked annoyed and, for him, slightly flustered. His eyes followed Tory as she stalked out of the restaurant, and then he saw Neal. He nodded distantly. On an impulse Neal called, "Hi, Alex. I need to talk to you."

Alex's bony face—so much like Jannice's, and so different—closed tight, but his voice was even: "Of course, Neal." As the other man approached, he said, "Maybe we should adjourn to the yacht club."

"This is fine," said Neal with a cheerfulness he didn't feel. "I might even eat that hamburger, if you don't want it."

Alex's look said he'd sooner devour a tarantula. "By all means. Help yourself."

He sat down, radiating attentiveness, and Neal dropped on the chair Tory had occupied. He realized he had no idea how to begin or exactly what he wanted to say. Fortunately Alex had his own opening remarks ready.

"We can clear the air quickly, I think," he said. "You are sorry Jannice is dead. I am heartbroken"—his face was expressionless—"but I don't think for a moment you did it."

"I'm glad of that," said Neal.

"You should be. Now, what did you want to know?"

Alex's waspish tone was bracing. Neal found he had no difficulty producing his first question: "Rudy McKay says Jannice was hurting for money. True?"

"Well, he should know."

Neal had the sense he was being tested, according to Alex's personal set of rules. And he knew that losing his temper would be losing the game. "You mean Rudy should know how hurting for money feels?"

Alex produced an acid smile. "He has lots of clients, and they hang on his investment advice as if it were Holy Writ. Or so he tells me."

"And he makes money on commissions, so it doesn't matter if the market goes up or down."

"It *shouldn't* matter," Alex raised an admonitory forefinger. "But if one's clients are elderly—and most of Rudy's are—they tend to freeze when the trend is down. Still, he should have enough capital to ride out a dead spot or two."

"Then he's not in trouble?" said Neal through slightly gritted teeth.

"Not at the moment, I should think. Still—did you hear he'd sold that fantastic new Maserati of his?"

"The noisy red one?" Neal replied.

"Yes, that delicious rumble. When he stepped on the accelerator, girls wet themselves for blocks around. It must have broken his heart."

"Rudy's overextended, then."

"I didn't say that."

Alex's disclaimer was perhaps a half second too quick, Neal decided. "But he's vulnerable."

"Aren't we all, in one way or another," said Alex. Something in his manner, an imperceptible tightening of his muscles, told Neal he was getting closer. "And in California, the precipice is always yawning at a married man's feet."

So that's it. "Jannice never told me anything about a divorce."

Alex's eyebrow lifted a sixteenth of an inch. "Don't take it personally, Neal. They agreed to keep it secret. Rudy felt they'd get much better prices for the community property if buyers didn't think they were under the gun."

It made sense, in a cold-blooded way. But it also opened up some unnerving possibilities. "You heard it was a fire bomb aboard *Finish Line*?" Neal asked.

Alex's face looked as if it had been carved in marble. "I hadn't, actually. Is that official?"

"So I hear—at second hand." I can be as detached as you, Neal thought. "I've been suspended."

"Have you?" Alex pursed his lips, nodding. "So. Ms. Acevedo makes her move."

"Officially, I'm taking a leave of absence. To convalesce."

"And Walt d'Andrea interposes," Alex added smoothly. "A clever response. But you won't be reinstated, you know."

His calm assurance shook Neal more than he wanted to admit. "We'll see about that, won't we?" he said, and took a deep breath. "Do you think Jannice torched *Finish Line*, and it went wrong?"

"No, I do not." Alex's husky voice was even quieter than before, but his eyes were blazing, his composure gone. "She would have told me." The curtain fell again, but Neal sensed Alex would have wished the last sentence unspoken.

"Well, somebody set that fire, and it wasn't me. If it wasn't Jannice, then who's left?"

"Who indeed?" said Alex. Neal could see there would be no more emotional slips, and he could also see that Alex was framing another speech. He waited.

"I meant what I said about reinstatement," said the other. "What will you do, Neal?"

"Thanks for the concern," Neal replied cautiously. "I don't know. Head west, I guess."

Alex's smile was mocking. "That's what you do, isn't it? Head west."

"It's always worked before." Surprising how hard it was to sound cool, but never more important.

"There are other jobs here in Santa Barbara, you know."

"For a cop under a cloud? Name one."

"You underrate yourself." Alex pushed back his chair. "You're living in paradise, my friend. Don't be too quick to move on." His wallet looked slim to contain the deck of credit cards he extracted from it. "I'll be in touch."

"Sure," said Neal, getting up.

"No, really. After all, we have a common problem."

"Do we?" It seemed polite to play straight man, and he was curious to hear the way Alex would phrase it.

"Oh yes," said the other. His icy smile had nothing to do with the rest of his face. "Getting Jannice's murderer."

"Catching, you mean."

"Whatever."

Marine Safety Detachment Office;
1415 hours: Tory

"For you, Lieutenant. Says he's a fisherman, but he doesn't want to give his name."

"Thanks, Chief." She reached for the telephone with one hand and with the other plucked from the row of publications in front of her a hand-annotated copy of "Federal Requirements for Commercial Fishing Industry Vessels." It would, she assumed, be one of the usual—a fisherman who knew his boat was in violation, hoping against hope for some loophole in the equipment regs that he could wriggle through. Brisk, she instructed herself. Bright. Positive. "This is Lieutenant Lennox. How may I help you?" Silence at the other end. *Damn. When will I learn? Skip the "lieutenant."*

At the other end of the line, someone cleared his throat. In the background she heard boat engines, the rhythmic thump of a power-driven pump, and a burst of conversation that sounded like German.

He's at the pay phones on the pier, she thought. "Hello?" she said. "Anyone there?"

"This is Tom," said a hesitant, slightly blurred baritone.

"Hello, Tom. Got a problem with your boat?" *Lord, I sound like a kindergarten teacher.*

"Not anymore, I don't."

I know that voice. But from where? "Well, that's good, Tom." She was half prepared for a sudden barrage of obscenities: it had happened before. But somehow she didn't think she was being set up.

"You passed my boat for me," Tom volunteered, and now she knew who her caller was, even if she couldn't remember his last name. The face was clear in her mind: rough and reddened and extremely hairy, with puzzled, almost pleading brown eyes.

"The . . . *Norma K.* I remember." Tom fished alone, one of the very few. Crab pots: you could smell his boat a hundred yards away, by the not-quite-sealed drums of rotting bait.

"That's right." Tom sounded pleased. "I just got back in. Been stuck behind Harris Point for two days."

Harris Point? What on earth was a crabber doing way out on the west end of San Miguel? And why was he calling her about it?

"I got blown there," Tom answered her unspoken question. "But two nights ago, I was in Prisoner's. They said you were looking for boats been out to Santa Cruz the other night. And I saw something . . ." He trailed off, sounding uncertain.

"Yes?" she said, trying not to betray the thrill that ran like an electric shock up her spine. Prisoner's Harbor, on Santa Cruz Island, was only a few miles from where *Blue Thunder* had sent her Mayday.

"Like, when the easterly swells come up, my anchor dragged."

"I see," she said, swallowing her impatience. Tom, as she remembered him, only got confused if you tried to push him, had to work at his own dead slow speed.

"So I figured maybe Chinese'd be better," he droned on. "But it wasn't. Swells just lapping right around Coche Point, you know?"

"I know," she said. She was on her feet now, the phone at the end of its cord, as she stretched to see the wall chart that showed the channel and its islands. There was Chinese Harbor, a right-angle indentation on the northern side of Santa Cruz. And Coche Point. "So what did you do then?"

"Well . . ." He dragged out the syllable for a full second, "I figured maybe Potato'd give me a lee."

Right, she thought, another mile toward San Pedro Point. We'll get there yet, if Tom's got enough change. "And did it?" she asked. As if invoked by her thought, the telephone burped. Through gritted teeth she coached Tom into depositing more money. "You were in Potato Harbor," she reminded him.

"No," he said. "I was *heading* for Potato."

"Oh, right."

"That's when I saw them—these two boats." He laughed. "Thought at first it was one boat, real weird looking."

He chuckled again, and Tory had the sinking feeling that his account might stall out right there. "So what happened, Tom?"

"One of 'em sank." His tone was so matter-of-fact, it took her a moment to appreciate what he was saying.

"Sank?" she managed at last, her voice a squeak.

"Yep. One sank and the other sailed away."

She could feel the blood racing in her veins, but she forced her tone to match his. "The boat that sank, Tom. Did you get a good look at it?"

He seemed to consider her question for some time before he spoke. "Not really. Like, it was night, and overcast. Besides, they were right close together. But it sank all right."

"Okay. Where did it sink?"

"Just off Cavern Point. In close to shore: water's five, six fathoms."

About thirty-five feet, she thought. That would be close indeed—probably closer than Dave had taken the *Hampton*. She focused on the chart: Cavern Point was a steep-sided, irregular triangle thrusting north. "That was the west side of the point, Tom?"

"Just inside the tip, on the west."

"What about the other boat? What did it look like?"

"Some sailboat," he said. "I don't know anything about sailboats. Well, I gotta run. It's been nice talkin' to you." And he was gone, leaving her staring at the handset in numb amazement.

What to do first? Call Long Beach, probably. They'd be able to produce a small patrol boat that could work in close to shore—a forty-four-footer would be best, with this nor'wester blowing. And divers . . .

The door opened, and Neal Donahoe stepped in. A different Neal Donahoe, looking miserably unhappy and slightly stunned. "I came by to apologize," he said.

Tory and Chief Washington regarded him warily. Something had gone out of him, Tory decided: the spark of hidden amusement he'd always carried was quite extinguished.

He turned to the chief. "I acted like an asshole this morning. And then I lost my temper and made it worse. I'm sorry."

"Hey, man," said the chief, looking uncomfortable. "I wasn't exactly a hundred percent myself. Forget it."

"Same goes for you," Neal said to Tory. "I must've seemed like the nursemaid from hell."

"More like the chauvinist from the black lagoon. But you're forgiven." A suspicion struck her with unexpected force. "You're quitting."

"I can't quit. I've been suspended," he said, smiling sourly. "Or allowed to go on sick leave—a camouflaged version of the same thing."

"Jannice's death?" She was appalled.

He nodded. "I'm not accused or anything. Yet."

"But I just told Steve Merriam it wasn't you who attacked me. And that guy must've been the same one who . . ." She pulled herself up, too late, remembering her promise to the detective. But Neal, she saw, already knew what she was talking about.

"Not necessarily," he said. "Anyway, it's all mixed up with politics. Your friend Alex Tallant says I'm done for."

She bristled at "your friend" but decided to let it pass. "And you're just going to take his word for it? Let yourself get pushed out?"

"Listen, if pushed out is the worst that happens, I may be lucky." Perhaps he meant his smile to soften the words, but bitterness seeped through it. He seemed to read her expression and added, "I just wanted to wallow in self-pity a while. I'll rise and fight again."

"See that you do."

"You seem perky enough for two," he said.

"Well, I've just had a break." She glanced toward Chief Washington, who was shuffling papers industriously.

He looked up, produced an unexpected, complicitous wink, and said, "I might just take the rest of the afternoon off, Lieutenant."

"Uh, great. I mean, that'd be fine. If you feel . . ."

"*Hasta la vista*," he said, picking his cap off a hook on the wall.

"I'll be damned," said Tory as the door closed behind him. "He must've been taking friendly pills. Anyway"—she turned back to Neal, whose smile looked somewhat more lifelike—"let me tell you what happened."

Halfway through her excited account, she realized he wasn't catching fire. "What's wrong?" she demanded.

"That wouldn't be Tom Kerrigan, would it?"

"Kerrigan. Sounds right. His boat's the *Norma K*."

"I don't want to rain on your parade, Tory—"

"I can feel the first drops."

"But Tom's one of our harbor's registered colorful characters. You want to take Tom with about a pound of salt."

"Oh, come on, Neal! He's a little slow, I know, but—"

"Slow's not the problem. Tom's an old-time stoner: his brains ran out his ears back in the seventies."

His bitter amusement was more painful than his depression, but he wasn't going to drag her down. "What he said wasn't craziness. It had . . ." She groped for the phrase, found it: "It had internal consistency, and it fit the known facts."

"Did you know your jaw sticks out when you get angry?"

"I'm not angry!" she blazed.

"The thing is," he said gently, "Tom wants to be helpful—and that's when you've got to watch him. You need a sunken boat near San Pedro Point: he'll supply you with one."

Her heart was sinking, but she wouldn't surrender without a struggle. "He saw two boats at the right time in the right place. It's worth checking out."

"Maybe you ought to check him out first."

"What do you mean?"

"You could start with Camarillo State Hospital. Tom's spent a bunch of time there, off and on."

He wasn't laughing at her. If anything, she could feel his sympathy, and it put her back up. At the same time, she could imagine the reception Long Beach would give to a hot tip from a certified loony.

"Promising lead goes sour—it happens to everybody," Neal was saying. "Just write it off and plug on."

Her head was shaking "no" by itself, the way it had when she was a child. "I believe him," she said, hearing the stubborn defiance in her own voice. "I've got to see for myself. I'll get Tom to take me out there in his boat."

"You're a diver?" He seemed amazed—which was, she thought, only to be expected.

Her thought hadn't got that far—it was, she knew, dead against service policy—but she heard herself say, "I've got an open-water card."

He bored in relentlessly: "Have you done any underwater searches? Have you got dive gear—regulator, weights, tanks? How about a wet suit? That water's fifty degrees."

"No, no, and no," she burst out.

"I hate you" was eating its way through the lump in her throat, when he shrugged and said, "Well, I've got my own stuff, of course, and most of what you'll need. The wet suit we can borrow from Joan Westphal—she's about your size."

Her mind, which had been sliding into its own slough of despond, couldn't grapple with such a turnaround. Her only coherent thought was that Officer Westphal was two inches shorter than she, at least ten pounds lighter, and had no chest to speak of. "You mean you'll come with me?" she said.

"No, you'll come with me, on *Carpe Diem*," he said.

"But—"

"We'll head out a little after midnight, let this northwesterly give us a lift before it starts dying down. You can sail, right?"

"Of course I can. But if you're so sure it's a waste of time, why . . ."

"What have I got to lose?" His grin was a little forced, but there was a shadow of the old lazy humor in his eyes. For an absurd moment, she thought she might hurl herself into his arms.

ABOARD *CARPE DIEM*; 5:30 P.M.: NEAL

On the tape deck, Lucia di Lammermoor had just gone out of her mind, and Neal was wondering if he was far behind. It wasn't that Tory Lennox had been convincing—he could see the holes in her case from across the room—but she was so determined, so bubbling over with sheer willpower, he'd been unable to resist her.

Was I ever like that? he asked himself. Did I ever think I could make things happen just by wanting them to? Have I ever cared that much about anything—or anyone?

No, he decided. At least not yet. Even Jannice's murder—if that was what it was—didn't ignite him the way Tory had been galvanized by the deaths of three DEA agents she'd never even met. But commitment wasn't his thing, never had been. Seeing hers made his own lack even more apparent—and, in a curious way, made him regret it. Though for someone who had next to no faith in what he was doing, Neal thought, he was certainly acting like a believer.

Retrieved from the wedged-in stowage of *Carpe Diem*'s after cabin and spread out on the main cabin's faded carpet were two arrays of dive equipment. He'd set the better of his two regulators in Tory's pile and his only reliable buoyancy vest. The random assortment of belt weights he'd picked up over the years was divided into approximately even heaps. Wrapped in the flush of Tory's enthusiasm, Neal had rented three air tanks from the harbor's dive shop to complement the one he kept aboard. His mask and fins, plus a pair of goatskin work gloves, lay with his gear; Tory had assured him she could supply her own.

The only remaining question mark was a wet suit for her. Neal's ancient quarter-inch White Stag, a black, crocodile-skin number patched and repatched at knees and elbows, was entirely serviceable, but when he'd held up Joan Westphal's shocking-pink farmer john and tried to picture Tory in it, the image had refused to coalesce. He'd fallen back on the spare one-piece suit he'd bought at a garage sale years before: the chest, at least, was right for Tory, even if the legs and arms were a little long. The neoprene was a lighter weight than he liked, but women were supposed to retain body heat better than men anyway. He hoped she wouldn't mind the smell—"musty" was the politest word that came to mind.

"Going diving, Neal?"

Between Joan Sutherland's Lucia and his own swirling thoughts, he hadn't heard his visitor come aboard. Crouched in the companionway, Sid Seligman looked like an eighth Disney dwarf. His eyes, nose, mouth, and especially his fleshy ears were all too big for his head, and he was swimming in a vast smock shirt over a pair of sweatpants. The only thing missing, Neal thought, was a floppy conelike hat to cover the aureole of white hair.

Yet he was anything but comical. What looked like near panic flickered in his darting, red-rimmed eyes, and his small, neat hands gripped and twisted at each other.

"Diving?" Neal repeated. Turning off the tape player, he found himself oddly unwilling to confide in his neighbor and finally said, "Just checking stuff out. How're you feeling, Sid?"

Bea appeared in the hatchway, looming over her husband. "He's fine, Neal—a little weak is all. What in God's name are you doing?"

"As I said to Sid, checking over my dive gear."

Bea, typically, was not so easily put off. "You're not going diving—it's much too rough out there."

And just as typically, Neal heard himself taking evasive action: "It'll calm down eventually. Probably by tomorrow morning."

"So where are you going?"

"If I go, probably out to Santa Cruz," he said.

"You'd be crazy to dive out there, with the great white eating that diver," Bea said.

"That was at San Miguel," said Neal. "Months ago and twenty miles away."

"For a great white, twenty miles is a walk before breakfast," she said. "And the breakfast could be you."

When Bea had made up her mind, Neal knew, opposition only dug her in. *Just agree and do what you were going to do, but quietly*, Sid always advised. And it was, by Neal's observation, a dictum the old man practiced as well as preached. "Okay, Bea, I won't go diving at the islands," he said, and glanced quickly to Sid. The old man was staring at Neal, tears coursing down his face.

"What is it? What's wrong?" Neal said, taking a quick step forward.

But Bea was already there, embracing her husband and blocking Neal with her shoulder. "There, there, old guy," she murmured softly. She looked up at Neal. "Maybe he's not so good after all. I'd better get him back into bed." She stood up, her arm supporting her husband, and looked down at Neal. "I think we'll postpone the dinner," she added. "If you want, I'll bring the logbook for you to look at."

"Forget it," he said.

Scotland through a Verdi filter, he decided, was just too gloomy for his present state of mind. Scanning his collection of tapes, most of them recorded off the local classical station's *Live from the Met* broadcasts, he found a two-year-old *Marriage of Figaro* and popped the initial cassette in the player.

Definitely better, he thought as the first, pulsing chords of the overture washed over him. And then he began to see his error: he'd wanted only a musical sugar coating for his depression, but Mozart clearly had no use for apathetic acceptance. Besides, something was eating at Neal from another direction, an uneasiness he didn't want to identify.

The unwelcome thought was just beginning to take shape when it was short-circuited by his cellular phone's burbling ring. "Harbor Patrol. Donahoe," he said automatically.

"That's not what I hear," said an almost familiar voice.

"Who's this?"

"Never you mind." A half second's pause, then: "You got a cellular phone on that boat, don't you?"

Mystified, Neal said, "That's what I'm using."

"Good." He heard the intake of breath, thought, He's nerving himself up for something. "I can make a hero outta you, Donahoe."

"That so?" Neal said as he replayed hero to his inner ear: *a southerner.*

"For sure." Another hesitation. Neal sensed his caller's courage leaking away.

"I wouldn't mind being a hero," he prompted.

"I know how Cowboy Daniels worked it," said the voice. "All the details."

Cowboy Daniels? That was *Blue Thunder*'s skipper—so this must be the missing agent's informant. Neal felt his breath coming fast and shallow. "And you want to make a deal, right?"

"Could be."

Neal knew he was on the verge of pushing too hard. "We need to talk," he said.

"Tonight. Shoreline Park—by the parking lot. The one nearest to the harbor."

"Okay," Neal said. "What time?"

"Ten. But hold on. You know the chain-link fence along the bluff?"

"Sure."

"Well, you climb over that fence, between the clump of trees and the john, and you stand with your back against it. You don't turn around, no matter what. And you come alone."

Time spent in reconnaissance is never wasted. Where had he read that? Neal swung the pickup into the parking lot at the top of the hill and climbed out. The narrow green strip of park that bordered Shoreline Drive ran for about half a mile along high bluffs, with a breathtaking view of the channel and the islands, twenty-five miles away. The park's southern perimeter was marked by a waist-high chain-link fence, put there by the city presumably to make sure that only the able-bodied could hurl themselves off the cliff to the rocky beach below. At two points along the way were one-story stucco structures with red tile roofs—the kind of municipal rest rooms early Spanish colonists would no doubt have built, had the thought occurred to them.

The northwest wind had blown away the normal channel fog, and in the vibrantly clear light of dusk the sharp ridgeline and deeply etched hillsides of Santa Cruz looked close enough to touch. The usual knots of sunset watchers lined the fence at the park's western end, and the seemingly endless procession of dogs paraded their owners along the paths.

Neal walked slowly to the fence between the nearer bathroom building and a towering clump of eucalyptus. His initial suspicion—that someone might be setting him up for a shove and a drop—faded as he considered the site. The fence at that point was several yards back from the bluff's edge. From his caller's point of view it offered reasonable privacy, little chance of an ambush, and, thanks to the parking lot, quick access and retreat. Probably worth taking at face value.

All the same, it would be nice to have a backup—but who? He certainly couldn't involve any of the kids on the patrol, and he didn't quite trust Steve Merriam. Well, what about Tory? he asked himself. This wasn't exactly her line of work, yet he suspected she would be tough and resourceful in a tight corner. At the same time, if the meeting went sour, he was reluctant—more than reluctant—to have her in the middle.

No, he concluded, this had to be a single-handed job. If it crashed, as was more than likely, he wouldn't be in any more trouble than he already was. And if it worked, he would have the singular pleasure of shoving his achievement up Feltrini's nose.

But what really drove him, he suddenly realized, was the

need to prove himself. Is this how it feels to be ambitious? he wondered. Probably not, he thought, because the only person he needed to convince was himself. And maybe, just a little, Tory Lennox.

Quarter of ten, and the park's lot was empty, except for a single RV from out of state. Neal had been standing in the shadows across Shoreline Drive for half an hour, having hiked the uphill half mile from the harbor. Here on the bluff, the northwester was still blowing hard, but not at its previous steady, unrelenting, postfrontal intensity. It would, he thought, gust out well before dawn.

Time to go. He hitched the Kevlar vest into a slightly less uncomfortable position under his windbreaker and started across the street. Except for the clasp knife in his pocket, he was unarmed. The fact didn't bother him. Around salt water, even the Harbor Patrol's stainless-steel automatics were just another damn thing to rust solid.

He paused behind the RV, which showed a single dim light through a crack in its drawn curtains. On the grounds that it couldn't hurt, he wrote down the vehicle's color and make, and the numbers on its Oregon plate, in his pocket notebook. He walked slowly across the ice plant border toward the fence, feeling his confidence—or was euphoria a better term?—ebbing fast.

As he scrambled over the fence, his pants caught on a wire prong, and he had to balance precariously while he worked the cloth free. This is like being one of those ducks in a shooting gallery, he thought. In the diffused glow of a streetlight, the dim edge of the bluff looked a lot closer than it had at sunset.

He was breathing hard when he finally placed himself with his butt against the links, as instructed. It was a much more exposed, even helpless, position than he'd thought. And then there was nothing to do but wait.

He never heard the approaching steps. The wind in the nearby trees must have blanketed the crunch of feet on ice plant. "Don't turn around," said the voice of his telephone caller, sounding scared—and angry about it.

Without the phone's distortion he instantly recognized

the mechanic T.J. Wellcome, figured there was no point in revealing that fact. "I won't," he said, and waited.

"You want to know what happened to *Blue Thunder*." Since it wasn't a question, Neal didn't answer. "Well, Cowboy set one of his traps, only he fell into it himself," T.J. continued. "Trapper turned out to be the trappee, you might say." His giggle was pure nervousness.

"How about a few details?" Neal demanded.

It became clear after a few minutes' verbal shuffling that T.J. wouldn't—or couldn't—be specific. "But I do know who did it," he insisted. "Oh, yes—I know that."

"So you're selling the killers' names? Is that it?"

"Never said there was more'n one," T.J. snapped back. "Anyway, what I got's much better."

"Tell me," said Neal.

"All those busts Cowboy made? There's a whole lot bigger hauls than those, never get caught." T.J. paused, clearly waiting for applause.

"No shit," said Neal coldly.

"What I mean," T.J. continued, his voice rising, "what I mean is that Cowboy was making it look like the water route into the county was blocked, when that's the way the heavy stuff's coming in."

"So Cowboy's busts were like decoys," Neal said.

"Now you got it, man. Little, diddly-squat stuff—but enough of 'em to make Cowboy look straight."

"Diddly-squat unless it was your boat got impounded." He could taste the acid in his own voice.

"Listen, man, what d'you care about those little dweebs? They done the crime, let 'em do the time," said T.J. angrily.

Control yourself, stupid. "So who set up those decoy busts?" he asked. "Must've been somebody who knew what was going down here."

"Forget that," snapped T.J., inadvertently giving Neal his answer. "What you want's the major dudes, the big shippers. I'm the man can break the whole thing open for you."

"For a price," Neal said, thinking how perfectly placed T.J. Wellcome was to have set up Cowboy Daniels's busts. People were grateful when a mechanic turned up, expected him to poke and pry around their boat. If you were feeling generous and he'd done a good job, you might even offer him a toke.

"For a *big* price," said T.J. "Enough to get me far away from here. You can hang around and take all the credit."

"Uh-huh," Neal said. "Do you seriously think anybody's going to lay out a lot of money on your say-so?"

"I already thought of that," said T.J. quickly. "I can give your bosses something—an appetizer, like—to show I'm serious. You check it out, and then we'll talk turkey."

"Okay," Neal said. "You tell me exactly where *Blue Thunder* sank."

HARBOR PARKING LOT; 0015 HOURS: TORY

Why am I doing this? she asked herself as she slid the Honda into a parking space a discreet three rows from the Marina 2 gate. Her mind was still reeling from her conversation, three hours before, with two Harbor Patrol officers she'd sought out to contradict Neal's opinion of her star witness. But when she'd floated Tom Kerrigan's name past them, the results were pure disaster.

"You mean Two-Tiller Tom?" Taffy Hegemann whooped. "Stay far away from that cuckoo, Tory—upwind, if possible."

Her partner, a strikingly handsome young man named Dalleson, smiled and nodded for a minute, then said, "Word is he's here on a green card from the gamma quadrant."

Wonderful. Yet here she was, positively rushing to make a fool of herself in front of a man who . . . Who what? It was a question that tantalized her, yet she didn't want to confront it just yet.

As she slipped from behind the wheel, the unaccustomed constriction at her elbows and behind her knees was a reminder that she'd indeed thrown her money—$149.95, plus tax—as well as her professional reputation to the winds. Swallowing an unladylike remark, she reached over the seat back and grabbed the net bag that held her foul-weather gear, a folded chart, and her mask, snorkel, and fins.

This wild-goose chase had just one thing in its favor, she decided: it would be underwater and thus invisible. Or maybe two things: it would also give her a chance to sort out her feelings about Neal.

Carpe Diem's diesel was turning over quietly as Tory padded down the wooden planks of the walkway. Neal was standing on the deckhouse, peeling back the mainsail cover. He was wearing mismatched foul-weather gear that looked, even in the semidarkness, about a million years old. On his head was a shapeless navy blue watch cap, on his feet a pair of knee-high black fisherman's boots. He looked utterly at home.

"Permission to come aboard?" said Tory.

He saw, thank God, that she wasn't entirely serious. "Permission granted," he said. Despite the clumsy boots, he dropped, catlike, from the deckhouse to a cockpit seat. His perfect teeth, bared in a welcoming smile, caught the light. "You can drop your stuff in the cabin."

She followed him below. The cabin's transformation was striking: the card table had vanished, along with the loose cushions on the settee. Dive gear littered the carpet, and clipped to the chart table was a large-scale chart—twin to the one she'd brought aboard—showing the west end of Santa Cruz Island.

"This pile here's for you," he was saying. "It's a little beat-up, but everything works."

She eyed the heap of gear, concealing the apprehension that swept over her. Since qualifying back in boarding school, Tory had dived only once or twice a year, always at resorts whose solicitous divemasters assembled the top-of-the-line equipment for their clients. The battered junk on the Oriental carpet (and where had *that* come from?) looked as if someone had been beating it with hammers. What was more unsettling, something seemed to be missing.

Neal had dropped to his knees. With quick, sure hands he fitted the elements together, then rocked back on his heels. "There you go," he said. "Regulator, pressure gauge, BCD, tank: all accounted for."

"Yes," she said, meaning the opposite. She was sure some important element wasn't there, but she couldn't remember what it was—and couldn't bring herself to ask.

"I put fifteen pounds of weights on the belt, but it was just a guess," he said.

"That should be fine."

"I was going to borrow Joanie Westphal's suit for you . . ." he began, and seemed to dry up.

His ears turn red when he's embarrassed. Interesting. "Officer Westphal is a sylph," she said. "There's no way I could fit into a wet suit of hers."

"Well, maybe not," he said. The scarlet had spread to his cheeks. Tory pursed her lips to keep from laughing aloud. "I've got this backup suit," he continued, lifting a dreadful, limp garment from the carpet. A distinct odor of drains filled the cabin. "What do you think?" he asked, his eyes anxious.

"I think it's revolting," she said.

"Oh."

"But fortunately, it's not necessary," she added, unzipping her coveralls in a single dramatic swoop. "Voilà!"

The look on his face, as she shrugged the shapeless garment from her shoulders, was enough to set her ego up in business for itself. His lips shaped the syllables for "son of a bitch," but not a word emerged.

"You approve."

He nodded, then managed a feeble, "Oh, yes."

She stooped and pulled the coveralls back up. "Then let's roll."

Neal was obviously so accustomed to leaving the slip single-handed that Tory quickly saw she could only get in his way by trying to help. Instead she positioned herself in the companionway and watched with professional interest as he cast off the lines, swung himself back aboard, and grasped the huge oak tiller with one hand. He glanced at the glowing instrument panel, then scanned the ketch from end to end. Apparently satisfied, he put the engine into reverse.

Carpe Diem began to move astern. When she was about halfway out of the slip, Neal pushed the tiller over hard. "We'll make sail outside," he said. "From aft forward, of course."

The words barely registered as Tory watched the sterns in the opposite slips approaching inexorably. Neal never even glanced over his shoulder but, at the last possible second, pushed the gear lever forward and dragged the tiller across.

Carpe Diem answered slowly; halfway through her turn, with room again running out, Neal had to back her down.

"A long, straight keel—right?" Tory said.

This time he threw a quick, appraising stare aft as the ketch's broad stern swung around ponderously. "The length of the underbody, and six feet deep back at the transom," he replied.

Well, that would account for the boat's behavior, Tory thought. "I expect she holds a course by herself, though," she said.

"If you can get her balanced," Neal said. "There's too little sail forward—she really needs a bowsprit."

Once free of the slips, he tapped the gear lever with his foot and the engine picked up speed. "It's a single-lever control. Farther forward is faster ahead, farther back is faster astern . . ."

"And straight up and down is neutral idle," Tory supplied. "But I didn't feel it go into gear—is the shift hydraulic?"

"Right. It can fool you." She sensed his approval. It confirmed her suspicion that this conversation was class and test combined. She could handle that.

Down at Neal's feet, Walt d'Andrea's tired voice said: "Going far?"

Neal laughed, bent forward, came up with a hand mike. "Just for a ride. Lieutenant Lennox is aboard—want to talk to her?"

"I can see her from here. Take care of him, Tory. . . . Take care of each other."

The northwester faded about five miles short of the island's high, sere bluffs, but by then Tory knew most of what she needed to know about *Carpe Diem*. The ketch was hard mouthed—not a boat to be mastered by plucking delicately at the tiller. And she needed a lot more sail and half a gale to pull her deep, heavy hull through the water at any speed. On the other hand, her big Perkins diesel and three-bladed propeller could punch her surprisingly fine-lined bow through steep seas, and she was both dry and stable. Not, Tory thought, a boat she herself could love—but someone else might.

About *Carpe Diem*'s skipper Tory was less certain. He was an instinctive sailor, which said nothing about him as a man: she had encountered a number of rats who were also natural-born boat handlers. What puzzled her was that none of the really good sailors she'd known would have tolerated a vessel like this—solid and seaworthy, but undercanvased and slow to respond. A heavy clunker. And she didn't even know for sure how Neal felt about *Carpe Diem*. She detected a certain fondness for the boat, but nothing close to either passionate love or loathing, the normal owner's emotions.

The sky was already lightening in the east, and Tory could see Neal's lean features clearly when he turned to her and said, "We'll heave-to here, I think. Have breakfast and get squared away."

Clearly he had thought it out. With *Carpe Diem* riding easily in the light breeze, under her strapped-in mizzen, Neal set about producing a lumberjack's meal while firing instructions up the companionway to her. She furled the mainsail on its boom; flaked, folded, and bagged the too small genoa jib; coiled down the sheets and tucked them out of the way. She unrolled the ketch's eight-foot-long inflatable tender, pumped it up, and launched it (remembering at the last instant to tie off its towline). She brought the dive gear up into the cockpit and wedged it securely with life preserver cushions.

Tired, sweaty, and ravenous, she went below. Neal had somehow found time to climb into his own wet suit, an ancient black jacket and high trousers with a lumpy finish that looked like crocodile skin: she had never seen anything like it. Squares of a different sort of neoprene decorated the elbows and knees. Old glue stains suggested these were not the first patches to cover the vulnerable points.

He was unshaven, and his eyes had dark circles beneath them. Even so, she found him ravishing. His unzipped jacket revealed a smooth, hard, tanned chest—not the disgusting pneumatic pecs of a weightlifter, but real working muscle. His legs, slightly exaggerated by the quarter-inch fabric of his suit, were lean and powerful, and her one quick glimpse of his ass made her determined to get a better view at the earliest opportunity.

Tory had shed her coveralls and unzipped the neck of her one-piece body suit as far as she dared. She felt in some danger of liquefying, and sweat had matted her hair and run in streaks down her face. If Neal noticed, it didn't seem to put him off. His eyes wandered from her cleavage to her thighs and back again, settled at last on a point above and slightly to the right of her head.

The cabin was awash in odors—pancakes and coffee battled with old wet suit and a faint tang of diesel. Tory fumbled in her net bag and extracted the chart. Tucking it under her arm, she grabbed a mug of coffee and a plate piled with pancakes and quickly climbed back up the companionway into the fresh air. Neal emerged a moment later with a handful of cheap stainless-steel utensils, an oversize mug, and his own heaped dish—twice what she was eating.

She had already unfolded the chart on which, earlier in the evening, she'd blocked in a creeping line pattern oriented on the shore at the eastern end of the island. That was before her meeting with the two Harbor Patrol officers. Now, as she considered her meticulous chartwork, she thought of her source, and her heart sank. "I'm afraid this could be a big waste of time," she said.

"It won't be."

His tone was buoyant, and she looked at him more carefully. Under his fatigue she could feel a vibrant, barely suppressed excitement. Thinking back, she realized it had been there all night. "What's going on?" she said.

He grinned around a mouthful of pancake and shook his head.

"I mean it, Neal. You're up to something, and I want to know what it is."

He swallowed with an effort, washed it down with a gulp of coffee. "We're going to find that boat," he said.

She wanted to believe him, but the doubt had set in too far for her to regain her confidence—a confidence that seemed to have migrated over to him. Still, she would play out the hand. She always had.

He shook his head at her carefully drawn search pattern. "It's much too big for two swimmers. We've got to cut the area down to something manageable." He stepped up to the deckhouse roof. Balancing easily, he shaded his eyes with one hand. "There's got to be some surface trace of *Blue Thunder*," he said. "We'll start close in to the point, over there, and work our way east along the five-fathom line. Look for an oil sheen, floating debris, anything at all that doesn't belong."

The first discovery—his own—was a floating fender. He fished it out with a boat hook. "In the water a couple of days at most, which is right on. But it's too small," he said after a minute's silent consideration. The second sighting—Tory's—he rejected out of hand. It was a life preserver cushion with, as he pointed out, hairlike green weed forming on its underside. "Been floating a week, anyway," he said.

He was steering the boat, his eyes flicking to the depth sounder and then back to the water, when Tory called out hesitantly, "That could be oil—two o'clock, about fifty yards off."

"I don't see it." But he throttled back to bare steerageway.

"Wait," she said. "The sun'll catch it again."

"Yes." He took the engine out of gear, and *Carpe Diem* slid up alongside the iridescent, multicolored stain. To starboard, breakers broke heavily on the rocky shore, altogether too close for comfort. "Forty feet," Neal announced. He had the boat hook in his hands, was tying a rag to its end. "See if you can dip up some of that stuff."

The boat hook was too short, but on the third try she managed to poke the rag through the sheen. As she withdrew the boat hook, a second stain blossomed across the water's surface, six inches from the first. "It's coming from right below us!" she called out. At the same instant she lost her balance and began to slide beneath the lifelines. Her nails clawed at *Carpe Diem*'s smooth sides, finding no grip at all.

But a big, powerful hand clamped onto her ankle and dragged her back, scraping painfully, over *Carpe Diem*'s toe rail. "One hand for yourself, one for the ship, Lieutenant." He sounded amused. "Don't they teach you that at the academy?"

She managed a weak grin. An image of the young DEA agent—Huggins, wasn't it?—was still clear in her mind.

Had he felt as helpless, as foolish, just before he hit the water? "Here's the sample," she said. "Smells like diesel to me."

Sitting in *Carpe Diem*'s inflatable, ready to roll backward over its gunwale, Tory ran a quick, final inventory of the gear that festooned her partner, sitting across from her to balance the dinghy. And at that moment she realized what had been bothering her about the scuba rig from the moment she'd set eyes on it. "You don't have an alternate air source," she said. "Come to think of it, neither do I."

Neal's expression, with the mask covering most of his face, was unreadable, but she could feel his impatience. He pushed the mask up on his forehead. "You mean an extra mouthpiece, on its own air hose? No, I don't." He paused, arranging his thoughts. "Look, when you're down there, you're on your own. If something bad happens to another diver, I'm not going to let him—or her—start grabbing at my air hose."

"You sure know how to make a buddy feel good," she said. "In the class, they showed us—"

"In the class," he interrupted, "they don't show you two dead divers tangled in each other's hoses, because one panicked."

The sudden layer of steel under the sunny California surface didn't surprise her, she realized. Somehow she had always known it was there.

"Sorry, but that's how I feel," he said. And he was sorry, she saw—but not about to give in.

Without a word, she pulled down the mask, put her other hand over her mouthpiece, and tipped back into the water.

7:15 A.M.: NEAL

Neal hit the water a couple of seconds after Tory, feeling the chilly Pacific seep through the wet suit as he followed *Carpe Diem*'s anchor chain down to the bottom. The heavy plow anchor was wedged between two boulders—not the secure lodging he would have chosen, but good enough as long as the wind didn't change. Above him, Tory hovered uncertainly, fiddling with the valve of her buoyancy vest. The shimmering body suit was really too light for this temperature, but her appearance in it had simply taken his breath away. She hadn't dived much or recently, he guessed, but she was clearly at home in the water, and the techniques would come back to her quickly enough.

He somersaulted a few feet off the bottom and finned back with the current. Visibility was good—about forty feet, he judged—and *Carpe Diem* lay with her stern only a few yards from the tiny oil seep. No wonder the Coasties hadn't seen it, especially in driving rain, with the water's surface covered in whitecaps.

Behind him he heard a hollow, metallic *thunk, thunk* and looked quickly around. Off to his right, Tory was waving at him, her sheath knife glittering in her gloved hand. He kicked easily in her direction as she pointed inshore and downward.

It hadn't occurred to him that *Blue Thunder* was actually blue, but she was—a dark shade that was almost black underwater. Her underbody was painted an even darker color, the whole merging with the boulders on which she lay. She had come to rest more or less on her starboard side, with her stern propped above her bow by a pile of rocks—an uneasy position.

With Tory following close behind him and just above, he finned slowly around the dead hulk, looking for signs of damage. Aside from a long white scar where some bottom paint had scraped off against a rock, she seemed intact. No, he corrected himself, not quite. He kicked a little closer. One panel of the glass windshield was gone, seemingly knocked right out of the frame. He grasped the steering wheel and pulled himself closer.

As he'd thought, something—a shotgun blast, or maybe two—had chewed up much of the dashboard and riddled the small VHF radio set into it. Tory's head appeared beside him, and he pointed to the damage. Eyes wide behind her mask, she nodded comprehension.

She made the thumbs-up gesture that indicated she wanted to surface, but he shook his head and continued his examination. The companionway hatch was closed, its padlock snapped shut—to hide what? he wondered. Or maybe closing the lock had been an automatic gesture on the killer's part, to shut away something he didn't want to think about.

Tory tugged at his sleeve and pointed. On the cockpit sole, winking dully, a big-barreled revolver—a Magnum, he thought. He stuck the blade of his knife through the trigger guard and retrieved it. *Now what do I do with the damn thing?*

But Tory solved the problem for him. Untying the pull cord from her BCD's deflation valve, she strung the pistol from it. Again she signaled to surface, and again he shook his head "no." Something at *Blue Thunder*'s bow had caught his eye on his first, cursory tour, and there was enough air left in the tank to have a look. Tory, however, pointed to the revolver dangling from her inflation vest and repeated her thumbs-up.

Fair enough, he thought and accompanied her slowly to the surface. Deprived of speech for an eventful half hour, she seemed ready to burst. "Terrific!" she exclaimed as they bobbed alongside the dinghy. "Wonderful! We did it!"

Her enthusiasm was nearly irresistible. "Let's get that damn gun off you," he said, grinning. "I'd hate for you to shoot yourself in your moment of triumph."

"Oh, right." And then, of course, she couldn't untie the water-soaked knot and he had to do it, equally conscious of the loaded gun and her shimmering body.

A couple of minutes later they were in *Carpe Diem*'s cockpit. As Neal had expected, Tory could barely wait to get on the radio. "Let's hold off a bit," he said, taking the microphone from her hand.

With her eager face and the water gleaming on her crisp golden hair, she looked like every sailor's dream. "How come?" she demanded. "Don't you want to start rubbing it in?"

"Oh, absolutely," he agreed. She was watching him closely, and behind her warm smile he thought he saw the tiniest shadow of doubt. "Look," he said, "before we get the DEA and the U.S. Coast Guard out here, I want to go over *Blue Thunder* myself, stern to stern, and we can do that underwater damn near as well as on top."

She cut right through his smokescreen: "Who don't you trust? Feltrini?"

"Him for sure—he's got an agenda a yard long and God knows how convoluted."

"Someone else?" The smile had evaporated. "You're not telling me something, Neal."

Of course he wasn't, but this didn't seem the ideal moment to spring T. J. Wellcome on her.

"And come to think of it, how'd you know exactly where to look for the boat?"

Just what he'd been afraid of. "Hey, your man Kerrigan gave you the position," he objected.

"No, he didn't. He just said inside Cavern Point, but you dropped *Carpe Diem* practically on top of the wreck—as neatly as if you'd buoyed it."

He tried a winsome smile. "Just lucky, I guess. But listen"—as her eyes narrowed—"if you want to call Coast

Guard Long Beach or Station Channel Islands, be my guest. Just do it on the cellular phone—we don't want every urchin diver on the coast in our laps."

He waited until she'd punched in the number, then unobtrusively switched to a fresh air tank. She was barely into her explanation of their discovery when he pulled his fins back on, slipped into the backpack, and cinched it. She looked up as he rose. "Hey, what're you doing?" she said.

"Going to have another look," he said. "Join me when you're through." He picked up the small pry bar he'd taken from *Carpe Diem*'s tool chest and took a single long step over the side.

He had, he figured, at least half an hour and probably twice that before anybody from the mainland reached them—but once the major league forces of righteousness arrived, he wouldn't be allowed within a mile of *Blue Thunder*. And if his reasoning was correct, somebody in marine law enforcement had a personal interest in tidying up the DEA boat. Feltrini was his own favorite candidate, but it was too easy to be misled by loathing. Even if Feltrini were honest, his first priority, as a good federal bureaucrat, would be making sure his own agency came up smelling like a rose, no matter who else took the fall.

And what if it wasn't Feltrini? What if it was somebody Neal hadn't even heard of—or someone he already knew? Walt d'Andrea, for instance. Or even Tory Lennox. His every instinct rejected the notion out of hand, but what did he really know about her? She was certainly better off than any Coast Guard junior officer he'd met, but where did her money come from? She never talked about it, and Steve Merriam's assumption it was family money was just that—assumption. Anyway, why was somebody with her looks and style, somebody who radiated ambition, in a job like hers?

His unsettling thoughts had ridden him back down to *Blue Thunder*. Her bow was right below him. Around the foredeck cleat was a piece of nylon line that ended not in a loop but a spliced-in eye, tightly fitted around a metal thimble. An anchor line, probably—but *Blue Thunder*'s anchor was still in its deck chocks, still shackled to its own rode. The cleated line trailed over the bow, and when he pulled it in, he saw it had been hacked through about twenty feet from the eye splice. Without quite knowing why, he uncleated the line and wrapped it like a sash around his own midsection, then finned back to the chase boat's cockpit.

He was just fitting the pry bar under the companionway padlock's hasp when the final and most disturbing notion bubbled up: Tory had been right in saying that Neal had pinpointed the DEA boat's location—but her own calculated position hadn't been that far off; they would have found the wreck inside a couple of hours.

Had she really gotten her information from the harmless screwball Kerrigan, or had she known all along? Savagely Neal levered the hasp out of the flimsy wood, which yielded so easily that he fell over backward. From the corner of his eye he saw Tory kicking down toward him.

As he righted himself, he thought he felt *Blue Thunder* shift slightly underfoot. But now Tory was in his face, quite literally. Even allowing for the mask's distortion, her determined expression was impressive. She pointed to herself, then to the companionway hatch.

You want to go in first? He shook his head. *Not a good idea.* But she persisted. *All right, have it your way.* He unclipped his flashlight and handed it to her, slid open the hatch, and sketched a sweeping gesture with his free hand.

She eyed the dark opening, and he could feel her hesitation. Then she nodded abruptly, switched on the flash, and kicked through. An instant later, as he swung himself around to follow her, he heard a hard thump of metal tank against fiberglass and saw an explosion of air bubbles burst from the companionway. With a grinding rasp, *Blue Thunder*'s keel slid off its rock, and the boat's stern dropped a good four feet. As Neal watched, frozen, and the air bubbles continued to erupt from the companionway, the chase boat teetered on her keel and then fell over on her other side in a cloud of silt.

Grabbing the sides of the hatch, Neal pulled himself into the cabin. The only thing he saw clearly was the flashlight, rolled down into a corner. Diving to grab it, he hit something heavy and soft with his shoulder. He groped for the light, his fingers clumsy in the work gloves, picked it up at last, and swung around. The figure sprawled against the bulkhead had been a man, but now it had no face. Only a pale pink chaos of flesh studded with white splinters of bone. Neal felt his gorge rise, and he swallowed desperately.

He pushed away, swinging the light around the cabin. It lit a second figure, around whose shoulders floated a shredded blue jacket that might have had white lettering across the back. And then he saw Tory, pressed into the cabin's farthest corner. Her eyes were wide with horror, her mouth clamped shut. Her air hose and mouthpiece were nowhere in sight.

Neal grabbed the shoulder strap of her BCD, and when her hand locked on his wrist, he wrenched it free. As he backed across the cabin, dragging her behind him, his shoulder struck something hard that bobbed away. His heels found the companionway steps, and he pulled himself and her up them. His tank caught on the hatchway frame, and he forced himself to stop and carefully disengage it.

Now they were in the open water, surrounded by so much silt that it was hard to be sure which way was up. But at least he could reach over Tory's shoulder and locate her air hose. He held the mouthpiece in front of her face, but she didn't seem to see it. He rapped it on her faceplate. She shuddered in his grasp, and her mouth opened. Quickly he shoved the mouthpiece between her lips. She coughed and choked but managed to retain it as he pressed down on the inflation button of her BCD.

They exploded to the surface together, and as her head cleared the water she spat out the mouthpiece and vomited. He dragged her, retching feebly, into the dinghy, tore off the constricting BCD and weight belt. After a while she looked up at him. Her face was paper colored, her lips faintly blue. When she spoke, her voice was a hoarse whisper. He had to lean forward to hear her.

"I panicked. Sorry."

"Understandable," he replied. How would he himself have reacted, confronting that shredded face?

"You saved my life," she said. It was hard to be certain, but she sounded more surprised than anything else.

Probably she was right, but there was no response he could think of. "You just take it easy," he said. "I'll be back in a few minutes."

0800 HOURS: TORY

For a moment she was sure she'd misheard him, but he straightened up and pulled on his mask. "You're going back down?" she cried. "What on earth for?"

"I want to see why she sank," he replied. She could see he wasn't telling her everything, but before she could challenge him, he'd flipped backward over the dinghy gunwale.

She wanted desperately just to lie there mindlessly in the bottom of the inflatable a few minutes more. But she knew perfectly well what she had to do, if she planned to continue inhabiting the same skin with herself. "Oh, shit," she said, and sat up. The moment the light breeze hit her skin, she began to shiver: the body suit was too thin. *Serves me right, buying for looks instead of function.*

With painful reluctance she rinsed off her mask and mouthpiece, poised herself on the dinghy gunwale, and rolled back. The water felt a lot colder than it had the first time. She gritted her teeth and finned downward. *I really don't want to do this.*

Blue Thunder was lying nearly level now, on her port side. There was, she assured herself, no chance the boat would subside farther. *But if I hang around until I believe it, my air will be long gone.*

The companionway hatch was open, and she thought she saw a flicker of light inside the cabin. *He must be in there—but doing what*? One way to find out. Deliberately, she lined up the opening and made herself kick through it cleanly, knowing that if she paused in the entrance, she'd never go inside.

It was dark, but the two huddling bundles that had been human were all too recognizable. No sign of Neal, and then she became aware of the generalized glow from forward. Hand over hand, she pulled herself through the low main cabin. Against the overhead small buoyant objects bobbed and a flattened air bubble quivered. An open door: *Must be the head compartment.* It was, and the light was coming from inside.

Neal was floating head down in the narrow space, shining the flashlight into a corner next to the toilet. He saw her through the side pane of his mask, and when he turned his head his widened eyes were still registering his surprise. She half expected him to wave her off, but instead he motioned her closer. With some awkwardness she half somersaulted forward, to hang parallel to him. Even with several inches of water and two layers of neoprene separating them, she was very aware of his body's closeness.

Blue Thunder's marine toilet was old and, Tory noticed automatically, technically illegal. Instead of leading into a waste tank, the discharge hose went straight through the hull, with a valve to close it off. But the heavy rubber hose had been hacked through right at the seacock, well below the waterline. With the valve open, water would have rushed into the hull and filled the boat in a matter of minutes.

Now Neal was indicating another, smaller-diameter through-hull valve: the toilet water intake. Its hose, too, had been cut through. She nodded comprehension, but he hadn't finished. With the flash he indicated the narrow band of hose still surrounding the larger pipe, then pointed the light down to reflect off a serrated metal collar lying on the floorboards, next to a rusty hacksaw.

I don't get it, she thought. Somebody had gone to the trouble of unscrewing the clamp that sealed the discharge hose to its seacock—and then, instead of pulling the hose free, had hunted up a saw and cut it through.

Now he was pointing toward the head compartment doorway. She pushed back and up, and her tank hit the door frame. The sound and shock of it were like a trigger: a white streak of fear shot up her spine. She felt herself go rigid, but his hand was on her biceps, squeezing firmly. She realized she was panting hard, knew there was no quicker way to use up her air. With an effort she unlocked her fingers from the handrail she'd been clutching and pulled herself back into the main cabin, her eyes fixed on Neal.

He moved easily down to one of the two bodies and put the light on it. Not, thank God, on the ruined face, but on the shredded jacket across the other man's back. Determined not to flee, she could not bring herself to come closer. Neal lifted the tattered cloth gently upward, then turned the light on what lay beneath. Tory's eyes unfocused themselves. After an hour—or, more likely, a couple of minutes—he pulled back and turned to the other corpse, taking it gently by the hair, turning its head to bring what had been the face into the beam of light. It was more than Tory was prepared to endure. She pushed off from a bulkhead, kicked out the companionway, and finned upward toward the shimmering surface.

"Here they come," she said fifteen minutes later. Swathed in a heavy towel, she was standing on *Carpe Diem*'s deckhouse, training Neal's binoculars on the white bow punching through the seas toward them. "It's *Point Morris*, the eighty-two from Channel Islands."

He had just pulled himself into the inflatable and was shedding his dive gear. "Quicker than I'd have thought," he said, looking up at her.

"They were probably out already, running search patterns," she replied. "I'll give them a— Say, what's that around your waist?"

"Piece of line," he said, continuing to unwrap it.

"I can see that. What's it for?" He didn't want to answer, she was sure of it—and she could think of only one reason: "It's off *Blue Thunder*, isn't it?"

"Yes." His flat stare challenged her.

"Why'd you take it?" She sounded, to her own ears, exactly like her mother.

"I'm not sure," he replied.

She didn't know why, but she believed him.

"You did a nice job of covering for me," Neal said, breaking a half-hour's silence. He'd been staring abstractedly at the horizon as he steered *Carpe Diem* with one foot on the tiller, and Tory sensed he'd been reviewing the hectic hour that had begun when *Point Morris* had swung alongside and Feltrini had leaped aboard the ketch, firing off questions at machine-gun speed.

You're right, Tory thought. For a gal who's such a clumsy liar, I was pretty smooth. But Feltrini wasn't through with them, of that she was sure. He'd swallowed her reasons for deciding to conduct a private search for the missing DEA boat and for using Neal Donahoe's ketch as a dive platform. But later, when he had time to consider the details, he'd check and recheck their stories, and check them again.

Right now he obviously wanted nothing more than to have *Blue Thunder* on the surface, preferably within the next five minutes. Years of experience in the federal bureaucracy had enabled him to tie the Coast Guard up in knots, and he was treating *Point Morris* like a taxi and her crew like his personal serfs. Coast Guard divers had already removed the two corpses and marked the wreck with floats. With the seacocks shut, it would be easy enough to pump *Blue Thunder* dry once she was raised to the surface—and a Coast Guard buoy tender was under way from Long Beach to do just that.

"What I don't understand," Neal continued, "is why you did it."

Their eyes met. He knows all right. Just wants me to go first. "Let's say I think we're headed in the same direction."

"If that's so, we might do better working as a team," he offered. "Share what we know and press forward faster."

"I show you mine, you show me yours—is that it?"

His grin was broad and complicitous, and she almost trusted it. "Something like that," he said.

"You first." *This must be how spiny sea urchins get to know each other. How bloody tedious for them.*

He didn't reply immediately, just stood on the cockpit seat with one arm draped over the furled mizzen, apparently considering the horizon. Behind him, *Carpe Diem*'s arrow-straight wake stretched back across the glassy calm water, pointing at the tiny white silhouette of the eighty-two-footer, with the island's bluffs rising stark behind it. The only sounds were the low rumble of the ketch's diesel and the hiss of water at her bow.

She couldn't take her eyes off him, knowing in her heart that when he spoke, she would have to trust him now or write him off. I could be a lot more detached, she thought, if he weren't so damn gorgeous. Though gorgeous wasn't the right word, she decided an instant later. Certainly not in his present red-eyed, unshaven state, wearing only the lower half of his disreputable wet suit.

He'd made up his mind, she saw. His tired eyes were hard. "Okay, here's what happened. I got a call yesterday . . ."

The story was more than she'd expected, and less. No name for his source, though from the context it was clearly someone he knew. No names at all, for that matter. But it hung together, made sense. Cowboy Daniels had been a crook, and maybe his crew had been bent, too. Essentially small fry—almost as small as the hapless dimwits who'd served as decoys. Neal's source didn't seem to be high on the food chain, either—though he was definitely a key player. But the ones Tory wanted were the orchestrators, whoever they turned out to be.

"When will you see your mysterious caller again?" she said. "Better get to him soon, before Feltrini starts breathing down your neck."

Neal shrugged. "My guy's in a hurry, too. Trouble is, now he'll want a deal, and I'm not exactly placed to set one up for him."

The hint was clear. And if Neal had seen through her cover, so would others. Coming clean with him was still a risk, but on balance it was worth taking, she decided. Still, she would play it his way: no names.

When she had finished, he was wearing a faint smile. "What's funny?" she said.

"It's Goodell, right?" he said. "The Republican Lady Macbeth."

A sputtered denial was even less use than a helpless glare. The two combined were utterly pointless. "How'd I give it away?"

"Sexist pronouns: you called your rabbi 'he' until you really got warmed up. Then a couple of 'shes' slipped through. And it's the authentic Goodell style: conspiracy everywhere."

She felt the blood rush to her face, already reddening in the morning sun. "You don't believe it, then—that somebody in law enforcement's involved."

"Somebody was," he pointed out. "Whether there's others . . ." He shrugged. "That's the thing with dope: it corrupts everybody."

"Not everybody. Not me."

He regarded her thoughtfully. "No," he said slowly, "not you."

But there was a more important point to make: "When you see your contact, I want to be there, too," she said.

She half expected him to object, but he only said, "He specified I was to come alone."

"Maybe so, but you need a witness, Neal. Someone who's on your side."

"I do indeed," he agreed. "I hope you're it."

"What do you mean?"

"Well," he said mildly, "I don't want to be just a marker on your road to an admiral's flag."

I should be outraged. I want to be. But she couldn't. "I think it'd be better to change the subject," she said.

He was looking a little abashed, she thought. "Maybe just as well," he agreed.

"I want to hear your version of what happened to *Blue Thunder*," she said.

His relief was plain. This was something he could deal with. "The general outline's pretty clear, I think. You can pick it up from where your own reconstruction left off: *Blue Thunder* ambushes the other boat in the dark, off San Pedro Point. But the other guys have been tipped off, and they're waiting. Or Daniels's crew are careless. Anyway"—he drew a long breath—"anyway, as they board, Daniels himself is shot in the face—a shotgun, at close range, is the only weapon I know that'll make a mess like that. Huggins goes overboard. The third guy . . ."

He hesitated, and she supplied it: "Ericsen, the ex-Coastie."

"Right. He's at the helm. He's broadcasting the Mayday when he gets it, right in the back. Okay so far?"

"I'm with you."

"The killers know they've got to buy time to get away—maybe they think the whole Mayday got through, I don't know. Anyway, they decide to sink *Blue Thunder* with the bodies on board."

"Wait, wait," she interrupted, her head spinning. "You're going too fast. What about the second guy, Huggins?"

"I don't know," Neal admitted. "My guess is he fell between the boats in the fight, and they couldn't find him afterward." He apparently saw she had another question and waited.

"I agree with you about hiding the bodies by sinking the boat," she said. "But why sink it in—what, thirty-five feet?"

"Six fathoms. Yes."

"I mean," she continued, "a quarter of a mile away from where she went down, it's more like three hundred feet."

"Easily," he confirmed. "Fifty fathoms, or even more." He was vamping, she realized, while he decided whether to peel another skin off the onion. "Okay," he said suddenly, and she knew he'd made up his mind. "Here's what I think happened: The shooting's over, and the killers are a little dazed. Not thinking too fast—not moving too fast, either. They lug the guts into the neighbor room . . ."

"What?" she said, then the quote came to her. "Oh: *Hamlet*. Pray continue."

"And then they try to figure out how to sink the boat. But it turns out to be harder than they'd expected. They back off the hose clamp on the head discharge, but it's so tight, and been on so long—"

"That they can't pull the hose off the seacock pipe," she finished triumphantly. "So they've got to find a hacksaw, because the damn hose is wire reinforced."

"And that takes more time," he picked up. "The upshot is, the water's finally pouring into *Blue Thunder*, and they realize the southeasterly's pushed them right into the shallows. So they get a line on the bow—"

"The line you took off."

"Right. And they start to tow her into deep water. But it's too late. Down she goes—so fast, in fact, that they have to cut their own towline before their victim pulls them under."

"Fantastic!" she exclaimed. Before she knew what she was doing, her arms were around him, her lips shaped for a kiss. His skin was salty and hot, the muscles beneath it like wire. His hard mouth was on hers, his beard rasping her cheek, and suddenly she was terrified: it was far too intense for a first kiss—out of control at the start. She pulled back as quickly as she'd embraced him. His bloodshot eyes were wide, but he shuddered and blinked, and it was over.

She started to speak, realized she was breathing too hard, shook her head. "I'm sorry," she managed at last.

"I'm not," he said.

CARPE DIEM, SANTA BARBARA HARBOR; 5 P.M.: NEAL

It was a piece of ordinary three-strand nylon line, half an inch in diameter and about twenty feet long from the eye splice to the raggedly cut end, whose strands had splayed out wildly. Half the boats in the harbor used half-inch nylon, and probably a quarter of them had anchor lines that size.

Neal lifted the hacked end—it was still damp—from *Carpe Diem*'s deck and held it up to the light. Each of the three strands was a slightly different length, which strongly suggested they'd been cut one by one, while the line itself was under load. From the ragged look of the fibers, they'd been sawed by a knife that was only moderately sharp.

He smoothed a cut strand between his fingertips, watched the fibers quickly unravel into individual yarns—cheap stuff, to lose its shape so easily. But that could mean either an ignorant purchaser or a cost-conscious one.

What about the other end? The small size of the eye and the fact that it had been spliced around a galvanized liner called a thimble told him he was almost certainly looking at a chunk of anchor line. The thimble itself was clean, but the galvanizing had nearly worn away, undoubtedly abraded by the shackle that had secured it to its anchor or a piece of connecting chain.

The splice was neat enough, though with each tuck the individual strands had lost a little more of their shape. A workmanlike job, he thought, but the unknown sailor had wrapped the line tightly with black electrical tape at the throat of the splice, where the end reentered the rope's standing part. A practical way of keeping the thimble from escaping, but less than artistic.

Something about the line . . . He rolled it between his fingers. The eye itself showed signs of wear, the small abrasions of sand and mud where it had lain on the sea bottom, moving slightly with each surge of the vessel. A working anchor line, then, and not someone's rarely used backup. But it lacked the telltale look and feel of deadness that nylon acquired when it lay in the sun for extended periods, so it was a line that lived in a locker. The anchor—assuming it was the boat's working anchor—was more than likely stowed on a bow roller or in chocks on deck, connected to the line by ten or twelve feet of chain leader. And now it was an anchor line that was twenty feet short. Under his breath the melody of "Voi che sapete" took shape in a nearly soundless whistle. He sensed he was missing something—maybe looking right at it and not seeing it. Or missing something he didn't want to see? That was possible, too. He coiled the line with quick, automatic movements and laid it on the chart table. Whatever it was would come to him eventually, he knew—but later rather than sooner if he kept trying to force it.

"Walt d'Andrea's a friend of yours, right?" Steve Merriam addressed the steaming black surface of his coffee, as if reluctant to put too much of himself behind his words.

"I'd say so," Neal replied warily. "Why'd you ask?"

"No reason," the police lieutenant said, and added, "He talks about you a lot."

What's that supposed to mean? Neal wondered, then decided Steve had dropped into the private, half-spoken language of city employees—a language Neal had never bothered to master, composed largely of allusion and veiled reference. "So what brings you to *Carpe Diem*?" he asked after a half minute of mutual silence.

"*Carpe Diem*? Oh, your boat." Steve's double take was nicely done, but not quite convincing.

"My boat," Neal said, and waited.

"Yeah. Well, I probably shouldn't be doing this, but everybody says you're the best source around." He was rummaging in the oversize shopping bag at his feet as he spoke. "Here, what do you think?"

Neal accepted the heavy, oddly shaped package wrapped in newspaper and sealed with tape, hefted it in his hand as Steve watched him expectantly.

Slitting the tape with his clasp knife, Neal unfolded the paper. The shards of plastic inside were torn and partly melted, the two lumps of bronze blackened and twisted. He laid them in a row, then looked up at the cop. "Used to be plastic pipe, threaded at both ends—looks like about one-inch diameter," he said. "The bronze caps ought to fit those threads. The bomb, right?"

"Part of it," said Steve. "The igniter, they tell me—blasting caps with an electrical detonator, inside the pipe. Hole drilled through the plastic for the wires, sealed with fiberglass resin." He fumbled in the shopping bag and came up with another piece of plastic, red where it hadn't been scorched black, and melted around the edges. "Recognize this?"

Neal took the piece and turned it in his hand. "Not to swear to, but from what you just told me, I'd say it was part of a plastic jerry can."

Steve's smile was sour at the corners. "Give the man a Kewpie doll. My experts say it came from a standard five-gallon container."

"Of course," said Neal. "I've got one myself, for my dinghy's outboard."

"You and a million other boaters. It's got a wide mouth, for a regular gas pump's nozzle—"

"I get it," Neal said. "The built-up cylinder with the detonator inside goes right into the gas can. Cute."

"The idea, my tigers think, is that the plastic was supposed to melt in the fire," Steve said. "But it blew apart so completely, there were pieces left."

Neal pushed the fragments back across the table. "And why are you showing them to me? Seems like you've got everything figured out."

"Not quite everything. We've tried a couple of plumbing supply stores, and the bronze caps are pretty standard. But the plastic pipe isn't. Occurred to me it might be some material specific to boating."

Neal poked at one of the plastic shards with the point of his clasp knife, then got to his feet. "Wait a minute," he said. But it was more like five minutes before he returned from the after cabin carrying a wooden box labeled "SPARES." He tipped the contents onto the card table, saying, "Every skipper I know has a container like this somewhere. Stuff you haven't any use for"—he stirred the heap with his forefinger—"but you can't bear to throw out. . . . Ah: here we go." He extracted a short length of plastic pipe threaded at both ends and laid it next to the fragments on the table.

"Looks like the same thing to me," said Steve. "Where'd it come from?"

"Right here," Neal replied. "See—it's still got the Chandlery's tag on it. But it could've come from any of half a dozen mail-order houses."

"Great."

"Let me finish," said Neal. "Look, whoever built this bomb probably made it out of stuff he happened to have on hand. But he might've had to buy the parts—maybe everything all at once. And if he did, he sure wouldn't have bought it locally."

"So you think he'd have used one of these mail-order places?"

Neal spoke to Steve's expression rather than his words: "Sure, it's a long shot. But nobody keeps better records than a catalog house—it's how they build a mailing list—and the customer's got to give them an address to send the merchandise to."

Steve looked unconvinced, but he said, "How do I get a list of these places?"

"Here." Neal turned to the chart table. While he'd been talking to the cop, Atrocious the cat had wandered in and curled up inside the coil of rope. As Neal gently raised the table's hinged top, she looked up at him with territorial displeasure. He reached inside and pulled out, one by one, four thick catalogs.

"Start with these—they're the biggest," he said.

Steve regarded the catalogs doubtfully. "I suppose it's worth a try. But how do I know what to ask for?"

"You really are a helpless son of a bitch," said Neal. "Do your suspects always have to do all your work for you?"

"You're confusing helplessness with delegation," Steve replied. "Here, use my notepad."

Five minutes later, Neal sat back and read off the list he'd composed: "Two bronze caps with one-inch threads, one plastic one-by-one hex nipple . . ."

"You're kidding."

"That's what the tube's called. One red, five-gallon polyethylene jerry can . . . What about the wire?"

Once more Steve dove into the shopping bag. "Here. This is just a sample."

"Okay." As he wrote he spoke: "Two-conductor wire, looks like fourteen- or sixteen-gauge—your mechanic can measure it for you—red-and-black insulation, tan cover. And whatever the total length was."

"Got it."

"What about the timer?" Neal said, and saw Steve's face close up.

"It's not something off a boat," he said.

"So?"

"In fact," the detective continued, "I probably shouldn't have said even that much."

Pushing, Neal saw, would get him nowhere. He waited.

"We've got it down in the evidence room, locked up tight. It's the key to the whole thing. . . ."

"But there's something screwy about it," Neal said, staking everything on a guess.

Steve looked so startled, Neal knew he'd got it right. "We're not completely sure," he said. He glanced about him quickly, as if for eavesdroppers. "I could get in real trouble," he said. And then, "Dammit, I'm sure you're innocent, Neal."

Almost there. Don't spoil it now.

"All right," said Steve, as if capping an argument with himself. "Here, look at these."

When Steve pulled the envelope from his pocket, Neal knew he'd always intended to. The indecision had been just an act, but for whose benefit wasn't clear.

The piece of blackened junk that had been photographed from six different directions and at three exposures was a ruined clock. The first two shots showed it in one piece, with a pair of wires, one red and one black, emerging from the back and diving into a tan sheath. "Runs on regular current or a nine-volt battery," Steve said. "The model's about ten years old, out of production for seven. See the hand?"

"Two forty-seven. That's about right for when it went off."

"No, no," Steve said impatiently. "Look at the alarm hand."

"Three-thirty," Neal said softly. "We'd have been in bed together."

"That's probably what she expected."

The next couple of shots showed the timepiece with its cover removed. "Follow the wires," Steve said, unnecessarily.

"They go to the battery first, then to the alarm," said Neal. "Clapper hits the bell and completes the circuit."

"Now look at this one," said Steve.

The camera had been too close to begin with, and the enlargement emphasized the original picture's fuzziness. But the photographer had the angle right, and the clapper looked as big as a baseball bat. "It's bent," said Neal. "Looks like it touches the case."

"It does," said Steve, his voice grim. "And the case touches the bell."

"So how . . ." Neal's mind was reeling.

"A couple of those twist-on pigtail connectors," Steve said. "Connect the red to the red, the black to the black. The wires from the bomb itself were short, so whoever hooked it up had to be very, very close."

"Jesus," said Neal softly. "A booby trap."

"Maybe, maybe not. Could have been a mistake or an accident."

But Steve clearly didn't believe it any more than Neal did. "So the idea," Neal said slowly, "was to make it look as if Jannice rigged a bomb to torch her boat for the insurance, and blew herself up by accident."

"That's how I read it," said Steve. He waited as Neal forced his mind to complete the necessary thought.

"And she *did* plan to torch the boat, with me supplying an alibi," Neal said. "Dimwit of the year, that's me. I guess she figured her regular lovers were too smart."

"Well, let's just say her regular lovers knew her too well," said Steve, avoiding Neal's eye. "And you made a hell of a beard for her, being chief of patrol and all."

"Yeah," Neal said heavily. Idly he turned over the last of the photos. After a moment he realized it was the underside of the clock. On the base, slightly off center, was a rectangle with charred edges.

"A paper label," said Steve, following Neal's eye. "Price tag of some kind. We brought the writing up: dollar sign and the number five."

"Five bucks?" said Neal. "Seems low."

"When they were in the stores, they listed for $12.95. Probably a garage sale tag. And you can forget what you're thinking," the lieutenant added quickly. "There aren't enough agents in the entire FBI to check out this city's garage sales."

It was true, Neal thought. Some weekends it seemed as if every second person in Santa Barbara had slapped price tags on all his earthly possessions and stacked them in the driveway. Next weekend, the same stuff would be on display again, in somebody else's driveway.

Steve had gotten to his feet, repacked the shopping bag. "Thanks for the help," he said. "I'd as soon you kept this quiet: officially, you're still a suspect."

"Steve, why in God's name would I have killed Jannice?" Neal demanded.

"You took the words right out of my mouth, pal. But somebody thinks you did—or at least he's sending my boss anonymous notes saying so." He paused by the companionway ladder, watching Neal from the corner of his eye as he stroked Atrocious, who barely twitched. "Looks like you've got a new girlfriend—and she's got herself a nest," he said. "So long, Neal."

Marina 2; 1845 hours: Tory

"Hello, Steve," she said, holding the marina gate for him. "Been visiting our friend?"

The police lieutenant coming up the ramp was carrying a shopping bag. In the twilight he looked slightly embarrassed at seeing her. "Evening, Tory," he replied, stepping through. And when she didn't start down, he finally said, "Yes, as a matter of fact."

She had the feeling that once he'd acknowledged her, he might open up. Releasing the gate, she turned toward the parking lot and swung into step beside him. "So how's your case going?" she said. "Neal and I had a real breakthrough this morning."

"I heard." He stopped by his car, fumbled with the keys. His eyes swept her, head to toe, and she was suddenly conscious that she was wearing more makeup than usual, and while her tan slacks and the dark sweater over her shoulders were certainly unexceptionable, the tie-dyed blouse she'd bought in Guadeloupe was perhaps a tad dressy for the docks. "You called Neal 'our friend' a minute ago. Mind if I ask how friendly you two are?"

She minded quite a lot. But she knew this was a question she had to answer—and maybe not just to Steve Merriam. "That's hard to say. Hard for me to define, I mean."

"I think I know what you're saying."

"I'm not sure I do," she said. "I really enjoy his company"—*You're weaseling, Tory*—"but I'm not sure if I completely trust him. Yet."

"Exactly," Steve said. "You have a feeling he's holding something back?"

"He's holding himself . . . his, I don't know, personal self back, if that's what you mean." *My God, when did I start speaking Valley Girl? And so fluently.*

Steve was looking at her narrowly. "I was a little more concerned about him holding back facts," he said.

She felt her face go hot. "Those, too," she said.

"He's got to decide who his friends are, and commit to them." He opened the car door and tossed the shopping bag in the backseat. "Maybe you could get him to see that."

Maybe I'm the last one who could. "Good night, Steve."

"So you think it was sailboat people who sank *Blue Thunder*?" Neal asked. He was standing at the galley counter, stirring a simmering pot of chili with a huge, charred wooden spoon that Tory decided wouldn't bear closer examination. "What makes you think so?"

"Well, it's a little complicated," she began. *And now that I think about it a second time, pretty farfetched.*

"Try me," he said, dipping up a spoonful of chili. He tasted it, blinked rapidly several times, and took a hasty gulp from the mug of beer on the counter.

She gathered her thoughts for a moment, decided there was no way she could bolster her ideas. "Okay. Now, everybody knows the best way to sink a boat is by opening the seacocks—right?"

"Unless you happen to own a torpedo, opening seacocks is certainly the MO of choice," he said, his face deadpan.

He was not taking her seriously, she saw. Mentally gritting her teeth, she continued: "Well, the engines have raw water intakes that could be used the same way, and they're under the cockpit. Given a choice, which would you prefer—futzing around below decks, with the water rushing in around you, or just lifting a hatch and yanking the hoses?"

"So you think the killers opened the head seacocks because they didn't know enough about engines to realize there was another way?" He pursed his lips. "It's possible."

"But you don't think so. Why not?" And why did she have to sound so belligerent just because he wasn't jumping to embrace her theory?

He was spooning the chili into big ceramic bowls as he answered: "Raw-water intakes aren't that easy to get at, especially with the engines hot—and they must've been. Besides, the engine compartment in those cigarette boats is bulkheaded off from the main part of the hull. It'd take about twice as long to sink."

"Oh."

Without further comment, he set the bowls on the card table. Garlic swept across the cabin in a wave. "Beer?"

"Please." From a plastic bucket full of ice he extracted two dark brown bottles, uncapped them, and poured the contents into a pair of exceptionally ugly plastic mugs decorated with dubious-looking sea creatures. "I guess it wasn't much of a theory," she said.

"You could be right, though," he said. He had produced another bowl from the icebox. "*Raita*—cucumbers in sour cream," he said. "Helps put the fire out."

She nodded, her mouth aflame, her eyes full of tears. "Delicious," she gasped.

"Glad you like it," he said as the cellular phone's burbling ring cut him off. Their eyes met. "Could be," he said. He picked the handset out of its cradle. "Donahoe." And a moment later: "It was there."

Tory raised her eyebrows questioningly, and Neal's lips formed the words *It's him*.

The conversation was short and almost entirely one-sided. Neal made only three more contributions: "That's okay"; a warning "Not on the phone"; and a closing "I'll be there." He hung up and, infuriatingly, took a healthy spoonful of his chili and a swallow of beer.

"Well?" she said.

"He wants to meet. Tonight. Told me, 'Come ready to wheel and deal.' " He shrugged.

"You said, 'Not on the phone.' What was that about?" she asked.

From the way he looked at her, she knew her tone had been too peremptory. "He wanted to start negotiating right then. He's scared." Neal stared off into the middle distance for a long two seconds, then added, "I'd guess he's feeling heat from somebody. Since it's not us, it has to be the people he's working for."

"And you're going to meet him," she said. "Even though you can't offer him a deal."

He looked surprised. "Of course. I can listen to what he wants—that doesn't cost anything, and it'll buy a little time for me to find somebody who can deal."

"I'm coming with you," she said.

Her words were no surprise, she saw. "Like hell you are," he said. "He told me to come alone. Specifically."

She doubted it. "Nevertheless, I'm coming."

"This is a desperate man, Tory—"

"All the more reason not to go alone," she said. She knew she was right and was reasonably sure he knew it, too. On the point of saying so, she was interrupted by a knock on the hull.

"Oh, Christ," said Neal under his breath. And louder: "Who's there?"

Bea Seligman's lined face appeared in the companionway. She looked a hundred years older, and her smile was visibly forced. "Is this a lovers' quarrel, or can anyone join?" she said with ghastly coyness.

"Come on in," said Neal, clearly meaning the opposite. But Bea stepped carefully through the companionway. She was wearing faded blue jeans that hung on her skinny shanks and a souvenir sweatshirt from Bodega Bay, way up the coast.

Her eye fell on the coiled furry bundle occupying most of the chart table. "I was just looking for Atrocious," she said, and bent forward to scoop up the cat. From where Tory was sitting, she saw the older woman suddenly freeze and the color drain from her face. *Heart attack* was forming in Tory's mind as Bea staggered, blindly putting out a hand.

Neal, whose back was to the companionway, saw Tory's expression and whirled to his feet, his folding chair spinning away to crash against the galley counter. Before Tory could rise, his arm was around Bea's shoulder. "What is it?" he said. "D'you—"

"I'm fine, I'm fine," Bea was insisting, but her skin was the color of parchment, and she was gasping. "Bad cat!" she cried to Atrocious, who had sprung to the back corner of the chart table and was standing straight legged, her back arched and her single eye blazing.

"What happened?" said Neal, sounding bewildered.

"She tried to claw me," said Bea. "For no reason, she tried to claw me." And to the cat, who looked fully capable of dealing with a mountain lion, "You stay here, you ungrateful bitch."

"At least sit down till you get your breath back," said Neal. "You look awful, Bea."

"Always the diplomat," Bea said to Tory. "I maybe had a little turn, is all. I'm not as young as I used to be." And indeed, Tory saw, her color seemed to be returning to its usual faded mahogany.

"Would you like a drink?" Tory said. "Maybe a sip of my beer—it's nice and cold."

"No, no." Bea waved Tory's offered mug away. "I didn't know I was interrupting your dinner. In fact, now that I think, I'd better get back to *Iolanthe* and make something for me and Sid."

"You could take Sid some chili," Neal offered. "I made extra."

This time Bea's smile was a little closer to human, though still less than natural. "The way Sid's feeling, it wouldn't be a good idea," she said.

"Still not good? Maybe you ought to see a doctor." His dark eyes were concerned. I didn't realize how fond he is of her—of both of them, Tory thought.

"He's just nervous. Things are a little hectic, you know."

It was obviously a code phrase, because Neal nodded his understanding. "Sure. No turnaround yet, I guess."

"Not yet." Bea shrugged. "But some good signs." She turned to Tory, who was still half out of her chair. "You look lovely, my dear. Doesn't she look lovely, Neal?"

"Oh, just great." He hadn't even noticed, she was sure.

"So, good evening to both of you," she said, but her eyes, imploring, were locked on Tory's.

Neal insisted on accompanying Bea to the pier. When he slipped back down the companionway, Tory was standing by the chart table, stroking Atrocious. The huge cat had settled back into the coil of rope it had been lying on and was emitting a sound that reminded Tory of the badly tuned diesel in her mother's Mercedes.

"The cat didn't try to claw her," Tory said.

"I beg your pardon?" *He knows.*

"You heard me. Atrocious was just lying there. Bea took one look at her and almost passed out. Why?"

Neal looked a shade paler himself, or maybe it was the oil lamp's misleading glow. He sat down and emptied his beer bottle into the hideous mug. "It's vertigo," he said. "Hits her sometimes. She hates people to notice."

I probably ought to just say "You're lying" and get it out there, she thought. But it makes more sense to take one thing at a time. "That's the line you took from *Blue Thunder*, isn't it?"

"Yes."

His defenses were up, but she had already backed down once. "It's a clue, I know. Are you going to tell me about it?"

"Yes, but not just yet," he said. "Please, Tory—don't push me."

A point-blank appeal. And from the heart, unless my ears deceive me. She could almost put words to what he didn't want to face, and part of her wanted to press in for the kill. *If I do, I lose him—in more ways than one.* "All right," she said, picking up Neal's chair from the deck. She set it at the table, resumed her own place, and began to eat.

He watched her for a moment. "What're you doing?"

"Eating my dinner," she said. "It's really delicious, Neal."

They finished their meal in near silence and cleared the table without a word. Only when they were standing side by side behind the counter—she washing, he drying—did she decide to risk it all. "Meeting's at the same place?"

"At midnight," he said. Her heart was sinking, when he continued: "If you get there really early—by ten, say—"

"Nine," she said, hiding her triumph.

"Okay, nine. But you stay hidden no matter what—no heroics. Agreed?"

"Heroics? Little *moi*?"

His grin was nearly out of control. "You heard me: No guns, no rockets, no cavalry."

And then, with no transition at all, she was in his arms. His lips were as firm, his mouth as demanding, as her fantasies had made them. His hands were amazingly gentle, yet she could sense the strength in them. Two more seconds and she would be lost. . . . "Enough," she said, gasping only slightly. He released her slowly, with clear reluctance.

"Not enough, but time out," he said, laughing breathlessly.

SHORELINE PARK; 11:45 P.M.: NEAL

Where would Tory have hidden herself? Neal strode up the hill, forcing himself not to scan either the bushes to his left or the darkened houses on the far side of the street. The wind was nearly still, and at the base of the bluffs the sea was chewing noisily on the land. Slightly winded—he had been nearly trotting up the steep slope—he paused at the crest that overlooked the glittering harbor a quarter mile behind him. Without warning, a surge of protective affection for the place swept over him, but he thrust it aside.

Tory was probably in the large stand of trees, he decided. There was enough underbrush around them to provide good cover—as there wasn't around the stucco rest room building. Important not to stare at the trees, though. He continued his walk, trying to look like an ordinary citizen out for a stroll in the middle of the night. He had left the protective vest behind this time, since T.J. had every interest in his survival and the damn thing was just too hot and constricting to bear.

At the fence this time he put both hands on the support at the top and vaulted neatly over. *I wonder if she's watching.* But she must be, unless she'd fallen asleep. She'd been there for nearly three hours by now—long enough to chill down even her enthusiasm. He felt himself smile at the recollection of how she'd thrown herself into the preparations for the stakeout. *God, I hope she didn't bring a gun.* Though it was exactly the kind of prop she'd feel was appropriate. What would she be wearing? Not that outfit she'd had on at dinner, for sure. Probably her Coastie jumpsuit and, if she had any sense, a watch cap to hide that golden hair.

With the wind calm, he heard the brakes on T.J.'s van squeal as he pulled up in the parking lot. Slam of a door, then nothing. It was ridiculous to keep on pretending he didn't know who he was meeting with, but if playing games kept T.J. from freaking out, it was worth it. The mechanic had sounded right on the edge of panic when he'd called.

Footsteps on the concrete path, then the crunch of vegetation. "Don't move," said a voice so wound up with tension that Neal barely recognized it. Then: "Put your hands where I can see 'em."

Neal pulled his hands slowly from his pockets, placed them on the upper edge of the fence. "Relax, for Christ's sake."

"You here alone?"

He'd expected the question, and his matter-of-fact "Just like you said" sounded natural to his own ears.

"You found *Blue Thunder*. You and the Coast Guard bitch. Right where I said it was."

"We found it," said Neal.

"So you know I'm playin' it straight. You can trust me."

"Sure. Unless you get a better offer," Neal said.

Silence behind him for a few seconds. "Things are moving," said T.J. at last. "I mean, they are *moving*. You ready to climb on board?" He sounded a little less terrified, Neal thought, but still tense enough for two.

"Explain," Neal said. "In English."

"There's a big delivery coming down. A double."

"Tell me about it."

Maybe the sound T.J. made was intended as a scornful laugh, but for a moment Neal thought he was choking. "Hell, no. Not till we make ourselves an arrangement."

"A deal, you mean."

"Abso-fuckin'-lutely. Now, there's three things I want—money, immunity, and anna . . . ano . . ."

"Anonymity."

"That's it. If my name comes out, I'm dead. And I don't plan on being dead for a long, long time."

"When you say money, what kind of ball park are we in?" Neal asked.

"Half million," T.J. snapped. "That ain't negotiable, either. And it's cheap, for what I'm gonna give you."

"So what do I get for that kind of money?" Neal asked.

"The whole package: how the stuff comes up the coast from Mexico without getting stopped, who's runnin' it at both ends, and a major bust to use for evidence. You'll be famous, man—the city'll be fallin' all over itself to reinstate you."

"I bet," said Neal—but he knew there was a good chance T.J. was right, and the possibility gave his spirit a tweak.

"And I'm throwin' in an extra," T.J. said.

Something in his tone raised Neal's hackles. "What kind of extra?"

"Why, the people who sank *Blue Thunder*, man. The dirty cop killers. If you want 'em, that is."

An unvoiced snigger hung behind T.J.'s words, but there was only one possible response: "Of course I want them."

"Just so's you're certain," said T.J. "Cause I'm gonna hand 'em over wrapped so tight they'll never wriggle free."

A flash of insight lit up the dark plain of the last three days, and Neal's stomach knotted. "You do that," he managed to say.

Something in Neal's voice may have told T.J. he had the whip hand. He sounded nearly condescending as he went on: "Thing of it is, I'm callin' the shots now. I'm talking to the top man here, just like Cowboy used to. Man wants a pickup boat, a cover bust . . ." He giggled as a thought struck him: "Who d'you want to get stuck with that one, buddy? How about we set up that prick Feltrini? He gets a handful of uppers and you get a couple hundred keys. Six o'clock news time!"

The mechanic's nasal voice had risen with each sentence until he was almost shouting. "Shut up!" Neal snapped. "You'll have half the town out here."

"Yeah, we don't want to go off half-cocked, do we, ol' buddy." T.J.'s manic glee was ebbing, but not quickly enough.

"When's all this happening?" Neal demanded.

"Soon as you come through," T.J. replied. "Details're all in my hands. My man's a major dude here in the city, but he can't set up something like this without ol' T.J."

Waves far below, and T.J.'s heavy breathing right behind him. "No big deal. You'd have had to tell me sooner or later," Neal said soothingly.

"Yeah, but I'd sure have liked later," T.J. replied. His voice had gone flat. "Man, that was dumb."

"Don't worry about it," said Neal. "You'll be free and clear inside a week."

"You really think so?"

A complete turnaround in ten seconds, Neal thought. Wonder what he's on. "For sure," he said, forcing confidence into his tone. "How can I get in touch with you?"

"Well, hell, man—you know my goddamn phone number now," said T.J. "I'm in the book."

Neal didn't try to hide his incredulity. "You mean you're running this operation on your business phone?"

"It's okay—I've got a cellular, like yours," T.J. replied, sounding sullen. "I'm careful."

"Stay careful," said Neal, thinking once the case broke open, he wouldn't give a nickel for T.J.'s chances. Or care, either. "I'll call you as soon as I've got what you want."

"For Christ's sake, make it fast," T.J. said. His emotional roller coaster was clearly running downhill. "I got to get back to my man in the next day or so. Stuff's already in the pipeline."

"Just stay cool," Neal said. "It'll work out." Something told him he was talking to the air, and when he turned his head he saw T.J.'s shadowy figure loping at speed across the grass toward the parking lot.

He waited on the outside of the fence until the mechanic's van had cleared the lot, then called, "Tory?"

"Over here."

Her voice came from the direction of the rest rooms. He jumped over the chain-link fence and started across the ice plant. "Where are you?"

"Up here."

A scraping noise from the tiled roof directed his eye. "D'you need a hand getting down?"

She must have heard his reluctance. "If you wouldn't mind."

Standing beneath the low eaves, he caught her ankles as she slid down the steeply pitched tile, but she was already moving too fast. They wound up on the dirt, with Tory sitting on his chest.

She was laughing as she got to her feet. "Sorry about that. I hope you didn't get too dirty."

"Oh, that's all right," he said from the ground. "At least I'm not covered with seagull shit."

Marine Safety Detachment Office; 0100: Tory

"Well, of course I noticed the smell," said Tory indignantly. "I just didn't connect it with—what was on the tiles."

Neal might, she thought, have shown a little sympathy. Instead he was grinning like an ape. "You're lucky it rained hard a couple of nights ago. God knows what that roof's usually like," he said.

Rise above, Tory, she told herself. If only I could. Ugh. She glanced down at the front of her coveralls and wished she hadn't, considered stripping it off then and there. But she was wearing two sets of long johns underneath, and she was deeply reluctant to have him see her in those totally unappetizing garments.

Neal, on the other hand, looked immaculate, even after rolling around in the dirt. It was a gift—no, a knack—that senior petty officers seemed to develop somewhere along the way. Had Neal been in the service? she wondered. She knew practically nothing about his past and felt a sudden need to be familiar with every detail. That was a symptom she recognized in herself only too clearly; Gilles had often laughed (and sometimes bristled) at what he called her "*interrogatoire perpétuel.*"

"Could you hear what was going on?" Neal was saying.

She pulled herself back to the present. "Not very well," she admitted. "The tone of voice, but not the words. When he started yelling I could hear, of course. What did he mean by 'six o'clock news time'?"

Neal's ears reddened slightly. "Oh, that was just his way of saying he was going to make me famous."

"So he's ready to cooperate," she said, adding, "What did you say his name was?"

"I didn't."

"But you know."

For a moment she thought he was going to deny it. "Yes, I know him," Neal said slowly. "So do you, I expect."

Was he teasing her? She waited.

"T. J. Wellcome. He's a boat mechanic, works out of his van. He's around the harbor all the time."

She couldn't put a face to the name, though she had an idea she'd heard it from one of the fishermen. "What's he look like? Besides being thin and short—I couldn't see his face."

"Like a weasel," Neal replied. "No forehead and not much chin. His face comes to kind of a point. Funny pale eyes."

"Yes," she said as memory kicked partway in. "I think I may have seen him a couple of days ago, aboard a dive boat. An unpleasant little man. . . . He was trying to needle me about something."

"That sounds like T.J. And he's ready to cooperate all right—for a price."

"What does he want?"

"The usual: immunity from prosecution, total anonymity, and a pot of gold. In return for which he'll turn in everybody he knows." Disgust dripped from every word, but she didn't think all of it was directed at T. J. Wellcome. Neal was poised on the edge of a great comeback, yet the prospect clearly repelled him. Why? In his place she'd have been driving hard for the finish line, and heaven help anyone in her way. Well, it was her finish line, too, and if he didn't want the prize, she certainly did. But how to handle him, in this strange mood?

"It doesn't sound impossible," she said. "Give me the details, and I'll make a phone call. At the least, we ought to get a counteroffer we can toss at him."

"I don't know, Tory." He sounded utterly depressed. "Maybe the smartest thing would just be to turn the information over to Feltrini, let him run with it. He and T.J. ought to get along perfectly."

"Feltrini? I don't understand you. This is your road back, Neal," she said.

"Maybe it's a road I don't want to take. Maybe I don't want to go back." Was he just being petulant? she wondered. No, it went deeper than that. But why? "All right, if you don't want to follow through, let me handle it," she said.

"Handle it how?"

"I've got the representative's home number," she said. "I'll put this guy's proposal to her and see what she says. If it flies, you just pass Mr. Wellcome on to me, and I'll play him myself." But as the words tumbled out of her mouth she saw how crazily unworkable it would be. No matter what Goodell said, Tory was going to have to open up to Long Beach at some point, and she could imagine the reaction when her superiors learned she'd made an end run around the chain of command. Even if a hundred headlines blossomed, her service future would be mud—or seagull shit.

Neal was watching her closely, and once again she had the sensation that he was reading her thoughts on her face. "Do you seriously think you could get Goodell behind you on this?" he asked.

Definitely a flicker of interest there. If only Neal would front for her, Tory thought, she could get credit with her rabbi and not stir up trouble under the flagpole. And of course Neal would be reinstated—which he certainly wanted, no matter what he said now. "Yes," she said firmly.

"All right," he said. "Here's my proposition: You tell Goodell whatever you have to, but make sure she understands that I'm the one who sets up the bust." He sounded as if the words were being winched out of him one by one.

"A minute ago you didn't want any part of it," she said.

"That was before I realized it's going to hit the fan, no matter what," he said, and smiled bitterly. "I might as well join the gathering crowd. Do well by doing good, as they say."

She didn't believe him. "But how can you—"

"Leave that to me," he said. "And don't worry: you'll get whatever brownie points there are."

It was exactly what she'd hoped for, but his manner stung her more than she cared to admit. "You're on," she replied. "Now, what exactly does Mr. Wellcome want, besides immunity and an impenetrable mask?"

"Half a million dollars," Neal replied. "He said it's non-negotiable."

"Well, what did you expect him to say—half a million or nearest offer?" She reached for the phone, expecting him to get up. He didn't. "Is there something else?" she asked.

"No," he replied innocently. "I thought I might get to see how a real wheeler-dealer operates."

"We wheeler-dealers do better without an audience," she replied. When he still didn't move, she said, "I have the feeling you don't trust me."

"Well . . ."

And why should he? she thought. Gritting her teeth, she dialed the number and only then glanced at her watch: 1:15.

Two rings, and an icy, "Yes?"

"Representative Goodell? This is Victoria Lennox, from the Coast—"

Warm, friendly, nearly overwhelming: "Of course, Tory. Wonderful to hear your voice, and congratulations on your . . . discovery."

It was like having a door swing open before you touched it. "You heard?" she said.

"Oh, my spies are *everywhere*, Tory." A peal of silvery laughter. "Now, I bet you've got something even more exciting to report."

"It's progress, Ms. Goodell," she said cautiously. "At least, we think so."

"We? Who's 'we,' Tory?" Was that the slightest chill coming over the wire?

"I'm working with a local peace officer," she replied. "I don't know how much we want to get into names on this line—I'm calling from my office, down at the harbor."

Silence for a second or two. "You're probably right, Tory. In fact, I think you'd better not go any farther. . . . Tell you what," she continued, "climb into your car and find a pay phone uptown. Call me from there, but not at this number. Do you have a pencil?"

The number Tory wrote down was not only a 301 area code, but the same prefix as Rep. Goodell's home phone—probably just down the street.

"You'll have to use your calling card," Goodell continued. "You do have one, don't you?"

"Oh, yes, Ms. Goodell," Tory replied, thinking, So it's a pay phone, too, followed by, This paranoia gig is really rather fun.

"Super!" A half-beat pause. "And Tory? I think we could drop the Ms., since we're teammates."

"Of course . . . Linda," she replied, and, looking up into Neal's astonished eyes, almost burst into helpless laughter.

"One other thing, Tory." Here comes an order, Tory thought. "I think you'd better ditch your friend—the peace officer you mentioned? We don't want any weak links in our chain."

"I quite understand, Linda," she said, thinking, This is going to take some fast talking. "But I'm afraid he's indispensable, at least for now. Our contact on the . . . other side won't deal with anyone else."

Neal, she saw, was following her perfectly. And enjoying it.

"Oh," said Goodell, clearly disappointed.

"It's a sort of chauvinist-to-chauvinist thing," said Tory, and when Neal made a face at her, continued, "But I don't think it's sexual—not overtly, anyway."

"I don't suppose anyone's put you over his knee lately," said Neal as Tory hung up.

"Not in the last twenty years or so," she replied. "Come on, you're going to drive me uptown."

"I am?"

"Unless you're willing to have me negotiate with my buddy Linda alone."

"Let's go."

Carpe Diem; 6 a.m.: Neal

It was just forty nautical miles from the red-and-white sea buoy off Santa Barbara to Cuyler Harbor on San Miguel Island, and the urchin divers began heading out in the predawn twilight. The grind and roar of their engines—mostly eight-cylinder, three-hundred-horsepower MerCruisers—kicking over reluctantly was the day's usual starting signal, one that live-aboards like Neal could sleep right through.

This particular morning, however, had found him sprawled on his back, staring up at the raw fiberglass deck and thinking of Tory Lennox. Not the early-morning erotic daydream that had already been and gone, but a replay of her second phone conversation with Representative Linda Goodell. The politician had done most of the talking, of course, and even with one ear cocked near the receiver Neal couldn't make out her exact words. Not that he really had to: like many professional speakers, she let vocal tone carry much of the freight, and the words were only a sort of counterpoint.

Her talk with Tory, he realized quickly, was for Goodell more an exercise in benevolent browbeating than a negotiation. Probably that was the way things worked in D.C.: first establish moral superiority, then get down to business. But in Tory Lennox, Goodell had bitten off a particularly intractable morsel who politely declined to be bullied, cajoled, or flattered. And in the end, the young lieutenant had mastered the congresswoman—which did not, Neal saw, seem to surprise Tory herself.

"It was very simple, really," Tory had said around a mouthful of blueberry pancakes (the pay phone being in an all-night restaurant on upper State). "I had all the cards: Wellcome, you, and being on the ground while Ms. Goodell is in Washington. She had to see it my way, if she wanted to move."

"Aren't you afraid—" Her eyes narrowed, and he quickly rephrased: "Has it occurred to you, if you really piss her off, you might wind up in charge of a loran station in Greenland?"

She raised a finger to stop him while she chewed and swallowed. "That's a risk one has to take. But when I was stationed at Buzzard Point—Coast Guard headquarters in Washington—I learned one thing: If you make a politician look good publicly, they'll forgive you almost anything."

"Well, if this caper works, she'll be on every news show in Southern California," he said.

Tory was assembling a forkful as he spoke—bacon, pancake, and a dollop of syrup. When she'd cornered it, she said, "That's the way it's got to be: she runs the press conference, but you run the operation." She popped the food in her mouth and began to chew, her eyes never leaving Neal's.

"So Goodell gets a big news break, right at the beginning of her reelection campaign," he said. "I get reinstated—if I want it." (*Is she laughing at me around all that pancake?*) "What do you get, Tory?"

She swallowed convulsively. "A steering wheel," she said, and her face lit up with the thought. "Command of a cutter. That was Goodell's promise, when I took this assignment."

"Her promise," Neal had said. And because he wanted to remember Tory's face aglow like this, he swallowed the quotation that leaped instantly to mind: *Who compels us to keep the promises we make?* Heinrich Himmler had said it in an unguarded moment, and he was speaking for all politicians in every time and place.

The congresswoman's promise for T. J. Wellcome sounded good, too: he could walk, "always assuming" (a nice qualifier, Neal thought) he wasn't immediately involved in the murders on *Blue Thunder*—though he might have to testify at one or more trials. In any case, Goodell had said, he'd get a complete makeover from the Federal Witness

Protection Program. As for what she called "a monetary recompense," there would certainly be one or more, and the size would directly reflect the importance of the bust T.J. led the authorities to. "Tell your little friend," Goodell had explained, "the more coke, the more cash."

A siren wailing down Cabrillo Boulevard snapped Neal out of his reverie, and when his ear followed it into the parking lot at the eastern end of the harbor, he sat up and swung his legs out of the bunk. Then he realized, as it moaned down to silence, that whatever it was didn't concern him. The knowledge stung. "All right," he growled to his shaving mirror. "I do miss it."

As he set water to boil for the morning's first mug of French roast, he was considering how early to call T.J. Going strictly by personal appearance, the mechanic ought to be a nocturnal, and Neal had tentatively decided to shake him out of whatever lair he inhabited around ten in the morning, when his overnight anxieties had had time to fester a little.

Tory wanted to be present, of course, and she, after all, was still employed. Ten A.M. would give her enough time to dispose of the Marine Safety Detachment's more pressing concerns.

He was pouring the boiling water into the coffee filter when he became aware of the vibration up through the soles of his still tender feet. A boat engine, coming nearer. He glanced out *Carpe Diem*'s main cabin port just in time to see *Harbor 2*, with a white-faced Taffy Hegemann at the helm, spin neatly around just astern of his slip. Taffy's stricken expression was not one he'd seen in the two years they'd worked together, and it sent him up the companionway steps in one bound.

"Thank God you're awake," she said. "We've been trying to call you for half an hour."

"What—"

"It's Walt." She touched the shift lever to back the boat a foot or two nearer. "He collapsed right in his office. They think it's a coronary."

"When?" Neal demanded.

"Hour ago, maybe more. Lance was on the phone, didn't hear him call out or anything. I went in to take him some tea—and there he was, kind of folded up in his chair." Her voice was steady, but she was blinking back tears. "I was trying to get him off coffee. He was as bad as you with that stuff." She shook her head.

"That siren a little while ago, was that the ambulance?"

"Right. The EMT didn't seem too worried." She managed a watery smile. "It was just such a surprise, someone you actually know."

Neal flashed on the number of his own friends, mostly down in the islands, who'd come to sudden grief one way or another. I guess that makes me some kind of ancient, he thought. But Taffy was right: every time it was a surprise. "I appreciate your coming by," he said. "I'd offer you coffee, but under the circumstances . . ."

"Oh! I almost forgot," she said. "I'm supposed to bring you back, right away."

"You are?" He was mystified.

"In uniform," she continued.

"Who says?"

"Ms. Acevedo." She rolled her eyes. " 'Tell him to get his Anglo ass up here on the double.' That's what she said."

Two black widow pols back to back, he was thinking as he pulled on his blue uniform trousers. If he had to choose, though, he'd deal with the waterfront director over the congresswoman anytime. Maria Acevedo might slit your throat without a second thought, but you knew where you stood with her.

Of course, where you stood was likely to be up against the wall, he reflected, checking his reflection in the ripply mirror. Especially if your job application read "Neal Machado Donahoe." "What's that supposed to mean?" she'd said the first time they'd met. And when he'd explained, she'd just shaken her head, contempt clear in her heavy-lidded eyes.

When he stepped aboard *Harbor 2*, Taffy gave him a quick once-over. "I suppose you've still got to wear those sandals," she said, sounding concerned. "They look kind of weird."

But when he stepped into the patrol office, which resembled a kicked anthill, no one seemed remotely interested in his feet. Bill Jacobson, who looked as if the flu had taken five pounds off his face, looked up with obvious relief. "Am I glad to see you," he said. "You take your phone off the hook?"

"I forgot to charge it," Neal replied. "Where is she?"

"Sitting at Walt's desk, like a damn vulture," Jacobson replied.

"She said she's going to can half of us," chimed in Lance Dalleson. "Well, she can start with me—I'll see her in court."

"Nobody's going to get fired," Neal heard himself say. "Just calm down. Has everybody around here forgotten how to make coffee?"

Gruff, he reflected, might not turn morale around, but at least it seemed to settle things down a little. Shaking his head in mock disgust, he strode down the hall toward Walt's office. The door was open, and he decided not to knock.

Maria Acevedo was indeed seated on Walt's desk chair, inspecting the contents of his desk drawer with interest.

Every other time Neal had seen her, the waterfront director had been dressed formally, usually in blue or gray jacket-and-skirt combinations and always a frilly blouse and high heels. She wore her hair—as dark and straight as Neal's—nearly shoulder length, framing her unremarkable face and unforgettable eyes.

This morning, presumably yanked straight out of bed by the emergency, she was in jeans and a sweatshirt, no makeup and her hair pulled back. She looked more like the gardener's maiden sister than the scourge of State Street. And, he sensed, she was angrily aware of it. She looked up through thick-lensed glasses—he'd never seen her wearing glasses—and said, "Oh, there you are," exactly as if he were a box of paper clips she'd momentarily misplaced.

"You might as well sit down," she added. "Assuming you can find someplace to sit in this garbage dump."

It wasn't exactly fair: two of the five chairs had nothing on them. Neal chose one, behind her and to one side, and lowered himself onto it. Not much chest and too much ass, he was thinking. So that's why she dresses the way she does. She spun around, and he saw she'd caught and read his automatic appraisal. The lenses made her heavy-lidded eyes seem twice as large as usual. "You don't look sick," she said.

It wasn't quite an accusation of malingering. Maybe she'd taken his leave of absence at face value. "I'm fine. As long as I don't have to run the hundred in less than a minute," he replied.

She didn't even look at his feet. "That's settled, then." She took off the glasses, returning her face to something like normal, and he guessed she was about to deliver a prepared speech. "We won't know about Walt for a couple of hours." She sounded annoyed—whether at the doctors or the victim was unclear. "But he'll be out of action for a while, no matter what."

This was a little cold-blooded even for her. Neal saw his face must be showing his feelings.

"Look," the waterfront director continued, "you don't have to like me, any more than I have to like you. But I think we can work together, as long as we keep a couple things straight."

"Work *together*?" Neal said.

She smiled her comprehension. "That's just a manner of speaking. I run this department, nobody else. But you have a free hand with the harbor, as long as you don't surprise me."

"Wait a minute," Neal said. "You mean—"

"Acting harbormaster," she said. "But you draw salary as chief of patrol."

Bedroom eyes in an executioner's face. The words popped into his head as if from outer space, but he realized they'd been taking shape for some time. And he suddenly felt surer of himself than he had in a while. "I don't want the job if it means stabbing my boss—my real boss—in the back."

"You won't have to," she replied. The ambiguity hung between them, and she looked amused.

"You ought to know—"

"I know everything," she said, cutting him off. She rocked back on Walt's chair. "Here's how it is: I'll handle Lieutenant Merriam and what's-his-name Feltrini, keep them off your back so long as you don't mess with their work. You screw up, and I'll throw you to the wolves—you're d'Andrea's appointment, so it won't reflect on me."

She paused, watching his reaction. "You're very . . . outspoken, Maria," he said, testing the feel of her name.

Her fleeting smile told him she knew exactly what he was doing. "That's my reputation, Neal."

He hoisted himself from the chair and walked over to the window. In an unexpected way, he found himself stimulated by her brisk near hostility. He stared down the axis of the harbor, the water gleaming in the morning sun. His eye went automatically to *Carpe Diem*'s oversize mainmast, sticking up from the smaller spars around it like a Douglas fir among saplings. And a couple of slips away he could make out the masts of *Iolanthe*, varnished spruce, almost unheard of these days.

I should walk away from this, he thought. It's a temptation I can't handle. Maria's intent face was faintly reflected in the dirt-streaked pane. He moved slightly to bring the reflection into sharper view. Turning abruptly, he said, "I'll do the job, but I won't promise anything beyond that."

Her face had colored slightly. "Fair enough," she said. She rose, and he saw her hips were not as heavy as he'd thought, though blue jeans were definitely not for her. She was, in fact, surprisingly sensual—if your definition of sensual included a dash of man-eater. Their eyes met, and she murmured, "I like yours, too."

"What did you say?"

"I said I'll tell your staff. About your appointment."

Breakwater Restaurant; 9:30 a.m.: Tory

Feltrini did not so much enter the restaurant as burst through the door, drawing startled looks from the handful of midmorning customers dawdling over their coffees. At her corner table across the room, Tory could see he was spoiling for a fight, and he erupted as his backside touched the chair. "I'm telling you, I just don't understand that dame," he said without preamble, his face darkening with recollected rage. "I spent half an hour with her, explaining the problems her Keystone Kops were giving me, and then she goes and promotes one of 'em."

No encouragement was required, but Tory offered a politely noncommittal "Oh?" while she tried to track into what the DEA boss was ranting about.

"Not just promotes," Feltrini railed on, to the fascinated interest of the waitress standing over him with a coffeepot. "*Harbormaster* she makes him! Jesus *Christ!*"

"I beg your pardon?" said Tory, blinking. "I heard about Walt d'Andrea, but—"

"I know he's a buddy of yours," Feltrini snarled. He glanced up at the waitress—"Coffee, black"—and turned back to Tory.

"Well, a friend, maybe," she said, "but I'd hardly call him a buddy." *Him or anyone: vulgar word.*

Feltrini's snarl transmuted itself to a leer—an unnerving spectacle—and his voice dropped to what he presumably thought was a confidential level. "Hey, this is your uncle Gus you're talking to. I saw the way you were looking at him."

Angry and bewildered, Tory knew her face had turned scarlet. She drew a deep, steadying breath, fixed her mind on Katharine Hepburn, and said, "Mr. Feltrini, I've spent the last two hours in a truly loathsome fishing-boat bilge, so I've obviously missed something important. I'd love to know what it is, preferably without a coating of sexist innuendo." Not bad, she thought. Especially the sexist innuendo.

Feltrini's mouth was working, but for once no sound emerged. At last he croaked, "You didn't hear about Donahoe?"

A surge of amazed delight formed just below her rib cage, but she managed to keep her voice cool. "Not a word."

"Well, when d'Andrea folded, that Acevedo c—" He swallowed hard and just in time. "Sorry. That Ms. Acevedo not only reinstated Donahoe, she appointed him acting harbormaster. Exactly one day after I tried to straighten her out about him."

As the only alternative to a hoot of laughter, Tory buried her face in her coffee cup and pretended to take a long, meditative sip. When she had fully savored the image of Feltrini telling Maria Acevedo how to run her department, she set down the cup carefully and said, "Mr. Feltrini—"

"Gus, for Christ's sake."

She bestowed a smile. "Gus. I am no friend of Ms. Acevedo"—*for whom, in fact, the c-word is entirely apt*—"but I can assure you of one thing: She's far too ambitious to stick her neck out for any employee, especially one who was hired by a man she hopes to dispose of. If she promoted Neal, even temporarily, she's pretty sure he won't embarrass her."

It was, Tory saw, the kind of reasoning Feltrini could understand. "Maybe," he said reluctantly. And then his saturnine face broke into a considering smile. "But that wimp d'Andrea didn't officially suspend Donahoe, so Acevedo might just be giving him enough rope to hang himself—and d'Andrea, too." The thought clearly appealed to him, and Tory, recalling her own encounters with the waterfront director, had to admit he might be right. But Neal would be able to deal with Acevedo, she told herself. He'd worked for the city—and under Walt d'Andrea's wing—long enough to know how that game went. Or so she hoped.

Feltrini was watching her narrowly, and she decided a change of subject was called for. "Tell me, Gus, what did your people find out about *Blue Thunder*?"

His condescending smile told her he'd seen right through her. "*Blue Thunder*? Well, the short answer is they think you diagnosed it right."

"Ambushed while boarding a suspect?"

"Looks like it," he agreed. "I'm hoping the autopsies on Daniels and Ericsen will give us a little more to go on, but a shotgun . . ." He shrugged.

"If the killers had any brains, they chucked the gun over the side in a hundred feet or so," Tory put in.

"Where they should've sunk *Blue Thunder*," Feltrini said. "Yeah. Between us, I think we've just got to wait for the next opportunity—the next shipment. If I could only talk your bosses into a full-court press on the whole channel, I know we could pull it off."

Tory, who had heard this pipe dream before, took another diplomatic swallow of rapidly cooling coffee. She'd still been at the academy during the high tide of Zero Tolerance, but the furious echoes from the entire maritime community had penetrated even there. Regional surveillances and indiscriminate mass boardings cost a fortune and accomplished little beyond infuriating the Coast Guard's natural constituency, the pleasure-boat owners and commercial fishermen. Not that the Coasties' nominal allies, Customs and the DEA, cared. If anything, they probably favored seeing a competing agency take a fall. Anyway, the really rewarding drug interdictions happened, year after year, because one of the players felt he was being screwed by his supplier or saw a chance to sell out a competitor. Feltrini must know that even better than she did. But Feltrini didn't have a dissatisfied druggie ready to turn on his associates—and she did.

The train of thought had flashed through in less than two seconds, but not so quickly that Feltrini had missed it. "Something's going on in that head of yours," he said. "Care to share it?"

"Not yet," she said. She fixed him with her widest blue-eyed stare. "I've got something cooking, Gus, but it's just too faint a trace to talk about yet."

"You're not going to freeze me out?"

Mostly a question, but the threat was there, too. "Of course not," she said.

"Because when this breaks open, there'll be pieces scattered all over the place," Feltrini continued. "Some of them may surprise you."

He had that right, Tory reflected as she tried to concentrate on phrasing her report so the skipper of the dragger *Magnificent* would come back for a reexamination and not just change his boat's name and skip to another harbor. "Balls," she said, and looked up in time to see the expression—shock, fading to amusement—on Chief Washington's face. "Sorry."

"No problem," he said.

Is he laughing at me? Well, I guess he's entitled. She shrugged off the thought and reached for the phone. After five calls she instantly recognized the voice of the harbormaster's administrative assistant—Neal's assistant, now. "It's me again, Shirley."

"He's still in the meeting, Tory. Probably will be right till lunchtime."

"Oh."

"He usually goes back to his boat to eat," Shirley confided. "You might be able to catch him there."

Tory suspected Shirley Dodge was the kind of instinctive matchmaker she'd always avoided. Today she didn't mind. "Thanks, Shirley. I appreciate it."

At 11:30, Chief Washington closed the folder he was working on. "Guess I'll eat right here, Lieutenant."

"What?" Tory pulled back from an elaborate daydream in which she was just about to rescue Neal from the entire DEA fleet.

"In case you wanted to go out," the chief said.

"Oh. Right." She forced herself to straighten the already symmetrical piles of paper on her desk. "Well, maybe I will. Go out—for a little while."

"We got to look at that well head down in Carp," the chief replied. "But that's not till sixteen hundred."

In the bad old days of oil exploration in Santa Barbara Channel, drillers had closed off dead wells by driving wooden plugs into the pipes. It was a postponement, not a solution, and the bills were now beginning to come due. The potential mess on Carpinteria's beach would be nothing, Tory suspected, to the legal mess involved in settling who would pay for the cleanup—though of course in the end it would be the public, one way or another.

The prospect of a summer of disclosure hearings was enough to draw a curtain of gloom across Tory's perceptions that cleared only at the sight of *Carpe Diem*'s spars down the pier. She slipped her key—a rectangular slip of metal with rounded corners—into the gate's magnetic lock, twiddled the key until it seated properly, and quickly pulled open the heavy wire gate. As she strode down the ramp she could see the big ketch's companionway hatch was closed and locked, and she slowed to look automatically at the boats on either side.

Iolanthe was in her slip, but reversed so her stem was up against the pier. On one of the cockpit seats a figure engulfed in coveralls almost as large as Tory's own, with a watch cap pulled down over its ears, a painter's mask, and immense rubber gloves almost to its elbows, was on hands and knees beside a bucket. The rasp of a stiff brush and a stabbing, acidulous whiff was all the explanation Tory required.

She considered the shape of the bottom stretching the coveralls and said, "Bleaching the teak, Bea?"

The figure rocked back on its haunches and pushed up the mask. "It never stops," she said. "Exhaust from the cars on 101, I think. Wood turns gray in a week."

"The boat looks beautiful, though," Tory said.

No more than the required minimum, but Bea's lined face formed what looked like a genuine smile. "Thank you. Like to come aboard?"

It was an automatic response, Tory knew. Not meant to be taken seriously as an invitation. But she heard herself say, "I'd love to." An expression, quickly veiled, widened the other woman's eyes. She wishes she hadn't said that, Tory thought. I ought to back out graciously. But something propelled her down the finger pier. Reaching out, she grasped the mizzen upper shroud and swung herself easily aboard.

"It's a real mess," Bea said, getting stiffly to her feet. "Live-aboards get like that."

Live-aboards often did, Tory thought, but on deck at least, *Iolanthe* looked ready to sail. "She's a Cheoy Lee, isn't she?" Tory said. "No other builder does teak over fiberglass that well."

A boat owner's pleasure—keener than any parent's—at a knowledgeable compliment was just about uncontrollable, Tory knew, but this time it seemed streaked with caution. "That's right, one of the old Bermuda thirties," Bea said after a minute.

"Of course," said Tory, looking around her with interest. The yacht was at least twenty years old, she guessed, and had been maintained with extraordinary care. The raw teak decks were nearly white, but without the lifeless, gouged appearance of careless bleaching. And the coamings and cabin sides—veneers, actually, over fiberglass—had been oiled to a golden brown gleam, like a surfer's skin.

"My dad had a Cheoy Lee," Tory remarked. "One of the old Lions—all teak, before they started doing wood over glass." Her father scorned boats like *Iolanthe*. "Half-breeds" was the nicest thing he said about them, but he could well afford to be a purist; he'd never personally bleached a deck in his life and never would, as long as he could hire someone to do it for him.

"Is that so?" Bea said. And then, perhaps feeling something more responsive was called for, she added, "It's the spars that kill you. That spruce dents if you look at it cross-eyed, and you have to varnish every year, in this climate."

"You do the work yourself?" Tory asked, though the finish on the mainmast answered the question for her.

"I do the varnishing," Bea said with a sour smile. "Sid could get sand in the varnish if he did it in the middle of the Pacific."

Not quite enough money, Tory decided. When it comes to boat maintenance, love and skill help, but it comes down to money in the end. She stepped carefully across the cabin top, aware of Bea's sharp-eyed watchfulness. It was like the old kids' game: Bea's suppressed alarm grew more tangible with every step her guest took toward the bow.

But the foredeck, when she got there, was entirely ordinary. The working anchor, an ancient Danforth, was in chocks on deck. Its shank had been bent and roughly straightened, but there was nothing unusual in that. The shackle was properly wired to keep its pin from backing off, and the chain it was attached to led below, through a hawsepipe.

Tory touched the chain with her sneakered foot, heard what might have been an intake of breath behind her. And suddenly she thought of the chunk of line—of anchor line—Neal had brought up from *Blue Thunder*. "Do you use an all-chain rode?" she asked.

"You're kidding," said Bea. "At half a pound per foot? Do I look like a Schwarzenegger?" Her laugh was forced, unconvincing. "Just ten feet of chain, and then two hundred and fifty feet of nylon."

I'd give anything to see that line, Tory thought. But how? "I suppose you've got a regular chain locker in the forepeak," she said, groping for an opening.

"Of course, with an elegant little door, has an anchor shape cut in it, for ventilation," Bea said. "But you must remember about those anchor shapes, from your father's boat."

She did. "What's the layout down below?" she asked.

"Pretty straightforward: vee berth forward, thwartships head compartment, two berths in the main cabin, with the galley aft," Bea said. She paused, and for a second Tory thought the invitation she'd been angling for was forthcoming. "No surprises, but it works."

"I'm sure it does," Tory agreed. "But with Hong Kong yachts—especially the Cheoy Lees—there were always those funny little touches that made it special. The carvings and all."

"I'll bet you'd like to see the cabin," Bea said. Her gaunt face was drawn into the semblance of a smile, but her words were unmistakably a challenge.

"Well, I would, for old times' sake," Tory said.

Bea's head went back, almost as if she'd been struck. "Come on, then—if you have a couple minutes."

The interior was exactly as Bea had said, though the warm waxed teak of the cabin took Tory instantly back to girlhood. The knees ostensibly supporting the cabin roof—pure decoration, since the fiberglass beneath the veneer was a one-piece molding—bore intricate carvings in the shape of Oriental dragons.

The space was narrow by current design standards, just barely big enough for two people with minimal possessions—a clock-and-barometer set, a shelf with half a dozen paperbacks, a framed photograph of a young couple with children. The man had Bea's features. On the back of the hanging locker's narrow door was a complicated wood construct that only someone familiar with Hong Kong-built yachts could have identified as a folding table.

Tory was barely aware of Bea's stilted running commentary. *She knows I'm looking for something. And she knows I know she knows.*

The V-shaped forward cabin was entirely filled by the berth mattress and a tumbled mass of bedding. "Where's your husband?" Tory asked, barely remembering to add, "I hope he's feeling better."

"Much better, thank you," Bea responded, her harsh voice dripping acid. "Sid's up on La Cumbre Peak."

"The mountain? You mean he's hiking?" Remembering Sid Seligman's fragile manner, it seemed inconceivable.

"Not really. Sometimes when things get too much for him, he likes to go up there and just sit." She seemed to be looking right through Tory, back down a corridor of years. "It seems to help, I don't know how." She shook her head.

"But how does he get there?" Tory asked.

"Oh, that. We don't own a car these days. He has a friend drives him up and waits."

"I see," Tory replied.

"I have to get back to my teak," Bea said. "You let it dry out, you've got to start all over." Looking Tory in the eye, she said, "Just look around all you want."

Not a challenge this time, Tory thought: pure defiance. "Thank you. I will." *I'm doing what I have to do. Why do I feel small and mean?*

The old woman didn't look back as she climbed the steps to the cockpit. Tory waited until she was outside, then kicked off her sneakers and lifted herself up onto the mattress. The door to the chain locker, as Bea had said, had a traditional anchor shape cut through it for ventilation. Through the hole came the faint smells of mold and dead marine life. *Do I really want to do this?* Bracing herself, she pulled open the square panel.

Inside, the locker was a raw fiberglass triangle, with an untidy heap of still damp line at the bottom and a short length of chain leading down to it from the hawsepipe in the deck. Tory's fingertips followed the chain to its shackle—wired, like the other—and drew out the attached line. It was half-inch nylon, three-strand like the piece aboard *Carpe Diem*. And like that piece, it ended in an eye splice around a galvanized thimble. She looked more closely at the splice, saw it had a misled tuck at the eye's throat, the universal error of the inexperienced splicer.

The ends of the three strands, protruding from the standing part of the line, had been neatly burned, to keep them from unraveling. A very different style of work from the one Neal had retrieved. She drew out a little more line, and her eye was caught by a flash of color. More line, and she found herself looking at a faded piece of yellow plastic that had been woven between the strands so its ends stuck out on both sides of the rope. Holding it up to the light, she could just make out the faded *10* on each end, dimly pink numerals that had once probably been bright red. She turned back one of the strands around the plastic. Under the protecting nylon, the tag was still yellow, and the rope itself retained the tag's shape: it had been in this place for a long time.

On an impulse, she took the tag in the fingertips of her right hand, ran the line through her other hand until her arms were at full stretch and the line was taut across her chest. Like most experienced sailors, she'd found the distance of her outspread arms—four and a half feet, almost exactly—was a convenient measurement. Two full extensions and about a half more, and the splice was in her hand. Ten feet, so the anchor marker was in the right place. This was not the line from *Blue Thunder*.

Or this end of it wasn't. . . . What if Bea had simply swapped ends? On her knees, Tory lifted out the rest of the line in an untidy heap. No need to search for the other end:

it finished in a splice, damp and stained with ancient mildew, around a rusty ring set in the thick fiberglass of the boat's bow. A splice, unprotected by a thimble, whose inner side was worn by years of slow chafe against the ring.

Back in the cockpit, Bea looked up from her work. Between the watch cap and the mask only her faded eyes were visible. Tory was unable to read their expression, but it was not the anger and contempt she had expected. Suddenly Bea looked past Tory, who followed her glance.

Neal was standing on the pier, looking at the two of them, deep concern in his eyes.

IOLANTHE, 12:15: NEAL

He felt his stomach clench when he saw the two women, frozen in a moment that simultaneously joined and separated them. "Hi, guys," he said, wondering if he looked as inane as he sounded.

Tory's face, as she turned to him, was strained and pale. "Hello, Neal. I came down to see if you were free for lunch, and Bea was showing me her boat."

Bea, still on her knees in *Iolanthe*'s cockpit, pushed the painter's mask up on her forehead. "I heard Walt had a heart attack," she said. Her eyes, starkly tragic, seemed fixed on some middle distance.

"That's right. But he's not dead yet," Neal said. "I mean, you two look . . ." His words trailed off.

Bea's grim stare never changed, but Tory reddened. "How is he?" she said.

"Still in intensive care, but it doesn't sound as bad as it might," he said quickly. "Shirley, in the office, has a friend works for the hospital."

"The secretary underground," said Bea. "Only reliable source." She shaped a thin smile. "Well, the harbor underground says you're in the driver's seat, thanks to Black Maria."

Tory looked startled, and Neal hastily put in, "That's Bea's sense of humor. Works better in New York than California."

Bea pursed her lips dismissively. "But it's true: she did appoint you harbormaster."

"Acting and strictly pro tem," he said, feeling as if he'd been saying it for weeks. "It's still Walt's job, soon as he's on his feet."

"Of course. Unless the blessed nonvirgin finds a way to hang you and Walt both together."

"Put a sock in it, Bea." And to Tory: "My new boss goes at something of a discount here in Marina Two."

Tory seemed on the point of contributing something, then clearly changed her mind. "Did you plan to eat at all, or just nosh on gossip?"

"Definitely eat," said Neal with relief. "Want to join me—both of you?" Bea shook her head. "I'm sure you two have so much to talk about." Her smile looked as if it belonged on a monument.

Tory regarded the other woman for a moment. "Thank you for the tour, Bea," she said. Her voice was prep school prim, yet there was an undertone Neal could not identify.

"So what was that all about?" he said as he sliced a block of Vermont cheddar. He glanced up at Tory, perched on the edge of the settee, staring thoughtfully out the companionway.

He was about to repeat his question when she said, "I just made a fool of myself. I think."

"How?" He halved a Granny Smith, quartered each half, and removed the core, never taking his eyes off her. He could, he decided, watch the play of muscles along her jaw all day and half the night.

"With Bea," Tory replied. "I more or less invited myself aboard *Iolanthe*, and then pushed her into letting me look around below."

"And?" If she'd found something—anything—he told himself, she wouldn't be sitting here so calmly. Or was she calm? Might that be the shock of discovery? He looked down, pulled back just in time to prevent the end of his left forefinger from joining the neat stack of apple segments on the cutting board.

"It was the damned anchor line," she was saying. "I mean, I saw that chain leader going down the hawsepipe, and instantly I turned into Sherlock Lennox." She shook her golden head angrily. "There was something about her, Neal. I just knew . . ."

"So what did you find?" He set out the apples, cheese, and half a baguette and only then realized he was holding his breath.

"A plain-vanilla anchor locker," she said. Her wry grin made his heart turn over. "Utterly innocent: anchor wired and shackled to the chain, which was wired and shackled to a slightly botched splice at the end of the rode—"

"Botched how?" he said, knowing the answer.

"The usual way," she replied, laying a slice of cheese onto an apple segment. "The third strand in the first set of tucks led in backward. Same mistake we all made the first time."

"Same mistake Bea's been making ever since I've known her," he said lightly. "I'm having a fake beer. How about you?"

"Fake as in nonalcoholic? That'd be great," she said. "And the rode spliced to an eye in the hull looks as if it'd been there since the boat was built."

"Only three years. I did that splice myself," said Neal. He took two bottles of Haake Beck from the icebox and uncapped them. "You want a glass?"

"Please," she said, but her abstracted look told him she'd detected a false note in his manner. And since she was Tory Lennox, she wouldn't let it pass. "Why so pale and wan, fond lover?" she asked suddenly, and just as suddenly blushed beet red.

He let a raised eyebrow stand for a reply, and she rushed on: "I just mean, you seem kind of down. Thought you'd be all keyed up, first day on the job."

He could be honest about that, at least: "I'm beginning to see where Walt's coronary came from. Christ, I've got half the population of Santa Barbara after me for free rooms in the old Naval Reserve Building, and the other half wants to natter about the Harbor Festival, which is three months and two goddamn weeks away. Plus some guy wants to know why the dredge can't pull clean sand from the harbor entrance instead of smelly mud. *And*"—he raised his voice over her clear laughter—"and your Chief Washington wants me to know—unofficially, of course—that if I don't do something about it, the *Amazon Queen* is going to sink right in front of my office."

"Sounds like a busy morning," she said. "By the way, this cheese is excellent."

"Right off the shelf at Lucky's," he said. "A lot of the hassle is just being a new face: people want to make sure you remember who they are." And a lot more, he might have added, stemmed from Walt's policy of keeping every ball in the air as long as possible, or even a little longer. Neal had known in the abstract how much his boss loved talking to people about their problems, but he hadn't imagined what a drain it could be.

"You can handle them," Tory said offhandedly. And he realized with a spurt of pleasure that she meant exactly what she said. "By the way, have you called T. J. Wellcome yet?"

"Not from the office. Too many people around." Which was a good enough excuse, but why did he need one? "Do it from here before I go back."

She nodded, her mouth full, and they chewed in companionable silence for a minute or two. "How's Sid?" Neal asked abruptly. "Was he there when you went aboard?"

"No. Bea said he'd gone up on the mountain. Made it sound like some kind of mystical rite." The thought was bothering her, he could see. "Neal, something's going on with them. They're both so strung out they'd twang if you touched them."

Sooner or later, he'd known, they were bound to circle back to this. "Well, maybe Bea thinks you're trying to lay a triple murder on her. Might make anybody a little tense."

He knew it was a misfire the instant he opened his mouth. "Oh, come on," she said. "I'm just doing my job. It's not as if I accused her of anything. And anyway, she was on a tightrope the minute she saw me."

"She's worried, is all," he said weakly. "Got a lot on her mind, and Sid isn't much help."

He had deflected her slightly, he saw. "I suppose it's money," she said.

"It shows on the boat, doesn't it?" he replied.

She nodded. "Just little things. And the way she said 'We don't own a car these days': kind of defensive."

He smiled. "If you don't own a car in California, you've got a lot to be defensive about."

"Sure, but not down here," she said. "That's one of the better things about the harbor. People here aren't afraid to be different. Just looking at the boats tells you that."

It was a discovery Neal had made nearly four years before, and he had looked forward to presenting it to Tory, as a gift. "People down here stick together, too," he said.

"Oh, boat people always—" she began.

"Not exactly that," he interrupted. "Let me tell you a story."

She sat back obediently, popped an apple chunk into her mouth, and fixed her wide blue eyes on him.

"When I first moved down here, I'd been working for the Waterfront Department in maintenance," he said. "People kind of kept me at a distance—not unfriendly . . ."

"But they didn't let you get too close to them," she put in, grinning. "Tell me about it. I go shopping at Von's and the checkout gal spends five minutes telling me about her hysterectomy. Down here, they just nod and smile and keep on moving."

"Exactly. Well, I was doing a small rebuild on my diesel, and I had an arrangement with one of the city mechanics to give me old parts they were throwing away. Subassemblies that were too worn to repair, but with working parts I could scrounge, if you follow me."

The knowing half smile that accompanied her nod suggested she had another version of the story, but he ignored it. "Anyway, the word got around that I was stealing engine parts. And the way stories move in the harbor, pretty soon people were convinced I was heisting whole engines out of city buses. Didn't make my neighbors any friendlier—but not a word went beyond the gate."

"Us against them," she said, nodding more emphatically.

"Yes and no. The 'us' doesn't imply a lot of buddy-buddy neighborliness. Just that what goes on in the harbor is the harbor's business. Nobody else's."

"You know I can't go along with that, not professionally," she said. She didn't move, but he could feel her backing away.

"I'm not asking you to. Just be aware it exists." He waited for the question he knew was coming.

"What about you?" she said. And then, "Lord, I sound like Feltrini. And I hate that."

"But he was right," said Neal. "From his viewpoint, anyway. The answer is, right now I don't know. I've got one problem's a lot closer to home than this *Blue Thunder* thing—"

"Not to mention Sid and Bea are your oldest and closest friends down here," she said.

"Oldest, yes," he said. "I haven't got any close friends."

"Well, that's a problem for another day," she said, getting to her feet. "I have to get back to my shop."

He couldn't let her leave in this mood. "Don't you want to wait till I call T. J. Wellcome?" he asked.

"Are you sure you can do that? Isn't he part of your magic circle?"

He was astonished at the ice in her eyes. He flipped open the cellular phone and picked out T.J.'s number. "No answer," he said after a dozen rings. "I'll keep trying and call you."

"You know where I am," she said.

"Is this the acting harbormaster's office?"

Neal looked up from the stack of papers he was sorting. "Afternoon, Steve."

The police lieutenant stared around him in mock disbelief. "Three hours on the job, and you've made more of a dent in this place than Walt has in three years."

Neal pushed wearily back on his chair. "Doesn't take a whole lot of talent to throw out wastepaper. And that's what nine-tenths of the stuff was."

Merriam dropped onto a chair. "If you can distinguish the nine-tenths junk from the one-tenth that just might be important, you've got the job knocked," he said. "You obviously can, so why don't you look happier?"

"Cares of state," Neal replied. "Are you going to lay another of them on me?"

"Actually, no," Steve replied. "Just a progress report, of sorts. We've traced the pipe, thanks to you."

It took Neal a second to make the connection. "The bomb, you mean?"

"The bomb that Jannice built," Merriam said. His smile appeared and vanished. "One of those catalog houses with the alphabet names—E&B, M&E, I forget. It's on the East Coast. Point is, all that stuff was in the same order, two weeks ago—the bronze caps, the plastic hex nipple, the plastic gas can, the wire—all of it."

"And?" said Neal. "I have the feeling you're setting me up for something."

"Shut up a minute," Steve said. "This stuff was ordered on an order form clipped from the catalog, paid for with a money order bought for cash at the P.O. on Canon Perdido Street, and addressed to Jannice McKay at General Delivery in Ojai. Picked up by her a week ago—by some woman with her ID, anyway. Jannice was on the company's catalog list—on six others, too—and she'd bought things from them before, but always by phone with a Visa number."

"Handwriting on the coupon and the money order?" Neal said.

"You ought to be a cop," said Merriam. "The coupon was all block letters, with a ballpoint pen. Almost certainly a woman's writing, very probably Jannice's. On the money order, the amount is machine printed, of course—it was a couple dollars more than the order. The payee's name and address were just like on the coupon."

By the end of Steve's account, Neal was sitting bolt upright, his brain seething. But the detective waved him silent. "There's more. The bomb construction, my FBI sources tell me, is very close to one described in a book called *Getting Even: The Frustrated Activist Bites Back.* Santa Barbara Public Library has a copy, and those pages have been razored out."

Neal slumped back. "Sounds like a dead end to me."

"That's because you haven't hit any real dead ends. These are still hot leads." He read the look on Neal's face. "Maybe lukewarm leads. Look, to tell you the truth, I think you just don't want to face the facts: Jannice tried to torch *Finish Line*, with you as her alibi, and she screwed up."

"What about the clock?"

"Ah, yes. The clock," Steve said. "Or Merriam's fucking clock, as some of my colleagues are now calling it. Well, if you assume it was bought about the same time as the other stuff—say, between three weeks and one week ago—and that it came from a garage sale, we've struck out."

It had been a long shot from the start, but Neal hadn't realized how much he'd been banking on a miracle. "You checked the garage sales," he said.

"All hundred and eighty-three that were advertised in the *News-Press* during that period," Steve said. "Of course, that leaves out a lot, but there's no earthly way of tracking them."

"Secondhand stores?" Neal asked.

"Before we did the garage sales," Steve replied. "I'm sorry, Neal, but that line seems to be played out."

"What about garage sales more than three weeks ago?" Neal said. "That's pretty arbitrary, three weeks."

"Give me a break, will you? That clock could've been sitting around the killer's basement for years. It's window dressing, remember—it wasn't really part of the bomb at all."

"Maybe not," said Neal. "But it was important enough so the killer came back to retrieve it."

"What if it wasn't a killer?" Steve said. "What if it was Jannice's accomplice—somebody who helped her out with the bomb and then panicked afterward?"

"Is that the official line, Steve?"

"Hey, we're looking at everything. We have to. But it's not pointing at you anymore, Neal. You ought to feel good about that."

Sure I ought to, he thought for the tenth time. But he didn't.

"Where you going, Neal?" Taffy Hegemann called from her desk.

"To the library. I'll be on my boat later."

As a new arrival in Santa Barbara with time on his hands, Neal had made the rounds of weekend garage sales for their entertainment value. But when he found himself actually buying things, he quickly recoiled. It had been four years since he'd succumbed to the lure of a heap of junk in someone's driveway, but clearly the attraction was still alive for a lot of people. The previous Friday's edition of the *News-Press* had a separate column of classifieds devoted to garage sales, with thirty-nine entries giving the sale's address but not the seller's phone number. Saturday, in a display column, the listings swelled to sixty-four. Another, shorter column in Sunday's paper duplicated many of the Saturday ads, while including a few new ones, for Sunday-only sales. And then, as if the situation weren't sufficiently overwhelming, a solid page of free, single-item ads called Classified Attic ran on Tuesdays—but these at least were listed alphabetically by item, so nearly all of them could be discarded off the bat.

Bearing a fuzzily copied list of the weekly ads for the three weeks before the period the SBPD had covered, he adjourned to *Carpe Diem*, armed himself with a beer (real, this time) and a reverse phone directory he'd borrowed from the harbormaster office, and began to dial.

A couple of facts emerged quickly: Some garage sellers were more or less permanent businesses, replenishing their stock from other sales and repricing it; some were highly specialized—dive gear or car parts—disdaining anything outside their own narrow line of interest; and more than a few were insane.

He used up one week's column by four in the afternoon, counting ten people who hadn't been home and two whose phones had been disconnected. Pushing back a wave of despair, he picked up the classified page from five weeks before *Finish Line*'s fire. He considered a second beer and decided in favor of an entire pot of coffee. He was measuring out the grounds when the phone burbled.

He picked it up with his left hand, reaching for the list of callbacks he'd prepared, but it was Alex Tallant's eerily familiar voice, sounding huffy. "I've been trying to get through all afternoon," he said.

Maybe it was unfair, but the fact that Alex sounded so much like his dead sister only made Neal's nerves crackle. "I've been on the phone a lot," he said. "What's up?"

"I hear the city police are losing interest in Jannice's death," Alex said.

Alex's contacts were probably as good as any in Santa Barbara, Neal thought. There was absolutely nothing to be gained by lying to him. "Losing interest is a little strong. They've run down just about all the leads there are, and the trail keeps doubling back to Jannice herself."

Alex's cold anger came through the phone like icewater. "If they think she killed herself, that's bullshit."

"Not killed herself deliberately," Neal said. "*Finish Line* was arson: that's for sure. The leading theory seems to be that Jannice torched the boat and was killed in the process."

"No." But not, Neal thought, as positive a "no" as it might have been. "What about Rudy? Has anybody checked him out?"

"I'm sure they have. . . . Checked him out how?"

"I heard he'd been talking about marrying again—one of the chickies in his office. But of course he'd have to divorce Jannice first—and a community property split wouldn't have helped his credit rating."

The venom in Alex's slightly hoarse voice seemed to drip from the phone. "Did Jannice ever talk to you about her marriage?" Neal asked.

"Well, of course." Alex sounded surprised. Then he chuckled. "I take it she didn't share her inmost thoughts with you."

"Not hardly," Neal replied.

"No, I don't suppose she would have," he said thoughtfully. "She could keep a secret. And men for her were—I hope this won't come as too much of a shock, Neal: for Jannice men were, well, *appliances*."

It was more relief than shock, though Neal was not about to say so. "She felt that way about Rudy, too? She seemed to think he was so smart."

"Oh, absolutely." Alex sounded coolly amused. "Your computer's smart. But that doesn't make it your soul mate."

And I have an idea who her soul mate was. "What did you think of Rudy? Before Jannice's death, I mean."

"I barely thought of him at all," Alex replied.

"You thought he was an . . . adequate husband for your sister?"

"Let's stop thrashing the shrubbery, shall we?" Alex said, his manner turning briskly dismissive. "Did I approve of Jannice marrying Rudy? Well, she was determined to marry *someone*, and equally determined to continue living here. As you may have noticed, Santa Barbara is a very small town. Her choices, as I recall, included a car dealer and the owner of an advertising agency. In that company, Rudy McKay seemed respectable enough. And it was only marriage, after all—neither of us considered the legal implications."

Neither of us. But what about Rudy?

"Enough of that," Alex said. "I suppose you realize Maria Acevedo is using you for a stalking horse."

"To get at Walt? Several folks have shared that thought with me."

"She's about as subtle as a train wreck," Alex said. "But don't underestimate her."

"Alex, I don't underestimate anybody," Neal said. "Especially you."

CARPINTERIA BEACH; 1830 HOURS: TORY

"How much did they allocate to seal those old well heads?" Tory asked as she kicked caked sand from the cleats of her heavy workboots.

"The state? Hundred thousand, I think," Chief Washington replied. He was putting the finishing touches to a sketch map of the beach, with each of the plugged pipes noted by a black *X* and the rusted-out ones indicated by a red circle around the *X*. "They're in for a shock, when they see how many of these suckers there are." The idea clearly pleased him.

"Well, before you get too happy, remember who gets called at zero-dark-thirty when one of them lets go," she said.

"There is that," he said. "You all set, Lieutenant?"

She glanced at her watch. "Time sure flies when you're having fun. Let's get out of here."

And she had been having fun, she realized as she slipped the Honda into the westbound stream of 101. Chief Washington was no conversationalist, but he was a meticulous, conscientious worker who knew what he was doing. In the last few days, he seemed to be accepting her as a partner he could work with—if senior in rank, junior in knowledge and experience.

"How you getting on with Mr. DEA?" the chief asked innocently.

"Up and down," she said. "He can't quite accept that other agencies aren't wholly owned subsidiaries of Drug Enforcement."

"Man takes his job seriously," the chief said. "Not too many do, anymore."

It was the closest they'd come to conversation since Tory's arrival, and she wanted it to continue. "You do," she said. "Take your job seriously, I mean."

"Yup," he agreed. After a full minute he added, "So do you."

She could say something polite and meaningless or see if this was a real opening. "You didn't think so at first."

She glanced across to see how he received it, thought she saw the flicker of a smile. "That's right." Again the extended silence, but now she felt comfortable with it. "Coast Guard's such a small service," he said at last. "I thought the marines was just a family, but it's ten times bigger."

She thought she saw what he was driving at, decided to gamble: "Reputations spread pretty fast."

"You got that right."

"I'm curious. What do they say about me?"

It was shockingly out of line, and she could think of at least three of her academy instructors who would have gone into coronary arrest to hear her, but the chief merely nodded and, after another while, said: "Smart, wise-ass, real ambitious. And rich."

"Rich?" she repeated.

"Like *loaded*. That's what they say."

Well, she'd asked for it. "And you figured rich equaled lazy."

"Not exactly lazy." She saw he hadn't finished and waited, fascinated, to see what he would come up with. "Not sure it's the right word, but I think, you know, *frivolous*."

Her amazement nearly put the Honda into a bridge abutment. "Sorry about that," she said, and then heard herself add, "You know, my mother would pay through the nose to find a man who thought I was frivolous."

"Well, that was what I *thought*. But I was wrong."

"And what does rich equal? In your reconsidered opinion."

"Having more money than me," he said.

As the 101 widened to three lanes through downtown Santa Barbara, she said, "I'll drop you off at home."

"That's good." By now she almost heard the quiet wheels turning. "They going to catch those bastards?"

"Who?" But by the time the word was out of her mouth, she knew: "The ones who sank *Blue Thunder*?"

"Ones who killed Swede Ericsen," he corrected her.

"You knew him?"

"We were on *Morgenthau* together. He was an MK-one, as high as he got. And a Dane, not a Swede: the nickname pissed him off no end. But an okay shipmate. I hope they catch the ones who did it."

"Yes," she said.

She dropped the chief off at the entrance to the little Coast Guard housing development and resisted the temptation to keep on going, down Shoreline to the harbormaster office. Besides, she assured herself, if anything had happened, Neal would have left a message on her home phone.

He had not. The unblinking red 0 on her answering machine lowered her spirits more than she had expected, and even a hot shower failed to raise them.

Food: an empty stomach was well-known to cause depression, and hers was growling. She emptied a can of Campbell's cheddar cheese soup into a saucepan and only then looked at the label and realized she didn't have the necessary milk to complete it. "Water," she said firmly. "Water will work fine."

It didn't.

But when the phone finally rang, she knew who it had to be.

It wasn't. "Tory, *mia bella*."

"Oh, hello, Alex."

"Well, I've never had that effect on a woman before."

"It's been a long day. Sorry."

"In that case," said Alex, "I won't ask if you're interested in a postprandial excursion up State Street."

"Maybe another time," she replied.

"I shall ask again," said the sly, hoarse voice, "when you've got the water cop out of your system."

Wonderful, she thought. I'm part of the rumor mill.

Carpe Diem; 8 P.M.: Neal

"A clock?" said the wispy voice uncertainly.

"An electric alarm clock. One that worked on batteries and house current both," he said wearily.

"No, I don't have it anymore."

"Sorry to bother—" He froze. "But you did own one?" He felt like a fisherman with the faintest vibration of a nibble.

"Oh, yes. It was in the sale." In the background he could hear vaguely familiar music. He associated it with a movie but couldn't remember which one.

"I'm sorry to bother you, Mr. Fox," he said again. "Do you by any chance remember the make—the brand name?"

" 'Forever,' " the wispy voice said, then corrected itself: "No, but a name like forever. Now, let me see . . ."

Under the rules of the game, it was cheating to suggest the answer, but that didn't mean you couldn't move your lips to form the name you wanted desperately to hear.

" 'Eterna.' That was it."

And you couldn't jump up and down or applaud, either. "You're certain," he said.

"Oh, yes. It was right at my bedside for three years, till I couldn't stand that awful alarm anymore." A dry, rustling sound that might have been laughter. "I even warned him about the alarm, but he didn't care."

"Him?" said Neal.

"The man who bought it. He was so nice, I didn't think it was right to sell the clock without telling him why."

"Do you remember"—his mouth was suddenly so dry, the words seemed to stick to his palate—"what he looked like?"

"Not really. He had one of those caps, you know, pulled down over his eyes, and a jacket with the collar turned up. It wasn't cold, though."

This close and washed out. It isn't fair. "Anything at all, Mr. Fox," Neal insisted. "Tall or short. Fat or thin."

"Kind of medium. A reddish face. Or maybe that was the man who bought the guitar."

"If you saw him again . . ."

"I really doubt it," said the wispy voice. "I'm so far-sighted these days, and he was so close. Quite in my face, as they say—though he was very nice about it."

"What about his voice?" *I'm pressing too hard.* "Could you recognize that, if you heard it again?"

"Oh, dear. It was just a voice. Quite like yours, really. Do you mind if I ask why you want to know, Officer?"

He had already explained once. Or had he? "The clock may be evidence in a case. Would you be able to recognize it again?"

"You mean, tell it apart from all the other Eternas? I don't see how."

"No, I guess not."

"You know, I did notice one thing that might help. . . ."

And hope really does spring eternal. "What was that? Please."

"His car. A foreign car—I don't know the make, but one sees them from time to time, a wonderful dark green."

"You'd recognize the car, Mr. Fox?"

"No," said the voice cheerfully. "But the license plate. It was so appropriate for someone buying a clock. Now, let me see . . ."

You could hold your breath only so long. He heard small clucking sounds—the not quite meshing of the gears in Mr. Fox's memory.

"No," said the wispy voice. "I can't summon the exact word. But I do remember it was very apropos. When you find the car, you'll see."

"Yes," said Neal heavily. "I expect we will. Thanks for—"

"Wait," said Mr. Fox, sounding almost excited. "I just remembered. Or almost remembered. The license plate read 'tock'—as in tick-tock?"

"Tock?" Neal repeated.

"Well, that wasn't all of it. But tock was definitely part of it."

"I see," Neal said. And then, in memory, he did: an actual photograph. Framed in teak, on a white bulkhead. The front of a hunter green Jaguar XKE, with a license plate that read BUYSTOK. And standing proudly beside it, the owner: Rudy McKay.

Harbor Parking Lot; 8:30 p.m.: Tory

His phone had been busy so long, she figured there might be something wrong with it. And if that were the case, she told herself, it was only right to trot by and tell him, in case an important call was trying to get through. Unless, of course, he'd taken it off the hook to keep her at arm's length—but you couldn't take a cellular phone off the hook. Or could you?

She pulled in next to a fisherman's three-quarter-ton, full of barnacled buoys, that screened the Honda perfectly. Neal's little Toyota pickup was in the next lane, so he was probably still on his boat. She turned off the headlights and engine but found herself making no move to leave the car. *He'd have called me if he reached T.J. He'll just think I don't trust him.*

She turned the ignition key to wake up the car radio and listened to five minutes of Beethoven. *The thing is, I'm not sure I do trust him.* Beethoven thundered to its familiar end. The announcer promised Charles Ives, "after these messages." Tory didn't particularly like Ives, and he made her homesick for New England. *I just want to be with him. That's okay, isn't it?* She clicked off the key and opened the Honda's door when she heard the marina gate clang shut, an unmistakable metallic crash.

She recognized him immediately, even though his face was in shadow and he had the collar of his jacket turned up. It was the way he walked, she realized—the way Indians were supposed to, with his feet toed in just slightly. And he was in a hurry, looking to neither side, as he strode toward his truck.

He didn't notice the light in Tory's Honda, though she pulled the door quietly closed to kill it the instant she recognized him. Something heavy on his mind, she thought.

Her hand was on the ignition key as he slammed the truck door, and she turned it as she heard the Toyota's starter grind. He didn't wait for the pickup to warm up but flicked on his lights, backed out of the parking slot, headed up the row of cars, turned, and rolled right down past Tory. She caught a glimpse of his profile as the truck went by: head slightly forward, jaw hard, eyes straight ahead and a hundred miles away.

At the end of the row he turned toward the parking lot entrance, as she'd known he would. She pulled back, turned, and after a second's thought put on her own lights: at this hour the harbor was still fairly active, no reason for Neal to wonder at a car behind him—if he even noticed.

The attendant in the little hut must have recognized Neal's truck, because the candy-striped barrier began to swing up when he was still fifty yards away—and before Tory had even begun to fumble for her wallet. The elderly attendant took her ticket and her money, making change so slowly that she was on the point of shouting "Keep it" when she realized that would only delay her even more.

It seemed forever before the barrier went up. She tramped on the gas and the Honda leaped forward, scattering a quartet of diners wandering boozily back from Brophy's. As she turned toward the harbor entrance, followed by a chorus of angry yells, she saw Neal's taillight turn right onto Cabrillo Boulevard.

He's found out where T.J. parks his van, she thought. The traffic light at the entrance was red, and she glanced left up Cabrillo. A car was coming, but she could beat it. The other driver thought so, too—and accelerated. Tory gritted her teeth and spun the wheel. The Honda screeched around the corner, and a horn blared right behind her.

As a transplanted New Englander, Tory had accumulated the standard repertoire of California driver stories. Now, she realized, she had become one herself, under the general heading "stupid woman driver." She giggled unsteadily. The post-dinner crowd on Cabrillo paid her no attention, though, and the car behind stayed a discreet distance back. Maybe that heading should be "crazy woman driver," she was thinking as Neal swung without signaling into the left-turn pocket at the State Street intersection. She slammed on the brakes and swung left just in time, glimpsed from the corner of her eye the frightened face of the driver behind her as he sailed past.

Waiting for the light to change, she had a chance to catch her breath. Lower State was alive and throbbing, with a super-amplified big beat thundering out of one restaurant's open doors and windows. To her right, Stearns Wharf stretched away across the harbor mouth. Every couple of seconds a car rattled out or back, its tires shaking the loose planking. I like this town, she thought, watching a scurry of wide-eyed tourists crossing the wide street.

The green arrow lit up at the head of her lane. Before the car ahead of it began to move, Neal's pickup was inching forward impatiently. She knew where he was going, now: he would cut right on Yanonali, just below the freeway, where the uncertainties of redevelopment had created a maze of back streets, ephemeral (not to say fly-by-night) businesses, and empty, unsurfaced lots. Scrofulous RVs and broken-down heavy equipment lurked there, as did a scattering of boats on trailers.

But his truck sailed right by Yanonali and under the freeway overpass, to turn right on Haley, one of the city's few really disreputable streets. It was not a neighborhood Tory was familiar with, but even Santa Barbara's worst was a vast improvement on much of D.C. and most of lower Manhattan. Left onto Santa Barbara Street, heading north through the center of town, riding the staggered traffic lights. Past the huge county courthouse—Disney out of Torquemada, a design so preposterous that it made her grin every time she saw it.

She turned her attention to staying on the pickup's tail without letting another vehicle slip between them—or getting so close that she'd ram him if he braked suddenly. It was a nice judgment, but she managed to keep her position until they were out of the commercial district, when without warning he dodged into the right lane, only inches in front of the car beside Tory.

Her first thought was that he'd spotted her and was trying to lose her. The intersection ahead was where Santa Barbara Street, hitherto one-way northbound, changed to a two-way street: a two-way street with a pair of blazing headlights coming right at her. The intersection was a four-way stop. Neal's lane could turn right or continue straight—as he did. Tory's lane could only go left, while oncoming traffic had the choice of turning either way.

The vehicle facing her—a four-wheel-drive high-rider—was signaling a left turn. The car on her right looked to be continuing straight ahead. Almost a block beyond, she saw Neal's turn signal begin to flash. "Shit," she said aloud, stamped on the accelerator, and cut diagonally across, just as the high-rider began to move. Its bumper was higher than the Honda's trunk, and its left front wheel thudded into her car's side.

She kept her foot down, but the high-rider's driver lost his nerve and stalled. The Honda was doing nearly fifty by the time she reached the corner where Neal had turned. When Tory braked to follow, her car spun a complete circle in the center of the intersection, then leaped ahead as the tires bit into the asphalt.

He was still in sight, moving past the old mission's twin towers and bearing left. From a side street a car pulled out quickly and dropped behind Neal's truck. No chance to pass here—the road was too narrow and there was too much coming the other way. Where could he be going? she wondered. The mission was nearly at the city's northern edge, and while some roads snaked up into the foothills, she couldn't imagine T. J. Wellcome stashing his van so far from the harbor.

At a T intersection the car in front of Tory turned left. Neal had gone off to the right, but now two more vehicles had squeezed between Tory and him. In the dark she was completely lost, able only to remember that downtown was to the right, the hills to her left. At the last instant she realized Neal had just made a sharp left, off the main road they were on, heading up one of the canyons. In the dark and concentrating on his taillight, she was unable to read the street signs. At a Y, Neal went left and the only remaining vehicle between them went right. The road was rising, with a steep hillside on the left, losing itself in the darkness. House lights here and there, set well back from the road. They were definitely out of town now.

Left around a sharp bend. Neal was driving more slowly now, even erratically—and then she realized he was braking to check the numbers on the mailboxes. He had an address, she decided, but he didn't know the house. Against instinct she dropped back a few yards. Suddenly he speeded up around a bend, and she responded, to miss his truck by inches as it pulled off the road onto the unpaved margin.

She kept going around the next bend—another hundred yards at the most—pulled off and parked, careful to check her rearview mirror first. She debated locking the car, decided finally not to: she might need to get out of there in a hurry. The asphalt surface of the road was so gritty from the recent rains that her sneakers rasped as she half ran, half skidded back down. She pulled up just short of the bend and scurried across to the far side before continuing more slowly around the curve.

He was standing with his back to her, no more than thirty feet away, staring fixedly up a steep, winding driveway. There were no lights at the top, or none that she could see, but she could sense a big, sprawling house perched on the hillside. Suddenly, as if he had arrived at a decision, Neal started up the driveway, loping silently. She waited until he was just visible near the top, then hurried after him. The drive was asphalt like the road, but so steep that it had run clean, at least in the middle.

The pale stucco house at the top of the drive was two stories high and blocky, with huge windows upstairs and a thicket of wildly inappropriate pillars across the front. To the left was a two-car garage with a single wide door. Neal was standing in front of the door, his dark figure clear against the light-colored paint. Tory faded silently to the side of the driveway, where untrimmed bushes overhung the curb, and froze.

Just in time, too: Neal turned and surveyed the drive for several moments, then walked slowly around the side of the garage. She was beginning to wonder what had happened to him when she heard the sharp, musical sound of breaking glass, followed a few seconds later by an unearthly screech that made the hair on her neck stand up. Metal on unoiled metal, she told herself, and hoped it was true.

Then silence—or, rather, the sounds of a California night: a distant coyote, a heavy vehicle shifting down, the dry rustle of the warm wind. She waited two endless minutes, timing them by her watch, then edged on up the drive and around to the side of the garage. It was almost at the edge of the hill, which fell away in great rolling swoops to the city, a magical pavement of lights seemingly miles below. Whoever owned this place, it certainly wasn't a mechanic who worked out of his van.

No sign of Neal, but a faint gleam was visible inside the garage, and one pane in its two side windows was darker than the rest—was not, she realized, there at all. The light seemed to be flickering—had he set the place on fire? Then it dawned on her that it must be moving, a flashlight. Stepping lightly, she made a wide circle to come at the broken window while looking through it. Now she could indeed see a pool of light that swung and fixed and swung again. It drew her like a magnet. This is exactly what killed the cat, she thought. But she could no more have gone back down the hill than taken wing from the crest.

She inched her way to the window, and something grabbed her ankle. She gasped, almost cried out. But whatever was holding her wasn't dragging her down or even moving. She bent slowly, slowly, and extended her hand until she touched waxy-textured leaves, interspersed with small, hard, round fruit and long thorns, one of which had gone right through the fabric of her coveralls.

By the time she had pulled it free, Neal's flashlight had stopped moving. He had set it on top of what looked like a steel filing cabinet with shallow drawers, so its beam lit most of the garage. The building, she saw, was only half garage—the side nearest her, bare and clean except for the shiny black smear of an oil stain on the floor. The other side was an elaborate workshop, with a row of big power tools—she recognized a band saw and a drill press—and a wide, heavy wooden work surface, backed up by steel boxes that probably contained smaller tools and their accessories.

An ordinary plastic toolbox—no, larger than the usual—was on the counter with its top tilted back, and Neal was extracting its contents, item by item, holding some of them up to the light, then setting each down on the counter. A minute more, or perhaps two, and she knew she could work out what he was looking for. But down at the foot of the driveway a double beam of light cut sharply around to light up the hill. She heard an engine hesitate, then roar as a driver goosed the accelerator.

The light played across the concrete apron in front of the garage, then lit the hill beside it, as Tory flattened herself against the stucco wall. The engine roared more loudly, and suddenly the whole building began to vibrate in sympathy. But it was only the wide garage door, lifting to the signal from an electric opener. And as it lifted, the garage lit up like an operating theater.

Through the stucco Tory heard the car slide into the garage, heard the engine's deep rumble quit abruptly. The well-oiled click of a car door opening and then an explosive "What the hell?" that echoed hollowly off the rafters.

She wanted desperately to see, had to see, no matter what the risk might be. Pivoting among the bushes, she pressed her chest against the rough stucco, edged her head past the window frame just as Neal's voice, calm and surprisingly loud, said, "I've been waiting for you, Rudy."

Rudy. The name dissolved all her caution. She stepped to one side, and the scene lay before her. In the foreground, the elegantly rounded shape of a Jaguar sedan. The driver's door was open, and standing behind it was the solid, powerful figure of Jannice McKay's husband. He was staring over the car's roof toward the workbench, littered now with what looked like a large collection of mechanical parts—most unidentifiable, some clearly nautical. She couldn't see Neal at all, but when he spoke again, his voice was coming from the shadows behind a hooded band saw.

She missed his exact words—something about a clock—but she saw Rudy's left hand, behind the door, clench on the handle.

"I don't know what you're talking about," Rudy said calmly.

"That's all right," said Neal's voice. "You made a wonderful impression on Mr. Fox—he remembers you."

"Mr. who?" Rudy sounded genuinely baffled.

"The old party who sold you the clock," said Neal. "The garage sale man. And we all know how shaky an ID can be in court, but he also remembers your beautiful car and your clever license plate."

"My license plate?" Rudy echoed. He sounded distinctly shaken. "Well, maybe I did buy a clock. For the boat. . . . Jannice wanted it—" His voice was picking up speed as he spoke and, with the speed, confidence.

"Did she want some wire, too? And some plastic pipe?"

"You're crazy," Rudy said. "Breaking into my garage for God knows what reason. Accusing me of . . . of . . ."

"Of murder, Rudy." Neal appeared from the shadows, walking forward slowly. "I found what I was looking for. This." He was holding a coil of stiff rope—no, wire—in his hand. "Unusual stuff. Expensive. Too bad you didn't throw out the extra, after you wired that clock to make it look like a timer."

"That's just goddamn wire," Rudy snarled. "Nothing so friggin' special about it. . . ."

"You want to bet, Rudy? Because that's what you'll be doing," Neal said. "Betting that a microscopic analysis of this coil won't show it's the same metallic composition as the timer wire. Compared to DNA analysis, this is basic stuff."

"Well, even if you were right—which you aren't—you'll never get that into evidence. Not after you broke in here and stole it. If you didn't plant it, which raises—"

"You keep forgetting Mr. Fox," said Neal, who seemed quite unmoved. "And a trial's not the real point. You're finished, Rudy. When word of this gets out, you won't have a customer left. Just Alex Tallant. And Alex really cares about who killed his sister."

"Maybe he should've married her," Rudy burst out. His face was scarlet, the veins at the sides of his head like knotted cords. "He's the one she always wanted. Never me, never any of the others. She didn't want you, either—except as a fall guy."

Neal's even voice never faltered. "So she did plan to torch *Finish Line*."

"Of course she did, the greedy twat." Rudy was shaking with rage. "I had to go along with it, or she'd have filed for divorce. She was a silent partner in my business, you see. Her family put up money to help me get off the ground. I paid it back long ago, but community property would've killed me."

"So you decided to up the ante," Neal said. He seemed to Tory only mildly interested.

"It was like blackmail, don't you see?" Rudy demanded. "Once she started, there'd be no end to it. Can you blame me?"

"Rudy, you burned her alive," said Neal. "You rigged that so-called timer so she'd have to stand right in front of the gasoline. It was all over her, and I saw it. I'll never forget it as long as—"

With a dull click the garage lights shut off, leaving Neal silhouetted in the Jaguar's headlights. Rudy's left hand darted downward into the car's door pocket, came up holding something shiny. He was firing as he raised the weapon, an ear-shattering crash in the enclosed space, with the simultaneous *whump*! as the round hit something in the back of the garage. The second round caromed off metal with an echoing clang and screamed away.

Neal had dived for safety behind the band saw, but in the blaze of headlight she saw his foot catch in the saw's power cable, and he sprawled on the floor, momentarily helpless.

Moving fast for so bulky a man, Rudy stepped from behind the car door. He was holding the pistol—an automatic—in both hands now, bringing it down, as Tory, only three feet behind him, bellowed: "Freeze! Police!"

Instead of freezing, he spun in his tracks, and Tory saw the gun swinging toward her. In the instant of time, she saw his eyes were wide and glazed, knew he would shoot. Knew she was going to die.

NEAL

As he hit the garage floor, his conscious mind was still two steps behind, blank with surprise that Rudy had come unglued so quickly. The impact of his chest on the concrete made him gasp, but the only pain he felt was just below his rib cage, on the right side. *My gun* was forming in his head even as his right hand, clawing the fabric of his jacket, dragged the automatic from his pocket. He knew it was too late, but his body was making its own decisions.

"Freeze! Police!"

He barely heard the shout—it might have come from another planet. He was still rolling over, bringing up the gun, as he saw Rudy turn away toward the dark garage window, in which a white blob had appeared.

The nine-millimeter automatic bucked in Neal's hand, the flat bellow deafening him. He had no idea where the bullet went—or what the weapon was pointing at when he pulled the trigger again. But a windowpane exploded in a shower of fragments, and someone screamed.

"Rudy!" Neal shouted. The other man was rigid, his broad back hunched as if against a storm. "Drop it!" Neal heard his own voice crack, and maybe that was what tipped the balance.

The clatter sounded right for a gun landing on concrete. "Hands up!" Neal ordered. "All the way up!"

Slowly Rudy straightened. Even more slowly his hands appeared, fingers spread wide. "All right," he said, his voice flat. "That's enough."

Only now did the shout from outside the window fully register.

"Who's out there?" Neal called. "Show yourself." On his knees, he shuffled sideways to keep the bulk of the band saw table between him and the shattered window. His ears were ringing badly.

"It's me." The voice came not from the window, but from the open garage door. "Easy does it, lover," said Tory, stepping slowly into view.

"I take it firearms are not, shall we say, your forte?" she said. She was standing at the counter in her apartment's tiny kitchen—so tiny that Neal had not even tried to squeeze into it with her.

"I hate guns," he said. He was shivering again, though he wasn't at all cold. He looked idly around him at the high-ceilinged living room. It was basic stucco and black wrought iron—very Southern California—to which Tory had added a black leather sofa, a delicate mahogany side table, two wide bookcases along one wall, and a New England landscape over the fireplace, a historical painting of Nantucket harbor in the last century.

"That's probably just as well," she was saying. "Between you and Rudy, it's a wonder half a dozen innocent cactuses weren't blown away." She appeared in the doorway, holding a wine bottle. In spite of dirt smudges and a large, not-too-clean bandage near her hairline, concealing a very small cut from flying glass, she looked remarkably neat and entirely composed.

"This time, you saved my life," said Neal. "I haven't had a chance to thank you properly."

"You will," she said. "I'm deciding exactly how."

Far too composed, he decided. She'd politely endured the hamhanded first aid of a firefighter who had mysteriously appeared at Rudy's even before the county sheriff's people; had sailed right through the necessary interviews, statements, and paper passing that followed Rudy's arrest; and had managed to get herself and Neal out a side door right under the noses of the local TV station's mobile unit. It was a tour de force by any standard, but she was bound to crash sooner or later, and Neal was determined to catch her when she did.

If, of course, he didn't crash first. "D'you want me to open that?" he asked. His voice was level, anyway.

"That would be nice," she said. "Would you like something to eat?"

He was ravenous, he realized—and why not? It was nearly eleven, and he hadn't eaten since lunch, ten hours before. "What have you got?"

For the first time she seemed uncertain. "I'm not very good about keeping food in the house. Breakfast stuff, mostly." She tipped her head in thought. "I'm afraid it'll have to be guacamole and chips, unless you're up for major thawing."

"Sounds fine to me."

"Good. You can make the guacamole while the wine breathes and I clean up."

A person's library was supposed to be a key to their character, Neal recalled from somewhere. The same might be said of some kitchens—but Tory Lennox's was merely bewildering. On the one hand, her cupboard shelves displayed a fearsome order—jars, bottles, and cans, arranged by size and dressed to the right in neat rows. The bleakly standard contents could be interpreted as reflecting lack of imagination, disinterest, or ignorance; yet a few surprising touches suggested depths yet to be plumbed. Like eight sealed pouches of crystallized Australian ginger in the refrigerator; or a nearly full case of canned evaporated milk under the sink.

The wine selection was simply huge. Neal's own knowledge of wine was restricted to red, white, and something in between that was always too sweet. Still, he remembered a remark of Walt's that you could often judge really good French wine by the stodginess of its label design, and Tory had a wide variety of the most suppressed labels Neal could remember seeing, as well as some California varieties whose price stickers made him purse his lips in a soundless whistle.

The bottle she had left on the small dining alcove's table was French, and the name—Château Margaux—sounded vaguely familiar. He found a complicated corkscrew in one of the drawers and opened it. Smells like wine, he thought. Smells like very rich, smooth, probably expensive wine.

A bowl on the sideboard contained an arrangement of avocados, bananas, and oranges that he suspected might be there for appearance rather than food value. But two of the avocados were ripe, and there was onion in the refrigerator, as well as half a container of salsa that had just begun to ferment. Not ideal, but it would do.

He was just finishing up when she reappeared, gleaming pink and blond, wrapped in a terrycloth robe. She looked good enough to eat, and he was on the verge of saying so when he saw the angry fear in her blue eyes and realized she was shaking. "I know it's just shock," she said. "But I can't make it stop."

He wanted desperately to take her in his arms, but something in her manner told him that would be precisely the wrong move. "You're running about half an hour behind me," he said lightly. "Probably the difference between being shot at by accident and on purpose."

She managed a smile that was only slightly strained. "What happens next? You look all right."

"I am all right—now," he replied. "Have something to eat."

Alcohol, he remembered, was not a good idea for someone in shock. But there was alcohol and alcohol, and how could something with a castle on the label be bad for you? He poured each of them a glass.

She raised hers, tiny ripples on the wine's surface. "Oh, *damn* it," she said, and took an appraising sip. "Not bad for grape juice."

It was like drinking red velvet, he thought. "It's wonderful. Maybe a little high class for guacamole, though."

"I know a Frenchman who'd agree with you," she said, and colored. "By the way, the chips are in the hall closet."

They were, enough ten-ounce packages of blue corn tortilla chips to feed half the state. "I guess you must like these things," he said, emptying an envelope into a bowl.

"Live on them," she said, crunching as she spoke. She held out her hand, fingers extended, and considered it. "That's better."

He wanted to take it in his. Instead he took another long swallow of wine, thinking it might go better with a slightly less spicy dish than guacamole, especially guacamole whose spoiled salsa had been covered by extra onions.

"Weren't you taking a big chance, sticking it to Rudy like that?" Tory said suddenly.

"So I found out," Neal replied, laughing. "Sure, but I didn't have a case that was going anywhere. Mr. Fox would dry up and blow away on a witness stand. I needed to make Rudy jump, but I wasn't exactly ready when he did."

"It was the garage light that did it," Tory observed. "When the timer turned it off, you were standing there in the headlights like the world's biggest target. It must've been irresistible."

For a second he was back in the garage, squinting into the lights as Rudy fired. He shivered. "Christ. You've got me started again."

She smiled sympathetically, but he could see she wasn't diverted. "Why'd you take the chance, Neal? Did you love her that much?"

"I didn't love her at all," he said, jolted into bluntness. "Any more than she loved me. She needed me for her little plan, and I . . ."

She let the silence hang, then addressed the contents of her wineglass: "Boys just want to have fun."

"I guess so." It was close enough.

"So it wasn't lover's revenge that sent you after Rudy," she prodded.

"No. Or only a little." He could see the question was important to her, sensed it should be to him, too. "I put myself in Rudy's face because that was the only thing I could think to do." He paused, glanced at her. She was sitting with her chin on her interlaced fingers, watching him intently. "He was messing with my harbor—well, both of them were. It needed to be straightened out."

A slow smile spread across her face. "Sounds like a cop to me."

He pushed away the empty bowl. "Not the best guac I ever made," he said.

"You're a better cook than I am, Gunga Din," she replied. She got to her feet in a single quick movement. Before he could guess what she intended, she was standing over him, smelling of shampoo and skin lotion. She took his chin in her hand, tilted his face up to the light. "Something I've wanted to ask you."

He felt breathless, suspended outside of time. "Ask away."

She hesitated. Ran the tip of her forefinger across his lips. "Are your teeth capped?" she asked, and burst into laughter.

He was laughing, too. Maybe a little harder than necessary. "Matter of fact, they are," he said at last. "Present from my grandfather, the eminent Chicano shyster." He deepened his voice: " 'Only thing my Mick son-in-law ever gave his kids—Irish teeth.' "

He could see from her eyes that the implications weren't lost on her. "Well, they're beautiful now," she said, and kissed him.

The kiss was nothing like what he'd expected. As accomplished as Jannice's, but far more subtle—it conveyed real affection, passion held in check, even a sense of fun. He let her guide them both, then took the lead when she relinquished it. He surfaced with a gasp. "Don't tell me they taught you that at the academy."

She smiled and straightened, taking his hand. He followed her up the stairs to the bathroom. "The green bath towel is for you," she said. "My room's through that far door."

The green towel was around his waist when he entered. It was a large room, very much a woman's bedroom, but all he really saw was Tory, lying on a double bed among a heap of pillows. She was wearing a black nightgown and a smile that lit up her eyes.

"My God," he said.

"Enough of this badinage," she said. "Come here."

"May I say you're amazing?" he called from the kitchenette.

"You may." But he detected a slight hesitancy in her voice.

He turned to look at her, and his heart jumped. She was sitting at the dining alcove table, once again wearing her bathrobe and a well-scrubbed look. Watching him with open affection and, he thought, just a touch of wariness around the eyes. "What is it?" he asked.

"Morning afters are always tricky, I think. Especially after a first night like last night." She paused, smiled past him, then continued in the same meditative tone: "I know the question you're dying to ask."

Her eyes met his. He felt his ears go hot and then his cheeks, but he said nothing.

"He was older than I, and he taught me a lot—though we had a lot in common, too. Ambition . . ."

She stopped herself in midbreath, and he said, "Background?"

He saw he'd guessed right. She colored and smiled again, a private smile this time. "In a way."

"Where is he now?"

"Back in . . . home. Our careers diverged, and they were the most important thing."

Was that a warning? It sure sounded like one. Behind him, the teakettle shrieked a warning of its own. "Coffee coming up," he said. And two minutes later, "Breakfast is served."

"Those pancakes were magnificent," she said, setting her knife and fork neatly across the empty plate. "I've never had anything like them."

"I can give you the recipe," he said.

"Thanks, but I think it'd be simpler just to retain the cook. Simpler and a lot more—"

The kitchen phone cut her off, and she reached out to pick it up. "Lieutenant Lennox." Her eyebrows rose. "Good morning to you, Officer Ortega. What can I do for you?" Neal knew what it was going to be, even before Tory rolled her eyes in mock despair and said, "It's for you."

"That you, Neal?" The voice on the other end of the line was very young and not a little nervous.

"It's me," he said. "What's up, Gaspar?"

"None of us wanted to bother you, but Taffy said it was real important, so we drew straws and I—"

"And you lost," Neal said firmly. "So what is it?"

"You said to keep an eye out for T.J. Wellcome's van? Well, we were making a dawn tour through the lot, and we spotted it tucked between a couple of urchin boats on trailers, over by the launch ramps."

A dawn tour. Neal glanced at his watch: about an hour ago. "You're sure it's T.J.'s van?" Tory, who had been clearing the table silently, dropped a dish.

"Positive."

"He in it?"

"Not's far as we can tell." Neal shook his head "no" at Tory, poised intently in the kitchenette doorway. "You said not to approach it or anything, so we just rolled past. Taffy's out in the channel in *Harbor 3*, just doodling around, keeping an eye on it."

"Tell her to get the hell out of there. Any idea when it came in?"

"Wasn't there at midnight," said Gaspar. "We checked with the gate, and they don't remember seeing it go through—but he's got a sticker, of course."

"Of course." And when the gatekeepers saw one of the harbor lot parking stickers on a vehicle's windshield, it seemed to cancel out any other recollection. "Just out of curiosity, whose idea was it to call here?" This time Tory's jaw dropped, and her expression looked like genuine dismay.

"Jeez, I couldn't say, Neal." The answer came so fast, Neal knew the young officer had been prepped for it, and he could guess by whom.

"Okay. I'll be down in fifteen, twenty minutes. Don't anybody go near that van till I get there." He started to pass the handset back to Tory, then remembered: "And Gaspar? You did the right thing, whoever's idea it was."

Santa Barbara Harbor; 0715: Tory

"You can just see it from here," said Taffy Hegemann, standing at the helm of *Harbor 3*. "Look between the big blue Radon and the Skipjack, third vehicle in the row."

"Got it," said Neal. He passed the field glasses to Tory. She found the trailered boats easily enough, but the van's faded, grayish blue paint job was an almost perfect urban camouflage.

"What now?" she asked. She could feel Taffy's eyes on her, wondered what was going through the other woman's head. If it was resentment, it certainly didn't show. But ever since Neal's triumphant arrival at the harbormaster office, Tory had felt like one of a conqueror's trophies, and to her mingled annoyance and amusement, it stung.

"I think we'd better have a closer look," he said. "Taffy, drop us on one of the finger piers."

"You want me to come along?" the young officer asked hopefully. "Since neither of you is armed."

"I don't think so," said Neal. "Between us, Lieutenant Lennox and I should be a match for anything."

She supposed it was meant to be a compliment, but somehow it came out condescending. Or am I just being postcoital petty? she asked herself, and received no answer.

They walked side by side up the asphalt launch ramp toward the parked van, and she almost reached for his hand—not for reassurance, she told herself, but just for the feel of it, firm and powerful and sensitive. She had put on a regular undress uniform—light blue short-sleeved shirt and dark blue trousers, and her MSD Santa Barbara ball cap—instead of the coveralls she usually wore around the harbor, but it hadn't provided the expected lift. Neal was wearing the same clothes he'd had on last night, minus as much of the grime as she'd been able to brush off in five minutes. He looked dangerously alert, and she had the sense he was enjoying himself.

"Nobody's in there. I'd bet on it," he said quietly after they'd walked completely around the van and its flanking boats.

"What makes you say so?"

"Morning's already heating up, and it's sealed tight. Must be like an oven in there."

It was, she saw, an old step van. If you looked at the side from just the right angle, the name RYDER was faintly visible under at least two coats of slightly different colored paint. Both front doors were shut and locked, and the windshield and side windows were so dusty that it was almost impossible to see into the cab. Moistening a finger, Neal wiped a streak of windshield clean, but it was the dirt that seemed to interest him. "What is it?" she said.

"Reddish dirt," he replied. "If you'd read my monologue on western dirt, Watson, you'd know instantly this comes from California. Or maybe Hawaii."

"Red dirt's more common up in the foothills, isn't it?" she asked. "There was a lot of it on your clothes this morning."

"Trouble is, a lot of the foothills are down in the valleys since the rains," he said. "It'd take a laboratory to say for sure where this van's been lately."

He had edged between the van and a boat trailer and was standing at the rear doors. He knocked once and again; called, "Anybody home?" and then, "T.J., you in there?" Idly he pushed up the handle with one finger. "Well, now."

"It's open," Tory breathed. "Can we go inside?"

"I'd say yes: he's illegally parked—this is a trailers-only space—and anyway, it's full of valuable and potentially dangerous tools. Some kid might hurt himself."

She glanced at him sharply. "When did you make that up?"

"Just now, but it sounds good," he replied. "You got a handkerchief?"

"A lady always has a handkerchief," she said, passing it over.

Wrapping it around his hand, Neal pulled one door open by its jamb and peered inside. His grunted exclamation sounded like surprise, and after a moment he opened the other door. "What do you make of it?"

The smell alone—long unwashed male, with a strong underlay of gasoline and WD-40—was enough to make her recoil, but the sheer chaos of the van's interior stunned her. "I don't know—explosion in a secondhand tool shop," she said. "You tell me."

Using his handkerchief-wrapped hand, he pulled himself up into the van and stood, rocking on the balls of his feet, at the very back edge. For about a minute he surveyed the interior, humming tunelessly under his breath. Tory, watching him from below, found herself thinking of a hawk circling. Abruptly he turned and held out his bare hand. "Come on up. It makes a lot more sense when you're looking down at it."

She took his hand, raised one booted foot to the fender. Without apparent effort, he pulled her up. "Just stand back here," he said. "Don't touch anything."

"You think—"

"I don't know," he replied. "But I do know Steve Merriam's boys get very testy when you mess with their evidence."

It was hard to concentrate with him so close. "It still looks like a shambles to me."

"That's the military mind," he said.

She could hear a note of amused satisfaction in his voice, and it should have annoyed her. "Explain, Sherlock."

"Okay. From left to right, like a photo caption," he said. "On this side, tool storage—wrenches, socket drives, drill bits, all that stuff. Also parts, mostly in boxes from the factory."

She could follow him partway: secured to the left-hand side of the van was a tier of shallow cabinets, their double doors hanging open. Inside some of them were arrangements of hooks and pegs that might indeed have held tools in place, while other lockers contained only empty, closely spaced shelving. "But the tools and stuff are on the floor," she objected. "Well, most of them are."

"Look closer," he said. He squatted, pointing. "All those filters—the little square boxes—see where they are?"

He was pointing to a row of cardboard containers labeled FUEL-WATER SEPARATOR. "Yes."

"And the Racors—the larger boxes. See them?"

"Yes. They're all on the floor."

He must have heard the forced patience in her tone. "That's the point," he said. "All on the floor, nearly in a row. They all fell off their shelves together. . . ."

He paused deliberately, and she picked it up: "When the van hit a bump—"

"Or went around a bend—"

"Because the lockers were open." She nodded. "Like the tool cabinets."

"Good," he said. "Now look up to the front."

"A folding cot, I think. And a revolting sleeping bag. And I suppose that's a pillow."

"I'm afraid you're right," he replied, laughing. "What does it tell us?"

"That he lives here," she said. "Clothes in those open drawers under the cot. They look as if he just threw them in there any old way."

"Or someone else had been pawing through them in a hurry," Neal said. "What else?"

The impossible confusion was beginning to make sense, now that he'd given her a lead. "It looks as if the other side of the van serves as his office," she offered. "All those bills and receipts and things. And his kitchen—here's a portable propane stove on the floor, too."

"Sailed off the counter," he said. "Lucky the gas bottle didn't break off."

She was getting into the exercise. "Isn't that red container an ice chest?" she said. "Looks as if it'd slid out from under the counter on the right side."

"Forget the food," he said. "What strikes you about the papers?"

It was clearly a test, and tests had always brought out Tory's competitive spirit. "Well," she said slowly, "from here they do look like business documents. His bill head . . . Six Harbor Way—isn't that the mailbox place?"

"You got it."

But not the right *it*, she saw. She stared at the drift of multicolored receipts, bill copies, shipping orders. Manila folders, too, labeled with boat names, some of which she recognized as those of commercial fishing vessels. "They're his files," she said at last, "but beyond that . . ."

"I'll give you a hint: How were they filed?"

"In those open-topped cardboard boxes," she replied, feeling that the answer was almost within her grasp. "All the office supply places have them, for temporary file storage while you're moving . . . Oh."

"Right. They're—"

"Still in place, but the papers are all over," she said triumphantly. "Therefore, the tools and parts *fell* out, but the papers were *pulled* out. By somebody who was looking for something."

"That's more or less how I read it," he said.

"More or less? What did I miss?"

He regarded her with mock alarm. "Hey, don't bite."

She forced herself to take a deep, steadying breath (and noted that his eyes still went automatically to the V of her blouse). "Sorry. I get carried away sometimes."

"It's part of your charm," he replied, then added quickly: "The way I see it, somebody searched the whole van—T.J. may be a slob, but he's a professional mechanic. Those tool and parts cabinets all have catches, but the doors were open when the van drove off. And the clothes drawers look as if somebody'd poked around in them, too."

She thought she saw where he was heading: "But a half-hearted search. They didn't really expect to find anything there. The papers were what had their real interest."

"Exactly. And another thing: The parts locker looks like it came off a boat, or maybe a boat cabinetmaker built it, with a lip on each shelf."

He paused, and she jumped in eagerly: "So the boxes wouldn't have fallen out unless the van was really rocking and rolling."

"That may be a stretch," he admitted.

"But what were they looking for?" she asked. "What kind of papers?"

"That's the question, isn't it?" he said. But she sensed he had at least the beginning of a suspicion, and he didn't intend to share it.

"Looks like it's decision time," she said.

"Say again?"

"You want me to quote the great Feltrini at you? As in which side are you on?"

His angular face went deep red with anger. "You don't give people much room, do you?"

"I am a pushy broad, if that's what you're edging around." Her voice, she noted, was calm and even, and he couldn't see the fingernails digging into her palms.

He turned and jumped to the ground. Like everything physical he did, it was smooth and controlled and a pleasure to see. Looking up at her, he said, "Close the doors when you leave." His face had closed off, in that infuriating way he had. She felt her heart turn to lead.

"Where are you going?"

"See you around," he said, and walked away.

Camino Cielo; 10 a.m.: Neal

Ahead of him and to the right, the summit thrust upward; he spotted the turnoff leading to the small picnic area from which, on a rare crystalline day, you could see past the four nearer Santa Barbara Channel islands to their misty outliers south and east. He knew exactly where he was going now and steered the pickup left along the twisting main road.

I shouldn't have left her like that. He could still see the angry hurt in her eyes as she stood on the back of T.J.'s van. *Last straw or final push, it's the same thing.* The sequence had been running through his head all the way up 154 and across the ridgeline. For the first time in his trips to the top of La Cumbre, he hadn't even noticed the panorama of the channel, spread out like a rippled mirror four thousand feet below.

As always, the trailhead was past before he recognized it. He spun the pickup around and found a reasonably shaded spot under an outcropping to park. He forced himself to concentrate on the smallest details—cranking the driver's window shut, carefully folding his jacket on the seat, locking both doors. What he had to do—this part of it, at least—was best done on autopilot.

Within the first fifty yards of cindery ground, he regretted his boat shoes. *I really shouldn't go farther in these. Go back and get proper boots.* But if he did, he knew he wouldn't return.

The trail had been gouged and sluiced by the winter rains, but it was still familiar from the surrounding landmarks, the dry, rocky upthrusts and the predatory underbrush. He slipped and fell three times, none of the actual falls as painful as when he slipped again, caught his balance at the last instant, and pulled a muscle in his back. What's the goddamned rush? he asked himself. But he couldn't stop pressing forward, and the pitch of the slope hurried him on.

The fifth time he slipped, he let himself fall limply. He landed flat on his back, knocking the wind from his lungs. He lay in the cool sunlight, savoring the dry, pungent smell of the breeze. After a minute or two, he sat up. He was still panting, and he rested his forehead on his upraised knees. Looking down, he saw his dusty shoes and, between them, the print of another, smaller foot. No lugs or cleats on sole or heel, and though the powdered adobe was not quite fine enough to take the imprint, he could have sworn he saw the jagged serrations of a Top-Sider sole.

Not much farther, he knew, but the lone print had unmanned him. He felt sobs welling up and knew that if he gave in to them, he could never go on. The trail ran a few feet from the cliff's edge—in some places it was the cliff's edge, and crumbling, too. Then the outcropping, looking exactly as he remembered it, as flat on top as a stone diving board, jutting over the abyss.

Neal's fear of heights went back to his earliest childhood, but it was a thing he refused to give in to. Twice a year he made a point of ascending *Carpe Diem*'s mainmast, all fifty-four feet, ostensibly to check the halyard sheaves and the masthead light. Each time he returned to the deck dripping sweat and shaking. *Carpe Diem*'s mast was no height at all compared to the outcropping. The first time he'd forced himself to edge out on it—sitting down—his companion had been reduced to laughter.

Now he'd suppressed fear enough so he could walk out, if someone were watching. Since no one was, he scuttled forward ignominiously, like a spider upside down, until he was seated at the very end, his feet dangling. Only then did he remember the winter rains and wonder just how much the rock's balance point might have shifted.

Not a thought to dwell on. He opened his tightly shut eyes and considered the distant scene. The spine of Santa Cruz

Island was quite clear, even the deeply channeled slopes. And Santa Rosa, too, but San Miguel was invisible, wrapped in its own haze. The channel shone like metal, and set into its shore the harbor was a perfect miniature of itself, with the double track of a single boat carving the water out and south. From up here you couldn't distinguish the boat itself or separate the mass of vessels inside the breakwater, though the larger individual craft anchored off East Beach were quite visible.

He dropped his gaze a little lower, over the red tile roofs of the city and the single houses that straggled up the foothill canyon. Rudy's house was down there—in fact, Neal was almost certain he could pick it out. But that was not what he was looking for. Lower still, until he was staring straight down between his knees, down and down the steep and rock-jagged slope, to where a shapeless dark blue heap had come to rest against the base of a clump of poison oak. A couple of crows were standing on a nearby rock, eyeing it with interest.

He sat for several more minutes in the increasing heat, considering his options. He could go back to his truck and use the cellular phone to call the rangers at the Los Padres station back on Camino Cielo. Or he could call the county sheriff's department or the SBPD. Or he could do what he already knew he had to do.

"Oh, shit," he said to the crows, and began to work his way back to firm ground.

Gaspar Ortega looked up from paper he was reading with his lunch. "*Santa Maria!* What happened to you?"

"I had a fight with some bushes," Neal said, thinking that he certainly should have gone back and showered before coming in. "What's happening?"

"Lot of calls. Some reporter from the *News-Press*, three times already, and KEYT says they're going to miss the six o'clock if they can't talk to you. And Walt called from the hospital—he wanted me to tell you he can see visitors. Other messages are on your door. Oh—Taffy left this list you wanted before she went off duty."

As he took the neatly printed sheet, he could see from Gaspar's expression that there was something else, but right now he didn't feel up to hearing what it was. He was numb with fatigue, hungry, more than a little dehydrated, and thoroughly miserable. "Okay," he said. "No calls."

Taffy's list swam before his eyes as he walked down the hallway. He took three steps before he saw she'd alphabetized it. His door was ajar and nearly hidden by phone message slips taped to it. He snarled at them as he stepped through.

Tory was standing by the window, her face pale and tense. She had changed back into coveralls, he saw—a fresh set. "I'm not going to let you walk out on yourself," she began.

"You were right," he said.

But her prepared speech was already tumbling out: "You don't owe me anything, but you—What did you say?"

"I said you were right. With the obvious corollary that I was wrong." Just seeing her again, his heart wanted to soar, but he kept his tone icily detached. Reminded himself that by the end of the day she wouldn't be able to stand the sight of him. Her mouth was open, but no sound emerged. "Did you want specifics?" he asked.

"No," she managed finally. "I think that covers it."

"And you're still in this."

His manner had penetrated, and she matched it. "Of course." A pause as she took in his appearance. "What on earth have you been doing?"

"Playing in the dirt." He lowered himself carefully onto Walt's swivel chair and put the sheet of paper Gaspar had given him on the desktop.

"What's that?" Tory asked without moving from her position by the window.

"A list of all the file folders in T.J.'s van. Taffy put it together while I was . . . busy."

She stared at him as if she'd never seen him before. "You told me not to touch anything in there."

"That's right. I changed my mind." While she digested that, he scanned the paper carefully. Clearly, consistency had not interested T.J.: half his customers were listed by boat, the other half by their own names. Two clients were listed both ways. When he saw which file was missing, he tossed the paper down and turned back to Tory. She was still standing by the window, young and beautiful and determined.

"Look," he said, "if you come with me, the next hour is going to be really ugly. It might be dangerous."

Her chin was up, and he realized he'd just destroyed any chance of keeping her clear. *Maybe it's better for her to see this. Get any lingering traces of romance out of her system.*

"But you're not going to hand it off to Gus Feltrini or Steve," she said.

"It's my mess, and I'm going to clean it up," he replied.

"Or compound it," she said.

"That's a possibility." He pushed the chair back and unlocked the desk drawer. Taking out his automatic, he slapped a new clip into the butt, chambered a round, and jammed it into his belt.

As he got to his feet, he saw she was watching him with cool concern. "May I make a suggestion?" she said.

He picked a lightweight windbreaker from a hook on the back of the door and shrugged into it. "Sure. What."

"Put the safety on."

"Jesus." He withdrew the gun gingerly, clicked on the safety, and replaced it. "Thanks."

"*De rien,*" she said. "What's the plan?"

He was unable to hide his bitter amusement. In his place she would've had a blueprint with every *T* crossed. "It's pretty flexible," he said.

"What do you want me to do?"

Just stay out of the way. The last thing he could possibly say. "What I mostly want is a nonthreatening witness."

"Understood."

"And no heroics," he added. "Stay behind me. If anything goes wrong, jump for cover."

"If you start waving that gun, I promise you I'll jump for cover," she said.

At the base of the steps outside the harbormaster office, he said, "We're just going to Marina Two."

She fell in step beside him. "Yes. I've got to make a stop at my office—I'll meet you at the gate."

He glanced at her, but her face gave away nothing.

Five minutes later, as he pushed his gate key into the slot, he felt she was on the verge of saying something. Only when they were actually walking down the narrow ramp, him in front, did she speak: "Break a leg."

When they came abreast of *Iolanthe*, Bea was standing in the cockpit. He had a feeling she'd been waiting for him. "Afternoon, Bea. Sid around?"

"No. He went to the store." She spoke calmly and evenly, and he knew she was lying.

"May we come aboard?"

She straightened, and a muscle in her cheek jumped. "I think it might be better for you to stay on the pier."

"Suit yourself." His stomach had knotted itself into a hard ball. "Bea, I don't know why the hell you did it, but you and Sid killed those DEA guys and then sank *Blue Thunder*."

Behind him, he heard Tory's sudden breath. Bea shook her head. "No," she said. Under the tan, her face had gone gray.

"Here's what I think happened," he said, his eyes locked on hers. "They tried to board you off Santa Cruz. Came up on you suddenly, after dark. Lot of bright lights and loud hailers and threats. You didn't know who they were—maybe you thought they were hijackers. . . ." He let his voice trail off, hoping she might jump at the faint hope he was extending.

But she was not the kind who was going to waver. "We were never anywhere near Santa Cruz. I told you—we were coming back down the coast from San Francisco. We have friends up there. They'll tell you—"

"I'm sure they'd back you up," he interrupted. "But I don't think you're going to stick friends with a perjury charge. Not you." Her mouth closed like a trap, and he continued: "You were set up. *Blue Thunder* was waiting for you. They knew what to expect, and it made them careless. You shot one of them, a second guy fell between the two boats in the confusion . . ."

I lost her on that one, he thought. Maybe she never saw him go.

"When the third tried to radio for help, one of you blew him away, too. Then you realized your only chance was to hide what you'd done by sinking *Blue Thunder* with her crew in her. So you dragged the two bodies below and opened the head seacocks. But you must've drifted in closer to shore than you thought, or else she went down quicker than you expected, because she sank in only forty feet."

"It's not true," Bea said "Not any of it." No outrage. No indignation. But he knew she would never be budged by mere accusations, however accurate.

"The thing is, it's so hard to kill somebody and not leave any traces," he said. "Practically impossible."

He waited for her response. She stood unmoving, gray as stone.

"The kid who fell between the two boats," he continued. "When he lost his balance he grabbed for support. One of your mizzen shrouds, to judge by the gash on his hand. You want to bet there's no blood and tissue—not the tiniest, microscopic bit—between the strands of that wire?"

From stone gray she had gone ash white, but she was still shaking her head "no," and he went on: "When he fell into the water, he tried to claw his way back up the hull. Tore out his fingernails trying—but I wonder if maybe he didn't scratch off some of your boot topping or your antifouling paint."

Bea shuddered at that image, just as he'd intended her to. The taste of bile was sour in his mouth. He felt Tory shift from foot to foot behind him, probably in disgust. Well, she had a small part to play in this piece of destruction. "And last but not least, there's the anchor rode. The piece I took off *Blue Thunder*—were you trying to tow her?—and the rest in your rope locker. Lieutenant Lennox told me about the old anchor rode marker, but she's an easterner. She forgot that charts out here are in fathoms, not feet. It didn't occur to her that the ten on that marker should've been sixty feet from the eye splice, not ten."

Bea's face looked like death itself, and Tory made a faint sound that could have been a moan. "You threw that new splice, Bea. The one in the line I took from *Blue Thunder* has a proper eye in it—Sid made it; I watched him. But the one in your rope locker had that same mistake you've been making for years."

He hadn't expected, even for a moment, that Bea would fold under his assault. He had been speaking to the other presence he sensed aboard *Iolanthe*, and maybe Bea realized that. She said, "Are you going to arrest me, Neal?"

"I haven't finished," he said. "There's still yesterday."

She sat down abruptly. "What do you mean, yesterday?"

"Yesterday, you told me Sid had gone up to the mountain."

She nodded, apparently unable to speak.

"And you said a friend gave him a ride."

She didn't even nod. Or couldn't.

Neal pitched his voice a little louder. "I went up there myself this morning—where Sid used to take me. You know what I found, don't you?" He reached into his jacket pocket and pulled out a worn black wallet, the kind with a chain that clipped to a belt loop. Opening it, he leaned across the gap between pier and boat and laid it on the seat in front of Bea, so that T. J. Wellcome's ferretlike face was looking right up at her.

As Neal raised his eyes to Bea's face, a creaking voice said, "I'm sorry, Neal." Sid Seligman was standing a couple of feet back in *Iolanthe*'s cabin. The shotgun in his unsteady hands looked as big as a howitzer, and Neal could see straight down both rusty barrels.

Tory

Her attention was so tightly focused on Neal and Bea that she hadn't even seen Sid rise from where he'd been sitting, on the near berth in the main cabin, out of sight from the finger pier. Now that he was standing, he and the old double-barreled shotgun were clearly visible through the big dog-house ports—as visible to Tory as she must be to him.

She had known in her heart what Neal was going to do, even before he told her where they were going. Had prepared her mind to accept the idea of Sid and Bea as murderers. What she wasn't ready for, she discovered, was the effect on Neal: his voice had been calm, even detached, throughout—but the skin of his face seemed drawn tight over his bones, and his eyes were liquid with pain.

Unobtrusively her right hand slipped into the pocket of her coveralls, closed around the butt of the nine-millimeter Beretta. The cool weight of the automatic restored her self-control, even as it brought the situation fully home. Numb a moment before, her brain began calculating chances, measuring odds: If she and Neal simply dropped flat on the finger pier, Sid couldn't possibly hit either of them from inside the cabin. But if they didn't move simultaneously, he might blast the one who was slower.

Or if Sid kept his attention on Neal, Tory could get at her pistol without Bea seeing it. Maybe. *With luck, a clear shot at a target no more than five feet away—but what about the heavy, tempered-glass window? Never mind: the exploding glass alone would throw Sid off. Or would it make him fire?*

A wild round in the crowded marina could hit any one of a hundred people. A blast—two blasts—from a shotgun could mow down half a dozen.

"I'm sorry, Neal." Sid sounded a hundred years old and utterly determined.

"So am I, Sid." The agony was plain on his face. No one, she thought, could possibly doubt it.

"It was my fault—all of it. Bea was just trying . . . I can't let you send her to prison."

"Maybe if you told me what happened—right from the beginning—we could figure something out," Neal said gently.

"You know there isn't any way out," said Bea, just as quietly. "I shot the one who was steering. I had to. And I sank the boat."

Ten yards away two couples walked by, carrying bags of groceries. "Hi, Neal," one of the men called. "Great job. Congratulations."

Neal glanced up, managed a nod and an artificial smile. "I can't let you just sail away, Sid."

"Then what do we do?"

"Talk," said Neal. "The three of us. What have you got to lose?"

"Wait," said Bea. She turned to Tory. "What are you in this?"

"A cop. Like Neal," Tory replied. A trickle of icy sweat ran slowly down her spine. She wondered if the flak vest's outline showed through the coveralls. *Damn thing makes me look like a pouter pigeon.* And would it even do any good? She tried and failed to keep her mind's eye from bringing up a picture of Cowboy Daniels's ruined face.

"But not just a cop where Neal is concerned," Bea said. Her eyes, dead a minute ago, now glittered. "Both of you, come aboard. First you, Neal—very slowly, and leave your hands where I can see them."

"What is this, Bea?" Sid asked.

"Wait," she said. "I have an idea. Neal, sit down. Now lean back against the coaming. Spread your arms out along it."

"Damn sheet winch is right in my back," said Neal. "Just let me shift—"

"No," Bea snapped. "Stay like that. Now you . . . Tory, isn't it? You come aboard, too."

Sid might have the shotgun, Tory thought, but Bea had the brains. And the control. Tory stepped carefully over the lifelines, moving slowly. She felt tuned to a higher pitch, but not really frightened. "Shall I sit down?" she asked.

"Don't sit," Bea said. "Go down below, into the cabin."

"Bea, what're you—" Neal began. Tory, with one foot on the companionway ladder, paused.

"Shut up," said Bea. "Tory, go down the ladder backward. When you get to the bottom, stop there with your hands on the hatch sill." The old woman's instructions were too clear for pretended confusion. Tory obeyed. "Sid, see what's in her pocket. On the right side."

"It's a pistol, Bea." The old man's voice, from just behind her right ear, sounded bewildered and querulous. His breath was rank with fear.

"Take it. Tory, sit down on the port berth. Stretch your arms across the top of the cushions, like Neal is doing."

Sitting spread-eagle, her breasts pushing against the vest, she was nearly helpless. Live and learn, she thought.

Bea came slowly down the companion ladder and took the pistol from her husband. "So," she said to Tory. "One big happy family." Her brow furrowed. "My dear, you've got a wonderful bosom—but maybe not quite that wonderful. Are you wearing some kind of bulletproof vest?"

"Since you ask, yes," Tory said.

"Good," said Bea, and, seeing Tory's surprise, added: "You're smart and you're careful. You might even live through this."

If Bea's remark was meant as reassurance, it had exactly the opposite effect. For the first time, Tory realized she was in the presence of a woman for whom the end of the road was in sight.

Never taking her eyes off Tory, Bea said, "Neal, can you hear me all right?"

"Perfectly." By turning her head, Tory could just see Neal's legs from the knees down. She didn't have to see his face to imagine his tight, watchful expression.

"This is what's going to happen," Bea continued. "You're going to get off the boat, and we're going to sail out of here—Sid and Tory and I. You're not going to raise an alarm, and you're not going to follow us. Because if you do, I'll shoot Tory, just the way I shot that man in the boat."

"How far do you think you can go, Bea?" Neal asked wearily.

"Far enough," she said. "When we get where we're going—might be a week, even ten days—I'll let her go."

"Bea, Tory's a Coast Guard officer," said Neal. "She can't just vanish for a week. They'll come looking for her."

"Then you'd better stop them," she said. "Because I meant what I said. I hope you believe me."

She was looking at Tory as she spoke. *I believe you.*

"But I can't—" Neal said. Bea's face was suddenly still and dangerous.

"Neal," said Tory. "Do what Bea says. Please."

"Like I said, you're a smart girl," Bea said.

Sid took *Iolanthe*'s tiller, and Neal cast off the lines. To the liquid sputter of the engine, the little ketch backed out of her slip, turned, and headed out of the harbor. From her seat on the berth, Tory caught a last glimpse of Neal, standing on the finger pier holding one of the docklines. He'll come after me, she thought. And when he does, somebody's going to get killed.

As *Iolanthe* cleared the breakwater, Sid asked, "Do you want to make sail, Bea?"

"I think we'll motor for a while," the old woman replied. More to herself than Tory, she said, "What a mess. What a goddamned mess."

"How did it start?" Tory asked. Fear was creeping through her system like icy water, and she knew if she succumbed to it, she'd do something foolish.

"Money," Bea replied. "Or no money. I suppose Neal told you about Sid and me."

"Just a little."

Hesitantly at first, and then in a torrent of angry, passionate words, Bea poured out the story. How she and Sid had liquidated everything back east and come to Santa Barbara on the crest of the eighties' real estate boom and how they were left high and dry when it broke, nominal owners of nearly a dozen properties, all mortgaged beyond the hilt. One by one the houses had gone down the drain, but they thought they'd salvaged enough to eke out a frugal retirement aboard *Iolanthe*.

"We planned so carefully," Bea said. "Every penny. The only thing we didn't plan was us."

The ghost of a smile twisted her thin lips. She saw the question in Tory's eyes and spoke to it. "People get old. Old people get sick, and not as strong as they used to be."

How old was Bea? Tory wondered. Seventy, at least. What must she have been like at forty? Or Tory's own age?

"Not me," Bea said. She nodded in the direction of the cockpit. "Him. I'm tough as an old boot. Sid is the delicate one."

It was hardly the word Tory would have chosen. "Delicate how?" she asked.

"A little arthritis, a few skin problems—a pretty big ulcer, from the real estate." Bea's eyes were moist, but her harsh voice never wavered. "It was the damn prostate that finished us."

Tory looked past her into the cockpit, where Sid was standing at the tiller, steering with just the pressure of his thigh against it. From this angle he wasn't a worried, funny-looking little guy. He seemed larger, almost an elemental figure.

Bea had followed Tory's eyes. "That's where he belongs," she said. "Not in some prison hospital." Again she read Tory's quizzical expression. "Cancer." Like Tory's parents, she was of the generation that lowered their voices for the angel of death.

"I'm sorry," Tory said. Her obviously genuine sympathy softened Bea's hard face.

"Until that, in spite of everything we had a good life," Bea said. "Then, it came apart."

Now, said an inner voice. "And T.J. Wellcome . . ." Tory murmured.

"He was right there, waiting." Bea's voice was puzzled. "How could we have fallen for such a *cockroach*?"

"T.J. was your mechanic?" The mist was beginning to thin, but Tory wanted to be certain.

Bea snorted. "The only one we could afford. At first his bills were so low, but there was always something else—a new voltage regulator, rebuild the carburetor. Just one more little repair, and the engine would be fixed. He never pressed us, let the tab get bigger and bigger, and then—boom. Pay up or he puts a lien on the boat."

"You couldn't get a loan from someone—your kids?"

"The ones in the picture?" Bea's eyes flicked to the bulkhead. "Sid would sooner die than ask. Maybe he'll get the chance."

"When you told T.J. you couldn't pay, what did he offer?" Tory said.

"If you already know, why ask?" Bea retorted.

"I don't know," Tory said patiently. "I'm just guessing. Maybe he suggested a way to clear the debt."

"Of course. Only a favor for a friend, he said. Not enough to make any difference."

Enough what? The quantity should give the answer. "From Mexico, I suppose."

"Not the first time. From Mission Beach."

Near San Diego. A transshipment. "You said it wasn't a lot. . . ."

"Fifty pounds, maybe. Wrapped in black plastic—smelled up the whole forward cabin, just the same."

Square grouper, they called it in south Florida. A bale of marijuana, the small change of the drug business. "And you turned it over to T.J.?"

"No, no," Bea said impatiently. "We were told to meet a couple of guys in a Boston Whaler, off Goleta."

There were no harbors west of Santa Barbara, she remembered—but there were a couple of state park piers with derrick booms, to launch fishermen's outboards. And miles of empty shore. Safe enough for a quantity like that. "What happened next?"

"Nothing," said Bea. "For six months, nothing. Oh, T.J. tried to give us a couple funny cigarettes, but I told him where to put them."

I'll bet you did.

"And then, the prostate. We decided against the operation, but the tests alone, and the medications . . ." She shrugged hopelessly.

"You were broke again," Tory said.

Bea nodded. "And we'd economized by not buying a what-d'you-call-it—an anode—for the propeller shaft. . . ."

"So the shaft corroded and had to be replaced." It was the old story, but none the less bitter for repetition.

"Instead of ten dollars, we wound up spending five hundred—five hundred we didn't have."

"And who should appear to bail you out, but T. J. Wellcome."

Bea nodded. "I don't even know how he heard we were having a problem. We never wanted to see him again. One more trip, he said."

"And this time?"

"This time, Mexico. A place called Bajamar, just north of Ensenada."

"Marijuana again?" Tory asked.

"I don't think so, but I'm not sure," said Bea. "We never saw it."

"How did they work it?" said Tory. "Just out of curiosity."

"The water tanks. We have two, under the main cabin berths. They're long and thin, about twenty-five gallons each. T.J. measured them before we left, and when we arrived in Bajamar, they had new ones for us. They held about five gallons of water, in one end, and the rest was . . . whatever it was."

Forty gallons of water would weigh about three hundred and twenty pounds. Cocaine packed nice and tight would probably come to at least two hundred. Not a major haul by any means, but worth the trouble.

Bea hadn't finished: "We cleared in at San Diego, no problem. Customs was very polite to us—two harmless old folks in their little cruiser. And a fishing boat met us off Ventura. Just pulled the tanks right out. We didn't have any water at all for the rest of the trip. Gave us a package of cocaine—I suppose it was, felt like powder through the plastic. A present for T.J., the guy told us. About half a pound."

Half a pound—a quarter kilo—would have been a worthwhile bust for Cowboy Daniels's team. And Sid and Bea, who knew much too much, would never have made it to shore. "What happened to it?" Tory asked.

"I threw it overboard."

They sat without speaking for five minutes or so, and Tory wondered what was running through Bea's mind. At last the old woman said, "What will Neal do?"

Silly question: she knows the answer as well as I do. "He's probably following us already," said Tory.

"He probably is," Bea agreed. A brief silence. "I was right, wasn't I—about there being no chance of a deal."

I am not going to lie to her, Tory decided. "No deal that'd make any difference," she said.

"Why do you suppose he let us go at all?" Bea asked, and quickly answered her own question: "Sid, of course. And that damned shotgun."

Tory had been following her own train of thought. "He'll come alone," she said. "Sometime after dark, before the moon rises." *And he's the worst shot I've ever seen.*

"He'll come for you," said Bea.

"Partly. And partly because he's decided which side he's on." *And partly some other reason, one that's just out of my sight.* She took a deep breath: now or never. "Look, Neal is doing what he has to. Please, please don't make him kill you. That would destroy him."

"You're a very intelligent young woman." Bea sounded slightly surprised. She looked through Tory for a long moment, waving the handgun absently, then said, "All right." Turning, she called out the companionway: "Turn around, Sid. We're going back."

Santa Barbara Channel; 4:30 p.m.: Neal

The ketch's two masts, which had been almost in line, began to separate. Changing course, Neal thought. Why? There was one possibility, but he refused to let the thought take shape. *Superstitious? Who, me?* He throttled back on the outboard, and the hard-bottomed inflatable dropped instantly off plane. *Iolanthe* was about a mile away, and from that distance—especially looking into the late afternoon sun—only a very sharp pair of eyes would be able to spot the small gray shape among the white-capped seas.

The masts came into line again—had the ketch turned back on her former course? The inflatable lifted to the top of a crest and Neal rose to his feet at the same instant, staring hard toward the distant yacht. Just as he and the little boat dropped toward the trough, he saw a V-shaped explosion of spray—*Iolanthe*'s flaring bows slamming into a sea: she was heading west, back toward Santa Barbara.

No need to be unobtrusive now. He twisted the outboard's throttle to wide open, and the inflatable roared down the seas toward the oncoming yacht. The two craft closed—*Iolanthe* pounding heavily to windward, the inflatable almost as wet, spraying sheets of water to both sides as it slid down the waves—and Neal saw Sid balancing easily at the helm, no sign of Tory or Bea. For an instant his heart sank, and then a golden helmet caught the sun and she waved from the companionway.

The ketch slowed until she was barely making headway. Sid headed her off the wind a few degrees, and Neal swung the inflatable around into the partial lee. With the two craft side by side and a foot or so apart, he took the inflatable's bow line between his teeth, killed the outboard, and stepped onto the little boat's gunwale. It flexed under his foot, and he sprang upward and across to the ketch, caught the mizzen upper shroud in one hand, and swung himself aboard.

Tory was in the cockpit. She made an effort to smile, but conflicting emotions showed in her drawn face. "Bea and Sid decided to come back," she said. "They know you can't make a deal for them."

Framed in the companionway, Bea looked a dozen years older, her face like eroded stone. Sid seemed lost in a private reverie, nodding rhythmically to a beat only he could hear.

Neal nodded a quick acknowledgment to Tory, aware that with the line between his teeth, his delighted grin was probably more like a leer. Stooping, he quickly tied off the dinghy to a stern cleat. Tory's automatic was nowhere in sight, but the shotgun lay seemingly unnoticed on the cockpit seat next to Sid. As casually as he could, Neal stepped inboard and placed one foot on the weapon. "I'm glad you turned around." And to Tory: "Everything all right?"

"She has her pistol back, if that's what you mean," Bea said.

"That's part of what I meant," Neal said. Tory's smile was a little more natural, but her eyes were full of unshed tears. "I need to talk to Sid. Would you drive?"

Before Tory could reply, Bea said, "I will." She put one gnarled hand on the oaken tiller, her manner challenging anyone to try taking the helm from her. Tory shrugged and stayed where she was, at the forward end of the cockpit.

Sid sat down abruptly, looking confused, and Neal took the seat beside him. "Sid, I want you to tell me exactly what happened yesterday, between you and T.J."

Sid stared straight ahead for several seconds, and Neal swallowed his impatience. "Yesterday," he began again, speaking slowly and carefully, "T.J. drove you up to the top of La Cumbre Peak. How come?"

He thought Sid wasn't going to reply at all, but at last he nodded, his eyes still fixed on the horizon. "His idea," he said, so softly that Neal barely heard him over the rumble of the engine and the whining wind.

"His idea. Okay. He wanted you to do something, didn't he?"

Sid shook his head, but so slightly that Neal wasn't sure if it meant "no" or was just a reflexive shudder.

"Sid, this is really important. What did T.J. want?"

Sid's jaw was set. He shook his head more definitely. After a minute Bea said, "Tell him, Sid."

The old man seemed to crumple inside his foul-weather jacket, and Neal thought he might collapse. Finally he spoke, too faintly for Neal to catch. He reached down and throttled *Iolanthe* back to idle. The ketch stemmed the big seas, barely making headway. Neal leaned down until his lips were right at Sid's ear. "T.J. wanted you to pick something up, didn't he? Take a load off a boat."

"Just an errand," Sid whispered. "Out and back in."

"Carrying what?"

"Didn't say. And I didn't ask. Because I wouldn't do it." Sid's voice was petulant, the willfulness of a child.

You didn't need second sight to know what had followed. "He wouldn't take no for an answer," Neal said.

"Told me we had to," Sid agreed. "Because of what happened before."

"With *Blue Thunder*."

Sid nodded. "Why'd they have to come at us like that?" he burst out, sounding more childlike than ever.

Because scaring the shit out of people made one of them feel important, he thought. But he said, "What did you tell T.J. then? After he said you had to run his errand."

"Didn't say anything for a while," Sid replied. "We were going down that first really steep stretch—what you and I used to call the slot, remember?"

A deep gouge in the trail, worn through the reddish earth to shale beneath. "I remember."

"T.J. was slipping and sliding all over the place." Sid smiled weakly. "Cursing and spitting like Atrocious when she gets splashed. Anyway"—he took a deep breath—"when we got to the lookout, I walked out on the rock. Thought he wouldn't follow me, but he did."

Just the thought of standing on the flat-topped rock made Neal's stomach turn over. "T.J. walked out behind you?"

Sid smiled. "Not him. He slid out on his seat, the way you do."

A little acrophobia was nothing to be ashamed of, but Neal found himself avoiding Tory's eye. "Anyway, he did get out on the rock. Then what?"

"I told him to leave me alone, but he wouldn't," Sid said. "Told me what I was supposed to do—"

"Which was?" Tory put in quickly.

The old man didn't seem put out at her interruption. "Sail out to Santa Cruz, he told me—Smugglers Cove—as if we were making a little cruise. Make sure we're there tomorrow night."

"You mean tonight?" Neal asked quietly.

Sid looked up, clearly surprised. "Yeah, I guess it is. Tonight. Anyway, we're supposed to drop anchor in close to shore and just keep our eyes open. The other boat'll find us. That's what he told me. No radio messages—too much danger of being overheard, he said. They'll know us."

"What kind of other boat?" Tory asked. Neal could hear the urgency in her voice, and maybe Sid could, too: a double furrow formed between his bushy eyebrows, and he blinked rapidly several times.

"Didn't ask. Didn't want to know," he said almost angrily.

"Do you know what the . . . cargo was?" she asked. "Where were you supposed to take it? Was T.J. going to pick it up?" Her questions were bubbling up uncontrollably.

But Sid just shook his head, muttering, "Didn't ask, didn't ask."

"Back off a little, Tory," Bea advised.

For a moment she ignored him, then sat back with a visible effort. "I'm sorry," she said. "It's just that we're so close."

And so is tonight, Neal was thinking. "You told T.J. you definitely wouldn't do it," he said.

"That's right."

An unequivocal reply—or was it? "What'd he say then?"

"He just kept right on telling me what to do—as if I hadn't even spoken."

"You mean, like where to deliver it and to who, that kind of thing," Neal said, trying to sound as if the information were of little interest to him. Across the cockpit, Tory opened her mouth, then shut it again.

"That kind of thing," Sid echoed.

Neal waited until he thought Tory might burst. "And?" he prompted.

"And what?"

"Where *were* you going to land it?"

"Wildest thing I ever heard of," said Sid, shaking his head in mild wonder. "Right on the beach in Montecito."

Neal was baffled: Santa Barbara's superrich suburb had at most a few hundred yards of narrow, gritty beach, all of it heavily built up: "In broad daylight?"

"No, no," said Sid impatiently. "He wanted me to pick up the load the next night—tonight—and land it by five A.M., just before dawn."

On the other hand, if the drugs in question were portable enough, it might make a kind of daredevil sense, Neal reflected. Certainly nobody would expect it. "Dawn tomorrow—Wednesday," he said.

Sid blinked twice and nodded. "Wednesday, right."

From the corner of his eye, Neal could see Tory almost vibrating with impatience, but he forced himself to focus on Sid. "This is important. Really important. Where exactly were you supposed to land this stuff?"

"Don't know."

Was that the faintest trace of satisfaction under the slightly surly reply? "What do you mean, 'Don't know,' Sid? Off the Miramar? Inside Fernald Point? In the Biltmore lobby?"

"I don't know," Sid repeated with exaggerated patience. "I told him to shut up. Yelled at him: '*Shut up, T.J.!*' "

"And did he?" Tory demanded, unable to restrain herself. "Did he shut up?"

"You might say so," Sid replied. "He fell off the rock."

SANTA BARBARA HARBOR; 1745 HOURS: TORY

As *Iolanthe* rounded the end of Stearns Wharf and headed up the entrance channel, Bea, still at the tiller, called to Neal, "I suppose you want to tie up at the Harbor Patrol pier?"

Neal, who hadn't spoken for fifteen minutes, was standing at the forward end of the cockpit with one foot up on the seat. He was looking over the bow, but Tory could almost hear his mind racing. He's up to something, she thought. But what?

"Neal?" said Bea.

"What? Oh, where to tie up." His brow furrowed as if in thought, but Tory saw he'd already made up his mind. "We'll go to your slip, Bea. Tie her up same as always." And "Tory, let me get at the VHF, please."

Iolanthe's transmitter was mounted just inside the companionway hatch, slung in a bracket from the overhead, where it was moderately safe from rain and spray yet accessible from the cockpit. Tory slid to one side and Neal reached past her, turned on the set, and plucked the microphone from its clip.

"Santa Barbara Harbor Patrol, this is *Iolanthe*, Whiskey Bravo Papa two three one zero, channel twelve. Come back, please."

"*Iolanthe*, Harbor Patrol," said a voice Tory didn't recognize. "That you, Neal?"

"Affirmative. Lance, I need you at the Seligmans' slip in about two minutes."

"On my way." But just as Neal was reaching to switch off the set, he spoke again: "Is Lieutenant Lennox by any chance with you? Over."

"She is." Neal looked to Tory with raised eyebrows, and she shrugged incomprehension.

"Man's looking for her—I'll bring him along. Harbor Patrol out."

The patrol's red-and-white pickup rolled up to the marina gate just as Tory, vaulting lightly over *Iolanthe*'s bow, picked up the two docklines and passed them to Sid. Officer Lance Dalleson, looking every inch a marine, came down the ramp at a trot, and behind him, radiating impatient energy, hurried Gus Feltrini. "You picked a hell of a time to go sailing," he called to Tory.

She glanced at Neal, who was standing by the main shrouds, and murmured, "Down, boy." To Gus she said, "It's not quite what it seems. You see—"

"Tell me later," Feltrini interrupted. "We've got something hot, and I figured you'd want in."

He was pointedly ignoring not only the Seligmans, but also Neal, and Tory felt herself bristling. "But you don't—" she began, only to be cut off again.

"Later, Lieutenant. This is really big," Feltrini snapped. "Where can we talk?"

She was on the point of suggesting her own office when mischief seized her tongue. "Right over there, that big green ketch—no, with the two masts, two slips down."

Feltrini shrugged. "Suits me. C'mon."

He turned away, and Tory said to Neal: "Coming?"

He was grinning. "Wouldn't miss it. Just let me talk to Lance a minute."

Feltrini, halfway to *Carpe Diem*, had spun around at Tory's invitation. He looked daggers at her but waited till she was within a step before he snarled, "Why him?" in a stage whisper that carried easily the length of the pier.

"It's his boat," she replied innocently, thinking that wide cornflower blue eyes sometimes had their uses. "Step right up on this box, Gus. Then over the lifelines," she said.

He was muttering under his breath as she led him below. He looked about him with unconcealed scorn and said, "Nice boat."

"It was good enough to find *Blue Thunder* with," she replied, feeling only slightly disloyal. "Now, what's happening?"

She watched as Feltrini swallowed his own reservations—a sour mouthful, to judge by his face—and said, "There's going to be a drop tonight, out at the islands. A big one—and we know where."

How did he find out? Her surprise clearly pleased him, and he rushed on: "Out at San Miguel Island, a harbor called Tyler something. You know it?"

"Bight," she replied automatically. "Tyler Bight." *What's he talking about?*

"That's the place," he said. "On the far side of the island from the mainland—a smart place. They're going to transfer from a deep-water carrier to a small boat and then run it into shore—land on the beach somewhere between Capitan and Gaviota. A truck's going to meet them: the 101 freeway's just a couple hundred yards from the water all along there."

He paused, and Tory, her head still spinning, said, "How'd you—"

Gus barked his humorless laugh. "At the press conference we'll call it sharp police work, but the truth is, we were dipped in . . . we got real lucky."

You had to give it to the druggies, she decided. They were really on the ball. But so was Gus. "Tell me," she said.

"Well, your friend Donahoe told the SBPD about this guy Wellcome and his van. So I got a search warrant and tore the thing apart." He laughed again. "Tore it apart again, I should say: you and Donahoe really trashed it."

"We didn't touch—"

"Well, maybe it was that kid with the German name. . . ."

"Officer Hegemann?"

"Whoever." Gus was clearly disposed to be forgiving in his moment of triumph. Tory could barely contain herself but realized that trying to break in was a loser's game. "Anyway," Gus was saying, "they missed it: the cellular phone. Must've fallen out of its recharger, but it was still blinking."

"You mean it was on," Tory said.

"Not just on," said Gus. "It had a message. Not exactly a message, but it was programmed to kick a caller over to voice mail, which the cellular company operates."

She had a vague recollection of how the service worked, but the details escaped her. "You mean—"

This time the interruption came from outside. She felt *Carpe Diem* shift slightly as Neal pulled himself aboard, and an instant later his face appeared in the companionway. "Congratulations, Mr. Feltrini," he said, stepping through the hatch. And, seeing Gus's shocked surprise, he added, "Officer Dalleson told me about finding T.J.'s phone."

Now, that's a big man, Tory thought. In Neal's place I'd be spitting bullets.

Gus seemed to think so, too. "Well, thanks, Donahoe." His city-pale face colored with pleasure. "I hear you made a good bust yourself."

Neal smiled. "SBPD did a lot of the groundwork," he replied. To Tory he said, "Did you tell him about the Seligmans?"

"I haven't had a chance." He took her meaning, she was pleased to see.

"What're the Seligmans?" Gus demanded.

"The elderly couple we sailed in with," Neal said. "They're the other drug couriers."

"That's the least of it," Tory began, but Neal, who was still standing on the ladder, shook his head sharply.

Gus, who was looking from her to Neal, seemed to miss it. "What d'you mean, 'other drug couriers'?" he demanded.

"Well, it seems there's two pickups and two drops scheduled for tonight," Neal said. "Trouble is, they're about forty miles apart."

Gus's fragile joviality had melted away, she saw, revealing the permanent combativeness beneath: "What the hell is this, Donahoe? You telling me those two little old folks are drug runners? Christ, they must be a thousand years each. That's ridiculous."

"Nevertheless," Neal replied. He seemed utterly unperturbed, Tory saw. Even pleased.

"T. J. Wellcome was blackmailing them," she said. "He knew they were—"

"Desperate for money," Neal interrupted. Ignoring Tory's amazement, he continued: "He wanted them to meet his long-haul boat off Santa Cruz tonight. Take on a load and bring it into shore. In Montecito."

"Montecito?" When he laughed, Tory decided, Gus sounded exactly like one of her neighbor's small, imperious dogs. "Monte-fucking-cito! Sorry, Tory." He laughed again, and Neal matched it with a vague smile. "You must be out of your skull, Donahoe. Montecito's crawling with millionaires and movie stars."

"It's a very upscale place," Neal agreed. "So what?"

"These two golden-agers tried to tell you they're going to load their sailboat with pot and land it on a beach full of people?" Gus's scorn was withering, but it seemed to wash right off Neal.

Tory, watching him more closely, suddenly began to suspect what he was up to. "But Neal, Sid told you he'd refused to take T.J.'s little assignment," she said.

Neal threw her a sharply appraising glance as Gus was saying: "You see? Even if Wellcome did approach these two—which I beg to doubt—they turned him down. By now, he's probably grateful he had to find somebody else."

By now? Does that mean Gus doesn't know T.J.'s dead? Neal caught her eye. She sensed that, for this instant, anyway, they were on exactly the same wavelength, even if she didn't know precisely what the messages meant.

"Tell me, Mr. Feltrini," Neal said, "just who was calling T.J.? Officer Dalleson wasn't too clear on that."

"His main man—who else?"

"Of course. D'you have a name?"

"We haven't had time to track him down—the call was only two hours ago," Gus said. The veneer of his good humor was restored. "I figure we'll have him in the bag tonight, anyway."

"Sounds like you've mounted a big operation," Neal said.

He sounded almost wistful, but Tory felt he was not looking at her on purpose.

"Big's an understatement," Gus said. "This is a major multiservice task force. I've got a Blackhawk from Customs ready to fly out to platform Hondo after dark, the county sheriff's people are spotted strategically all along the shore, the CHP's alerted on 101, and one of those little Coast Guard cutters is going to tuck itself into the harbor on the other side of San Miguel. I'll be on the cutter, so that's where the action will be."

If he had feathers, he'd be preening, Tory thought. I hope Neal knows what he's doing.

"Is that so?" Neal said. "Any way we can help?"

"Matter of fact, there is: have one of your people keep an eye on Wellcome's van. My guess is he'll be riding shotgun in the pickup boat, but if he comes back here, I want him grabbed."

"If he comes back, we'll grab him," Neal said evenly. "I guess you're not interested in following up on the Seligmans, then."

"Don't make me laugh," he said, and laughed anyway. "I don't know what you're thinking of, Donahoe, but I don't want you screwing up my operation." Neal remained silent. "Fair warning: You get in my way, and you'll get hurt—one way or another."

"I think you made your point," Neal said.

Gus turned to Tory and pasted on a smile. "You're invited, Lieutenant. In fact, I'd rather have you along than leave you behind."

Something in his voice put Tory's guard up. "What's that supposed to mean?"

"Oh, nothing," Gus replied. "Nothing at all." He bared his teeth in a ferocious smile. "Just remember, an old fox like me has friends all over. Even D.C."

Tory felt her face turn to stone. "Thanks for the tip," she said.

"Interservice courtesy," Gus said. "So, you coming? I've got to get down to Channel Islands Harbor and meet a boat."

Decision time. From a career point of view, it might make sense to side with Feltrini, even if he was going to come up dry—*especially* if he was going to come up dry. Nobody ever got in trouble lining up with authority, while there was practically nothing to be gained by bucking it. She stole a glance at Neal, who had a faint smile on his dark, angular face. *Damn you to hell and back, Neal Donahoe*. "I appreciate the invitation, Gus, but I think I'll sit this one out," she said.

6:15 P.M.: NEAL

"I hope somebody's still in the store," he said.

Tory looked up from his telephone. "In Operations? It'll be a full house. One of our boats is involved. Besides"—she smiled crookedly—"they don't really trust the DEA a whole lot."

Which is what you're counting on, Neal thought.

She rolled her eyes and punched in three more digits. "Automated switchboard," she said. "Hateful; stupid thing." And in an entirely different voice: "Captain Ward, please. This is Lieutenant Lennox up in Santa Barbara."

A long pause. Tory's voice hardened slightly. "I'm sure he's busy, Petty Officer—and I know why. This call relates to tonight's operation. It's very important I speak to him."

"What're you going to tell him?" Neal asked.

Her answer was what he expected: "Everything." And then, as she mentally rehearsed her argument, "Well, almost everything."

"He'll never go along with it. Not while the other operation's running."

He could see she agreed, but she said, "That depends on how good a pitch I can make." Her face was calm; her knuckles, on the hand cradling his phone, were white. "I'll keep holding, Petty Officer. Just find him," she said.

Another half minute slid glacially past. Neal wondered how much longer the cellular phone's battery was good for. At last Tory's stubbornness paid off. "Good afternoon, sir," she said.

Had she gotten to her feet out of long-distance respect for rank or because she preferred to stand when she fought? Neal wished he'd taken the extra few minutes to go over his plan one more time.

But he quickly saw that his concern—on that score, anyway—was needless. With a crisp precision that sounded as if she were reading from an outline, Tory explained the entire situation, gliding swiftly over Neal's failure to tell the DEA man about either T.J.'s death or the extent of the Seligmans' confession. He was so preoccupied watching her intent face, he was startled by the sound of his own name.

". . . Mr. Donahoe's sure the call Feltrini picked up was disinformation, sir. And so am I," she added with a moué of apprehension that made Neal grin.

Now she was listening to something—something extended—that clearly exasperated her. "Sir, with all due respect, that only supports my point: even if the smugglers have doubts, the drug shipment's already en route. It's more dangerous for them to send it back than to try outmaneuvering us. Besides, it's a worthwhile gamble for them, sir, assuming it's not too big a shipment."

Her eyes widened, and she put her palm over the mouthpiece. "Intelligence thinks it's cocaine," she whispered. "A couple hundred keys, at least." She addressed the phone again: "Sir, submit it's a worthwhile gamble for us, too. Cover all our"—she hunted the word, found it—"bases. And no more assets are required. Sir."

She had shot her bolt. Now she listened, biting her lower lip. Suddenly he saw her eyes light up. "Sir, if what our informants say is correct, we have to use the civilian boat named *Iolanthe*. That's the vessel the carrier expects to see."

And Sid and Bea on it, Neal thought.

"Sir, recommend we go for the small solution," she said. "Just grab the drugs and the smuggler. Let the rest . . ."

No. No. No. Neal's vehement headshaking finally caught her attention. "Uh, could you wait one, sir?" Again she put her palm over the mouthpiece. "What is it?" she whispered.

"Tell him I'll get word to the sheriff's people," Neal said. "The CHP, too. We can't give them a precise landing spot, but they—"

She waved him silent. "Sir, Mr. Donahoe will liaise with the county and state police." A pause, which the handset punctuated with a musical tone. Tory blinked, but Neal recognized the set's low-battery signal. "No, sir," she said, three times. Then, "Understood, sir. I have Chief Washington, and the *Hampton*'s crew is available, since she's in Charlie status."

He's going for it.

She was listening again. Suddenly she went scarlet, starting at her hairline and running right into the V of her coveralls. Neal found himself wondering how far down a blush went, but Tory was spluttering helplessly. "Sir, I . . ." she began, and lapsed into incoherence. After a final volley of "Yes, sir" and "No, sir" she sat down, nearly missing the settee. Her forehead was gleaming wet, and she was breathing hard.

"A little pep talk just before the big game?" Neal offered after a few seconds. " 'Come back with your shield or upon it'?"

"Not exactly," she replied. The color that had begun to fade darkened again. Abruptly she began to laugh; Neal had the feeling it was very close to tears.

He was mystified. "What?" he demanded.

"I should've known," she said, shaking her head. "I of all people."

"Known what?"

"It seems that Representative Goodell's office, like the rest of the Hill, is a sieve. Or maybe an echo chamber," she said with exaggerated precision.

"Long Beach knew about your . . ."

"My indiscretion," she said around a bitter smile. "I'm cooked, Neal. Finished." Her shoulders slumped, and he resisted the urge to put his arm around her.

"It can't be that bad," he said, hoping he sounded more convincing than he felt. "If we pull this off tonight . . ."

"Won't matter. You are looking at Lieutenant Pariah, USCG." With an effort that wrung his heartstrings, she straightened her back and thrust out her chin. "Self-pity is so demeaning," she said. "Let's put this show together."

Neal stood at the foot of the companionway ladder, his elbows on the hatch sill. "You're sure you want to do this?"

he asked. "Both of you? It's not part of any deal, you understand."

From the tiller, Bea glared at him. "You've already said that twice, Neal. What have we got to lose?"

Only your lives, and those are trashed anyway. Bea knew that, he was certain, but he wondered if Sid was really aware what was happening.

"D'you want to make sail?" Bea asked. "Or do we wait for this navy of yours? We haven't got that much time, you know."

No one knows it better. "Wait. They'll be along." He reached up to make sure the VHF was on. It was. And turned to the correct channel. It was. *Where the hell are they*? And then, *What if Tory couldn't get any volunteers?*

It was fully dark now, the inky blackness of the outer anchorage made more impenetrable by the blaze of windows behind Cabrillo Boulevard, the headlights moving along it. All around *Iolanthe* buoys and moored boats bobbed, invisible except when a reflecting surface caught a light from shore.

Taffy Hegemann's voice, right in his ear, almost made him jump out of his skin. "That you, right inshore of *Mr. Clean*?" She sounded tense and a little hostile. Surely she hadn't expected to come along on this harebrained venture.

He pulled the mike from its bracket. "Right here," he said. "Swing up into the wind and hold it," he called to Bea.

Harbor 3 swooped out of the darkness, her running lights off. Neal could see Taffy's face and shoulders behind the wheel, lit from below by the dashboard lights. With barely a glance she brought the police boat neatly alongside, so close it was only a short step for the boarding party, looming shadows in the cockpit.

"Go," he heard Tory say. Svoboda, *Hampton*'s second in command, was first, followed by a slightly built Coastie Neal recognized but couldn't put a name to. Svoboda, standing just inside the lifelines, said, "Pass it over," in a low, angry voice.

For a second no one moved, and Neal heard Taffy touch the patrol boat into reverse to maintain position. "Do it, Chief," said Tory. A square shape, like a towing bitt but taller, moved to *Harbor 3*'s gunwale. A linear parcel wrapped in a piece of nylon tarp came across the gap between the boats, followed by Chief Boatswain's Mate Brad Washington, looking entirely at home in camouflaged fatigues. A whispered, "Fucking showboat," hung momentarily in the cool, damp breeze, and then Tory stepped gracefully over.

She stood on the yacht's toe rail for a moment, her hand resting lightly on the shrouds, gazing up to the masthead, where a small white light illuminated a wind pennant. Then she shook her head and called softly, "Thanks, Officer. Wish us luck."

Taffy's voice was choked with emotion. "Knock 'em dead, Lieutenant. I wish . . ." Her wish was lost in the sudden wet rumble of *Harbor 3*'s twin engines, but Neal knew exactly what it was.

They were losing precious minutes. "We'll motorsail toward Santa Cruz," he said. "Bea, give it the gun. Sid, raise the mizzen. I'll put up the main and genoa. Everybody else—"

"I'll get the main," Tory said.

"Hold it!"

Tory and the others froze. *Hold it yourself. This is no way to start out.* "Tory, I need you on the sheets. Everyone else get below, please. You, too, Lance—but stand by the companionway."

"Right."

Dalleson, Neal had found, was at his best working with simple, unequivocal orders. Maybe it had something to do with having been a marine. Neal had made Sid and Bea his responsibility. "Just don't let 'em jump overboard," he'd said. Now he wished he hadn't been quite so precise.

Standing on the cabin roof, at the base of the mainmast, he cleated off the main halyard. Before he could look back to the cockpit, he saw the boom move inboard and the sail fill: Tory was right on his heels. He'd expected no less. He raised the genoa hand over hand, flipped the wire halyard over the winch, and drew it up tight. As he bent to secure the rope tail, he heard the sheet winch rasp. "Easy," he called over his shoulder. "That's perfect."

Iolanthe was heeling slightly with her sails drawing. More important, the sound of the water under her bow was much louder. From the feel of her, Neal guessed she was making a solid six and a half knots. Even subtracting half a knot for wishful thinking, that wasn't bad for a twenty-four-foot waterline. As he dropped from the cabin top to the cockpit, he saw that Bea was dragging at the tiller. Before he could react, Tory had eased the mizzen sheet a foot or so; the little ketch's lee gunwale rose slightly.

"Sid, you always sock it in too tight," Bea said, easing her grip on the tiller.

Tory's tight smile caught the red light from the compass. "She's really moving. I wish we could shut down the engine."

Neal held his watch under the binnacle. "We're running behind." Sensing that the atmosphere was already too tense, he said, "In case I forget to tell you later, you're a sailor."

This time the smile was unforced. "Thank you, kind sir. You're not exactly a landlubber yourself." She moved closer and said, just under the sound of the engine, "Do you think Sid's told us everything?"

Neal had been wondering the same thing himself. "Probably everything he remembers. I don't think he's planning to pull a fast one, if that's what you're thinking."

If the thought had even occurred to her, he saw, she'd dismissed it. "I just hate to go into this any blinder than necessary," she said. "You're a lot better with him than I am. Could you . . ."

Could I what? He wasn't really sure, but it was worth a try. Fifteen minutes later, however, he got up from his seat next to Sid knowing exactly as much as when he'd sat down. Not only was he getting nowhere, but with each dead end he could feel Tory's nerves stretching a little tighter.

Off to port, four oil platforms, lit up like cruise ships, were slowly moving into line as *Iolanthe* closed them. We're going too slow, he thought.

At his side, Tory said, "Bea, you don't happen to have a mizzen staysail, do you?"

Bea shook her head. "What you see is what we've got," she said.

Maybe it wasn't, though. "You didn't sell that old light-air jib, did you?" Neal asked.

"That old rag? Nobody'd buy it," Bea replied scornfully. "It's not as big as the genoa, anyway."

"No, but it's a hell of a lot bigger than the mizzen," he said.

Tory understood before Bea did: "Use it for a staysail?"

"Might work." And even if it didn't, he reflected, putting it up would keep Tory's mind from circling in on itself.

"Half a knot more," said Neal, sitting heavily on the windward side.

"Three-quarters, at least," Tory replied. It had taken them the best part of an hour to set the old jib, but *Iolanthe*'s speed had definitely increased. Privately Neal suspected the wind had picked up, too, but whatever the source of their speed, now there was a chance of their being at Smugglers Cove for their appointment. Assuming anyone was there to meet them.

"Time to address the troops," Tory said.

"You've got a plan?" he asked.

"Not the kind I'd like, but better than nothing. I hope."

He followed her down the companionway ladder, past the silently watchful figure of Lance Dalleson. A small oil lamp on the forward bulkhead cast a warm glow over the scene, making it seem less like a teak-trimmed flophouse than it otherwise might have been. On the leeward berth, presumably by virtue of seniority, Brad Washington lay wedged comfortably in the V formed by the mattress and the padded seat back. His eyes, which had been closed, snapped open at the vibration of feet on the ladder. The slender Coastie, whose name was Paul Abrams, was sitting on the windward side, reading a book with his feet braced against the opposite berth. There was no sign of Svoboda, but in response to Tory's questioning look, Abrams said, "He's sacked out up forward."

Movement from the darkened forward cabin resolved itself into the *Hampton*'s exec. For a startled moment Neal thought the burly boatswain's mate was wearing a fur scarf, and then he saw it was the cat, Atrocious.

"She really likes me," Svoboda said defensively.

"Clearly a cat of taste," Tory said, short-circuiting whatever Brad Washington was preparing to say. To judge from his sour look, Neal thought, it wouldn't have been a compliment. But he levered himself to a sitting position, and Svoboda sat gingerly beside him, with Atrocious still in position.

"Neal, why don't you sit next to Paul," Tory said. "Officer Dalleson, can you hear me from there?"

"Fine, Lieutenant."

She braced herself against the forward bulkhead. The gimbaled oil lamp, level with her head, drew golden glints from her hair every time it moved. "Okay," said Tory. "Here's the situation."

SMUGGLER'S COVE; 0100: TORY

With Sid at the tiller and Bea on the foredeck, *Iolanthe* glided slowly into the open anchorage. Tory was perched in the companionway with just the top of her watch-capped head showing above the hatch, surveying the scene with the yacht's 7 × 35 binoculars. The half-moon was up now, and its light was strong enough to make up for the cheap, fuzzy lenses. "Six boats at anchor," she reported to the cabin. "No cabin lights on any of them. Two urchin boats side by side—they're not the ones we want—and a sloop I recognize from the harbor, so it's not him, either. . . ." Pride and good sense clashed silently, and then she said, "Maybe you'd better have a look, Neal."

The words were barely out of her mouth when he was squeezing in beside her. He smelled, oddly, of coffee.

She passed over the binoculars. He peered through them, twiddled the focusing knob, and looked once more. "Can't really say I like any of them—though it could be the big catamaran," he said after a moment. "She's got room to hide stuff in those two hulls, and her hailing port's San Diego. The Chris-Craft is too small, and she hasn't got the range. The Grand Banks can run all year, but she's awfully slow." He handed back the glasses. "We may have missed them."

Just what I didn't want to hear, she thought. But it was all too possible. *Iolanthe*'s engine had begun missing about halfway across and had packed up entirely two hours before. It was still sputtering as Neal had the engine hatch open and was groping for the fuel filter. Crouched to one side of the hot engine block, with the boat corkscrewing briskly down the quartering seas, he managed after two failures to loosen the fuel filter and spin it free.

The flashlight held between his teeth kept him from articulating, but his wordless growl was eloquent enough that Lance Dalleson's, "Shit! It's solid rust!" was only a footnote.

Neal had straightened up slowly. "I'm not even going to ask if you have a spare filter," he said to Bea, and to Tory: "Loose rust from the gas tank. Filter's packed up pretty solid, but I'll siphon some gas from the tank and try to rinse the element out in a bucket."

She'd opened her mouth to agree but saw the lunacy of it at the last instant. What came out was a firm, "No!" followed a couple of seconds later by Neal's reluctant, "You're probably right."

They could still sail, and sail they did, as the northwesterly slowly failed behind them. So here we are, an hour late and a dollar short, she thought. She was exhausted, she realized, her brain too numb to construct the simplest order. At her side, Neal said softly, "Better get down, but don't move too fast."

It made no sense, and then she saw he was staring behind them, over *Iolanthe*'s stern. His face was taut, his lips drawn back in something very like a snarl. She followed his eyes. About a quarter of a mile away up the moonlight's bright path was a solid black mass moving toward them. Dropping down into the hatchway, she turned the binoculars on it, cursing their lack of definition. "A dragger. A big one." She handed Neal the glasses. "What do you think?"

He didn't take them. "Eighty, eighty-five feet, steel hull, twelve or fifteen knots—I think we may have a tiger by the tail."

Twice or even three times *Iolanthe*'s speed, and bows like a battering ram, Tory thought. If the visitor was in an aggressive mood, she could crunch the little ketch like an ice-cream cone. The smart move might be to get on the radio and scream for help. But sometimes a cigar was only a cigar, and she would look like the fool of the world if she called in armed assistance to deal with a hold full of dead fish.

"What do you want me to do?" Sid's voice was cracking with fear. Somehow it steadied her. She looked at Neal.

"Your call," he said.

Well, of course it was. Her brain was suddenly racing, thoughts tumbling over each other. Her original plan was in fragments—but it wouldn't have worked anyway. Not against this behemoth. "Sid, I want you to jibe around slowly," she said. "Come to a reach. Pass him close, port side to port side." Over her shoulder she called softly, "Brad, tell Bea we're going to jibe. As soon as we do, I want her to get aft, stand on the port side, right at the end of the deckhouse where they can see her."

"You're going through with it," Neal said. She couldn't tell if he approved, and it didn't matter. She felt *Iolanthe* start to swing away from the wind.

"Listen up, people," she said. It was unnecessary: every eye in the cabin was on her. "It looks as if we've got a nibble." Neal's eyebrows shot up his forehead, and she looked past him carefully. "We're going to let them make the first move. What I'm hoping is that they'll take pity on Sid and Bea and put a couple of their own people on *Iolanthe* to help with the loading. Mike, I want you and Lance to welcome them aboard."

Lance smiled thinly, and Svoboda emitted a short laugh that reminded her of Gus's bark. "The rest of the plan stands unchanged. Brad, you've got the M-16: I want you in the forward cabin, under the foredeck hatch. When I give the word, come right up through it."

"If you're going to shoot," Neal put in, "try for the wheelhouse."

"Right," said the stocky chief. "Just remember, that forehatch is pretty tight—I can't swing the M-16 too easy."

Svoboda bristled. "Wasn't for the *Hampton*, you'd be blazing away with handguns."

"Quiet!" Tory snapped. "Paul, you're on the radio—"

"*On board the ketch!*" The hail, seemingly from right alongside, froze everyone in the crowded cabin.

Tory drew aside a corner of the curtain covering the main cabin windows. *Iolanthe*, her jibe completed, was passing the dragger a few yards to leeward. As she watched, white water churned at the big vessel's stem, and the ketch shuddered to the vibrations of the reversing propeller. She looked toward the companionway, where Neal had stationed himself, and nodded.

"Luff up, Sid," Neal called. "Head up *now*!"

Iolanthe rounded into the wind, sails slatting noisily—but not so noisily that they drowned out the second hail: "We're the friends of T.J.'s you're waiting for."

"Wave to them, Sid."

The old man managed a feeble gesture, but it seemed to suffice. "Follow us around the corner to Yellowbanks," the voice called across the water. "More privacy there." The thumping propeller paused, picked up again in a slightly different rhythm: the dragger was going ahead.

"Wave again," said Tory. Bea appeared in the cockpit, framed in the hatchway. "You, too, Bea."

She watched the dragger swing wide, its white stern light coming into view, and aimed the binoculars at its stern. "*Wayfarer*," she said. "Portland, Oregon: write it down, Paul." She called: "Follow her, Sid. Bea, as soon as you've trimmed the sheets, come below."

The old woman climbed slowly down the companionway ladder. "This isn't going to work," she said as she shrugged off her faded red foul-weather jacket. "You don't look anything like me."

"Nobody looks like anybody in foulies," Tory replied. "That's what I'm counting on." Fortunately Bea's foul-weather trousers, from a different set, were yellow, like the ones Tory was already wearing. She tugged on the red jacket. It was tight across the shoulders and even tighter across the chest. "I can't breathe in this damn thing," Tory muttered. She extracted herself from it with difficulty. Quickly she flipped the suspenders off her shoulders and unzipped her coveralls to the waist. "Help me out of this vest," she said to Neal.

"Are you sure—"

"I'm sure. Hurry."

Without the Kevlar vest, Bea's jacket was just bearable, as long as Tory bowed her shoulders. She pulled the jacket's hood over her head, leaving it loose and, she hoped, shadowing her face. Climbing the companionway ladder, she reminded herself to move slowly, even stiffly. She sat down beside Sid. "I'll take the helm," she said. "You handle the sheets."

The *Wayfarer* was waiting, running lights extinguished, just around the point. Three figures were at the rail, and Tory thought she could see two more behind the wheelhouse windows. "Christ almighty," called a new, irritated voice. "Haven't you got an engine?"

Tory knew an old woman's shout wasn't in her repertoire. She nudged Sid: "Tell him the engine's broken down."

Sid looked at her vaguely. It was too dark in the cockpit to be sure, but his eyes didn't seem entirely focused. "Say it!" she whispered. "Engine's broken."

Sid's cracked shout sounded to Tory like a parody of age, but it seemed to work. "Well, shit," said the voice from the *Wayfarer*. "How you gonna make the run without an engine?"

Keeping her head down, Tory pointed up at the luffing sails.

The heads at the dragger's rail came together for a muttered conference, while Tory held her breath. On *Iolanthe*'s cabin top she thought she saw the slightest movement of the forward hatch. *Not yet, Brad.*

"Get some fenders over, buddy," came the voice from the dragger. "We'll scratch that pretty little toy of yours all to hell, otherwise."

"Where are they, Sid?" But he just stared at her—or through her. Fenders, she thought desperately. If I was a fender, where would I be?

Neal's disembodied whisper floated out the darkened companionway: "Portside seat locker, under Sid."

With a strength she didn't know she had, Tory half lifted, half slid the old man to one side. Raising the seat, she began to drag at the tangle of old rubber cylinders inside. "Easy, Tory. Slow and easy," came Neal's soft voice. *All very well for you to say.* But just hearing him gave her strength.

"Christ on a crutch, we'll be here till next week!" growled the voice from the *Wayfarer*. "Lloyd, Hawker—get on down there and give 'em a hand."

The dragger's propeller churned, and she slid sideways to within a foot or two of the ketch. A couple of burly, youngish men in yellow foulies perched themselves on her rail and, with perfect timing, jumped across and down into *Iolanthe*'s cockpit. Tory quickly retreated to the tiller as the two men hung out the fenders and then took lines thrown from the *Wayfarer*'s deck and made them fast. "Okay, swing it out," one of them called. A boom with a bulging net suspended from it swung out over *Iolanthe*.

"Goddamn sailboats got so much friggin' *rigging*," muttered one of the men, making a long step up to the ketch's cabin top. "Lower away." As he spoke, the ketch and the dragger rolled toward each other. In spite of the fenders, *Iolanthe*'s teak-trimmed gunwale scraped noisily against the *Wayfarer*'s steel hull.

"Hey!" said Sid. "Watch out with that!"

"Shut your face, old man," said the other hand from the *Wayfarer*, and added, "Grab it, Lloyd," as the cargo net jerked downward.

Lloyd's hands were on the net filled with burlap bags. The two vessels rolled into each other again, and this time the rusty rivet heads along the *Wayfarer*'s side caught on a piece of the ketch's teak trim and ripped it cleanly off.

"You stupid bastards!" Sid shouted, lurching to his feet. He was holding one of *Iolanthe*'s foot-long bronze winch handles. To Tory's shocked surprise, he slammed it into the other man's shoulder.

With a yell of anger, the man spun around and drove a punch into Sid's face, knocking him into Tory. He was moving in for another blow when there was a shout from *Iolanthe*'s cabin and a gray-haired fury exploded out the companionway and hurled itself onto the smuggler's back.

On the cabin top, Lloyd was grappling with the cargo net while trying to retain his balance. A cascade of burlap poured from the net. Oh, God, the evidence! Tory thought as she wriggled out from under Sid's limp form. "Neal, up on deck!" she shouted. "Chief! Now!"

Scooping up Sid's winch handle, she struggled over the figures writhing on the cockpit floor. On *Iolanthe*'s cabin top, Lloyd had abandoned the net and was trying to pull something from his foul-weather jacket. It was a pistol, she saw, and as the smuggler brought it to bear on her, she tripped and fell to her hands and knees. A flat crash right above her, and another, followed instantly by a gurgling scream behind her back. She rolled to one side, dragging at the automatic in her own pocket, as *Iolanthe*'s companionway hatch slid back with a crash.

It caught Lloyd, who was standing between its tracks, right above the ankles, scything him down. He fell forward, into a tangle of arms that dragged him, yelling curses, down into the cabin.

Behind Tory, a cry of pain. Without looking, she pivoted and swung the winch handle. It struck something neither soft nor hard that yielded with a breathless gasp. It was the other man, Hawker. He reeled back, his arms flailing for balance, as a shape she somehow knew was Neal shot past her. Ducking under the smuggler's awkward swing, he drove his shoulder into the man's gut, knocking him back against the cockpit coaming with a force that shook the boat.

From up forward, the stuttering blast of the M-16 and a booming voice—*My God, it's Brad*—shouting, "Coast Guard! Freeze! Freeze!"

Santa Barbara Harbor; 10:30 a.m.: Neal

"... a major example of interagency cooperation," Rep. Goodell was saying. It was, by Neal's count, the fourth time she'd used the phrase. "And here"—a sweeping gesture—"is what you might call the proof of the pudding: nearly three hundred kilograms of cocaine confiscated from the fishing boat *Wayfarer* by the combined efforts of the Drug Enforcement Administration, the United States Coast Guard, the United States Customs, the Santa Barbara County Sheriff's Department, and your own very fine harbor police."

This was the first postbust press conference Neal had attended, but he'd realized immediately it was a ritual as rigidly scripted and deeply boring as a coronation. Each of the named agencies had a representative behind the long table, facing some dozen journalists and twice as many shills hastily recruited to fill up the chairs in the low-ceilinged classroom, which was normally used for fishermen's meetings and boating safety courses.

Neal had found himself at the far end of the head table, next to a suit from the Los Angeles Customs Office. He could barely see Tory, seated at the right hand of power—and, he was delighted to note, upstaging it. In her freshly pressed uniform, gleaming with colored ribbons and a glorious bruise on her right cheekbone, she was the focal point of every camera, far more so than the five-kilo plastic packages lined up neatly on the table before him or the pile of weapons (including, Neal was amused to see, the cutter *Hampton*'s M-16) laid out beside them.

Rep. Goodell, perhaps sensing she was losing her audience, ground to a halt. "Any questions?" she asked.

The out-of-town reporters were swallowing the story without a burp, but in the front row the grizzled cynic from the *News-Press* put up his hand. "Question for Mr. Feltrini," he said mildly. "Let me make sure I've got this straight. The DEA and the Coast Guard cutter and the Customs helicopter and Uncle Tom Cobley and all were at San Miguel Island, and the actual bust was forty-some miles away, at Santa Cruz."

Feltrini's face darkened, but he nodded.

"And that was the work of Lieutenant Lennox and her pickup team, in a thirty-foot sailboat?"

Put that way, it sounded more than faintly ridiculous. Feltrini glowered, but Tory came to his rescue. "If I may, sir," she said. Neal leaned forward and peered around the Customs man. She looked no more than eighteen, earnest and sincere, and he would have cut his heart out for her. "A certain amount of misdirection was involved," she said. "I can't go into the details, but we did have all the bases covered."

"Well, somebody did," the reporter said with a faint smile. "Now, the woman who was killed, Beatrice Seligman: I understand she was shot to death by one of the smugglers? And was she involved in the smuggling, or an innocent bystander, or what?"

The color drained from Tory's face so completely that Neal was momentarily certain she was going to faint. But her voice, when she answered, was cool and entirely detached. "I'm afraid I can't answer that. It's still under investigation."

"How about her husband, Sidney Seligman?" said the reporter. "He's been arrested—is that right?"

"That's correct," Tory replied. "But any other details will have to come from Coast Guard District Office in Long Beach. I can give you the name of the public affairs officer."

"Oh, I expect we have his name," said the reporter, closing his notebook.

Neal poured the steaming chowder into two bowls and a cup. "It's ready," he called.

From her living room, Tory said, "So are we."

He turned, a bowl in each hand. She was enveloped in her terrycloth robe, pale but composed. Her eyes were red, the bruise on her cheek a startling purple. In her arms, Atrocious was producing a sound like a file on plywood.

"How do you feel?" Neal asked.

"Hollow, mostly. What a disgusting exhibition."

"The press conference?" He set the bowls on the table.

"I thought Goodell was going to award herself both ears and the tail." Tory put Atrocious on the floor, and the cat promptly leaped back into her lap.

"Just as well it didn't occur to her," Neal said. He placed the cup of chowder on the floor by the table. Atrocious regarded it for a moment, then jumped down and began lapping noisily. "What about you?" he asked.

"Me?" Her smile was a little shaky. "The reviews are mixed, you might say." He started to speak, changed his mind. After a long minute she said, "On the one hand, I seem to be some kind of media heroine. They said ABC picked up the local station's coverage and splashed it clear across the country. Your tax dollars at work."

He had already seen the televised news conference, including a quick glimpse of himself in one corner, looking (as Taffy Hegemann had said) like a corpse in search of an autopsy. Tory had been ravishing, Goodell had been genuinely impressive, and Feltrini, thanks to a wide-angle lens in his face, had come across as a rabid chipmunk. But Neal could guess what the down side was. "You're not the flavor of the week in Long Beach, however."

"Not exactly." Her smile this time might have convinced someone who didn't know her. "I can stay in, if I want to," she added, looking down into the bowl.

Something in her voice told him the obvious question was out of bounds. "This clam chowder's not great," he said.

"I told you it was canned," Tory replied. She placed her bowl on the floor next to Atrocious. "The person behind it all got clean away," she said. "You noticed the press conference didn't dwell on that."

"He'll be back," said Neal. "It's not a business people walk away from."

"You say 'he,' " Tory said. "Does that mean—"

"Just a manner of speaking," Neal replied. "Steve Merriam and I have got a little list, and there's a woman on it."

"So you're staying in the police business," she said. "I heard you'd been confirmed as harbormaster."

Neal grinned. "Just pro tem, until Walt decides whether he's going to retire. It's Maria Acevedo's way of saving the city a salary."

"Then we'd still be working together." She sounded oddly tentative, almost reluctant.

"If you stay in," he agreed. And, stepping carefully out on the limb, "More than that, I hope."

"I hope so, too," she said. He waited. "Right now, I don't quite know how I feel," she continued slowly. "I mean, this whole thing has worked out for the best, and I'm miserable." The tears welled up, overflowed. "I think what I need is comforting. Do you do comforting, Neal?"

He pushed the chair back. "I never tried. But I'll give it a shot."

Please turn the page
for a bonus excerpt from
Tony Gibb's newest
Harbormaster novel

Fade to Black

Available soon
from
The Mysterious Press

EAST CANON PERDIDO STREET; TUESDAY, JULY 16, 6:15 P.M.: JOCK FEVEREL

The window was dark, but the miniature spotlights that illuminated the paintings along the walls also silhouetted the new lettering on the glass, and Jock paused to read it again:

THE FEVEREL COLLECTION
OF
FINE ART

He still didn't like collection much, but he knew it was a hot word: everything was a collection these days, from condoms to real estate listings. Even if it didn't make much sense, it sounded classy—and in Santa Barbara, sounding classy was often an end in itself. Besides, the city already had a dozen places that called themselves art galleries, and if you were going to stay alive in this cutthroat business, you had to scramble for even the tiniest marketing ploy that would set you apart from the others.

Maybe, Jock reflected, it would read better without the OF. He couldn't quite visualize the change, but he'd have Wilbur scrape the letters off in the morning and see how it looked.

Speaking of Wilbur, where the hell is he? In the back room, no doubt. More than likely screwing up his own supposedly finished work. Wilbur Andreas might be employed as the gallery's night watchman, but he was a painter first—and a painter who simply couldn't pull the string on his paintings. Jock remembered with a surge of retrospective fury the time he'd just about sold Wilbur's epic parade scene, the 48" by 72" *Summer Solstice: State Street,* to a visiting Hollywood type, only to find Wilbur had sneaked in and changed the whole foreground, painting over the curbside figures the prospective purchaser had liked so much. A five-grand sale (two thousand of it Jock's commission) down the drain with a couple dozen brushstrokes.

Lately, though, Wilbur was different. There was something about him—something Jock couldn't define but made him obscurely uneasy. Like when Wilbur was supposed to be watching the shop, he now flatly refused to sit at the gallery desk, even though it was discreetly half-hidden behind an antique Chinese screen. "I can't stand it, being . . . *exposed* like that. Makes me feel like I'm for sale, too," he said.

But it was the way he said it—gritting on the words, as if they were sand between his teeth—that raised Jock's hackles. And Wilbur's round, Frans Hals face, its usual scarlet a pale mauve from barely suppressed emotion. Jock shivered at the recollection.

Wilbur was too much. He not only gave Jock the willies, he scared the customers. He would have to go. It was a decision that had been creeping through the tangled underbrush of Jock's brain, and now, fully revealed, it seemed inevitable. *I just have to tell Wilbur our arrangement is over. Tell him now.*

Propelled by his thought, Jock reached for the door handle. Pressed it without result. Now, what the hell: the tastefully lettered sign—Wilbur's work—read WE'RE OPEN TO SERVE YOU—PLEASE COME IN. But the door was locked. Grateful anger for this latest irresponsibility warmed Jock's soul. He fumbled his alligator keycase from his too-tight pants pocket and flipped it open.

The key turned and the bolt slid back, but still the door wouldn't open. Jock selected a second key and inserted it in the upper lock, thinking, *Well, he can't say he double-locked it by accident.* But the thought wasn't as comforting as he'd expected it to be.

"Wilbur?" he called. Thought he heard a noise from the storeroom in back. Like a groan. "Wilbur! That you?"

Jock stood frozen, his mind racing in neutral. Robbery? It was, alas, ridiculous: nothing to steal—but would a gangbanger up from Oxnard know that? The gallery looked prosperous, even wealthy. It was supposed to. But gangbangers would go for one of the convenience stores on Haley or Milpas. For sure they wouldn't knock off an art gallery around the corner from City Hall and three blocks from Police Headquarters.

The sound again. Definitely from the back, but hard to define. Not so much pain or fear as unbearable weariness. Sudden apprehension melted Jock's fear. He stepped through the curtain, ready for anything but what he saw.

Beyond the curtain, thick beige carpet gave way to

scarred flooring. The stark room, lit by a single bare bulb, seemed even smaller than it was. Roughly carpentered racks, filled with unframed canvases and prints, lined its two longer walls. In the narrow space between facing racks Wilbur Andreas lay on his side, curled in a tight ball. His head rested in an unspeakable pool, and as Jock stood frozen, watching, he snorted thickly.

"Wilbur. Oh, Jesus," Jock heard a voice say. His own voice, cracking. He stepped forward, dropping halfway to his knees before he remembered his new slacks. He squatted instead, balancing unsteadily as he lifted Wilbur's head. His forehead was wet, his face a purplish gray. He was breathing slowly. His eyes opened, at first unfocused, then recognizing Jock.

"Lost my nerve," he said, with a ghastly smile.

"Feeling better?" Jock asked, half an hour later. His initial concern had soured to exasperation, and he could hear it in his tone.

"Worse, actually," Wilbur replied. He was slumped in the desk chair, which Jock had dragged from the gallery to the storeroom—the last thing he wanted was Wilbur visible from the street in his present condition. "Guess I'll live, though."

"Well, that was why you stuck your finger down your throat: suddenly deciding you wanted to live." To Jock the very idea of suicide was incomprehensible. No matter how bad things seemed, there was always a way out. All you had to do was find it. A considerable number of his clients were heavily into self-dramatization, however; this was not the first suicide attempt Jock had seen. Still, Wilbur was hardly the person he'd have expected it from—or was that what he'd been edging up to these past weeks?

"Not exactly wanting to live," Wilbur said at last. "Scared to die, that's all."

"Oh, for God's sake," Jock exploded. "What on earth would make you feel like—" He pulled himself up short as the dreadful possibility occurred to him. "Is it AIDS? Is that it?"

Now it was Wilbur's turn to be annoyed. "No, it is not AIDS. It's . . ." He groped, shrugged helplessly as the words eluded him.

Not fully convinced, Jock tried another tack. "You polished off half a bottle of my Wild Turkey—you know that's for the customers, damn it—and all of a sudden you decide to kill yourself. Bang, just like that." He paused, waiting for a reaction, but Wilbur was staring into the middle distance. "Or were you just boiled out of your mind and swallowed two dozen of my Nembutals for the hell of it?"

Still no reaction. Jock continued: "Whatever it was, you must've changed your mind real fast—those capsules came back up as good as new, which is more than you can say for the booze."

"Look, I'm sorry," Wilbur said. "I'll replace the Wild Turkey, okay?"

"Forget it," said Jock. "It was cheap rye anyway."

"I know," Wilbur said. A tiny but genuine grin creased his cheeks. "I was here when you refilled the bottle."

"So you were. We've been through a lot together, Wilbur."

"That's why you should get it. You of all people,"

Wilbur said. "Remember when you said I was the best painter you ever represented?"

"Yes. And I meant it. Still do."

"But you don't sell my stuff," Wilbur continued. "I don't mean it's your fault," he continued, riding down Jock's automatic objection. "You've done your best, but it's this . . . this half-assed, watered-down, impressionistic shit that sells. If I see another view of Goleta Slough with the colors all wrong, I'll . . ." He trailed off. An expression Jock had never seen before turned his face to a mask of horror.

"What—" Jock began, but the other man held up his big hand for silence. After a long moment he spoke again, his voice hoarse.

"You know what I was going to do, when I found the sleeping pills?" Jock shook his head. "I was going to swallow them down and then, before I passed out, I was going to take that letter opener of yours and . . ." He shuddered uncontrollably. "The thing is, Jock, I'd be better off blind. I really would."

Portobello Mexican restaurant, State Street; 7:00 p.m.: Neal Donahoe

Outside, the Tuesday evening farmers' market was winding down. The farmers—jeans-clad growers and bearded hippies from up in the hills—were breaking down their stands and loading the unsold organic avocados and pesticide-free oranges back into their pickups; the customers, who had moved in purposeful, antlike progression from stand to stand, had begun trailing off to dinner.

But the Portobello's narrow, dark dining room remained nearly empty. It was often nearly empty, except on those less than rare occasions when it was totally deserted. The Italian chef had fled home to Connecticut a month ago, to be replaced by a French expat who lasted three weeks and was succeeded by a Mexican recruited from Taco Bell. The printed menus had disappeared, and the carte du jour now appeared on a chalkboard in the window, between an oversize sombrero and a wooden cactus.

Seated at the Portobello's best table, in front of the nonfunctional fireplace, Neal Donahoe reflected gloomily on the mistake he had made a week earlier, when he'd confided to his regular dinner companion, Tory Lennox, that the Portobello had just about run out its string, unless there was an unseasonally heavy run of German tourists, renowned for eating nearly anything and lots of it. His remark was meant to be harmlessly amusing, at a point in their relationship when neutral conversation was increasingly hard to come by.

But instead of a smile the line had earned Neal six consecutive Portobello dinners and a semipermanent case of heartburn. It wasn't the first time he'd been misled by Tory's reserved, coolly sophisticated, every-hair-in-place surface, under which lurked a fierce compassion for life's losers. That concern had been surfacing more and more frequently of late, and though Neal knew perfectly well what inspired it, Tory's career problems seemed to him a poor excuse for prolonging the half-life of another doomed Santa Barbara eating place.

Still, he wanted desperately to help her climb out of her despond, and not just on her own account. Until she was herself again, Neal's own life was marking time. There had to be some way to jolt her off dead center, but for the life of him he couldn't figure out how.

Through the course of the meal—for her, a stringy chile verde; for him, limp, greasy taquitos—her silences had stretched until he could no longer ignore them. "So what is it?" he demanded, raising his voice to carry over the TV behind the bar.

"I don't know," she said. And then, because waffling irritated her more than most other character flaws, she gave him a wry grin. "Oh, the usual. You must've had 'whither Tory' up to here by now. Heaven knows I have."

"Well, you know what *I* think you should do," he said, and took a long swallow of Negra Modelo to stop himself from telling her again: the subject of Tory's stalled Coast Guard career was an emotional minefield. She would talk about resigning her lieutenant's commission, but when Neal agreed it was the logical thing to do, she acted as if he'd suggested selling out to the enemy.

But they had had this conversation often enough, over the past couple of months, that the rest of the script was unnecessary. Tory's brows drew together in silent objection to Neal's unspoken prescription, and he could feel himself bristling at her rejection. Christ, he thought, we're like two old married people, and we're not even married.

From the bar TV, a wave of audience hysteria washed through the nearly empty restaurant. Neal rocked back in his chair. "Irma," he called, "could you—"

"Slack off, Neal," Tory interrupted. "It's just Making Things Right. Give the poor woman a break—it's her favorite program."

"It's a freak show," he snapped. "Who wants to eat dinner with a screenful of geeks looking over their shoulder?"

"They're just people," Tory said. "People with problems they can't solve by themselves."

Her voice was reasoned, gently firm, adult to child. Exactly like your mother, Neal thought. But the fact that she was nearly eight years younger than he, with the face and figure of a centerfold, sometimes made it hard to take her seriously. "Sweetheart, they are in fact geeks," he said, trying to match her tone. "If they weren't making faces at a TV camera, they'd be in some carny sideshow, biting the heads off chickens."

"That's disgusting," she said, but he could tell she was only half listening, and a moment later she proved him right: "What do you know about Alameda?" she asked.

Six years in Southern California had not transplanted Neal's East Coast worldview. "Up north somewhere. In the Bay Area, I think."

"Well, of course it is," she said. "But what kind of place is it?"

"Place?" He was baffled.

"To live."

She was looking not at him but down at the congealing mess on her plate. Her short blonde hair gleamed in the dim light, and he thought he detected a slight reddening under the smooth tan on her cheeks. I am in love with this woman, he thought. "Why do you want to know?" he asked, surprised at the effort required to keep his voice level.

"We got the official word today: Eleventh District headquarters is moving up there," she replied, raising her clear blue eyes to meet his wary dark ones. "Most of it, anyway—there'll be some folks left behind in San Pedro. The Safety Detachment will still be here, of course . . ." Her voice trailed off.

"But the good jobs are going north. The two-and-a-half-stripe jobs," he said. Himself almost without ambition, he often forgot how promotion obsessed her.

She glanced automatically down at the sleeve of her blazer, as if expecting to find her lieutenant's two stripes on the cuff. Looking back up, she saw Neal was reading her perfectly. "Not that it matters," she said, managing a tight smile.

Six months earlier, Tory had let herself be maneuvered into an unofficial operation entirely outside her jurisdiction. Highly publicized success had fended off the retribution that would otherwise have swept her out of the service. But within it, her reputation was frozen in mud, and she seemed doomed to wither quietly in the Santa Barbara Marine Safety Detachment, chasing oil spills and trying to keep ungrateful commercial fishermen from destroying themselves.

To the outside world she soldiered on with no trace of resentment or frustration. Only that afternoon Neal, walking the piers in his official capacity as Santa Barbara's acting Harbormaster, had overheard her lecturing a bearlike commercial fisherman as if he were a child of six. And making him swallow it with a rueful grin.

"Smooth work," Neal had murmured, falling into step beside her. "Toto Boyle would've pitched your predecessor into the drink for talking to him like that."

She had unleashed a dazzling smile that failed to light her eyes. "Toto's a pussycat, once you get to know him," she said. A moment later she added, her lips barely moving, "My predecessor, however, is the south end of a northbound horse. And he was just selected for lieutenant commander."

Neal had had no reply, and even now all he could say was, "Just be patient. They're bound to see they can't afford to lose people like you."

"Oh, but they can," she replied. "In fact, they have to."

"The Coast Guard has to cut four thousand regulars from a strength of thirty-nine thousand," Neal said. "You told me. What I meant was—"

"I know what you mean," she said quickly. "Unfortunately, my superiors don't see me the same way you do. Dangerously irresponsible is how I look to them. Insubordinate. And they're right."

She was quoting, Neal guessed, from the letter of reprimand she'd never let him read. "Dangerously irresponsible," Neal repeated. "Insubordinate. I like that in a woman."

"You're sweet. If only you were the admiral." This time her smile was real, and he decided to take the chance.

"I'd rather be your husband," he said.

"What did you say?" She clearly couldn't believe her ears, and he pressed in.

"Marry me. You know how I feel about you—and you've said you love me, too." But it was coming out all wrong, and he could sense her slipping away from him.

"I do love you, Neal," she said. He could see her choosing the next words with painful care. "It's just I don't know if I love you enough for marriage."

"There's one way to find out," he said.

"No," she said firmly. "That's not good enough for me—and it certainly shouldn't be good enough for you."

"After the first time, you mean?" He felt himself bridling. His divorce, years before, was something they had never discussed.

"Well, you don't want to make the same mistake twice," she replied.

"Is that different from making the same mistake over and over again?" he retorted. "That's what the Coast Guard is for you."

"Even if I thought you were right—which I don't—it's not much of an argument for marriage," she said.

He could feel the gathering chill across the table. "Marriage in general or marriage to me?" he demanded.

She took a deep breath before she replied. "Either way." And before he could say anything she went on: "Look, there's still a chance I can retrieve my career. But it means I've got to give a hundred and ten percent, and do it a hundred percent of the time."

He'd blown his chance, and the bitter realization made him snap out, "Why?"

He could see she was assembling an answer for herself as much as for him. "Why should I bother? Two reasons, I guess. The first is that I *hate* failure. Just hate it. I've never failed at anything I really put my mind to." She hesitated. "The second . . ." For several seconds she regarded him as if he were a stranger. "You'd laugh at me if I told you."

"You've got a thing for uniforms," he said. "I've noticed."

She blushed scarlet, and he suddenly recalled how she had hurled herself into his arms a few hours earlier, when he'd turned up at her apartment still wearing his Harbor Patrol uniform. "Not that way," she said quickly. And changed the subject.

They were still disconnected when they left the Portobello fifteen minutes later. Irma, the owner, was glued to the TV, tears coursing down her hollow cheeks. "Christ, Irma, what's wrong?" Neal asked, feeling for his wallet.

"It's just so beautiful," Irma said, beaming through her tears. Neal glanced at the screen, where a blotchy teenager, her face even wetter than Irma's, was clutching a tall blond man in an expensive suit. His handsome face registered deep self-satisfaction alloyed with a twinge of distaste.

"Freddy just turned her *life* around," Irma continued, her eyes overflowing. "I mean, she was ready to kill herself, and he just stepped in and fixed *everything* for her."

"I see," Neal said.

"It's like a *miracle*," Irma continued. "I don't know how Freddy hears about these cases, but he just turns up, like those Publishers Clearing House people, and makes everything right for them." She caught sight of the twenty in Neal's hand, and shook her head. "Dinner's on the house."

"Irma, you can't," said Tory.

"Sure, I can," Irma replied. "And you know why? Because this is my last night. The bank's closing me down tomorrow—one step ahead of the wholesaler and the linen service." Her gold-toothed smile, still brightening, collapsed on itself.

"Oh, Irma, I'm so sorry," said Tory, folding the other woman into her arms.

Neal stood irresolute as the two women embraced. He detested tears, yet suddenly felt his own throat blocking up. Looking away, his eye was caught by the man on the TV screen, who was looking straight at him with a knowing smile. Dropping the twenty on the bar, Neal fled blindly into the night.

Welcome to the Island of Morada—getting there is easy, leaving . . . is murder.

Embark on the ultimate, on-line, fantasy vacation with

MODUS OPERANDI.

in fellow mystery lovers in the murderously fun MODUS OPERANDI, a nique on-line, multi-player, multi-service, interactive, mystery game unched by The Mysterious Press, Time Warner Electronic Publishing and imutronics Corporation.

eaturing never-ending foul play by your favorite Mysterious Press authors nd editors, MODUS OPERANDI is set on the fictional Caribbean island of orada. Forget packing, passports and planes, entry to Morada is asy—all you need is a vivid imagination.

imutronics GameMasters are available in MODUS OPERANDI around the lock, adding new mysteries and puzzles, offering helpful hints, and takng you virtually by the hand through the killer gaming environment as ou come in contact with players from on-line services the world over. lysterious Press writers and editors will also be there to participate in eal-time on-line special events or just to throw a few back with you at he pub.

MODUS OPERANDI is available on-line now.

Join the mystery and mayhem on:

- America Online® at keyword MODUS
- Genie® at keyword MODUS
- PRODIGY® at jumpword MODUS

Or call toll-free for sign-up information:

- America Online® 1 (800) 768-5577
- Genie® 1 (800) 638-9636, use offer code DAF524
- PRODIGY® 1 (800) PRODIGY, use offer code MODO

Or take a tour on the Internet at http://www. pathfinder.com/twep/games/modop.

MODUS OPERANDI—It's to die for.